ALL THE WAYS WE SAID GOODBYE

A Novel of the Ritᶻ Paris

BEATRIZ WILLIAMS, LAUREN WILLIG, AND KAREN WHITE

wm
WILLIAM MORROW
An Imprint of HarperCollins*Publishers*

A hardcover edition of this book was published in 2020 by William Morrow, an imprint of HarperCollins Publishers.

FIRST WILLIAM MORROW PAPERBACK EDITION PUBLISHED 2021.

Designed by Bonni Leon Berman

Library of Congress Cataloging-in-Publication Data has been applied for.

ISBN 978-0-06-293110-8

21 22 23 24 25   LSC   10 9 8 7 6 5 4 3 2 1

ALL
THE
WAYS
WE SAID
GOODBYE

CHAPTER ONE

Babs

Langford Hall
Devonshire, England
April 1964

I T WAS ALWAYS worse at night. The shadowy figure that followed me each waking hour yet seemed just beyond my reach, just around the corner. That fleeting flash of movement out of the periphery of my vision became mortal at night. It slipped into my bed and rested its head on Kit's pillow, melded itself against my back under the counterpane, exhaled a breath against my cheek in the darkness.

Sometimes, if I was in that half-world between wakefulness and sleep, I'd imagine Kit had come back to me, that he slept in his spot on the bed that even a year later I hadn't encroached upon. Other times, like tonight, it would only remind me that Kit was truly and completely gone, and the tight ball of grief that resided in my chest would unfurl its sharp talons, stealing all hope of sleep.

With a sigh, I threw back the bedclothes and slid from the bed, shivering. I was always cold in the house, even more so now that it was almost unbearably empty. After sliding on my slippers and pulling on Kit's dressing gown that rested at the foot of the bed, I wandered aimlessly through the drafty, cold hallways and rooms of Langford Hall, Kit's ancestral home.

Although I'd been raised with three older brothers at the neighboring estate, I'd always considered Langford Hall mine as much as Kit's, having spent as much time growing up there as in my own home. Since the time when I'd been a little girl, I'd adored the elegant rectangle of red-brown Georgian brick, the three stories tucked under a hipped, dormered roof. The sash windows, twelve panes each, evenly spaced on either side of the door. Or maybe I'd simply adored it because it was where Kit lived.

I'd been in love with Kit since I was four years old and he'd lifted me up onto the saddle in front of him when I'd announced that ponies were for babies. When I was eight I'd told my eldest brother, Charles, that I would marry Kit one day despite our ten-year difference in age. He'd laughed but had promised to keep my secret. And he had, taking it with him when he'd been shot down over the Channel during the war.

Clutching Kit's robe tightly around me and trying my best not to personify a tragic heroine from one of my sister's novels—those gothic romances that she thought nobody knew she read—I walked slowly down the upstairs hallway and visited the three vacant bedrooms of our children, all but one away at school. Even the family dog, Walnut the whippet, had abandoned me, allowing pity cuddles now and again but vastly preferring the warm kitchen and the prickly housekeeper, Mrs. Finch. It made no sense that Walnut would choose to align himself with a woman who professed daily that she didn't like dogs, but I had long since given up trying to make sense of a world that refused to make itself logical.

Moonlight through the tall windows guided me across the foyer to the closed door of Kit's study. I paused, my hand on the knob, still feeling as if I might be intruding. I was beyond exhausted of feeling that way. Tired of pretending and acting as if everything were normal, that Kit had merely been away for a short trip and would be returning soon. But he wouldn't. I knew this, but I still found myself turning toward him in the evening to say something or tip-toeing past his office so not to disturb him. It was all so foolish of me, yet I couldn't seem to resurrect the sure-footed and unwavering young woman I'd been when I'd first married Kit. The same woman he might have even been a little in love with. Turning the handle, I pushed gently on the door and stood in the threshold for a long moment. The spicy scent of his pipe smoke wafted toward me and I found myself peering inside the room expectantly, as if Kit might be sitting at his desk or in his favorite reading chair by the window. But the scent quickly evaporated, and I was left with the empty room again. With a resolute jut of my chin for encouragement, I walked forward as memories like water threatened to drown me.

The large leather couch was where Kit had done most of his con-valescing in the year following the war. He'd been in a prison camp in Germany for nearly two years before that, and he'd been returned to Langford Hall with a racking cough and an insatiable hunger that merely tormented him as he couldn't keep down more than a spoonful at a time. His blue eyes had sunk deep into their sockets, his cheek-bones bird-wing sharp. His parents had hired doctors to oversee his care, but it had been I who'd slept on a cot beside him, first in his bed-room and then in his study when he'd threatened mutiny if he was kept in his bed one more moment, dropping water onto his tongue and feeding him soup until he was strong enough to hold a spoon.

It's where I'd cooled his fevered brow with water-soaked cloths, held his hand, and listened to his almost incoherent ramblings that only hinted at the horrors of what he'd experienced. Of how he'd prayed for death just to end the constant hunger, cold, and pain. He'd spoken of other things, too, things he never mentioned again. Things that I never brought up afterward, either. The absence of the signet ring with the two swans that he'd always worn was never mentioned as its memory, too, became entangled with his time in France. It was as if those years hadn't existed if we never spoke of them, surviving only in the occasional outburst fueled by nocturnal nightmares. And I found that ignoring unpleasant things made it easier to pretend they didn't exist.

I had always been a stickler for the truth, for facing unpleasantness and dealing with it forthwith. But I'd discovered that there were some things too fragile to touch, the threat of shattering too imminent. It's why when the letter arrived for Kit after he'd been home for nearly a year, after he'd slipped his mother's sapphire engagement ring on my finger and we'd made plans to marry in the new year, I had gone against everything I believed myself to be and hidden it. I was too pragmatic to destroy it, its continued existence a balm to my conscience, never truly forgotten but more like a ticking bomb whose day of detonation I knew would be as sudden as it would be devastating.

My gaze traveled to the study window, seeing the white path of moonlight that led to the folly where Kit's father, Robert Langford, had written most of his bestselling spy novels. In a testament to her grief, his widow, Tess, had ordered it locked up after he'd died. I stared at the gray glow of stone in the middle of the lake, like a monument to a broken heart. I had never considered myself the sentimental sort, but the sight gave me pause, made me wonder if I needed to make some grand gesture to acknowledge my own grief. Or if wandering Langford Hall like a nocturnal wraith might be sufficient.

With one last look at Kit's desk, where his pipe still sat in the empty ashtray, I let myself out of the study, then paused at the bottom of the stairs, loath to go up and return to bed. Maybe I could change bedrooms or rearrange the furniture. Or do what everyone had been telling me to do since Kit's death and the resulting taxes—deed the hall to the National Trust. But how could I? Langford Hall was Kit's legacy, the place where I'd fallen in love, where we'd raised our children. It was inconceivable, really, to imagine strangers traipsing over the Exeter carpets and staring at the portraits of the Langford ancestors that glared down from their perches.

My feet were already leading me away before I realized where I was headed. I pretended I'd heard Walnut whimper, which was why I needed to be in the warm kitchen, making sure he was all right and had water in his bowl. I would be the last person to admit that I needed the warm comfort of a living creature, even a four-legged one, to face the rest of the night.

I sat down in the chair at the marred kitchen table and watched as Walnut stirred from his bed. He lifted his head, his eyes martyr-like as he issued a heavy sigh before heaving himself out of his warm comfy bed to amble over to me. He dutifully sat down next to my chair and rested his head in my lap so I could stroke his silky ears. Tired now, I rested my head on the table, feeling inordinately comforted by the soft snoring and fuggy dog breath coming from my lap. I closed my eyes, my last waking thought wondering how on earth I was meant to face another day.

I WAS AWAKENED by the sound of the heavy slap of something hitting the table by my head. My head jerked up, and I regretted the quick movement as my neck revolted from being in an awkward position all night. My lap was cold; my canine companion had long since deserted me to the more comfortable confines of his bed and was enjoying the heat of the cast-iron stove that had apparently been lit.

"You shouldn't be sleeping in the kitchen, Mrs. Langford. It's not proper."

I blinked up into the pinched face of Mrs. Finch, the housekeeper's eyes enlarged by the thick lenses of her glasses causing her to resemble her namesake. She was of an indeterminate age, the tightly permed hair and shapeless housedresses giving no clue as to her exact age. Mrs. Finch's mother had been the housekeeper at Langford Hall for years until she'd moved to a cottage closer to the village and Mrs. Finch had taken over. Her mother had been called Mrs. Finch, too, and I rather hoped it was because the name came with the position rather than because of any improprieties in the family tree.

I blinked again, staring at the stack of post that had been dropped on the table beside me. "I'm sorry, Mrs. Finch. I just wanted to rest my eyes for a moment."

"You were up wandering again, is more like," Mrs. Finch said between tight lips. She jutted a pointed chin at the post. "That's been piling up for a week now. I'll put the kettle on and bring your tea and toast to the breakfast room, where you'll be more comfortable sorting through it all."

The kitchen was Mrs. Finch's domain and she resented any interlopers, including the mistress of the house. I could manage an entire cadre of forceful women in the Women's Institute, supervise dozens of small children and live barnyard creatures for the Nativity play at the local church, as well as organize the annual gymkhana on the grounds at Langford Hall with ease and aplomb, but I couldn't bear to argue with Mrs. Finch. Maybe it was because I always suspected that Mrs. Finch thought that Kit could have done better in choosing a wife. Someone who retained her good looks and youthful bloom and didn't "let herself go" as my sister called my lack of interest in clothes and other feminine things meant to retain one's attractiveness postchildren. And maybe it was because I knew that Mrs. Finch was probably right.

"Yes, of course," I said, looking down at my lap, mortified to see that I still wore Kit's navy-blue dressing gown. "I suppose I should wash and dress first."

Mrs. Finch looked at me with what could only be called disappointment and gave me a brief nod.

I grabbed the stack of envelopes on my way out of the kitchen, walking slowly toward the stairs as I flipped through each one to see if there was anything more interesting than the usual bills and the slightly threatening overdue notices that had been coming in with an alarming frequency since Kit's death.

It wasn't that I wasn't capable of handling the family finances, it's just that Kit had always taken care of things. Even my father had told me that I was very clever with maths, something that had made my perfect older sister, Diana, positively green with envy. As if having all the poise and fashion flair in the family hadn't been enough. I made a promise to myself that I'd finally sit down at Kit's desk and open up all the account books to see what was what. Soon. When I could summon the energy. I was just so tired all the time now. So tired of wishing each day I'd feel better, that there would be some hope or purpose on the horizon. That I'd rekindle the joy I'd once had in the busyness of my old life.

I stopped, noticing an unusual postage stamp on one of the envelopes. It was a red US Air Mail eight-cent stamp showing a picture of aviatrix Amelia Earhart. My name and address had been scribbled in barely comprehensible letters on the front in bold, black ink. Definitely not a graduate of a British boarding school, then, so perhaps not a school friend of Kit's offering condolences.

I looked at the top left corner to read the return address. *A. Bowdoin, Esq., Willig, Williams & White, 5 Wall Street, New York, NY.* I assumed Bowdoin was either a funeral director or a lawyer, having never clearly understood the difference between the two when it came to death and taxes.

Climbing the stairs, I slid my finger under the flap and began tearing the envelope, not wanting to go through the bother of retrieving a letter opener. Tucking the rest of the post under one arm, I pulled out a piece of letterhead paper and began to read.

Dear Mrs. Langford,

My condolences on the death of your late husband, Christopher Langford. I never had the pleasure of meeting him, but my father, Walter, was a huge admirer and shared with me many stories of your husband's bravery and courage during the war.

We only recently became aware of your husband's passing when an old war friend of my father's mailed him the obituary from the Times. It took a while to find us, which is why it has taken me so long to contact you. I realize my letter might be a surprise and might even be an imposition at best. But I hope you will bear with me so that I might explain myself and perhaps even enlist your assistance.

In the obituary, it mentioned your husband's brave exploits in France during the war as well as his involvement with the French Resistance fighter known only as La Fleur. As you may or may not be aware, she has reached nearly mythical proportions in French lore—to the point where some even say she never really existed.

My slow progress up the stairs halted, and I grabbed the banister, the other envelopes slipping from their hold under my arm before gently cascading down the steps. *La Fleur.* I closed my eyes in an attempt to regulate my breath before I passed out. Of course I'd heard the name before. But not from a history book or news article about the French Resistance. I'd once heard it on Kip's lips, when he was quite out of his head after his return and I wasn't sure if he planned to live or die, wasn't even sure which he'd prefer. *My Flower* is what he'd said in a near whisper, the words spoken as one would speak to a lover. I'd seen the name written, too. In another letter.

I leaned against the wall, listening to the sounds of Mrs. Finch in the kitchen and my own breathing skittering from my lungs like angry bees. Opening my eyes again, I raised the letter and forced myself to continue reading.

My father has had a stroke, which makes communicating difficult as he can barely speak or write. But when I read the obituary to him and mentioned La Fleur he became quite agitated and upset. After I'd calmed him down, I was able to understand that my father had reason to believe that La Fleur was no hero but the grandest traitor of them all—and especially to my father. She ruined his life—something I've only just begun attempting to understand.

My father was OSS during the war and was scheduled to receive an important drop from La Fleur. He was told only that he was to receive something very valuable to the Resistance, something containing rare and expensive diamonds and rubies. It was not explained exactly what he should be looking for as it would be too dangerous, and he was told only in a message from La Fleur to look for the "wolf with a cross."

La Fleur never appeared that night, leaving my father empty-handed. A few months later, however, the wives of Nazi officers began appearing in public with beautiful diamond and ruby jewelry leaving many to speculate that my father had lied and had profited from the treasure meant for the Resistance.

He was questioned relentlessly and his reputation permanently damaged, yet he consistently maintained his innocence. For all these years he has been dogged by not only La Fleur's betrayal, but how he himself was forced into the position of being hailed a traitor and a thief. Unbeknownst to me, he has unsuccessfully spent his entire life attempting to clear his name and find the elusive La Fleur. I'm afraid my father is near the end of his life, and it is his last wish that I might be able to succeed where he has failed.

I have sent many inquiries to various government offices both here in the States and in France for more information and have hit a brick wall, as many records from the war are still confidential. However, after doing quite a bit of research as well as trying to piece together my father's story, I came to understand that at least part of the answer might well be with your husband's effects, or even in any of the stories he might have shared with you of his war years.

I apologize if this letter is unwelcome during this time of your grief, but a part of me hopes that you are not only able to assist me, but also willing to revisit some of your husband's past.

I have arranged to be assigned to my firm's Paris office for a brief period of time starting April 20th. I understand that this is short notice and you most likely have a very busy life and would be unable to make the trip across the Channel. Yet I feel compelled to at least ask—very brazen and American of me, I know. But I believe that being in Paris while searching for La Fleur is what I must do, and it is my strongest wish that you might be able to join me in this quest. My father never met you, but he was certain that the woman Kit Langford married had to be a force to be reckoned with. I'm not a betting man, but I'd like to wager that he was right.

I will be staying at the Ritz and you may address any correspondence there as they have instructions to forward to my office if a letter arrives prior to my own arrival. I look forward to hearing from you or, even better, meeting you in Paris.

   Yours truly,
   Andrew Bowdoin, Esq.

My hands shook when I read the letter again, and then a third time. Then, carefully, I refolded the letter and returned it to its torn envelope. Ignoring the rest of the post scattered on the steps, I climbed the remaining stairs and headed down the long hallway to the door at the end, each step more purposeful than the last, my anger at the enigmatic woman I had been forced to share my husband with for almost twenty years growing with each step. *The grandest traitor of them all.*

I yanked open the door to the attic steps, ignoring the puff of dust that blew in my face and made me sneeze, the stale, icy air of the unused space making my teeth chatter. I made my way to the trunk in the corner, a place I hadn't returned to since I'd thought I'd buried the memory of La Fleur. *A ticking bomb, indeed.*

With another sneeze, I knelt down in front of the trunk, lifted the latch, and opened the lid. I pulled out a linen-bound book, allowing it to rest in my hands while I sat back on the floor, ignoring the coating of dust. Smoothing my hand over the title, I read it in the murky light. *The Scarlet Pimpernel.* It was the one thing Kit had managed to keep in the camp, hidden again and again to prevent it from being confiscated. Kit had once confessed that it had been his token of survival, his lucky card. When he'd recovered enough, he'd asked me to throw it away as it was a part of his past. And then he'd asked me to marry him.

I opened the front cover, reading the words stamped inside. *Le Mouton Noir, Rue Volney, Paris.* I began flipping through the pages until the book opened up to a folded piece of paper, another letter, this one sent to Kit a year after his return. I didn't need to read it to know what it said. I'd read the French words often enough that they were emblazoned on my brain.

My Darling Kit,

    Oh, how I have missed you. I have barely existed these past years after we last said goodbye, waiting for news of you, to know if you survived. It has been so long since I've seen your face, but I remember it as well as my own. I see it every night when I fall asleep, and it's as if you are next to me again, in Paris, where we found love amid so much destruction. When you told me that swans mate for life.

    Remember the promise that we made to each other? That if we are both alive we would meet at the Ritz. So, darling, meet me at the Ritz this Christmas. I will wait for you until New Year's and if you don't come, I will know that you have a new life and that I am no longer a part of it. I will not write again. My only hope is that you remember me and the short time we had together and know that I will always love you. Always. La Fleur

My anger exploded inside of me, fueled by guilt and betrayal and grief. By the irrefutable fact that I'd never been my husband's first choice. Shoving the letter back into the book, I slammed down the trunk's lid before hurrying out of the attic, *The Scarlet Pimpernel* clutched tightly to my chest.

I marched down to Kit's study and pulled out a pen and paper. Before I could stop myself, I wrote a letter to Mr. Andrew Bowdoin, informing him that I would book a room at the Ritz and would like to meet with him after my arrival on the twentieth. I signed it *Mrs. Barbara Langford* and sealed it into an envelope.

As I placed the letter on the hall table to go out with the outgoing post, I had a fleeting worry as to what Mrs. Finch might think, but then quickly brushed the thought aside. I was weary of wrestling with ghosts. It was time to lay this one to rest.

CHAPTER TWO

Aurélie

The Hôtel Ritz
Paris, France
September 1914

DARLING, DO TRY to rest. You're making me dizzy with your pacing. Wearing a track in my carpet won't drive the Germans away, you know."

"Neither will drinking champagne," muttered Aurélie, but her mother didn't hear her.

Her mother never heard her.

Even now, with the Germans a mere thirty kilometers from Paris, with trains running to the provinces to evacuate the fearful, with the government in exile in Bordeaux, her mother refused to allow anything to interfere with her precious salon. The treasures of the Louvre might be hastily packed in crates and shipped to Toulouse, that dreary Monsieur Proust might have taken his complaints and his madeleines and decamped to the seaside pleasures of Cabourg (and good riddance, thought Aurélie), but in the Suite Royale at the Ritz, the famed Boldini portrait of the Comtesse de Courcelles still hung above the mantel, the cunning little statuette by Rodin brooded on its stand near the fireplace, and the remains of her mother's entourage continued to admire the countess's elegant toilette, laugh at her witticisms, and eat her iced cakes.

Trust her mother not to allow a little thing like an invasion to discommode her.

When bombs had fallen from a German monoplane the week before, all her mother had said was, "I do hope they don't blow out the windows. I rather like my view."

The *bon dit* had already made the rounds of Paris, and Madame la Comtesse de Courcelles was being held up in the international press as an example of French fortitude, which Aurélie thought was rather rich given that her mother was American, an heiress who had married a French count and had never gone home. Whatever the early days of her parents' marriage had been, Aurélie had no idea; all she knew was that by the time she was four her father had taken up permanent residence at the family seat in Picardy, staying at the Jockey Club if business necessitated that he spend the night in town, while her mother, abandoning the Courcelles *hôtel particulier* in the Faubourg Saint-Germain, had established herself in the second most opulent suite at the Ritz, surrounding herself with artists, poets, and would-be wits, American expatriates, British aesthetes, and German philosophers. In short, the riffraff of Europe. Her mother, Aurélie thought in annoyance, was an American's idea of a Frenchwoman, impeccably turned out, always ready with a quip, urban to the bone, and about as French as California wine.

Through her father, Aurélie was a de Courcelles. She had made her debut at the *bals blancs*; she was invited to the teas and dances of the Faubourg, as was expected. But she knew that she was suspect, an interloper, alien among her own relations, that web of cousins that comprised most of the old nobility of France. The true old nobility, not those Bonapartist upstarts or the Orleanist arrivistes. But even though her blood on her father's side went back to Charlemagne, the whispers followed Aurélie through the drafty drawing rooms of the old guard: What could the girl be after an upbringing like that? All of Minnie Gold's millions couldn't make up for the taint—although those millions had done rather a nice job of restoring the roof of the château.

But, still, the daughter. Not quite like us. That was what they whispered behind her back. She might be tall like her father, have his straight, dark brows—de Courcelles brows, as distinctive as a royal birthmark, chiseled in stone on the effigies in the family chapel, immortalized in oils in portraits, displayed in the flesh on her father's beloved face—but her hair was her mother's, soft masses of fluffy ash-blond hair, like something out of an advertisement for soap. Common, they said. So like her mother, even though she wasn't at all, not really, not if one really looked. But no one did.

Aurélie wished she had been born a man, to prove them wrong. Then, she might have distinguished herself in battle, proved her valor in fighting for her country. She might have been awarded the Légion d'honneur as her father had been, when he was only fifteen and had lied about his age to take sword against the Prussians back in the war of 1870. Admittedly, the French forces had been repulsed and her father had been forced with the rest of the troops to retreat to Paris, where they had endured terrible privations under siege, but no one denied his bravery. It was the first thing anyone mentioned when speaking of her father: "Do you remember the battle of Mont-Valérien?" And they would wag their heads in admiration over his audacity, as though it had been five years ago and not close on fifty.

Here was France in peril again, and what was she, Aurélie, doing? Sitting in a sulk in her mother's salon while an elderly professor of ancient history droned on about Caesar's wars and how they wouldn't be in the bind they were in if only more military men had bothered to attend his lectures.

"Yes, but did Caesar have trains?" said her mother, taking the sting out of the comment by handing the professor another cake. Aurélie's grandfather had made his fortune in something to do with trains, just after the American Civil War. Her mother rather liked reminding people of that. "Rilla, darling, will you ring for more coffee?"

As Aurélie went to tug the bell, she heard the professor saying stiffly, "He had baggage trains, which was much the same thing."

"Somewhat slower, I imagine," said Maman.

"No slower than our army at the moment." Seizing the advantage, one of her mother's other guests leaned forward to grab the countess's attention. "Have you heard they haven't enough trains to take the troops to the front? They're requisitioning the taxis."

"With all the taxis gone, how will we get to the opera?" murmured Maman.

"But the opera is closed," said the professor blankly.

Maman briefly pressed her eyes shut. "Yes," she said gently. "I know."

It was, Aurélie knew, a dreadful trial to her that the clever men, the young men, had all gone off, most to war. Like Maximilian von Sternburg, fighting, one presumed, for the wrong side.

"Shall I see if the papers have come?" Aurélie said, too loudly, breaking into whatever her mother was saying. She wasn't sure what had made her think of Herr von Sternburg. Germans, she supposed. "*La Patrie* should be here by now."

Her mother glanced at the ornate ormolu clock on the mantel, a gilded Bacchus reclining on top of the clockface while two cherubs dropped grapes into his mouth. "It's four o'clock. We should have *La Liberté* as well."

Since war had been declared, they measured their days by the arrival of the papers, *Le Matin* with their morning chocolate, *Le Paris-Midi* at noon, *La Patrie* at three, *La Liberté* at four, and *L'Intransigeant* at six. It was the one sign Maman gave that she was at all concerned with the fate of her adopted country: the way her jeweled hands grabbed for the daily papers. Not that they were of terribly much use. The government had passed a law back in August banning any military information from the papers and anything that might serve to dampen national morale, which meant that one tended to read very little that actually mattered. But even that little was enough to make them check the clock and badger the porters for the papers.

"They're saying it will be another 1870," said the professor. "We'll be roasting rats for supper."

"I'm sure the chefs here can turn even rat into a delicacy," said Maman, never mind that most of the kitchen staff had been called up, along with the rest of the male populace of Paris.

"I remember the last time," said the professor gloomily. "The Germans at the gates."

"Plus ça change." Maman shrugged her narrow shoulders, and her entourage laughed, as though she'd said something dreadfully witty. Aurélie hated all of them: the men about town with their lilac cravats, the artists with their paint-stained waistcoats, the poets who thought themselves above the vulgarities of war. There were no captains of industry here, no men of action; her mother had had enough of those, she said, in her youth in New York. Instead, she entertained the philosophers and the *fainéants*, the men too old or effete to don uniform.

"That's not funny," protested Aurélie, her hand on the ornate doorknob. Whatever the papers said, however much they tried to boost morale, there was no getting around it. They were losing. The word had gone around, all available troops had been called up, all the reserves, all the able-bodied men, all to be rushed west to make one last stand to protect Paris.

Had the Germans already overrun Courcelles? Had her father raised his sword and swung into battle as he had before, one man against an army? There was no word, no way to receive word. All communications had been cut, all was in disarray. Aurélie had tried to use her father's position and her mother's reputation to extract information from the Ministry of War, but had been sent pointlessly from one department to the next, shunted along with a bow and a few polite words, before being told, after hours and hours of being shuffled here and there, that spies were everywhere and no information could be given.

I'm hardly a spy, Aurélie had protested. *I'm the Demoiselle de Courcelles.*

It was a name that ought to have some resonance. Her ancestors had fought with Joan of Arc.

But the official, a very minor official, had only shook his head and repeated that he couldn't tell her anything.

Can't or won't? Aurélie had asked desperately. *Do you know anything of my father? Anything?*

But he hadn't answered, had only flipped the tails of his coat and seated himself again at his desk, as though Aurélie weren't there at all.

She wasn't sure what was worse, that there might be news of her father, of her people, and she was not told, or that they didn't know, that the very Ministry of War was as much in the dark as the rest of them. It did not inspire confidence.

"If the Germans take Paris . . . ," she said, and broke off, not being able to imagine it.

"Then we'll treat for peace," said her mother matter-of-factly.

"What peace can there be with the Hun?" Her father's stories of 1870 mingled with the pathos of the papers, Belgian babies murdered, women violated, villages laid to waste and plunder.

"They're not all savages, sweetheart." Maman's lips twisted in a wry smile. "One can't believe everything one reads in *La Patrie.*"

Aurélie hated being made to feel young and naive.

"They're not all poets, either," she retorted.

Paris drew a particular type of German nobleman, or at least her mother's salon did. They all seemed to quote Goethe, read the poetry of Rimbaud, and have strong feelings about the works of Proust. It was very hard to imagine the Germans of her mother's entourage spitting babies on the spikes of their helmets.

But they were Germans. Goodness only knew what they might do. What they might be doing even now.

"No, I imagine not," said her mother. "But a man's a man for all that. When the war is over, one might even be inclined to like them again."

Like them? There were thousands dead, thousands more likely to die, whole areas of France overrun by soldiers. How could one forgive something like that? How could one take tea with a conqueror?

"If you were French—" Aurélie bit off the words, knowing she was only opening herself up to mockery. "Never mind."

"Will you pardon me?" With a gracious smile for her guests, Maman rose from the settee and came to stand by Aurélie. The smell of her mother's distinctive perfume, the particular way her silk skirts swished around her ankles as she moved struck Aurélie with a combination of old affections and resentments. Once, those had spelled comfort to her; recently, they had been the opposite. Aurélie stood stiffly as her mother set a jeweled hand on her arm. "Darling, I've lived in Paris since I was nineteen. More than half my life. Don't you think I care just a little?"

Yes, that her coffee not be served cold.

She was being unfair, Aurélie knew. Her mother wasn't like the Marquise Casati, who had gone into hysterics in the lobby last week— not because of the men dead or the babies butchered, but because the reduction of staff had meant her breakfast had been delayed. Her mother did care. In her own way.

"It's not the same for you," said Aurélie, hating her voice for cracking. "You're not a Courcelles."

Her mother glanced fleetingly across the room at a glass curio case lined with velvet in which rested a single item: the Courcelles talisman, a scrap of cloth dipped in the blood of Joan of Arc. One could hardly see the precious relic; her mother, as a young bride, had had it cased in an elaborate pendant of gold, studded with precious stones, so that all one saw was the glow of rubies and diamonds, not the frail remnant of the holy martyr.

Aurélie's father had been appalled, but he hadn't interfered: it was a tradition that the talisman was to be carried by the women of the family, ever since a long-ago Comtesse de Courcelles had knelt at the feet of the Maid of Orléans and tried to stanch her blood with fabric ripped from her own dress. The saint had blessed the comtesse, and, ever since, the talisman had protected the house of Courcelles, conferring victory in battle or safety to the bearer, depending on whom one asked.

The relic had been passed down in Aurélie's family ever since, carefully guarded—until her grandfather had lost it in a game of cards, and her father had suffered the humiliation of having it bought back by an American heiress, a bribe for a betrothal.

"I know I'm not a Courcelles. I gave up trying to be a long time ago. It wasn't worth the effort." Maman looked up at Aurélie, twin furrows in her celebrated forehead, uncharacteristically at a loss for words. "My dear, I understand your pride. I do. Your father was always rotten with it. No, no, we won't quarrel about your father. All I mean to say is, you mustn't let your ancestors rule your life. There's more to you than your lineage."

"My life *is* my lineage. I have a sacred trust. . . ."

"Over a bit of old rag?" As Aurélie glowered at her, her mother said gently, "It's a beautiful story. I was taken by the romance of it, too—when I was nineteen."

As if patriotism, as if service to one's country, were a child's game that one might outgrow!

"It's not romantic," Aurélie protested. "Not if by romance you mean it's something woven of untruths."

"It's woven of fibers," said her mother. "Like any other cloth. I'm not saying it's worthless. There's value to be had in symbols. But you can't really believe that a saint's knucklebone can cure a cold—or that a scrap of fabric can confer victory in battle. Not on its own. What is it Voltaire said? *God is on the side of the big battalions.*"

"Not always."

"No. Sometimes the smaller battalion has the better marksmen." Aurélie's mother touched her cheek; her perfume tickled Aurélie's nose. Part of Aurélie wanted to shake the hand off, the other wanted to lean against her mother's shoulder, as she had done when she was small, before she had grown taller than her mother, taller and more aware of the oddities of their existence. "A talisman is only so precious as the confidence it confers, nothing more, nothing less. Rather like a love potion."

Her mother would never understand. There was a discreet tap on the door. "That must be the coffee," said Aurélie, ducking away from her mother's touch and yanking open the door.

It was the coffee, but not brought by a porter. Instead, a man in uniform stood with the coffeepot, which he raised sheepishly in greeting. "When I said I was coming here, the maître d' asked if I'd bring this. I gather they're rather short-staffed?"

"Monsieur d'Aubigny!" Maman kissed Jean-Marie on both cheeks, deftly relieving him of the coffeepot. "I'd thought you were in the cavalry, not the commissary."

"Ha ha," said Jean-Marie uncomfortably. That was one thing Aurélie had always liked about him; he had never found her mother's jokes funny. "I've just come to say goodbye. I'm to leave tonight."

"Didn't your regiment depart last week?" Aurélie wasn't sure how her mother knew these things, but she always did.

"Well, yes," said Jean-Marie, "but I was given leave to stand god-father at my niece's christening. They've all gone away without me. I'm to join them at Nanteuil-le-Haudouin."

"How will you get there?"

"Take a taxi, I suppose." He wasn't, Aurélie realized, joking. "They're lining them up in the Place des Invalides. Someone ought to be able to squeeze me in."

"But we can do better than that!" Aurélie glanced at her mother, then flushed, annoyed at herself for looking to her for approval. "There's my car."

"There's no one to drive it," said her mother. "Gaston joined up weeks ago."

Gaston was her mother's chauffeur and had never, ever touched the Hispano-Suiza that was Aurélie's very own car, a gift last summer from her father, who, while old-fashioned in some respects, was a devotee of racing in every form.

"Jean-Marie can drive," said Aurélie. "After a fashion."

"That's not fair," protested Jean-Marie, but added, "I can't take your car. You'll never get it back again."

Aurélie felt a twinge at that. She adored her motor and not just because it represented a means of escape. But she was being selfish. "It's little enough to sacrifice for France. You're willing to give your life. I can give a chunk of metal and glass."

Her mother shrugged. "As you say, it's yours."

"I'll come with you to fetch it," said Aurélie, daring her mother to contradict her. Normal notions of chaperonage could hardly hold under these circumstances. Besides, she and Jean-Marie were practically betrothed; their fathers had decided it when they were still in their cradles, and Aurélie saw no reason to object. Jean-Marie never interfered with her. That was, she felt, an excellent basis for a marriage. "The garage mightn't let him have it otherwise."

"If you feel you must. You'll be back in time to change for dinner," said her mother. It wasn't a question. "I wish you a safe journey, Monsieur d'Aubigny."

"Thank you, madame," said Jean-Marie politely, and Aurélie's mother wafted away in a haze of perfume and silk, collecting her guests as she went and taking them through with her to the dining salon, where a cold collation had been laid out.

"Would you like to eat before you go?" offered Aurélie.

"No," said Jean-Marie, tucking his hands beneath his arms and hunching his shoulders. "If I'm going I should go."

Aurélie understood perfectly and respected him for it. One was always less afraid when one plunged forward, like jumping into cold water. It was the waiting that was always the worst. "Let's go, then." But at the door, she paused. "Go downstairs. I'll join you in a moment."

"If you don't want me to have it . . ."

"No, no. Nothing like that. I just want—a bit of bread," she improvised, and Jean-Marie didn't argue.

Back inside, she checked to make sure the dining room doors were closed before going, furtively, to the display case that held the talisman.

But why should she feel guilty? It was more hers than her mother's, even if her mother's money had brought it back into the family.

The legend had it that the prayers of a daughter of Courcelles, in possession—physical possession—of the talisman, would protect those she loved and spare them from harm. One version, that was. There were some who claimed that to hold it conferred victory, but Aurélie's grandmother, impossibly ancient and wrinkled and aristocratic, had told her, long ago, that they had it wrong. It wasn't victory in battle, but protection that it conferred. Protection for France. "France cannot fall while the Demoiselle de Courcelles holds the talisman," her grandmother told her.

Her father had carried it with him to Mont-Valérien, not encased in gold and jewels as it was now, but in the old setting, two pieces of crystal held together by thin bands of gold, the whole, he had told her, little bigger than a marble. It hadn't done any good. It wouldn't, of course; her grandmother had been quite clear about that. The talisman only worked when held by a daughter of Courcelles.

Defiantly, Aurélie pressed the catch that opened the case and snatched the talisman out. It was as big as her palm, the de Courcelles crest engraved on the back, the front adorned with jewels and a glass circle in which one could just glimpse the stained silk of the talisman.

Who had a better right to it than she? And when had there been more need for it than now?

Her mother had had it set with a loop and a thin gold chain, as though the honor of their house could be reduced to personal ornament. On the other hand, it did make a convenient way of carrying it. Lifting the chain over her head and tucking the talisman down under her chemise, Aurélie hurried down the stairs to join Jean-Marie.

"Where's the bread?" he asked.

"I ate it," she said shortly, feeling the jewels pressing against her breast.

Outside, the Place Vendôme felt foreign to her, no taxis queuing for passengers, no omnibuses wobbling along, no hawkers crying the day's papers. They had been banned, along with so many other things. The few men on the streets were old or lame; the city had become a city of women, women with their heads down, hurrying along as if life were no longer something to be celebrated, but to be got through as quickly as possible. Cafés were shuttered, shops closed for want of proprietors and customers. It was as though Paris had the life drained out of it, a thin, pale version of itself.

She had the power to change that. Taking strength from the talisman, Aurélie said, "Never mind about driving yourself. I'll take you."

Jean-Marie gawked at her. "Er, that's very kind of you, but I really don't mind."

"I'm a better motorist than you are, and you know it." They'd raced last spring. She'd driven Jean-Marie off the road and beat him to the finish. It was a measure of his character that he hadn't minded; he was used to her outrunning and outclimbing him from the time they were children.

Jean-Marie held up his hands in surrender. "I'm not denying it! But your father would have my hide if he knew I'd let you into harm's way."

"Who's to say I'm not in harm's way in Paris?" demanded Aurélie and knew from the sudden gravity of Jean-Marie's expression that she'd hit home. "They'll take Paris, won't they? That's what everyone says."

"Your mother has friends among the Germans."

"Didn't they say the same in 1870? It didn't matter who was friends with whom when everyone was starving in the siege."

"I'm not sure Paris has the defenses for a siege," said Jean-Marie helpfully.

"Is that meant to be comforting?"

"Yes . . . no . . . I mean, er . . ."

"At least you get to go and fight! I'll drop you at the lines and then drive sedately back to town. I have to do something."

"You're not planning to bind back your hair and put on a breast-plate, are you?"

Aurélie frowned at him. "I should think a breastplate would be rather conspicuous."

"You sound just like your mother—no! Don't hit me. I was only joking." Jean-Marie looked at her with bemused affection. "I should know better than to argue with you, shouldn't I?"

Aurélie had never been so fond of him as she was at this moment. "You won't tell my mother?"

"On my honor." He looked at her uncertainly, looking very young in his army greatcoat. "You know, I could just take a taxi."

"Get in," said Aurélie.

It was heaven to be at the wheel of her car, to smell the familiar combination of leather and dust. She shoved the goggles down over her eyes, tied a kerchief around her hair, and turned the car in a defiant circle that had Jean-Marie clinging to the side.

Aurélie laughed, a sound of pure joy, relief at being free, free of her mother, free of the Ritz, free of the endless waiting.

"Don't fret," she told Jean-Marie. "I'll have you to your regiment by midnight."

"No hurry," said Jean-Marie, clutching the seat, and Aurélie laughed again, tilting her face to the breeze, watching Paris fade behind them.

The stately procession of Renaults carrying the rest of the forces were confined to one route, moving slowly down National Road 2, but Aurélie slipped away down the side roads, bouncing down rutted tracks, cutting across fields.

The swiftly falling dusk was kind, masking abandoned houses and empty fields, farms from which all the inhabitants had fled, taking their livestock with them, but nothing could hide the rumble of artillery, the scent of cordite heavy in the air.

They spoke as she drove, the desultory conversation of old friends, jumping from this to that, interspersed with long silences. Sometimes they sang, bits of old nursery songs, popular tunes, "La Marseillaise." Aurélie felt the thrum of it, the road, the engine, the song, the battle in the distance, deep in her bones, and exulted in it, in finally being part of the war effort, the Demoiselle de Courcelles, bearing the talisman that would turn the tide of war.

It was an anticlimax to arrive, to find themselves in a confusion of cars and trucks and men rushing this way and that, tents hastily thrown up, doctors in stained aprons spilling out basins of goodness only knew what.

"I suppose I leave you here, then," said Aurélie, as someone gestured to her to stop and turn around.

Jean-Marie rose slowly from his seat, his movements stiff, with nothing like his usual exuberance. "I suppose so," he said.

Aurélie's euphoria faded. She rubbed her hands along her arms, wishing she'd changed into something warmer than the afternoon dress she had been wearing at the Ritz. "A Frenchman is worth ten Huns," she said fiercely. "Just remember that. You'll rout them and be home in a month."

Two months ago, she had believed that. Now, the words felt thin.

Jean-Marie ducked his head. She could see him swallow, his Adam's apple bobbing up and down. "You'll be all right getting back? I shouldn't have let you take me."

"You had nothing to say about it. I made you. And it is my car."

They looked at each other, ill at ease in a way they had never been before. The air was foul with mud and smoke and blood; the night was loud with gunfire. It didn't feel the least bit glorious or heraldic and Aurélie found herself suddenly afraid, afraid for Jean-Marie and afraid for France.

What was it her mother called it? A case of the willies? Some phrase like that.

"Don't die," she said, which was odd, because she'd meant to say something else entirely, something about being brave for France.

"I'll try not to," said Jean-Marie, and, awkwardly, leaned forward to kiss her, not on the cheeks, but on the lips, a tentative, fleeting pressure. He rocked back on his heels, shoved his hands in the pockets of his greatcoat, and said, "You will be all right?"

"Of course," Aurélie said, wondering if she ought to have protested or kissed him back. On the whole, she thought neither. Better to just leave it as it was. She grimaced to make him laugh. "Except when my mother gets hold of me."

Behind her, someone was beeping. "You! Out of the road! Paugh! Woman drivers."

"They've never seen you drive," said Jean-Marie ruefully, and then, "I guess this is goodbye."

A chill ran down Aurélie's back. Her hand rose to the talisman beneath her dress. "Not goodbye! Only au revoir."

But Jean-Marie was already gone, trudging off into the confusion to report to his commanding officer in one of those smoke-grimed tents.

Aurélie pressed her hand to her chest, feeling the bulk of the talisman between her breasts.

The road to Paris lay before her. Paris, and the suite at the Ritz, the endless salons, the waiting, the not knowing.

The car behind her beeped again.

Aurélie jerked the wheel sideways, spinning the car in an expert turn that made one driver spit at her and another applaud in admiration.

She didn't care. Above the sound of battle, she could hear a thin, high sound, like a hunting horn, and she thought, for a moment, she could see, like the figures in an old tapestry, men in armor with lances by their sides and women in tall, draped hats.

Instead of turning to the southwest, to Paris, she set her course north and east, around the battle, into the disputed land, where she knew she was needed, where she truly belonged.

Home. To Courcelles.

CHAPTER THREE

Daisy

The Hôtel Ritz
Paris, France
May 1942

To Daisy, the Ritz would always be home, even though she hadn't actually lived there since her marriage seven years ago. People used to think it was so strange, to grow up like this inside a hotel, like some kind of rare plant inside a hothouse, but then what could you expect from a girl named for a flower?

Her full name was Marguerite Amélie de Courcelles d'Aubigny Villon (this last patronym belonging to her husband) but everybody called her Daisy. That was Grandmère's name for her, because *daisy* was the English word for *marguerite*, and Grandmère had been born an American. Privately, Daisy hated the nickname, but she adored Grandmère so she let it be, as she did most things. When you possessed a grandmother as vivid and giant as Grandmère, before whom all of Paris trembled, you learned this happy method early in life. *Laisse-le vivre*—let it be—this was Daisy's watchword. She'd said it over and over (in her own head, naturally) as she left the bookshop on rue Volney and walked north until she reached the banks of the Seine, crowded with

German soldiers who smelled of cigarettes and sweat and sour beer, who laughed in their strange, loud, guttural way—to Daisy's delicate French ears, anyway—and crossed the Place de la Concorde toward the hotel's back entrance on rue Cambon. *Laisse-le vivre,* that was how you stayed alive in Paris, these days. Anyway, it was early May and Paris was blossoming in its heedless, abundant way, all buds and sunshine and sidewalks glossy from some recent shower, and when you drank in the air from the Tuileries it tasted of spring, as it did year after year, Germans or no Germans. What was the point in railing against fate? Against anything? It made no difference, except to get you in trouble. *Laisse-le vivre.*

Oh, but the sight of those crisp white awnings, that soot-smeared honey facade! A warm sigh escaped her. Grandmère had always preferred the grander main entrance on the Place Vendôme, but Daisy liked rue Cambon best, discreet and familiar, where nobody noticed you coming and going except the staff, and they were like family so Daisy didn't mind. Now, of course, the Luftwaffe was headquartered on the Vendôme side, and most of the civilian guests came and went from rue Cambon. *C'est la guerre.* Daisy crossed the sidewalk and almost leapt up the steps to the door, which opened magically as it always did, the magician's name being Bernard the porter. Daisy had known him all her life. He was large and dark-haired and fastidious, and he had once caught her rolling marbles outside Mademoiselle Chanel's shop across the street and hadn't told Grandmère, so she knew she could trust him.

"Hello, Bernard," she sang.

"Welcome, Madame Villon. She's expecting you." Bernard's gaze flicked across the hall to the Little Bar, which didn't mean that Grandmère awaited her inside—Grandmère would conduct this meeting from the comfort of her suite, of course—but that some German officers had wandered over from the Vendôme side for a drink or two, so watch your step, Madame Villon.

"Thank you, Bernard," she said.

In contrast to the grandeur of the Place Vendôme building, the wing fronting rue Cambon was built to a more human scale, which Daisy appreciated. Of course, this was human scale according to the Ritz. The staircase wound upward, the black railings gleamed, the lights cast softly upon marble and wood. From the Little Bar came the sound of primitive laughter. Good, let them laugh. Let them laugh and drink and pay no attention to some young woman scurrying across the entrance hall, books gathered to her chest, handbag dangling from her elbow, worn hat shading her face. Daisy had almost reached the staircase when a uniformed chest appeared in front of her.

"Mademoiselle?"

She looked up. The face startled her. Not because it was so typically German, or rather Prussian—those blue eyes, that straw-colored hair, that rigid something about the jaw and cheekbones could be seen everywhere in Paris now, most especially in the lobby of the Ritz—but because he was startled, too. His eyebrows slanted into an expression of stern surprise. She glanced at the stripes on his shoulder.

"Yes, lieutenant colonel?" she said to his nose, which was sharp like the beak of a predatory bird of some kind, she wasn't sure which one. A large, mottled scar disfigured the skin on the left side of his face, or else he might have been handsome.

"Your name, please."

He spoke sharply, and Daisy's palms, turning damp, began to slip against the bindings of the books. Still, she lifted her chin and edged her gaze upward a few centimeters to the space between his eyes. Not for nothing was she a Frenchwoman.

"I am Madame Villon," she replied, just as sharp. He seemed to be staring at her eyebrows. Daisy hated her eyebrows, which were straight and thick and several shades darker than her blond hair, like a pair of accent marks, *grave* on the right and *aigu* on the left. The eyebrows were a gift from her mother, who had died when Daisy was three years old, and there were many times Daisy angrily wondered why her mother couldn't have left her something useful and beautiful instead, not these two fierce, mannish eyebrows. Anyway, she disliked this German even more for noticing them, and he must have seen the dislike on her face, because his own expression softened a little, insomuch as it was possible for a scarred Prussian mask like that to soften at all.

"Your papers, please," he said.

"My *papers?*"

"Yes, please."

Daisy heaved a little sigh, just to show him how unreasonable he was. "You must wait a moment, lieutenant colonel, while I set down these books."

"I will hold the books."

She ignored that and bent to set the books on the floor. She had the feeling that Bernard was staring at them worriedly, that Bernard was in an agony, wondering whether he should sweep in to hold the books—service at the Ritz was a sacred thing, a holy calling, even in war—or whether he could better serve her by staying the hell away from this encounter. She prayed he'd stick to the latter resolution. The less attention, the better. She burrowed inside her pocketbook and produced her identity card and handed it to the German officer with a tiny snap of her wrist, the nearest Daisy had possibly ever come to defiance. As he held the official paper straight before him, squinting a little—he was at that age when a man has begun to require reading glasses and will not admit this truth to himself—Daisy noticed that his fingers shook a little.

"Marguerite," he said. "This is your given name, Marguerite?"

"Yes."

"D'Aubigny. This was your family name, before you married?"

Daisy aimed for a note of bored irony. "So it says on my papers, as you see."

"But is it *true*?" he demanded.

"True? I don't understand."

"Your father's name was d'Aubigny?"

"Yes, of course." She opened her mouth to babble out all the details, that her father was a soldier of the Great War who had died at Verdun before she was born, so she had never known him, had spent her entire childhood here at the Ritz with her grandmother, because this German was staring at poor Daisy like she had failed a critical examination at school and must be demoted to the year below, which made her panic. She stopped herself in time. It was Grandmère's voice in her head—*Don't babble, child!*—that saved her. (Also in obedience to Grandmère's voice, she straightened up, child.)

He spent a moment considering this. His lips were sealed tight, and his nostrils flared a little as he breathed. Finally he nodded. "I see."

He returned the identity card and she stuffed it back in her pocketbook. He was staring at the parting of her hair, she knew. As she fumbled with the old, worn clasp that wouldn't properly shut, he spoke again, and this time she noticed that his French was actually excellent, that he didn't have that usual awkward, guttural way with the delicate vowels. He caressed them almost as a Frenchman would, with reverence. Of course, this only made Daisy dislike him still more, if that were possible. How dare he lay some kind of ownership on her beloved native tongue! At last she forced the clasp shut and went to retrieve her books, but the German had already bent his long body and retrieved them for her, the final straw. She hated him. She snatched the books back and pressed them against her chest.

"If that's all, lieutenant colonel—"

"One more question, if you please, madame. What is your business here?"

"My business?"

"If you please, madame."

She wanted to say that she *lived* here, you German turd, this was her *home,* that was her business here! But that wasn't quite true anymore, and besides it would make him suspicious. So she said the truth. "I'm delivering some books to my grandmother."

"Your grandmother stays here?"

"Yes." Again, she bit herself off before she could babble out her grandmother's name and history and state of health.

Against odds, he smiled a little. "Your grandmother likes to read?"

"Yes."

"Then let us carry the books up to her together."

"No! That isn't necessary. I'm perfectly capable of carrying a few books up a few stairs."

"No doubt, but German chivalry demands that I don't allow you to."

Well! Her hatred was now so strong, it gave her actual courage, imagine that. Like a glass of good champagne, swiftly drunk. She gave this obnoxious fellow a look of French defiance such as even her grandmother would approve, one that must communicate through even the thickest German skull what Daisy d'Aubigny Villon thought of German chivalry.

She spoke in a voice that measured about zero degrees centigrade, although her insides shook a little. "I assure you, lieutenant colonel, I don't need any help."

"Madame, please. You must allow me—"

"You have far more important matters to attend to, I'm sure."

At that instant, there was a roar of laughter from the Little Bar, and Bernard appeared at her elbow.

"Herr Lieutenant Colonel," he said hurriedly, "there is a telephone call for you at the bar."

The German answered without taking his gaze from Daisy's face. "A telephone call? That's odd. From whom?"

"The party wouldn't say, I'm afraid."

"Yes. Very well."

Then the German did something strange. He lifted Daisy's right hand away from the books, so that she had to shift her weight to keep her grip on them, and he kissed the tips of her fingers with his thin, soft lips.

"Madame," he said, "you will please excuse me."

Daisy tore her fingers away and darted past him to the stairs. On the fourth step, she turned to thank Bernard with her eyes, but it was not the doorman who remained there in the hall with the chandelier glittering on his pale hair. It was the German officer, who had taken a gold watch from some inner pocket of his uniform and now stared at the open case, inspecting the hour.

Now, Daisy might have spent her childhood inside the walls of the Ritz Paris, but that was the Place Vendôme side, in Grandmère's permanent suite that was like an apartment lifted straight from the Palace of Versailles, except more homelike. (The Ritz liked to think of itself as a kind of grand country residence rather than a hotel.) This building, the rue Cambon side, connected to the main building by a long gallery that traversed the garden courtyard, wasn't nearly as familiar to her. In fact, so flustered was Daisy by the encounter with the German, she turned down the wrong corridor and spent an awful, dizzy moment in total discombobulation, imagining the entire hotel had turned on some new and previously unknown axis. Then recognition came to her in a flash—oddly enough, the memory of some childhood game of hide and seek—and she turned back and went down the correct corridor this time, humbled, heart still pounding against her ribs, mouth dry, fingertips itching where the German officer had kissed them. She found Grandmère's door and knocked on the louvered panel.

"Come in," came her grandmother's voice, almost inaudible because the doors at the Ritz were made of solid, heavy wood that actually hurt your knuckles a little when you knocked on them.

Daisy shifted the books to her left arm and used her right hand to turn the handle. Grandmère's apartment faced northwest, overlooking rue Cambon from the third floor. You could see Mademoiselle Chanel's atelier at number 31, now closed for the duration of the war. Only the perfume business remained open. Mademoiselle Chanel was too canny a businesswoman not to clear herself a fortune selling bottles of Chanel No. 5 to all the German wives. The afternoon light was just beginning to make itself known through the windows, illuminating the gilded Louis Quinze furniture—reproduction, but well-made reproduction, elegantly upholstered—and the two people who sat on the pair of sofas that flanked the fireplace, Grandmère and a man Daisy didn't recognize, wearing a dark, rather shabby suit. They both looked at her in the doorway. The man stood. Daisy had a fleeting impression of glossy brown hair—a little too much of it, really—and a dry smile as she passed her gaze over him to find Grandmère.

"Why, what's the matter?" asked Grandmère.

Daisy opened her mouth and glanced at the stranger. "Nothing."

"You look like you've had a fright."

"It's just the stairs. And I took a wrong turn."

"A wrong *turn*?"

"I keep thinking you're in the old apartment." Daisy stepped closer and set the volumes down on the sofa table. They made a soft, leathery thump on the wood, which was overpolished in the Ritz tradition. "Here are your books."

"Thank you, my dear. Give your grandmother a kiss, now."

Daisy smiled and bent to place a kiss on Grandmère's cheek. She smelled of powder and perfume and something else, a new and pungent scent, not native to her grandmother at all. "You're well?" she asked quietly.

"Quite well. Daisy, my darling, this is Monsieur Legrand, a friend of mine just arrived in Paris."

Daisy straightened and turned. The man still stood politely in place before the opposite sofa with his smile and his glossy hair. The light picked out some gold among the brown. His eyes, however, regarded her with gravity. She pulled the sides of her cardigan closer together. "Monsieur," she said, by way of greeting.

She gave him no hand to clasp, no cheek to kiss, so he just ducked his head briefly and widened his smile. His jacket was unbuttoned to reveal a knitted vest, as if he expected the weather to turn. "Madame Villon. It's a pleasure to meet you."

His French was exquisite, absolutely without flaw, but Daisy had some idea nonetheless that this Monsieur Legrand was not a Frenchman. It wasn't his voice but his bearing, his stance. Also the pipe, which she now noticed dangling from his right hand and recognized as the source of the unusual spicy odor, so out of place in her grandmother's apartment.

"A friend of my grandmother's? I don't recall her mentioning the name before."

"Ah. I suppose you might say I'm more of an acquaintance."

"A new and trusted acquaintance," said Grandmère. "Monsieur Legrand is a poet, darling. He's begun working at the bookshop to support his literary ambitions."

"A poet," Daisy said dubiously. "Is this really a proper time for poetry?"

"For poetry above all, Madame Villon. It's how we make sense of the world around us, isn't it?"

"*Good* poetry, perhaps."

He put his hand—the hand with the pipe—to his heart. "You wound me."

"I beg your pardon. I'm sure your work is wonderful."

"His work is tremendously important," said Grandmère, "which is why I'm afraid it's time for you to leave, monsieur, so you may return to it."

Monsieur Legrand spread out his arms and bowed extravagantly. "As you wish, madame."

"And you may return these books to the shop as well." Grandmére reached forward and picked up a pair of slim volumes that rested on the edge of the sofa table, next to the fireplace. "I've finished them both. Quite good. Tell Monsieur Lapin that I approve of his selections."

"I shall with pleasure, madame." Legrand lifted a glass from the table—cognac, Daisy thought—and finished it off in a flick of his wrist. For an instant, his eyes closed, bringing all his concentration to bear on this mouthful of spirits, and no wonder. Grandmère kept only the best cognac, and God help the Nazi who tried to confiscate her private store in the name of the Reich. Daisy found herself staring at the intersection of frayed white cuff and bare wrist. His skin was tanned, and it was only May. He set the glass down, and the wrist disappeared once more beneath the cuff.

"Don't forget your hat," said Grandmère.

"Of course. Good day, madame." He turned to Daisy and fetched up another smile. "Good day, madame. Until we meet again."

He stuck his pipe in his mouth and made his way to the door, hardly pausing to snatch his hat from the commode as he went. He closed the door with just enough force to make a decisive click of the latch, and at that exact instant the room dimmed a degree or two, like the sun had gone behind some cloud in the western sky.

"Glass of cognac, my dear?" said Grandmère. "You look as if you need one."

"No, thank you." Daisy lowered herself on the sofa, taking care to avoid the small, warm hollow left there by Monsieur Legrand. "I can only stay a moment. The children will be home from school."

"Yes, the children. And there is this dinner party to prepare for, no?"

"That too."

Grandmère pressed her lips together. She was a slight woman, shorter than Daisy by several centimeters, topped by a mass of fluffy hair that had recently—and rather abruptly—turned from its original ash blond, without a strand of gray, to a luminescent white. That was Grandmère for you, all or nothing. As always, she was a little over-dressed for the occasion, in a long dress of emerald silk topped by a short quilted jacket of aquamarine satin, a combination of colors that could never have worked on any woman except Grandmère, who had been born Minnie Gold of New York City and wore whatever the devil she liked. Now she stood in a rustle of silk and went to the liquor cabinet. "Cognac you must have, my dear, whether you want it or not. Actually, I suspect you *do* want it, only you don't think it's ladylike to ask."

"Oh, Grandmère . . ."

"Here. I've saved you the trouble." Grandmère returned with a snifter, which she handed to Daisy. The lamp made her rings glitter. The jewels used to be real, but Grandmère had sold them off, one by one, and replaced them with paste, which everybody pretended not to notice. Anyway, you couldn't tell unless you were up close and happened to know a great deal about gems. They were excellent fakes, the best. Grandmère would accept nothing less.

Daisy stared down for a moment or two at the amber circle between her thumb and forefinger. Grandmère resumed her seat on the opposite sofa. Daisy sipped. A very small sip, and then a larger one. Oh, the burn! But it was a nice burn, a good, expensive burn, a familiar burn that tasted of home. From the sofa cushions came a whiff of pipe tobacco.

"I need your help," said Grandmère.

Daisy glanced at the books on the sofa table. "I'm already helping you, aren't I?"

"It's not enough."

"You know I can't. It's risky enough, what I'm doing. Carrying your stupid books back and forth."

"There's no risk at all. Nobody knows what you're really carrying. Nobody would notice if they looked."

"They might. Germans are like bloodhounds. Have your new fellow do it. That's his job, isn't it?"

"My new fellow?"

Daisy nodded at the door. "Monsieur Legrand. He's one of your little army, I can smell it on him."

"That? That's just his pipe, my darling. He's a poet, as I told you."

"Oh, of course. A poet. Who just happens to have found work at your favorite bookshop."

"Well, Jacques needed someone to replace dear Émile, who—as you know—had to leave so abruptly because of his poor mother in Brittany. Someone with enough skill and knowledge to—"

Daisy held up her hand. "I don't want to know what he does. I don't care. I don't want to get mixed up in your crazy plots. I have a husband and children to think of. I'm just delivering books to my grandmother, that's all."

"Your mother would have—"

"My mother is dead."

She said this a little more sharply than she meant to, and Grandmère winced at the noise, or the sentence, or both. Daisy looked away, to the fireplace, where the familiar Rodin twisted its black, sinuous limbs on the left-hand side, just as it had in the old apartment. She set the empty glass on the sofa table and rose. The cognac was already making her dizzy.

"Stop," said Grandmère. "Please."

"I can't help you, Grandmère. I'm sorry, but I really can't. You're right, I'm not like Maman, I'm not brave or defiant or cunning. I can't do what she did. I'm just Daisy. And my children will be home soon, and my husband, and we're having some important people to dinner tonight, people who can help Pierre in his work—"

"Exactly, and—"

"And that's all I can do. I can't risk getting into trouble, helping somebody else's family. I'm sorry, but I can't. To protect my children, to keep my children safe, that's all I care about."

"Well," said her grandmother. "Well."

Daisy couldn't bring herself to look at Grandmère. That look of pity and frustration, she couldn't stand it this time. Instead she dragged her gaze along the wall until she found the curio case in the corner, old-fashioned not in the elegant way of the rest of Grandmère's furniture, but brown-legged and lined in faded burgundy velvet. She stared for a moment at the little halo of light on the glass cover. "I know I'm disappointing you. I know you wish I were like her."

"Like whom?"

"Like my mother. But I'm not a heroine. I am not capable of doing miraculous deeds. I just want to stay alive. I want my children to stay alive."

"And your husband?"

Daisy shrugged and returned her gaze at last to Grandmère's face, which was more tender than she expected. Maybe she was getting soft in her old age. Then Daisy caught the books with the corner of her eye and thought, *Maybe not.*

"Pierre works to protect us," she said. "Everything he's doing, he does to protect us."

Grandmère put her hand on the arm of the sofa and hoisted herself upward, and it occurred to Daisy that this everyday action seemed to cost her grandmother a little more effort than it used to. But there was nothing stiff or measured about Grandmère's movements as she walked down the room, following the exact line of Daisy's earlier gaze, until she came to the display case. Instead of unlocking the glass lid, however, and taking out the talisman within—something an astonished Daisy had seen her do only a handful of times, her entire life—she stuck her hand underneath the case, palm upward, and pulled open a small, unmarked drawer.

"What's that?" Daisy asked.

Grandmère drew out a piece of paper and walked back to the sofa. She set the paper on the table and resumed her seat, without saying anything, until Daisy felt morally obliged to sit down, too. She looked at the paper, and at Grandmère, and her eyebrows rose.

"My dear Daisy," said her grandmother, straightening her dress around her knees, "we are none of us safe, don't you realize that? When they come for one of us, they come for any of us, all of us."

"Grandmère, my heart breaks for the Jews, it does. Why, Madame Halévy and her sweet children, across the street, it doesn't bear thinking of. The Nazis are monsters, worse than monsters—"

"Darling," said Grandmère, "darling, don't you understand? Haven't you ever guessed?"

An icicle seemed to have found its way inside Daisy's stomach, where it melted slowly and leached its coldness throughout her middle. "Guessed what?" she whispered.

Grandmère nodded to the paper that lay between them atop the sofa table. "Did it never occur to you? Minnie Gold of New York City, rich as Croesus, weds the Comte de Courcelles of Picardy, France. Are you really so naive?"

Daisy, her mouth dry, her stomach cold, wished for another glass of cognac. Instead she reached out and grasped the corner of the paper and held it before her, fluttering until she took the other side with her left hand to hold everything steady, hold the world steady. She didn't read it, however. She didn't need to. She was not so naive, not really.

"You're a Jew?" she whispered.

"Naturally I am. I haven't been to synagogue since I was a girl, I confess, but you see the family tree before you. And there is nothing on that page, dearest Daisy, that an industrious public official couldn't discover for himself, if he had the curiosity."

Daisy set the paper back down on the table and looked up. "Pierre can save you. Pierre——"

"Pierre is interested in nothing but his own neck, my dear, which is something I tried to tell you from the beginning. If Pierre can secure his own standing among his masters, he will happily sell his wife's grandmother to them. With a red bow tied on top of my head."

"But he can't! To accuse you would be to accuse *me*, his own wife. His own children!"

"Ah," said Grandmère. "You're beginning to see the situation."

"He wouldn't do it."

"Maybe he wouldn't. But I doubt he'd be able to stop those who would. He's a minor official, nobody important, no matter how much he thinks he ought to be. And the Nazis have begun to get serious about this business of hunting down the Jews in France. Maybe they've run out of prey in Germany and need their sport, I don't know. But we've heard that——"

Daisy put her hands over her ears. "No, don't say it."

"But you must hear, Daisy. You must." Grandmère went to the edge of her seat and reached across the table to grasp Daisy's elbow. "We are none of us safe, do you understand me? None of us. This Madame Halévy, I know her. Do you know why she was arrested? Because Émile was caught with the papers he'd forged, and they never got to her, she couldn't escape with her children. We lost Émile and we lost the Halévys, and time's running out. They're planning something more, something bigger. Not to pick us off one by one, but all of us at once. To round up everyone. So you must help me, Daisy. You must. If not for others, then for yourself and the children."

Daisy stared at her. The coldness had faded, and now she was just numb. For nearly two years she had lived with fear, ever since the Germans had first marched into Paris, and her husband, Pierre, had been arrested in his office, his stupid little post in the civil service of which he was so proud. Then the Nazis let him go, which was a relief, and he went back to work, but this time under the supervision of the occupiers, in a new bureau they had set up for agriculture and supply, managing the rationing of food, exactly the kind of petty lickspittle rule-enforcement he relished. So the fear remained, only at a low simmer, and also this terrible sick feeling of dependency on Pierre, this knowledge that her entire existence and that of her children relied on her husband's ability to remain in the good graces of the Nazis who ran Paris. And meanwhile her neighbors were being deported, her friends and acquaintances arrested at night without warning, so that her street and her arrondissement and all of Paris, really, existed under this suffocating atmosphere of terror, of panic just barely suppressed. What would she do, Daisy wondered, almost absently, if the numbness left her and the panic took its place?

"But there's nothing I can do," she said. "I don't have any skills. I can't forge papers or—or listen through keyholes—"

"Of course not. But you have a husband who is climbing his way up the Nazi ladder, and tonight he's hosting a dinner. A rather important dinner, from what I understand. Several Germans of considerable rank will be gathered around your table, eating your meat and drinking your wine—"

"Grandmère, that's unfair. I had nothing to do with that."

Grandmère's hand went up. "I'm not accusing you of anything, Daisy. I know your heart. All I need to know is the names of the people at dinner tonight, that's all. Just their names. You don't need to do anything at all."

Daisy gnawed her lip.

Grandmère put her index finger down in the middle of the paper. "I never wanted you to marry Pierre. He's a weak man, Daisy. Like watered-down wine. But you insisted, God knows why, a man twenty years your senior. You wanted a nice, respectable husband. I suppose I can understand. A girl who grew up without a father naturally wants to fill this void in her life. And now you have your respectable husband, you have your dear children, God bless them. You have your comfortable apartment in the Eighth. And what has it got you, after all? You don't love him."

"Enough, Grandmère. You don't understand, not a bit. You never have. You don't know what it's like to grow up without a mother or a father, with all the rumors—don't think I didn't hear them—in this crazy place, this hotel, like an animal growing up in a zoo, an animal nobody wants—"

"Don't say that. I always wanted you. I raised you myself. When your mother died, I wanted to die, too, and you were the only reason I did not simply kill myself with grief, because you needed me, and you were hers. And now I need you, Daisy. I need you to help me."

"Grandmère—"

"Their names, that's all. Just the *names*. Please, Daisy. Help me."

Daisy closed her eyes and knit her hands together in her lap. She gathered up an image of her children's faces—round-cheeked Olivier and pale, thoughtful Madeleine—and in the absence of sight, the whiff of pipe tobacco came to her again, mixing up the two ideas, her children and this Monsieur Legrand whose name was almost certainly not Legrand. She opened her eyes again and stood.

"I must get home," she said. "I'll think about what you've said."

DAISY FOUND HER way back downstairs without difficulty, clutching the book that she was supposed to return to the bookshop the next day. As she crossed the entrance hall, passing over the very spot where the

German officer had stopped her, she felt a shiver on the back of her neck. She glanced to the left, where the noises of revelry still floated free from the Little Bar.

She thought she saw a face turn away and melt back into the throng of uniforms. But perhaps she was mistaken. Just nerves, she told herself. Now she was seeing Germans everywhere, even when they weren't really there.

CHAPTER FOUR

Babs

The Hôtel Ritz
Paris, France
April 1964

M Y NERVES BOUNCED and tapped on my skin like flies, but when
I looked down to slap them away, I was surprised to see they
weren't really there at all.

"Really, Babs, this is so unlike you."

I glanced at my sister, Diana, behind the wheel of her roadster, the
wind rippling her headscarf. She met my gaze briefly—at least I think
she did since her eyes were hidden behind very large white-rimmed
sunglasses—then returned her focus to the road, which, considering
how she drove, was preferable.

I didn't want to argue with her, knowing I would lose and then agree
that we'd best turn around and head back to Langford Hall. Instead, I
remained silent as Diana continued to race toward the local train station, as I clutched the side of my door while surreptitiously checking
my watch. I didn't want to miss my train to London's Victoria where
I would catch the Night Ferry and its train to Gare du Nord in Paris,
knowing if I missed it, I wouldn't find the courage again.

I knew I was mad, throwing away caution and my good sense to meet a strange man in Paris. It was the sort of thing my sophisticated and incredibly beautiful sister would have done in her single days. And perhaps that was the main reason why I'd decided to go.

We'd slowed behind an ancient tractor whose driver seemed even older than the vehicle. Diana pressed down on the accelerator, the silk ends of her scarf fluttering like angry doves, and passed the tractor, moving back into our lane just as another car approached in the opposite lane. My stomach jumped, lurching up into the place where I needed air to breathe, and I was suddenly very, very sure I was doing absolutely the wrong thing.

Who would manage the upcoming gymkhana? And who would handle the auditions for the nativity play? It was all very tricky with the feelings of the children's parents to contend with if their little angels weren't selected for the roles of Mary, Jesus, the wise men, and the shepherds. Perhaps they should add more characters that *might* have been present but had merely been ignored in the Bible? And how could I abandon my eldest, Robin, who'd been sent down from Cambridge for drinking? Drinking! The scourge of the Langfords, really. Excessive drinking had been involved on the night he'd been conceived, not that I would ever admit to such a thing. Because then I'd have to wonder if Kit had *needed* to be inebriated.

"I don't know why I'm aiding and abetting, but if it helps at all, Robin will be fine," Diana shouted over the wind. I didn't even blink at Diana's apparent ability to read my mind. It had always been that way between us.

"He simply misses his father," Diana continued. "But his uncle Reginald is more than happy to take him under his wing, I assure you. Reggie is thrilled to have a boy to take fishing and with whom to do manly things. I don't think he's fully forgiven me for giving him three daughters, so Robin is truly a balm to that sore spot."

I only nodded, unable to speak past the ball in my throat. I wouldn't cry. I was British.

Diana parked her car and despite my protests, insisted on accompanying me inside, although she allowed me to carry my worn valise. Diana, although four years my senior and a full head shorter, still maintained the grace and poise of the debutante she'd once been and had never handled her own luggage. She frowned up at me. "They might not let you into the Ritz, you know."

"Whyever not? I have a reservation."

Diana gave her familiar smirk, the one she'd been using since we were eight and four and I'd dared return to the house covered in muck acquired from playing with our brothers and Kit. "Really, Babs. Your valise looks like it was dragged behind a horse in battle. Why didn't you ask to borrow one of mine?"

"Do you think they really notice those things?"

"At the Paris Ritz? I'd say so." Diana frowned again. "Really, Babs. You have the most beautiful skin and such fine gray eyes. And most women would kill for your figure and bone structure. Why on earth do you hide behind all of those . . . tweeds? You dress like a ninety-year-old woman instead of the thirty-eight-year-old you are." With a quick tug, she removed my wool scarf, the last one I'd knitted while Kit had been ailing, and replaced it with her silk Hermès with the beautiful blue pheasants strutting all over a pale yellow background. As she gently looped it beneath my chin, she said, "There. Much better. Now you don't look like a refugee."

Her gaze traveled up to my hat—bought on sale at Debenhams—and then down to my legs and feet, respectably clad in lisle stockings and my best brogues. "Babs, I do wish . . ."

The *chuff chuff* of an approaching train made me jump, my heart racing now at the prospect of actually stepping onto the train and beginning my journey. The scent of Diana's perfume wafted up from the scarf, comforting me, allowing me a modicum of confidence. Despite my sister's shorter stature, she'd never lacked confidence and now, more than ever before, I needed that.

As the train chugged into the station, I turned to Diana. "Do you still think I'm being reckless?"

Diana pressed her lips together. "Most definitely." Then her mouth softened into a smile. "But I also think that recklessness might be the thing we need sometimes to see our lives anew." She put a hand on each of my shoulders then leaned in to kiss each cheek. "Godspeed, dear sister. And do write at least once. It will be nice to be living vicariously through your life for a change." She briefly raised her elegant eyebrows, then smiled reassuringly. "Remember you're wearing a Hermès scarf, and hopefully no one will notice your luggage. Or your shoes."

I remembered her words as my taxi pulled up in front of the Place Vendôme entrance to the Ritz, the white awnings and brass lighting fixtures reflecting the bright sun, making it appear as if those passing through the hallowed doors had somehow been anointed. My door was opened by a white-gloved valet and I realized his deep blue uniform with the gold edging was perhaps more fashionable than my tweed traveling suit. I hesitated for a moment, almost believing that if I cowered long enough in the taxi, the valet would forget all about me and I could simply find a side entrance in which to enter without any fuss.

"Madame?" A white-gloved hand stretched toward me.

Remembering Diana's scarf, I took a deep breath and placed my hand in his and allowed him to help me from the taxi. "Bonjour."

His eyes flickered imperceptibly. "Bonjour, madame. You are English?" he asked in English with only the hint of an accent.

"Yes," I said with surprise. "How did you know?"

His eyes flickered again as his smile broadened. "Just a guess, madame. This way, please." He was still looking for my luggage when I finished paying the taxi driver. Or, more accurately, staring at my valise as if it might bite. It was more than past its prime. It had once belonged to my mother and she'd used it as a schoolgirl. I'd brought it on my very brief wedding trip with Kit to the Peak District, and on our overnight trips to visit the children once they'd gone away to school. It was functional and served its purpose and I'd never once considered the need to replace it. Until now.

I was about to suggest I carry it so as not to sully his white gloves when I was distracted by a couple of women walking past us into the awning-covered arched entrance. They were both slender with short, shiny hair, white sunglasses, and long, bare legs that appeared longer because of the shockingly short hemlines of their dresses. Men's heads turned, yet the two women appeared unaware of the attention as they walked up the red-carpeted steps and disappeared inside. I glanced down at the thick hem of my skirt hitting my legs midcalf and felt those same men looking at me but not for the same reason.

I took a step back, ready to return to the safety of Langford Hall, and found myself facing the Place Vendôme. A tall column dominated the center of the square, and I recalled my brother Charles, who'd read history at Oxford and had thought everyone as fascinated with the past as he'd been, saying it had been fabricated by more than a thousand melted cannons captured by Napoleon's troops at Austerlitz. A statue of the emperor himself stood at the top, dressed as a Roman emperor, naturally.

The valet coughed politely, but I couldn't remove my gaze from the little man at the top of the column. There was something about his pose, or perhaps it was his legendary hubris, that gave me an odd burst of confidence. If a diminutive Corsican could conquer most of the world's armies, then surely I could step into the Paris Ritz with my tweeds and brogues. And Diana's scarf.

"Madame?" the valet repeated, his hand indicating the entrance.

I managed a smile, then followed in the footsteps of the two young women, feeling a lot like how I imagined Marie Antoinette must have felt on her way to the guillotine. I paused in the threshold, the scent of flowers wafting over me, allowing myself a moment for my eyes to adjust from the bright sunshine outside. I stood blinking like the village idiot, unable to move forward as two opposing thoughts collided in my head simultaneously.

The first was how opulent, how grand the crystal chandeliers, the thick rugs, the vases filled with elaborate floral arrangements, the gilded mirrors and the people walking through the palatial hall appeared to be. It all reminded me of the dolls and the dollhouse Diana and I had once played with as children, a fantasy world with imaginary people. The second was how absolutely out of place I was, how I had most certainly taken a wrong turn when I'd made the rash decision to shake myself from my melancholy. I should have opted for a weekend in the Cotswolds instead.

The bar to the left seemed filled with more well-dressed people, all having highbrow conversations because they looked the sort to know a lot about everything. A burst of laughter floated out from the dimly lit room, and I found myself cringing, certain that they must be laughing at me.

Another uniformed man approached and introduced himself as the hallway manager, his French name quickly forgotten in my embarrassment at being noticed, then escorted me to a desk near the bottom of the wrought-iron wrapped staircase. I peered past the enormous tapestry hanging on the stairwell wall, upward through the loops of gleaming brass banisters to the upper floors.

A woman's voice caught my attention. "I thought this was the Paris Ritz and not some hourly motel. Because I just can't understand why the flowers that arrive in my room in the morning are sad little crawdads on the wrong end of a fishing net by afternoon. You must be giving me day-old flowers, which isn't what I expected at all. If you can't get it right, then I'd prefer no flowers in my room at all." Her words were light and airy, carrying with them a strong accent that brought to mind Scarlett O'Hara. I turned with interest, as it wasn't just the accent that reminded me of that particular indomitable and stubborn heroine.

"Miss Dubose, I assure you," began the young man behind the desk in perfect English, his face a mask of understanding. "Our flowers are cut fresh every morning. Perhaps they're sitting in the sun in your room? We can certainly place the vase . . ."

"Pardon me," I said, a feeling of familiarity a welcome reprieve. If there was one thing I knew, it was flowers. I'd had my own flower patch in my mother's garden since I was small, kneeling in the dirt beside her as she worked. I was more at home with my hands in the rich soil than holding a delicate teacup. The hardest part about doing without during the war had been the requisitioning of my flower garden to grow vegetables.

The woman looked at me, and I realized we were both tall, our eyes level. She was older than me, perhaps in her late forties, but it was hard to judge by exactly how much because of her exquisite skin and flawless makeup. Beneath her elegant hat, her hair was that lovely color of blond that caught the light at every angle, and her slender figure was evident from her form-fitting silk skirt and jacket in the most extraordinary color that reminded me of the sunsets over the lake at Langford Hall.

She was looking at me expectantly, so before my better judgment could intervene, I pressed on. "You see, if one should sear the stems in boiling water, the blooms will perk up as if they'd just been cut from the garden. And a drop of bleach in the vase is all they'll need to remain shipshape for two to three days."

The woman didn't say anything as her gaze swept my person from head to toe and then back again. Then she turned toward the young man behind the desk and said, "That sounds like very good advice. I would appreciate it if your people would do as . . ." She paused, waiting.

"Mrs. Langford," I supplied.

"As Mrs. Langford has suggested."

The man nodded once. "Of course, Miss Dubose. I will see to it personally."

Miss Dubose turned to me again, her clear blue gaze on me. "You're British, aren't you, dear?"

I frowned, having the distinct impression that it hadn't been my accent that had given me away. "Yes, actually. I am."

She smiled tolerantly as if she might be speaking with a young child with food on her face. "Of course you are. I'm American. From Memphis, Tennessee," she said as if I'd asked. "Are you staying at the Ritz?"

"I'm just now checking in." I looked expectantly across the desk.

The young man handed me a key. "Everything is arranged, Madame Langford. Enjoy your stay."

Miss Dubose reached over and took the key from his hand. "Really, Jacques. Is that the best you can do for Madame Langford? She's come all the way from England, has just given you expert advice on keeping flowers fresh, and you give her a tiny room on the wrong side of the hotel? That won't do. Please find her another room—preferably one of the suites on the Vendôme side?"

"Oh no!" I protested. "That's completely unnecessary. I'm sure the original room is quite suitable."

"It isn't," Miss Dubose countered. "And this is simply what they do at the Ritz. They make their guests comfortable and happy. Let's allow them to do their jobs, shall we? I think they get quite upset if they believe we might be unhappy." She glanced across the desk, where the man stood absolutely still with a smile on his face.

"Of course," he said. There wasn't even a flicker in the man's eyes. He simply gave another single nod before referring to a large ledger on the desk and pulling out another key. Handing it to me, he said, "Enjoy your stay, Madame Langford. And do let us know how else we may serve you."

I turned to look for my valise but found it had disappeared—hopefully to the correct room. "Don't worry, Mrs. Langford," Miss Dubose said. "Your clothes will be unpacked and placed in your closets and drawers by the time you get upstairs. And hopefully they can work their magic on your valise, too, although I do say it's hopeless."

I was sure she'd just been insulting, but she was smiling so pleasantly that I wasn't certain. "It was a pleasure meeting you, Miss Dubose."

"How long will you be staying?" she asked, her words spoken slowly and with the irritating habit of consonants disappearing from the endings of her words.

"I'm not exactly sure. I'm here because . . ." I tried to find words for my reason to be in Paris, but found that I couldn't explain it even to myself. "I'm on a business trip," I said with confidence, imagining that's what Diana would have said.

"Ah, you're here for a man." The woman actually winked at me.

It felt as if someone had just immersed me in a hot bath. "No, no . . ." I flushed even hotter at my stutter.

The concierge chose that moment to interject. "One moment, Madame Langford. You have a message." He handed me a small envelope with my name written on the front in familiar bold, messy, and decidedly masculine handwriting. I peered up at Miss Dubose and found her smiling knowingly.

"Excuse me," I said, pulling out a piece of embossed Ritz stationery from the envelope.

Dear Mrs. Langford,

I trust that you have arrived safely from England. Allow me to suggest that you spend your first day acclimating yourself to Paris, and then we can

*rendezvous at the Bar Hemingway (on the Cambon side) at eight o'clock
tomorrow evening.*

   I look forward to meeting you then.

   Yours,

   Andrew Bowdoin

I stared at the word *rendezvous* and my cheeks flamed once more.

Miss Dubose patted my hand. "An assignation? How simply marvelous."

Assignation? That was even worse than *rendezvous*. It made my hasty visit to Paris seem so . . . sordid. "No, no . . ." I stammered again in protest. "He merely wants to rend . . . meet tomorrow evening at the Bar Hemingway . . ."

"How delightful. But, darling, you must allow me to take you shopping first." Her eyes flickered over me, her head turning from side to side as she studied my face and my hair that I'd piled into a functional sort of bun at the back of my head and tucked under my Debenhams hat. "There is so much here to work with and your skin is just lovely when you're flushing like that." She looked thoughtful for a moment. "I'm supposing that whatever you have in your valise isn't suitable to wear, either."

Her face brightened, her eyes widening, and I suddenly felt like a fox surrounded by barking beagles. "Meet me right here tomorrow morning at ten, and I will take you shopping at Printemps. I'll have you looking pretty as a picture before you go meet your beau."

"He's not my . . ."

Miss Dubose seemed not to have heard me and was waving at someone across the lobby. I followed her gaze toward a pinch-faced and gray-haired woman standing with a cane, wearing clothes that were even more out of fashion than my own. She appeared to be at least ninety years old and in a very loud and shrill American accent was demanding that someone—anyone—find her spectacles (perhaps the same that were currently hanging from her neck) and saying something about surviving the sinking of the *Lusitania*.

Turning back to me, Miss Dubose said, "I must go see to my friend, Mrs. Schuyler. It's been a delight meeting you, Mrs. Langford, and I honestly can hardly wait until our shopping trip tomorrow. You will be *transformed*. Goodbye for now." With a little wave of her fingertips, she walked away, her high heels clicking across the floor. Turning her head as she walked, she added over her shoulder, "And that's a lovely scarf—wear it tomorrow."

"But—" I closed my mouth, aware that others had paused to watch. Diana had always loved being the center of attention, but I had never appreciated being a spectacle simply because I hadn't wanted observers to be disappointed. Feeling the gazes of strangers, I abruptly turned on my heel, my brogues sticking stubbornly to the marble tiles and most likely scuffing the shiny surface, and made a hasty retreat out of the front door, my head down to avoid meeting anyone's gaze.

I walked blindly, somehow managing to avoid other pedestrians, simply eager to escape the Ritz and the knowledge that I'd made a fool of myself coming to Paris. I needed to go back to England as soon as possible. I would make my excuses to Miss Dubose in the morning and leave a note for Mr. Bowdoin, and then I would take the first train home.

Having reached my conclusion, I stopped in the middle of the sidewalk. A man bumped into me and said something in French that certainly wasn't *pardon*. I looked up at the blue street sign on the building in front of me, hoping I could at least find my way back to the hotel. *Rue Volney*. I stared at it for a long moment, wondering why it sounded familiar. A stream of angry French erupted beside me as an older man with a long brown cigarette and beret made an exaggerated show of going around me.

I apologized and moved to the edge of the sidewalk and looked up at the sign again. *Rue Volney*. I'd seen that name recently. And it had meant something to me, but I was at a loss now in recalling what it had been. A man with a pipe walked past me, heading toward the zebra crossing. I turned at the smell of his tobacco, the scent making my heart ache, my gaze following him across the street. When he'd reached the other side, he entered the corner door of a shop built into the bottom floor of a white plastered building.

A small table full of stacked books sat on the sidewalk to the side of the entrance, a sign directly over the door reading *Livres*. Glass-paned windows covered the two angled sides of the building, allowing passersby to view the piles of books inside. I lifted my gaze and there, dangling from the deep awning, hung a large wooden placard with the words *Le Mouton Noir*.

I recalled now where I'd seen those words. They'd been stamped inside the cover of Kit's cherished copy of *The Scarlet Pimpernel* that he'd bought in France during the war. Which meant he'd been to this bookshop, had walked through those doors, had slid a volume or two from the shelves. Had purchased at least one book in this very store.

I knew there would be nothing of Kit there still, but something—maybe it had been the pipe smoke—compelled me to find out for myself. I stepped into the intersection, looking right as I always did for oncoming traffic. Someone grabbed my arm from behind, forcibly pulling me back against a strong, firm chest that smelled pleasantly of soap. I opened my mouth to screech out a protest just as a lorry sped past me on the left, passing close enough that I felt the movement of forced air on my face.

"Are you all right, ma'am?" said a decidedly American male voice as the tight grip on my arm ceased. "I hope I didn't hurt you, but you were looking the wrong way."

My heart hammered wildly as I stared up into the face of my rescuer and for the third time in an hour, I found myself blushing profusely. I was a widow with three children and one should be expected at this stage in one's life not to be so easily ruffled. He was young-looking, with hair the color of hay, and eyes that were either green or brown—I was too flustered to look closely. He was a large man—not like a man who enjoyed his pints, but more like one who enjoyed sports and outdoor activities. Diana would call him *muscular* and a definite *looker*. Not that I'd ever use either word although in this case they were decidedly accurate.

"No. Of course. Thank you. I didn't see the lorry, you see, and I thought no one was coming, and I wanted to cross the road to the bookshop, and I'm British so I looked right . . ." The words tumbled from my mouth like dandelion seeds, spewing in every direction at an alarming rate.

A swarm of pedestrians moved toward the crosswalk at the light change, sweeping us across the street as if we were no more than pebbles in a downpour. The man held my elbow as if I were a feeble old woman, escorting me to the other side before making sure I'd safely ascended the curb. I began to tell him that it was all unnecessary and that I was perfectly capable of walking when a loudly gesticulating Frenchwoman speaking to a companion dislodged my hat and knocked it to the sidewalk and then carried on as if unaware of what she'd just done.

The American bent down to retrieve the hat before anyone trampled on it, pausing for a moment with a small smile on his lips. "I think my mother has this exact same hat," he said as he handed it back to me. His smile faded quickly as he caught a closer glimpse of my face, visible now without my hat.

"Oh, I'm sorry. I beg your pardon. I thought with . . ." He made a vague movement with his hands either indicating my shoes, my suit, my hat, or all of the above. "I mean, I thought you were older. My greatest apologies." With a deeply chagrined expression that somehow made him even more appealing, he pulled open the door. "You were headed to the bookshop? I am, too."

I glanced behind him to the crowded interior of the shop, the floor-to-ceiling shelves crammed with multihued volumes with more stacks of books on the floors crowding the aisles. I could not imagine being in that small space with this large man—not the least reason being that I found him attractive and he thought of me as elderly.

Clutching my hat to my chest and no doubt crushing it beyond repair, I shook my head. "Actually, I've changed my mind. Thank you again."

I turned on my heel, prepared to cross the street from where I'd just come.

"Look left," the man shouted as I once again approached the intersection looking the wrong way. Completely mortified, I pretended I hadn't heard him and instead of crossing the street, took a left down the sidewalk, intent on walking until I'd forgotten the scent of pipe tobacco, and the hazel—yes, they were definitely hazel—eyes of a particularly outspoken, well-fed, and well-groomed American. Except all I'd accomplished after an hour of walking was a pair of very sore feet and a memory that remained startlingly clear.

CHAPTER FIVE

Aurélie

The Château de Courcelles
Picardy, France
September 1914

THE TOWERS OF the Château de Courcelles stood out clearly against the gray-tinged light of dawn.

Aurélie could have sobbed with relief at the sight of them. She managed to turn the sob to a sort of half gulp, half hiccup, but she couldn't control the shivers that made her teeth knock together and her skin prickle beneath her too-thin clothes. She balled her hands together to stop their shaking, trying to find some, any, of that buoyant spirit with which she had set off the previous evening, back when it had seemed a brilliant gesture to thumb her nose at Paris and the Ritz and spin the wheel east, to Courcelles.

She had seen the battlefield and assumed that would be the worst of it.

She had been wrong. So wrong.

Aurélie yanked the corners of her thin jacket closer and tried to ignore the memory of a hand protruding from a ditch, an English soldier bloated with death and wastewater, his feet bare where someone had looted his boots.

The crows had been at him, even in the dark she could tell that much. The stench had been appalling. She had forced herself to stay and murmur a quick prayer for his soul—a very quick prayer. It seemed the least she could do. She'd had vague thoughts of covering him somehow, but then the sound of someone's motor had forced her to flee into the woods, and he had been left to the crows again.

It felt as though she had been walking for years, cursing the delicate shoes that had been fashioned for the thick rugs of the Ritz, not the viscous mud of Picardy. She had been forced to abandon her beloved Hispano-Suiza somewhere just north of Haudouin, after an anxious farmer, mistaking her for a German, put a bullet in the fuel tank and narrowly missed putting another one into her shoulder. When she'd shouted back that she was French, he'd not apologized, not really, only shouted at her that she was a fool to be about and made some rather alarming insinuations about her status and her level of virtue. Aurélie had deemed it wiser to depart than to debate the point.

The car was beyond saving. A sacrifice for France, she'd told herself, trying to make light of it, but she'd never imagined how dark the night might be, nor how small she could feel without that metal carapace between her and the world. She took to the fields, but it was slow going in the dark, and she'd found herself floundering about, her skirt knee deep in mud, terrified that she'd lost her way and was going in circles. She'd always prided herself on her sense of direction, but it was one thing to find one's way by road, another to navigate in darkness by the stars and the sound of shelling behind her.

She'd crept back to the road, but that had been a mistake. The Germans controlled the roads here. She spent a miserable hour in a ditch, shivering in the mud as a German convoy thundered past, sending troops to reinforce the line. She had simmered with frustration and shame, certain she should be doing something—but what? What use was she against a phalanx of Germans? She didn't even have a knife, much less a gun, just a miraculous talisman that might or might not confer some sort of benefit on the wearer. Her ancestors, she thought darkly, might have been more specific. It was a pity they hadn't taken something of more utility from Saint Jeanne. A sword, perhaps, or an arquebus.

The talisman dug into the skin between her breasts. Aurélie crossed herself and muttered a quick prayer of apology. The fault wasn't in the talisman; it was in her. Her weakness, her shame. Her father had flung himself into battle at the age of fifteen. Here she was, four years older than he had been then, cravenly crouching in a ditch, painfully aware of her own uselessness.

Never, ever before had Aurélie felt herself so completely powerless. Here, in the dark, caught between two armies, all of her father's noble blood, all of her mother's precious francs couldn't protect her. She was only a woman, alone.

Aurélie fled back to the woods, skulking past burned-out farms, creeping carefully around the outskirts of villages where the German imperial flag hung like a taunt above the *mairies*. Her stomach rumbled. Petits fours at the Ritz had been a very long time ago. She wished she'd had the sense to bring food, a proper coat, anything. She'd always thought herself a countrywoman at heart, but she had never experienced the country like this. How had she thought the countryside quiet? Every step made the brush crackle. A wolf howled and an animal let out a high-pitched squeal. The woods felt like something out of the stories her nurse had told her: Red Riding Hood and the wolf, Hansel and Gretel and the witch lying in wait.

A man approached her, a man in a British uniform. He spoke in what sounded like an educated voice but Aurélie shook her head and turned her back on him, walking very quickly away, resisting the urge to break into a run, to run and run with the twigs yanking at her silk stockings and the tree branches reaching clawing fingers toward her hair.

Would morning never come? The night seemed to go on forever, far longer than any night ought to be allowed; Aurélie began to fear it would never be day again. She grimaced at her own whimsy. Of course, day must come. Mustn't it? Just because she had been a fool didn't mean the earth would stop its spinning. She hoped. She felt like a medieval peasant, afraid of the dark, stumbling along in a fog of cold and fear, her entire being reduced to the animal instinct of avoiding pursuit.

When the sky began to lighten she scarcely knew it at first; her eyes were so firmly fixed on the path ahead. But there, there, the sky was surely more gray than black ahead. And was that . . .

Yes. Yes, it was. In the distance, the great tower of Courcelles, still a mile away or more, but *there*.

Her dress was in tatters, torn by twigs, her stockings glued to her heels by the blisters that had broken and bled, but Aurélie scarcely noticed the pain, buoyed by a relief so intense that she felt she floated rather than walked that last mile.

Home.

To the right, in the valley, lay the village of Courcelles, a cluster of brick houses with slate roofs, dominated by the substantial bulk of the *mairie*, tapering off into farmhouses toward the edges. To the left, up a deliberately steep road, loomed the Château de Courcelles, quiet in the gray dawn.

The village was beginning to wake; Aurélie could see the thin curls of smoke beginning to emerge from chimneys as ovens were lit. The smell of baking bread taunted her. But where were the men who ought, even this early, to be trudging toward the fields to harvest the hay? Where was the sigil of their house, flying from the tallest tower?

A terrible fear seized her. Over the course of the long, terrible night, she had seen so many homes burned, others abandoned or requisitioned. And that was to the west, closer to Paris. Courcelles was impregnable, so her father had always claimed, but that had been in the days of lances and siege engines, not now, not this.

Slowly, aware of every ache, every bruise, Aurélie began the long trudge up the hill she had so seldom traveled on foot. When she went to town, she drove the pony cart or rode one of her father's horses and people bowed as she passed.

A man emerged from the guardhouse, placing himself squarely on the path, a gun pointed at her chest. "Who goes there? *Kmint qu'os vos aplez?*"

The guttural tones of the Picard dialect made her weak with relief. The man was in the shadows of the guardhouse, but Aurélie knew his voice from the time she was little and he had put her on his shoulders to play with the weapons mounted on the wall in the hall.

"It is I." Her throat was so raw that the words came out as little more than a rasp. "Don't you know me, Victor?"

"Miss Aurélie?" Victor dropped the gun he had been holding, one of her father's fowling pieces, brilliant for making the lives of pheasants a misery, somewhat less useful for warding off invading armies. He grabbed her cold hands, chafing them for warmth. "Miss Aurélie! What happened to you? We thought you were in Paris!"

"I was." With difficulty, Aurélie withdrew her hands. "Don't fuss, Victor. *Cha va fin bien.*"

I'm quite all right. The old dialect came easily to her tongue, bringing tears to the big man's eyes.

"You don't look all right," he said, with the bluntness for which their region was famed. "You look like you had a fight with a hedge-hog and lost."

Aurélie gave a laugh that wobbled. "Close enough. Is my father here?"

"The seigneur is in the old keep." Victor followed after her through the gate and into the courtyard, forcing her to hang back. "Is it true the Germans are in Paris? Is that why you've come? We saw them go past—what they did in Catelet—" Victor spat on the flagstones.

Aurélie paused, looking over her shoulder at him. "They've not come to Courcelles?"

"Your father put a sentry on the road. Kill anyone who tries to come this way, he said," announced Victor proudly.

"Did they? Try, that is?"

"Well, no." Victor looked momentarily crestfallen. "They were too busy in Catelet. Beasts, they were. They shot Madame Lemaire Lienard through the throat—the throat!—as she lay hiding. There were beatings and men tied to trees and left to rot, houses looted, women— um, er. Well, then. But that was Catelet, not here. There were some as left the village when they heard the doings in Catelet. Fools. I told them the seigneur would protect them. Courcelles's not been conquered yet."

As far as Aurélie could make out, the last time anyone had tried had been roughly during the Thirty Years' War, but that was beside the point. Perhaps her father's reputation had preceded him. Perhaps the Germans simply hadn't wanted to climb the hill. Whatever the reason, she was grateful.

"Thanks be to God and Saint Jeanne. No, no, Victor," she remonstrated, as it seemed he meant to follow her and continue to regale her with horrors. "You mustn't leave your post. What if the Germans were to come and you were not here? There's no need to announce me. I know the way."

Every stone in the courtyard was an old friend; this had been her home every summer, while her mother enjoyed the more sophisticated pleasures of Deauville. Aurélie knew Courcelles as well as she knew the Ritz. Better. The Ritz belonged to the world, but Courcelles was hers, from the dent in the wall where a cannonball had landed during the Wars of Religion to the effigy of a long-ago lady of Courcelles in the chapel. There had been a gap by that stone lady's feet where Aurélie used to hide her childhood treasures, bits of feather and string, and, once, an ornament off the armor of a Merovingian knight, found by an archaeologist her father had benevolently allowed to poke about.

Ahead of her, across the courtyard, lay the family's living quarters, a manor house within the old walls, built in the baroque style and decorated during a period of relative affluence during the reign of Louis XV. It might be over two hundred years old, but it would always be known as "the new wing."

Her father, Victor had said, was in the old keep.

Aurélie turned left at the gatehouse, toward the round tower that dominated the countryside. It was, her father liked to boast, the largest of its kind in France, a great circular tower, hung with tapestries and the relics of old wars, a gallery circling the whole so that minstrels could play above and adoring retainers gawp and cheer. The great fireplace was a later addition, added in the fifteenth century, featuring larger-than-life figures of the Nine Worthies, all of whom were said to have been modeled after the daughters of the lord of Courcelles of the day, particularly the busty one at the end, which was also said to be the reason why the carving was never quite finished and the artisan left with a chisel in his backside.

There was no fire in the great fireplace today. Instead, Aurélie found her father directing the removal of antique weaponry from the walls, barking orders as axes long rusted to their stands were pried free and hauled down, joining antique muskets and ceremonial swords in a martial pile on the floor.

It was her father's wolfhound who gave her away, struggling up on his arthritic paws to wag his tail as best he could.

Her father frowned at his old companion. "Clovis! Clovis! What's got into you, you old so-and-so?"

"I have, I think," said Aurélie, and her father spun around, his face going whiter than the marble figures at the fireplace.

"Aurélie? Aurélie!"

"Father, don't, your heart, the doctor said . . ." Aurélie could have kicked herself for her own folly. She ought to have let Victor announce her; she ought—oh, she didn't know what she ought.

"Oh, bother the doctor," said her father irritably, and crossed the room in two strides, kissing her firmly on both cheeks before holding her out at arm's length, frowning at the scratches and tears, the burrs in her hair and smuts on her cheeks. "By all that's holy—I thought you were a vision."

"No, I'm quite solid, I promise you." Aurélie breathed in the familiar scents of tobacco and wet dog, molding tapestries and flaking paint. Her father was thinner than she remembered, his cheekbones sharper, his hair wilder, but he smelled like home. Nothing could be wrong when Courcelles was still Courcelles and her father ruled supreme. When she was little, when the priest spoke of God the Father, it was always her father she pictured, with his unbending posture, his autocratic voice, and his strong sense of noblesse oblige.

Her father frowned at her, those brows so like her own drawing together over his nose. They were, she noticed with a pang, entirely white now. Her father was thirty years older than her mother; he had been nearly fifty when Aurélie was born. But that didn't mean anything, she told herself hastily. He was still hearty, still vigorous. Nothing could daunt her father, not even a German invasion.

But his heart . . . She ought to have remembered his heart.

"What in the name of Saint Eloy brings you back here? Is Paris fallen?"

"No, no, nothing of the kind! I thought—I thought I'd come home." Put that way, it sounded rather unconvincing. Aurélie cleared her throat and tried again. "They're fighting for Paris right now. I drove Jean-Marie to join his regiment and then—well, I drove this way rather than the other."

"You drove Jean-Marie to his regiment?" After a moment of silence, her father exploded in a great bark of laughter. The men around them exchanged looks of relief and permitted themselves nervous chuckles, although they stopped when her father glared at them. He clapped Aurélie on the shoulder. "Your mother always said the Courcelles have more guts than sense, and you're Courcelles to the bones, my girl."

He didn't need to know how terrified she had been in the woods, how weak. "How could I leave you to face the Germans alone? How could I leave our people to them?"

"Bored at the Ritz, were you? There's work to be done here and plenty. The Germans will be back, and I mean to be ready for them when they do."

Aurélie looked down at the pile. "With Sigismund de Courcelles's tournament lance?"

Her father hefted the lance, the long shaft wobbling dangerously. "As good as the day he used it to break Raimond the Fat's shield."

It was a very nice lance, and Aurélie was sure that her ancestor had wielded it valiantly, but to charge a field gun with a lance seemed a bit optimistic.

"Maybe it won't come to that. Maybe they'll be driven clear back to the Rhine and all we'll see will be their backs as they run."

"Have you ever known the Hun to give up so easily? No, they'll be back as soon as food gets scarce. We've precious little enough for our own. The harvest is rotting in the fields. The idiots dropped their tools and ran to join up when they heard war had come."

"You would have done the same," Aurélie pointed out.

"I'm a knight of France, not a field hand. It's my job to fight for France. Their job is to thresh wheat."

That explained why there had been no men straggling toward the fields. "If the men are all gone, then someone will have to bring the harvest in," said Aurélie thoughtfully.

Her father looked horrified. "I trust you're not suggesting I do it."

"No," said Aurélie, who sometimes thought it a shame her father hadn't been born during the days of the Sun King. "I'm suggesting that I do."

Every man in the room instinctively backed away, waiting for the explosion.

"No," said her father. "I won't have you with your skirts kilted, burned brown—"

"I'll wear a hat. If the Germans don't kill our people, starvation will—and of the two, I'm not sure that wouldn't be worse. We can't let that happen. I can ask in the village. If the men can't harvest, we'll hand the women their scythes. They'll do it," she added, cutting off her father's protests, "when they see I'm doing it with them."

Her father was silent a long moment. He looked at Aurélie, his expression unreadable. "There are times," he said, at last, "when you're very like your mother."

"I'm not like my mother." Aurélie thought of her mother, all silk stockings and plucked brows, holding court at the Ritz. She couldn't imagine her mother threshing wheat. Any flailing she did was with her tongue. "I'm not!"

"How is she?" her father asked abruptly. "Your mother."

"My mother is my mother." Realizing just how ungracious she sounded, Aurélie flushed and plunged on. "She's well. Or she was well when I left her yesterday. She's holding court with what's left of her salon."

"That's one good thing," said her father grimly, turning away to survey the coat of arms engraved above the fireplace. "As long as the relic is with her, I don't have to worry about it falling into German hands."

Aurélie just stopped herself from putting her own hands to her breast, where the talisman hung heavy beneath her chemise, shirt-waist, and jacket. "You wouldn't rather have it here, at Courcelles, in case of need?"

"And have every fortune hunter in the Prussian army after it? No. It's safer where it is. One thing I don't doubt about your mother is her tenacity. What she has, she holds."

Except for her marriage. Except for her daughter.

With false brightness, Aurélie said, "Well, then. That's good then, isn't it?" She'd meant to present the talisman to her father like a trophy. Now it was contraband, something to be hidden. "I'll just say a quick prayer to Saint Jeanne, shall I, before I take the harvest in hand?"

"I don't think the saint's much to do with scythes," said her father drily. "You would have to ask Monsieur le Curé. If you can pry him from his devotions."

"I'll do that," said Aurélie, and left him discussing with the black-smith the best way of putting a better edge on a fourteenth-century sword.

The chapel lay outside the castle walls, a small, rectangular edi-fice made of the same stone as the keep. There was a parish church in Courcelles at which the villagers made their devotions; as a child,

Aurélie had joined in the processions on saints' days. But this chapel was for the family and their retainers. Effigies lined the walls, narrowing the nave. The original Sigismund de Courcelles, the one who had gone on Crusade with Louis the Fat, lay on a slab of stone, his wolfhound at his feet, his sword still in his hand.

But it wasn't to Sigismund the First that Aurélie went, but his wife, Melisande. She had a dog as well, but hers was smaller and fluffier. Aurélie had never been sure whether it was a miscalculation on the sculptor's part or design that had left a little alcove between the dog's tail and the lady's feet, entirely hidden unless one looked from just the right angle.

Aurélie knelt down beside the effigy, contorting her body into a space that had been much more comfortable for a five-year-old. Looking behind her to make sure she was still alone, she wiggled the chain holding the talisman up over her head. For a moment, the diamonds and rubies glimmered in the light slanting through the small, rosette windows. Mercilessly, Aurélie muffled their glow, wrapping the talisman in her handkerchief and thrusting the small bundle into her old hidey-hole.

Please let no one find it, she prayed to the saint. *Please let no one find us. Let the Germans stay away—and away from Paris, as well*, she added virtuously.

She felt a momentary pang for the anxiety it must have caused her mother when she emerged from the dining room to find Aurélie and the talisman gone.

But would she have worried, really? The talisman was insured, and it wasn't as though her mother had any regard for the saint, anyway. As for Aurélie . . . well, her mother would scarcely notice she was gone, would she? She would be too busy. She'd probably be glad of the extra seat in the salon.

It wasn't true, she knew, but it made her feel better to think so.

Aurélie rose, dusting the dirt of decades off her skirt—wherever Monsieur le Curé accomplished his devotions, it certainly wasn't here—and went to go set her father's affairs in order.

THE SOUND OF shelling became a steady accompaniment to the whistle and thump of the scythe. Aurélie rose exhausted and fell into bed exhausted. Her team of harvesters consisted of the baker's oldest daughter, who was very conscious of her own dignity; two ten-year-old boys; and a sixty-year-old sot. Kilting up her skirts, Aurélie did her best to lead by example.

Unfortunately, she had about as much experience with a scythe as with a plow, so her example was one, she rapidly realized, that no one ought to follow. But with a great deal of error and waste that made her wince, they made some progress, and the pile of bales in the carts began to grow. They weren't very shapely bales, but they were bales all the same.

It wasn't just the harvest, although to get even the barest fraction of the wheat in took cajoling and bribing and constant vigilance. No. Everyone looked to the lady of Courcelles for advice and reassurance. With the telegraph wires all cut, Aurélie was the first word from the greater world they had heard for some time. No use to tell them that they were as much in ignorance in the capital as at Courcelles; Aurélie began shamelessly making up stories, reinforcements from England, German spies uncovered, the Kaiser sick with food poisoning. That last was pure wishful thinking, but she certainly enjoyed the image, and she could tell her audience did, as well.

Perhaps saying it would make it so. She certainly hoped so.

Miraculously, the weather held. The only thunder was the constant echo of the guns, sometimes stuttering, sometimes in full volley, but never silent. To the west, the battle raged on and on, but Courcelles, in its valley, might almost have been Noah's boat in the storm, cut off from the world, bobbing along alone.

"Those are French guns," said Victor hopefully. "Can't you hear? It's our boys, routing the Hun."

To Aurélie, the guns sounded like guns, and she was so weary, she was about to plant her nose in her soup, but she nodded all the same.

On the afternoon of the sixteenth of September, ten days after her return home if one believed the calendar, a century or so according to her aching muscles, Aurélie was in the village, badgering the baker, when the sound of hoofbeats sent everyone running into the square. A French cavalry division thundered toward them. Chasseurs, cuirassiers, dragoons, cyclists, gunners all thronged the small square, bringing with them shouts of joy. The baker's wife rushed to bring them loaves of bread; the café owner hauled out bottles of wine.

"It's over!" called out a dragoon, as his horse reared back, hooves clattering on the cobbles. "You won't see anything more of the Germans but the back of them!"

"Praise God!" called out old Madame Lemaire, the baker's mother-in-law, dropping her false teeth in her excitement.

One of the cavalry officers reined in, dropping to his feet. "Aurélie?"

"Jean-Marie?" Aurélie embraced her intended on both cheeks. "Is it true?"

"I thought you'd said you'd go back to Paris." For a man celebrating a great victory, Jean-Marie didn't look joyful. His cheeks were sunken and his eyes haunted.

"What does it matter if the Germans are really gone?"

"I—" Jean-Marie cast a furtive look over his shoulder. "I'm not so sure they are, not really. It's—it's not what I thought war would be like."

Poor Jean-Marie, thought Aurélie with affectionate toleration, just like her father, caught in a chivalric dream of an era long ago.

"Who cares so long as it's over?"

"But it's not. We're still fighting. We've pushed them back, but . . . Do you think they'll give up that easily? The things we've seen . . . the things we've done—"

Aurélie squeezed his hand. "It's war," she said comfortingly. "The priest will shrive you."

"I suppose," said Jean-Marie doubtfully. "But—"

"Come to the castle," urged Aurélie. "My father would be glad to see you. He'll want to hear all about your battles."

"But I'm not sure I'd want to tell it," said Jean-Marie, with unwonted resolve.

He did not, realized Aurélie with alarm, look at all like the same man she had dropped at Haudouin ten days ago. It wasn't just the gray cast of his skin. It was something more, something behind his eyes. But that was silly and fanciful.

"Come," said Aurélie again. "Our hospitality isn't up to my mother's standard, but we can offer you a good, thick stew and a soft bed—with fresh sheets."

"It sounds like heaven," said Jean-Marie, and he sounded more like himself again, more like the boy she had always known. "But that's the signal. We're moving on. I can't stay. I—"

"D'Aubigny!" barked his commanding officer.

"You should be proud," said Aurélie, trying to raise his spirits. She stood by his stirrup as he mounted. "I always said one Frenchman was worth twenty Huns!"

Jean-Marie gave her a wistful smile. "Then it's a pity there are so many of them."

"Wrap up warmly," Aurélie called after him as he cantered away. He was probably sickening from something, that was all. But a vague feeling of gloom lingered, all the same, all through the festivities in the village that night, through the feasting in the castle, the bonfires and songs. Aurélie found herself feeling vaguely annoyed at Jean-Marie. He'd never been so faint of heart before. If they'd pushed the Germans back, well, then. Even if the war wasn't done, it meant it would be.

The talisman was at Courcelles and France could not fall.

There was no getting her workers into the field the next morning; there had been too much *genièvre* consumed the night before, the fierce, local gin that could send men mad—or at least give one a very bad head.

Rumors percolated around the village. Le Catelet had been liberated. The Germans were running away. The sounds of the fighting became louder and closer. French machine gunners dug in at a farm the next village over, holding off a squadron of Uhlans. Aurélie thought her father would go mad with the strain of inactivity, standing on the parapet with a telescope, scanning for uniforms, trying to figure out which way the fighting was going.

"Skirmishes," he said disapprovingly. "Skirmishes."

"It has to be over soon," said Aurélie fervently, thinking of the talisman in its hiding place. "It has to."

But when the troops came, they were the wrong sort. It was her father's shout that alerted them. Holding her skirts, Aurélie ran up the twisting stairs to the parapet. Her father handed her his telescope. His hands were shaking. Without comment, Aurélie snatched it from him, holding it to her eye.

They looked like ants. Lots and lots of ants. The road from the north was black with them, with motors and men and cyclists. On and on they came, in ordered rows, marching, marching, marching south and east, Germans upon Germans upon Germans, like a plague of locusts, covering the ground, making the sky dark.

Aurélie made a strangled noise deep in her throat and tried to turn it into a cough. "They said they'd driven them back."

"If they don't, we will," said her father grimly, and Aurélie had the vague suspicion that he was enjoying this, that he was looking forward to wielding his antique arquebus.

Her hands were suddenly very cold. She rubbed them together, wincing a little as the blisters on her palms stung. "Maybe they'll pass us by. They did before."

There was the sound of a motor gunning, of men shouting. Aurélie could hear Victor's voice, raised in remonstrance.

Aurélie didn't wait for her father. She took off down the stairs, spiraling down, down, down, bursting out of the narrow stairwell into the light of the courtyard, where Victor stood with his musket raised like a club, as if he could bar the entrance of the men who stood beyond by sheer will.

"Entry, pah! I'll show you where you can—"

"Stop!" Aurélie stepped forward before Victor could write his own death warrant.

She drew herself up, wishing she was wearing something more impressive than the old frock she had donned to work in the fields. She would have liked to have been garbed like Minnie, in her Paris best, or, even better, in breastplate and helmet.

"Who goes there?" she demanded, cursing the light that made halos in front of her eyes. They had the sun to their backs, rendering her sun-blind. "I am the Demoiselle de Courcelles and this is my land on which you trespass."

"Mademoiselle de Courcelles?" One of the Germans stepped forward, out of the mess of men. He had removed his hat and his fair hair shone in the sun. His French was fluent and cultured and alarmingly familiar. "Do you not remember me?"

"Why should she?" demanded Aurélie's father, arriving breathless beside her. He was toting a fourteenth-century sword so heavy that the point dragged in the dirt behind him. "And what are you doing here? I didn't invite you."

The German officer stood to attention, clicking his feet smartly together. "We've come to ask the favor of lodging in your castle, on behalf of my commanding officer, Major Hoffmeister. And by favor," the German added apologetically, "I mean that we've come to requisition it."

He had moved sideways, out of the sun. His hair was shorter than the last time Aurélie had seen him; it had been worn long then, curling at the collar. The image wavered in front of her, rain-streaked windows in the Louvre, a man standing beside her in a gray-striped suit, a posy in his buttonhole, gray kid gloves with pearl buttons holding a portfolio of rich leather stamped with gold.

"Herr von Sternburg?" she said.

CHAPTER SIX

Daisy

Rue Portalis
Paris, France
May 1942

"Von Sternburg," said Pierre. "Here, in my own home. I can't believe it."

Daisy set her hat on the hall stand and frowned at the appearance of a small new stain on the brim. How had it got there? And how was she to disguise this one? She said absently, "Von Sternburg? Who's this?"

"*Who's this?*" Pierre repeated, in his high, mocking voice. "*Who's this, Pierre?*"

Daisy turned to the children, who lingered behind her, slinging their school satchels wearily from their shoulders. "Olivier, Madeleine," she said. "Go to your room, please, and change out of your uniforms. Remember, dinner's early, in the kitchen, because of the party." She watched them trundle down the hall, Madeleine with her dark braids and Olivier cheerfully blond, and said to Pierre, more quietly, "I'm sorry. I just don't seem to recall the name."

"Oh, I don't recall the name! I've never even heard *of Lieutenant Colonel Maximilian von Sternburg!"*

Daisy turned to face her husband, who stood in the small, cramped foyer of the apartment, still clutching the scrap of paper that contained this information with which he'd greeted her. Some German fellow named Max von Sternburg had hastily inserted himself into tonight's dinner party, which seemed to Daisy like the worst kind of news, another mouth to feed when food was already scarce and expensive, when a single German officer might wolf down as much meat as three Frenchmen, no regard at all for the subtleties of taste and digestion, and lick his lips for more. How was she to manage another guest? Pierre's face was pink and shiny and round, his black eyes bright, his sneer familiar on his plump lips. The shirt collar looked as if it strangled him, so great was his contempt for his ignorant wife. Daisy, whose nerves had buzzed all the way home from rue Cambon, felt the old tide of weariness engulf her. She spread her palms. "I'm sorry. All those German names, I can't always remember which is which."

Pierre folded the paper and ran his thumb and forefinger along the crease to sharpen it. "Only one of the most important men in Paris, that's all, as anyone knows who reads a newspaper."

"I'm afraid I don't have much time to read the newspaper these days."

"Oh, I don't have time to read the newspaper. I'm so busy idling about the apartment all day—"

"Pierre, please. Won't you just tell me who he is?"

Pierre sucked in a little breath. He hated to be interrupted. In fact, he hated any gesture that smacked of disrespect, anything that pricked in any small way, real or imagined, at his own importance. Daisy braced herself, dug her nails into her palms, and cursed her hasty words, but the expected volley of mockery never arrived. Instead he turned away and said, over his shoulder, in a tone of deep contempt, "Max von Sternburg is the right-hand man of the commandant of Paris, as *everybody* knows, and he'll very likely be named commandant himself before the summer's out."

Daisy brushed back her hair from her forehead and followed her husband down the hallway toward the study. "Is he a big man?"

"Big? *Big*? What do you mean, *big*?"

"I mean, does he eat much? We have only a single ham for eight guests—"

Pierre stopped at the door of the study, opened it, and turned to Daisy. "My God, do you think I'm stupid? Do you think I haven't thought of that?"

"Of course not—"

"Then if it isn't too much bother, you *might* stop by the kitchen. If you look *closely*—closely, mind you!—you *might* discover a fine leg of lamb from that butcher on rue du Rocher."

"A leg of lamb! Pierre! But how? Where did you get the money? The coupons?"

Pierre brandished the paper in his hand and spoke again in his mocking falsetto. "*But how? Where?* My God, have you no idea how things *work* in Paris? I'm an important man now, don't you know that? Don't you *understand*? I work in the Ministry of Agriculture and Supply! If I want meat, I can get meat. Now do something useful—just *once*, that's all I ask—and prepare it properly, like a housewife should. A mint sauce. Yes."

"I don't think there's any—"

"And decant that Burgundy your grandmother gave us for Christmas. I want everything perfect."

"But—"

"Off you go. I've important work to do. Don't disturb me until our guests arrive."

Pierre stepped inside his study and slammed the door. Daisy stared at the louvered surface, the delicate grain of the wood. With her finger, she traced the swirl that always reminded her of the neck of a swan, traced the beak like a salient and wondered how it formed, what ancient, tiny impediment had changed its course.

"Is PAPA ANGRY at us?" Madeleine wanted to know, as she wriggled into her nightgown.

"No, of course not," said Daisy. "He's only worried about this dinner. So many important men are coming to see him! He wants everything to go well."

"So we are not to make a peep," said Madeleine glumly.

"And we are not to show our noses," piped up Olivier.

"And it's a shame, because they're very handsome noses." Daisy kissed the tip of Madeleine's nose, then the tip of Olivier's. "But children must go to bed, after all, so they get plenty of sleep before school the next morning. Now, how do I look?"

Olivier threw his arms around Daisy's neck. "You look *beautiful*, Maman!"

"You look *exquisite*," said Madeleine, serious as always.

"Why, thank—"

A heavy knock sounded down the hallway and through the door.

Daisy unwrapped Olivier's arms from her neck and rose to her feet. "I'd better answer that, before Papa—" She bit off the rest of the sentence by kissing Olivier on the cheek.

"Before Papa gets angry," Madeleine said.

Daisy kissed Madeleine. "Before Papa starts to worry. Now into bed, both of you! Into bed and sweet—"

"*Daisy!* What's the matter, are you *deaf?* They're *here!*"

"—sweet dreams!" Daisy switched off the light and hurried into the hallway, where Pierre glowered in his dinner jacket and his polished black shoes that—Daisy knew—contained hidden lifts, which Daisy couldn't quite understand because what difference did it make? These German soldiers towered over him regardless, and which of them would notice an additional three centimeters on this Frenchman scurrying below his chin? From Pierre's right hand burned the stub of a cigarette, which he stabbed out into the ashtray on the hall table. As Daisy passed, he hissed at her. "*That's* what you're wearing? It looks like a potato sack."

"I've lost a little weight, I'm afraid."

The knock came again, just as Daisy reached the door and drew back the bolt. She turned the handle and threw open the door before Pierre could say another word, and because she had grown wise about towering German officers by now, she knew to look up to find his face. So yes, she tilted her chin and looked up, expecting some grim, fair, blue-eyed stranger, and yes, his eyes were blue, and his hair the color of straw, but he had also a sharp, large nose like the beak of a predatory bird, and his scarred face—far from strange or grim—was both familiar and soft with kindness.

From behind her right shoulder, Pierre exclaimed, "Lieutenant Colonel von Sternburg! What an honor to have your company at my humble table this evening."

Von Sternburg, who wore a dress uniform and a pair of white gloves, lifted Daisy's hand to his lips and then sandwiched her fingers gently between those two large, gloved palms.

"I assure you, Monsieur Villon," he said, in perfect French, "the honor is all mine."

DAISY KNEW BETTER than to offer any conversation at the table. There were a great many Frenchmen who took pleasure and even pride in the wit and beauty of their wives, but Pierre was not one of them. He liked to make all the conversation himself. Daisy ate the lamb and the fried spring potatoes (Pierre had also brought home a lump of real butter, more precious than gold) and the puny boiled carrots, and she drank Grandmère's Burgundy, which was excellent and much the best part of the meal. And she listened. She listened with more attention than usual, and she took particular notice of each man's name, which she engraved on her memory, along with his face.

They spoke mostly in French, although only two of the Germans were really fluent—Von Sternburg and a plain, big-eared fellow with a face like a moon, whose name was Dannecker, and the two of them effortlessly provided the necessary translations. Daisy had worried that conversation would be awkward. What, after all, did one discuss with one's German conquerors? The weather? The food? It was Von Sternburg who rose to the occasion, beginning with an observation about the upcoming performances of the Berlin Philharmonic at the Palais de Chaillot—the Beethoven symphonies, all nine of them—for which tickets were nearly unobtainable. They discussed music for a bit, poor Pierre making valiant attempts to keep up, and then opera (who had been to see *Ariadne auf Naxos* at the Comiqué, and what was the opinion?) and the imminent opening of the Breker exhibit until Grandmère's wine had its loosening effect and they turned to gossip. Who was out, who was in, who was perhaps a little too brutal in his methods and who was not brutal enough. Who had made some unforgivable blunder and might be recalled to Berlin altogether. They talked as if Daisy weren't even present. Von Sternburg, who had discussed the peculiar narrative structure of *Ariadne auf Naxos* with animation, now sat back in his chair, idled his wineglass in his hand, and observed the florid, talkative Pierre. Daisy caught the eye of the passing maid— Justine, the fishmonger's daughter, who toiled in the Villon household four days a week in order to uphold the dignity of the family—and signaled her to pour the lieutenant colonel more wine.

But Von Sternburg, when Justine appeared with the bottle, merely smiled at her, shook his head briefly, and passed his hand over the open mouth of the glass. Justine backed away and moved to the next guest, and Von Sternburg lifted his gaze to fasten on Daisy. There was no time to look away. She'd been caught, fair and square. She made a tight smile with one corner of her mouth and turned to the fellow on her left before she had to endure Von Sternburg's answering smile. Without looking, she reached her shaking hand for her own wineglass and knocked it over in a spectacular red arc across the table. The voices stopped as if by thunderclap. Everyone turned to Daisy.

"I—I beg your pardon," she whispered. She pulled her napkin from her lap and started out of her chair to retrieve the fallen glass, to blot the mess.

"Daisy!" snapped Pierre. "Sit down." He gestured furiously for Justine, who darted forward with a dishcloth and sopped up what little wine hadn't already soaked through the worn linen. Daisy sank back and reached, reflexively, for the wine that wasn't there. Anything to keep her fingers busy. Anything not to look at the shocked faces around her.

Pierre made a high, saw-edged, grating laugh. "My clumsy wife. You'd never know she was the granddaughter of a count!"

The other men laughed along, while Daisy lowered her chin and watched the movements of Justine's bony elbow. She felt their laughter, their hot, sloppy gazes on her skin. The smell of meat and grease turned the air rotten, turned her stomach so she thought she might retch. Justine lifted the edge of a plate to blot the tablecloth beneath.

"The evening . . . the evening . . . ah, *mon Dieu*." Pierre could hardly speak through his ragged laughter. "The evening we met, do you know what she did? She was taking coffee from the maid, and she dropped it—dropped the entire cup—right on her lap!" Another burst of laughter around the table.

Justine straightened. "Here," Daisy whispered, handing Justine her napkin. "Lay this on top. We'll sprinkle it with bicarbonate later."

"And to think . . . listen!" Pierre was sputtering now, absolutely undone with success. He smacked his open palm on the table. "To think her mother—her *mother*!—was none other than the Demoiselle de Courcelles!"

Another burst of merriment, an undertone inquiry from one of the men to another (*Was ist die Demoiselle de Courcelles?*) into which Von Sternberg's voice—deep, sharp, devoid of amusement—inserted itself like a knife into a cake.

"I hope she was not hurt?"

The laughter died. Pierre wiped his eyes.

"Sir? Herr—lieutenant colonel?"

"Madame Villon. The coffee, was it not hot? I hope she wasn't burned."

"Why—why—" Pierre looked helplessly at Daisy.

"No," she said. "Luckily I was still wearing my coat."

"I am relieved to hear it. These accidents will happen, even to so graceful and charming a woman as you, madame. You must think nothing of it."

There was a deep, shameful silence. Someone cleared his throat. One of the candles guttered, so that the shadows of the men made grotesque distortions on the wall and the smell of burning wax flowered briefly. Justine reappeared with a fresh napkin in her hand. Everyone turned except Pierre and Max von Sternburg, who both stared at Daisy, one fierce and one gentle. Poor Justine stopped in her tracks, framed by the doorway, and looked to Daisy with a panicked expression, as if Daisy could help, as if Daisy could somehow repair this broken object that had once been a dinner party.

Daisy thought desperately, *What would Grandmère do?*

Of course, Grandmère would call for dessert.

So Daisy straightened her back against the chair and spoke in her most dignified voice, wobbling only a little: "Justine, will you please clear the table for dessert?"

AFTER DINNER, THERE was thin, watery coffee in the salon. The Germans gathered in a cluster near the window and spoke in their native tongue, to which Pierre grinned and nodded frantically as if he understood every word. All except Max von Sternburg, who approached Daisy in her chair and settled himself at the corner of the adjacent sofa, cradling his cup and saucer with one hand.

"Madame Villon," he said, "I wish to compliment you on the meal this evening. The lamb was exquisite."

"No, it was not. I am afraid the meat was not especially fresh."

"In these times, one is lucky to obtain meat at all."

"Lucky? I don't think luck has anything to do with it."

He sipped his coffee, taking his time, as if considering what to say. Daisy did the same. Neither had yet mentioned their meeting in the lobby of the Ritz earlier this afternoon, as if it had not existed, or was somehow beyond the pale of polite conversation. The memory hunched between them now, all the grizzlier for not having been acknowledged. Daisy squinted across the room at the back of Pierre's head, and then at the worn curtains, the flocked, old-fashioned wallpaper that had needed replacing eight years ago, when they had first married and moved into the apartment, after a brief honeymoon in Brittany. But then Daisy became pregnant with Madeleine, and Olivier had followed a year and a half later, and the Nazis arrived after that, and who had time to think of new wallpaper? To say nothing of the money for new wallpaper. Pierre had married her in high expectation of Grandmère's largesse, and now that Daisy thought about it—and she did think about it, often—that was when the trouble began, the tempers and the sneering. When Grandmère had made clear that this largesse did not extend to people who disappointed her, and that Pierre Villon—self-evidently, irrevocably—belonged to this unhappy tribe.

Von Sternburg set his cup in the saucer. "Your grandmother. Is she well?"

"My grandmother?"

"You were on your way to visit her this afternoon, isn't it so?"

"Yes," Daisy said.

There was a terrible beat or two of silence. They both sipped coffee. Von Sternburg said, in a voice that seemed strained, even anxious, "And your mother?"

"My mother? What do you mean?"

"Your—your husband called her . . . the Demoiselle de Courcelles. Is this true? You're her daughter?"

"You've heard of her?"

Von Sternburg had finished his coffee. He reached forward and set the cup and saucer on the sofa table, and Daisy was surprised to see that his hand shook, that the china rattled a little as he consigned it safely to the wooden surface.

"Yes," he said. "I've heard of her."

"How remarkable. I wouldn't have imagined she had a following in your country. Unless to vilify her, perhaps?"

"On the contrary. A woman of such courage is always admired, whether friend or foe." Von Sternburg covered his knee with his hand and rubbed the edge of the patella with a broad, sturdy thumb. "But perhaps it's not so easy to be the daughter of such a paragon?"

"I don't know what you mean."

"One always feels a certain . . . a certain urge, I suppose, to emulate one's parents. To follow in their footsteps."

Daisy's jaw began to ache. The muscles of her face and her neck, her fingers around the delicate saucer, had clenched almost into paralysis. She forced her teeth apart in order to speak. "I—I didn't really know my mother. She died when I was just turned three. The influenza."

Across the room, the men laughed at some joke. Pierre cast Daisy a sharp, curious stare, even as he laughed along.

"I'm sorry for your loss, madame," said Von Sternburg, very softly. "And your father?"

"Killed at Verdun." Daisy set down her cup and signaled to Justine, who had just entered the room with a tray. "If you'll excuse me, lieutenant colonel, I must help Justine."

As soon as the coffee was cleared, Pierre invited the officers into his study. For brandy and cigarettes, he said, winking one slow eyelid. With his hand he made a signal to Daisy that indicated she should disappear, into the kitchen or someplace, it didn't matter where. There was a general bustle of limbs rearranging, of bodies rising from chairs. Daisy turned obediently to leave.

"I'm afraid I must demur, Monsieur Villon," said Von Sternburg. "I have a very early meeting tomorrow morning."

"Of course, lieutenant colonel, of course," said Pierre. "Gentlemen, you'll excuse me—"

"Don't trouble yourself. Madame Villon will see me out. Won't you, madame?"

Pierre turned to Daisy and frowned. Bemusement or disapproval, she wasn't sure. She pressed her lips together. The salon was quite dim, only a single lamp lit, in order to save electricity. Was it only a trick of the darkness that the faces around her seemed so menacing? As if she were surrounded by a pack of wolves.

"Of course," she said. "This way, lieutenant colonel."

Von Sternburg followed her into the hallway and into the foyer. Because it was May, he hadn't brought a coat. He lifted his gloves from the tray on the commode and tugged them over his fingers before he turned to Daisy, who held his stiff officer's cap, and said solemnly, "Thank you, madame. It has been a great pleasure to spend the evening in your company."

Daisy held out the cap. "It was nothing."

Von Sternburg placed the cap on his head and drew the brim low on his brow. The ugly scar on the side of his face fell into shadow, so he seemed a degree less forbidding. He took her hand and kissed it, just as he had upon his arrival, and said, in a voice almost too low to be heard, "If you have need of anything, madame, anything at all, I hope you will not hesitate to find me."

Daisy withdrew her hand. "I can't imagine the necessity. Good evening to you, sir."

He stood another second or two, quite rigid, studying her expression as if he meant to continue the conversation, wanted to discover some common ground between them. But not for nothing had Daisy endured eight years of marriage to Pierre Villon. She schooled her features into impassivity, a complete absence of intent, of personhood. She refused to acknowledge the earnest blue of his eyes, or the stern cut of his features beneath the brim of his hat, or the curve of his mouth that seemed to be pleading with her. To all these things she returned nothing, not the slightest sign of recognition, not even her own breath.

He closed his eyes briefly and sighed. "Good night, Madame Villon," he said, and spun in an exact semicircle, opened the door, and left the apartment.

When the door clicked shut, Daisy let out all the air in her lungs. Her shoulders slumped. She put out one hand and leaned against the wooden panel, panting as if she'd just run a mile, as if she'd just dashed across Paris, all the way across France itself. Her pulse thudded in her neck.

"Madame?"

Daisy wheeled around. Justine stood a few meters away, holding her hat in her hands. She stared cautiously at the quick movements of Daisy's chest.

"I've finished the dishes. Is there anything else?"

"No thank you, Justine. I'll see you Monday."

"Yes, madame."

But Justine didn't move, and Daisy realized she was waiting for her wages. She hurried into the salon and unlocked the desk, where she kept her precious store of francs. When she returned to the foyer, Justine was adjusting her hat before the mirror. She was a short, sturdy, dark-haired girl, the kind who might have been stout if it weren't for the war and its shortages.

"Here you are, Justine. Good night. Give my greetings to your parents."

Justine counted the coins and put them in the pocket of her jacket. "Yes, madame."

This time, when the door closed, Daisy didn't hesitate. She took off her shoes and padded down the hallway to the study, the door of which was closed and probably locked, though she didn't try the handle. Instead she leaned the side of her head carefully against the hairline crack between door and frame. A low mutter of voices came to her, muffled by wood. She closed her eyes, so that every ounce of her concentration might pour through that little gap and gather up noise, gather up syllables and connect them into words, connect the words into sentences.

But the voices remained too low and too muffled. Daisy could distinguish only the smell of cigarettes, the clink of glasses, the occasional creaking of wood as somebody shifted his feet or his seat on a chair.

At last she stepped away and moved down the hall to the kitchen. Justine had left everything tidy, every dish put away, the table wiped and the floor swept, the lamp switched off, the curtains snug so as not to permit the slightest leak of warmth or light into the air outside. From the corner, the radiator groaned softly. Daisy turned and went back down the hallway, all the way to the end, where their bedroom lay. The men were still talking, and Pierre (she knew this from experience) would not want her to linger and wait, to add any feminine awkwardness to their masculine farewells. She changed into her nightgown, washed her face, brushed her hair and her teeth, checked briefly on the children—both sleeping peacefully—and crawled into bed. The sound of voices drifted through the walls, and as she lay awake on her thin pillow, staring through the darkness at the shadowed ceiling, she thought she heard the word *July*.

Possibly she fell asleep then, because she next became aware of Pierre banging open the door of their bedroom, reeking of cigarettes and brandy, humming something in his flat, tuneless way. He switched on the lamp carelessly and she opened her eyes a millimeter or two to watch him strip his clothes away, toss everything on the floor, piece by piece, necktie and collar and shirt and trousers, and clatter open a drawer for a pair of pajamas. She shut her eyes again and felt the sway of the mattress, the groan of springs as he settled in beside her.

"Daisy?" he said. "You're awake?"

She made a small noise that might mean anything. His hand found her hip and turned her over.

"Pierre, I'm so tired," she said.

To her surprise, he laughed and withdrew his hand, rolled on his back and switched off the lamp. "So am I, my dear. Very well. Let's go to sleep."

She stared at the faint gray outline of his nose. In the darkness, she couldn't quite tell for certain, but he seemed to be smiling.

"What's going on?" she whispered. "What does this mean?"

He laughed again, and it was not the way he had laughed at her earlier, like the edge of a saw. This laugh was soft and happy, like the laugh she remembered from their honeymoon.

"It means we are moving up in the world at last, my little wife," Pierre said. "It means, for one thing, we will soon be moving out of this stupid dump to the kind of apartment even your grandmother will envy."

CHAPTER SEVEN

Babs

The Hôtel Ritz
Paris, France
April 1964

I

T WAS FAR from a dump, but it wasn't Langford Hall, either. There were no drafts, or the sound of old, aching floors and walls gasping throughout the night. No sound of wind blowing down chimneys, and no windows rattling like ghostly visitors. No scratchy bed linens that had been left on the line in a rainstorm by Mrs. Finch rubbing against my skin. And no need for socks on my feet to keep out the chill as I slept. No, the Paris Ritz wasn't anything like home.

Instead, plush carpeting swallowed all sound, and when I flipped a switch, the light was guaranteed to turn on without a flicker or pop. The pipes in the bathroom didn't groan and rumble, and water was dispensed into the basin via a gold swan. I found I rather missed the gurgles, but as I sat in the heated water of the bath that was actually hot and remained so, I wondered if I missed it all because it was home, or because I didn't belong at a place such as the Paris Ritz.

By the time I'd bathed—making sure not to use more than one towel and face cloth despite the veritable pile of them heaped on the heated towel rack—and dressed, I'd confirmed my decision from the previous day to go back to England. Sitting at the desk and using the provided Ritz stationery, I wrote a note to Mr. Bowdoin explaining how I'd made a mistake and would not be joining him for a rendezvous or anything else that evening, and then another to Miss Dubose thanking her for her kindness, but letting her know that I'd be on my way home to England by the time she received my note.

I packed up my meager belongings and stowed them carefully in my valise. It had taken me a while to find it, tucked very far back in the large closet, itself hidden behind door panels that blended with the wall, as if the staff had hoped to hide it forever.

I dressed in the same tweed traveling suit I'd worn the day before and stood facing the mirror for a full five minutes debating on whether or not to wear Diana's scarf. In the end I knotted it at my chin, then left the room carrying my valise, pausing at the door briefly for one last glance at the tall ceilings, marble fireplace, and carved frescoes over the doors. Maybe if Kit had been with me, I would have seen it through the rose-tinted eyes of a woman in love. But now it looked only like a beautiful yet cold and sterile place to sleep.

The door shut softly behind me as I made my way to the mirror-paneled lift, the two sealed envelopes in my hand. When the lift opened into the lobby, I found myself tiptoeing toward the main desk as if I were escaping. Which, I realized, I was. From what or whom, I wasn't quite sure.

I'd almost reached the desk when I heard a familiar voice behind me. My brogues spun in an ungainly way as I twisted around to find Miss Dubose perched elegantly on one of the armchairs neatly arranged in the long-windowed hallway. Once again, she was dressed impeccably in a silk coat dress in that lovely sunset color she'd worn the previous day. Her slim ankles were crossed and her little finger extended as she took a sip from what certainly looked like a Coca-Cola bottle. I'd never tasted it, preferring Bovril and tea.

When she caught me staring, she raised the bottle a little higher. "I can't start my day without one of these, even in Paris. And they put in the salted peanuts just like I asked. Which goes to show you that you really *can* get anything you want at the Ritz."

I nodded dumbly, wondering if I should hand her the note I'd written for her, or simply leave it at the front desk as I'd intended.

She took notice of my traveling attire. "Not everyone can get away with wearing all that tweed, bless your heart," she said, her gaze once again taking in every inch of me as if she were Michelangelo and I a block of marble. Or a lump of clay. "At least you have on that lovely scarf. A gift, I'm thinking."

It wasn't a question. Nor was I quite sure of the meaning of her blessing, only that it didn't quite sound like she was blessing me.

"Yes, well, good morning, Miss Dubose. It was a pleasure to see you again." I took a step backward, deciding to leave her note at the front desk. "Have a lovely day." Clutching my disreputable valise, I began my retreat.

"Were the bath towels not to your liking? They're the most luxurious towels I've ever used, and they're peach because the Ritz has declared that hue to be the most flattering on a woman's skin."

I paused. "I found them quite lovely, thank you. Why do you ask?"

She looked perplexed. "Because I can't understand why you're leaving after just one night. César Ritz is turning over in his grave at the very thought of a guest choosing to leave early."

"It's just . . . ," I stammered, watching as she unfolded her lean form from the deep chair and stood to face me.

"I'm surprised you actually stayed the night. I had you pegged for a middle-of-the-night bolter. But I thought to come down here this morning just in case I'd misjudged." She smiled. "I'm very good at judging people and predicting what they're going to do next. It's a very useful talent."

I straightened my shoulders. "Well, you were wrong this time. Perhaps you're not as good at judging as you might think."

Her smile didn't falter. "Or perhaps you're not as convinced that you should leave as *you* might think."

Half of my mouth lifted of its own accord. "Touché."

She waved at a passing uniformed valet and a gray-mustached man approached. "Please take Mrs. Langford's valise back to her room."

With the certainty that I had no choice, I relinquished the grasp on my bag. The valet began his retreat, but Miss Dubose called him back. "And please take her hat, too. But find another place to put it besides her room." She reached up and unpinned my hat, considerably the worse for wear after yesterday's events on the streets of Paris.

"And where should I put it, madame?"

"Anywhere. Absolutely anywhere else besides her head or her room."

He bowed and walked away, not even looking back once.

"That was a good hat, I'll have you know," I said, less perturbed than I should have been.

"For an aged and blind fishmonger, maybe. We'll find you a new one today on our shopping expedition." She slipped her hand into the crook of my elbow. "But first we must eat. There's a lovely café very close by that has the most delightful hot chocolate. And there's nothing like a croissant or *pain au chocolat* to give us the energy we will need." Her gaze flickered over my outfit again and frowned. "Thankfully there are plenty of cafés in Paris. I think we're going to need at least two."

"Really, Miss Dubose. This is entirely unnecessary. I brought two perfectly good dresses with me."

"Call me Precious. It's what I've been called since five minutes after my birth when my grandmama took one look at me and called me precious. As for your perfectly good dresses, like I said, I'm a pretty good judge of people. And if I weren't a lady, I'd bet that those two dresses are at least ten years old and have been worn and mended dozens of times. In other words, they're not fit for any kind of rendezvous unless it's with a rag bag. If I'm wrong, tell me now and I won't force you to come out shopping with me today. But if I'm right, let's go to breakfast."

At the word *rendezvous* my cheeks reddened. "Fine," I said. And to avoid further discussion, I began walking briskly toward the entrance, pulling her along with me, the heavy trod of my brogues out of sync completely with the *tap tap* of her dainty heels and the gilded elegance surrounding us.

NINE EXHAUSTING HOURS later, I found myself in front of the dressing table mirror in my room at the Ritz, on my second glass of champagne—the bottle ordered by Precious, who'd declared it a necessity for a lady dressing for the evening—while she fluttered about like a hungry butterfly in a bed of daisies. What I'd thought would be an expedition to find two new dresses had merely been the edge of the rabbit hole into which I'd been pushed.

The poor valet had actually staggered as he'd gathered my shopping bags from the taxi—dresses, blouses, skirts, trousers, and shoes by the dozens filled the bags. But it hadn't just been my outer garments that Precious thought needed replacing. She had actually let out a cry of distress when she'd seen my underpinnings—alarming enough that the salesclerk had run to the fitting room.

"But they're sturdy and serviceable," I protested.

"So are ovens, but they're not meant to be worn."

After I had been measured at every dimension and juncture and touched in places I was quite sure—even after three children—I'd never been touched before, Precious then brought in little slips of lace, satin, and silk that looked more like tea cozies than something I should actually wear on my person.

"I'll freeze to death wearing those. How on earth am I meant to keep warm?"

Precious had smiled knowingly. "If you're wearing these, you shouldn't have a problem."

I'd blushed furiously, too embarrassed to protest when Precious told the salesclerk to take away what I'd been wearing and toss them in the rubbish bin.

Precious now glanced at the antique gold clock on the marble mantel in my room. "Good. You're ten minutes late. A lady should never be early for a rendezvous with a beau. It makes her appear too eager."

"It's not a rendez—" I began but stopped as Precious began applying lipstick to my mouth.

"There," she said, admiring her handiwork. "Pretty as a peach."

She stepped back and I stared at the stranger in the mirror with the black-lined eyes, long, thick lashes, and bright pink lips. And the shorter, sassier hair. After my experience at the lingerie shop, I'd been too numb to protest when Precious had suggested visiting her favorite hair salon. In my schoolgirl French, I'd suggested trimming my long hair just an inch. Raphael had pretended to agree and then set to work, Precious distracting me just long enough that I didn't notice the clumps of dark hair falling onto the salon floor.

When he was done I'd barely recognized myself. He'd cut my hair so that it hit at my shoulders, flipping up at the ends, and then framed my face with a side-swept fringe. I wanted to complain that I didn't think I could still braid it for when I went riding, but then Raphael had handed me a glossy magazine, pointing at the cover photo of a beautiful woman wearing a bikini.

"He says you look like Jean Shrimpton," Precious explained. "And I declare that he is completely right."

I wasn't sure who Jean Shrimpton was, but I looked nothing like the picture on the cover. At least I hadn't when I'd stepped into the salon.

But now, staring in the mirror and wearing the plush Ritz bathrobe, I wasn't so sure.

Precious went to the closet and pulled out a dress on a hanger. "This will be perfect. I know when you originally tried this on, you gave it a pass, but I thought you should reconsider."

I'd tried on so many things that I was no longer sure what was now hanging in my closet and what I'd rejected. I looked at the dress, trying to remember why I'd said no to it. It had a soft green almost transparent silk for the first layer, and on top was a pretty netlike fabric with a green leafy vine climbing across it. It had short puffy sleeves and a deep scoop neck, with an emerald-green velvet band that hit right under the bosom. I did remember the neckline, and how it had given me a décolletage I'd forgotten I possessed. Maybe that's why I'd rejected it.

She unzipped it and I let the robe fall, no longer shy. Precious Dubose had seen more of me today than Kit had in almost nineteen years of marriage. After much argument, I wore one of the new lingerie sets Precious had said I needed—which I actually did now that she'd discarded mine. She carefully slid the dress over my head so as not to muss my hair and makeup, then zipped up the back.

I stared in horror at my reflection. "Where's the rest of it?" The hem was a good five inches above my knees and remained so regardless of how much I tugged. "And I can't go out in public with this much skin showing on my chest. I've seen bikinis that were less revealing."

"You have gorgeous legs, Babs, and a lovely bosom. You shouldn't be hiding your natural assets under all that wool and tweed."

"Whyever not? I'm not a woman. I'm a widow and a mother of three. Er, not a woman who needs to wear . . . this." I pulled up the neckline, which only made the other problem much worse. Tugging down on the hemline again, I demanded, "Please unzip me. I'm going to be unforgivably late."

"Which is why there's no time to change. Here, put these on."

She handed me a pair of shiny white leather boots with square, flat heels.

"Did I buy those? I can't imagine why. It's not like I can wear them to muck out the stables."

"Exactly. Now put them on and we'll walk down together. I've arranged to meet with my friend Mrs. Schulyer and sit at a small table in the bar to give you moral support. But with that dress and boots, I don't think you're going to need it."

She actually winked at me, and I knew to protest that I wasn't having a rendezvous would simply be wasted breath. She handed me a delicate beaded purse, and then, when it was clear I wasn't quite sure what to do with it, she placed the silver linked-chain strap on my shoulder.

"No—wait. I need to bring my large bag. It has something in it that I might need for my meeting. It won't fit in this little purse."

She sighed heavily as she waited for me to make the switch then frowned down at my oversized cloth bag that I'd made from scraps during the war. "Good heavens, Babs. Whatever you do, keep it behind you so no one sees it."

I did as she asked and stood in front of her as if requiring an inspection.

"Perfect," she said as if she were a farmer and I a perfectly tilled field. "You look good enough to eat."

At the odd gleam in her eyes, I picked up my champagne glass and drained it. I wobbled a bit as I headed for the door, but Precious quickly steadied me with a firm grasp of my elbow. She didn't let go until we were stepping out of the lift and we could hear the chatter and laughter coming from the bar.

An elderly woman, the same one I recognized from the day before in the lobby, approached us, stabbing her cane into the floor as if she held a personal vendetta against it. I knew that I was horribly out of date when it came to fashion, but I was quite sure that the dark brown ankle-length dress she wore was something my grandmother might have worn around the turn of the century. In fact, there was a photograph of Kit's grandmother in her art studio around 1919 wearing a nearly identical outfit.

"I'm Mrs. Schulyer," the woman announced imperiously. "I'm sure Miss Dubose has told you all about me. Did she mention that I survived the sinking of the *Lusitania*?" She was shouting, and I wondered if she might be hard of hearing.

"Not now, Prunella," Precious admonished. "We are only here to offer support. Let's find a table so that Mrs. Langford can make her assignation."

"An assignation?" the old woman shouted.

"No, that's not . . ." I gave up as Precious propelled the woman and her cane toward the bar.

"Langford, did you say? Do I know a Langford? I seem to recall that I know a Langford . . ."

Mrs. Schulyer's voice disappeared into the crowded bar, leaving me alone staring into the entrance. I was suddenly conscious of the boots on my feet, as if I were a gladiator preparing to enter the Colosseum. It might have been my imagination, but it seemed as if there was less talking and heads turning in my direction. I looked behind me, wondering what they might be looking at, then turned back around and blinked with realization. I looked for Precious, not just to thank her for the champagne and the extra layer of clothing it seemed to have lent me, but also to find out if she might have more.

I took a step forward, wanting to get this ordeal over with. I had no idea what Andrew Bowdoin must look like, but the picture I had in my head was a grizzled barrister type with graying beard, bald head, and thick glasses. And definitely a tweed jacket.

In my champagne-induced fog, it seemed the crowd parted for me as I walked deeper into the dimly lit room with lots of varnished dark wood on most of the walls, vaguely aware of people staring as I looked for a paunchy, older man wearing tweed. My foot collided with the leg of an empty chair and as I apologized to it, I heard a familiar American voice next to me.

"*Pardonne-moi*, mademoiselle," he said with a terrible French accent that made everyone hate Americans. "Would you like to *s'asseoir* here? *Ici?*"

He was indicating the chair at the small table where he'd evidently been sitting, an empty wineglass at his elbow as if he'd been there for a while, a yet untouched martini glass full of a viridescent cocktail at the empty seat opposite. He grinned his American smile and it was excruciatingly evident that he didn't recognize me from the bookshop the day before. I suppose I should have been grateful.

"Would you like to *boire?*" He indicated the full glass on the table. "For *vous?*"

When I didn't respond because in all honesty I couldn't think of an appropriate response in any language, he continued with, "You are *très bon*. Very . . ."

His next word sounded very much like the French word for *tree*, which I didn't think was his intention. In an attempt to save him from embarrassing himself further, I said in English, "No thank you. I'm meeting someone. Another American, actually. They seem to be everywhere, don't they?"

He blinked, his startled expression rapidly turning into one of acute mortification and for once the tables were turned, where I was the confident one and my companion the personification of awkwardness. And he was rather adorable at it. It could have been the champagne, but I took enormous satisfaction seeing him bluster his way through his explanation.

"I apologize, I didn't recognize . . ." He shook his head. "You just look so . . . different . . . so much younger than you did yesterday, I mean, you changed your clothes and your . . ." His fingers gestured to his own thick head of hair. "It got shortened."

"Yes," I said, trying very hard not to laugh. "I did get my hair cut. Thank you for noticing. And now, if you'll excuse me, I do have a meeting, although he might have left by now because I'm frightfully late . . ."

I stopped at the strange look on his face.

"You're here to meet someone? Are you Mrs. Langford, by any chance?"

It was my turn to blink. "Yes, I'm Barbara Langford. And you are?"

"Andrew Bowdoin," he said. "Not related to the college."

"I beg your pardon?"

He waved his hand dismissively and I got the sudden impression that he might be nervous. About what, I had no idea. "Oh, it's just something I have to explain a lot when I'm in the States."

Good heavens. Not a paunch or speck of tweed. Good heavens, indeed. I swallowed. "Yes, well, it's a pleasure to meet you, Mr. Bowdoin."

"And you, too, although please call me Drew." He reached out his hand to shake mine—a terribly American thing to do—and his hand collided with the full martini glass, sending it airborne and tossing the entire contents onto my chest.

We stared at each other in stunned silence as I felt the cold, wet drops of the drink slip down my skin, between my breasts, and through the thin fabric of the dress. The conversation around us dimmed, a stray sentence carrying over from the far corner and a brief shout of laughter.

"I am so sorry," he said, reaching into his jacket pocket and pulling out a clean and pressed linen handkerchief. He immediately began dabbing it on the skin of my neck and chest, then started to rub in earnest on the actual dress. I was too stunned to protest and it took him a moment before he, too, realized what he was doing and stopped. "Here," he said, suddenly thrusting the sodden handkerchief at me. "Maybe you should do it."

A waiter appeared with fresh drinks and a towel to wipe down the table and chair, and collect the empty glass, but the damage had been done.

"At least it matches your dress," Drew offered with a weak smile as I ineffectively rubbed at my chest before sliding the handkerchief back to him. His eyes seemed focused on the stain on my chest. "Um, maybe you'd like to go upstairs and change?"

"No. I'm exhausted already so if it's all right with you, let's go ahead and compare notes. I don't know very much about my husband's time in Paris during the war, so I'm anticipating a short meeting."

"Sure. It's just . . ." His eyes fell to my chest again as his finger plucked at his own shirtfront.

Looking down at my chest, I saw the pale pink lacy confection of a brassier that Precious had forced me to wear on full display through the wet fabric of my dress. Completely defeated now, I picked up my drink and drained it. It was at that moment that I spotted Precious and Mrs. Schulyer sitting at a table in the corner with a direct line of sight. They must have seen everything because Precious actually gave me a thumbs-up signal.

Something warm and heavy descended on my shoulders and I looked up to see Drew carefully settling his navy-blue jacket on me. "Maybe this will help," he said, patting me on the back as if I were some faithful hound before settling back into his seat.

I made the mistake of looking at Precious again, where she and her companion were now giving me four thumbs-up. The waiter reappeared with two more drinks, another green martini for me and a glass of red wine for Drew. "From the two ladies in the corner," he said.

"Do you know them?" Drew asked, twisting in his seat and giving them a hesitant wave.

Ignoring his question, I thumped my large bag on the table, making sure to avoid our glasses. "Let's get this over with, shall we?" I picked up my drink and took a large gulp, appreciating the encroaching alcohol buffer between my true self and my current actions. I stifled a hiccup. "And since you've already seen my underpinnings you should probably call me Babs."

He choked a bit on his wine. Setting down his glass, he said, "Sure, no problem. Babs it is." His gaze drifted to my chest again between the lapels of his jacket and he quickly took another drink. "That's a delicious Bordeaux," he said studying the deep red of the liquid in his glass. "Great earthy notes, with a burst of fruit." He swirled the wine and held up his glass. "Juicy, full-bodied, and great legs."

Our eyes met and I watched the color slowly rise in his face as he realized what he'd just said. "The wine," he said quickly. "I was talking about the wine. I was president of the wine club back in college."

"Of course," I said, a little surprised. He seemed too big and too American to know the difference between a nice Bordeaux and a glass of grape juice. I slid the copy of *The Scarlet Pimpernel* from my bag, noticing the edge of the letter peeking out of the middle. I hastily removed it from the book and tucked the letter back inside my bag, hoping he hadn't seen it. I wasn't quite ready to share that bit of information with him. Or anyone. Or ever. I wasn't even sure why I'd brought it, except that at some point while packing I must have listened to my conscience. I opened up the front cover of the book, revealing the Le Mouton Noir address stamp in the front.

"That's why you were at the bookstore yesterday," Drew said.

When I nodded, he continued, "My father told me about the bookstore—how it was a hub of Resistance activity, and that La Fleur met many of her contacts there. I thought it would be a good place to start."

"Did you find out anything?"

"No. I didn't stay." He smiled sheepishly. "I was worried about you since you seemed so bent on self-destruction yesterday, and I followed you at a discreet distance to make sure you made it back to wherever you came from. When I saw you enter the Ritz, I figured you'd be all right."

I felt the blood rush to my face, embarrassed and yet a little bit charmed. "Yes, well, here I am. Safe and sound. And I'm afraid I don't really have any more information about this La Fleur woman."

He gestured with his hand for me to speak more quietly. "Be careful about mentioning her name. She's a national hero here in France for the work she did during the Resistance. Not sure if it's more legend than fact, but women have been naming their daughters Fleur for the last two decades in her honor."

A sour taste began at the back of my throat and I quickly washed it down with another gulp of my drink. "I only heard the name a few times. From Kit, right after he'd returned from the camp at the end of the war. He wasn't well, physically or mentally." I looked up at Drew Bowdoin and saw the compassion in his eyes, and knew that he understood. He was here for his father, after all. "He was delirious. Calling out in his sleep. It happened several times, but not in any context that I could make sense of. I wasn't even sure it was a person until I learned about who La Fleur was later. They must have worked together in the Resistance is all I could piece together."

"Yes, they did. According to my father, La Fleur began as a courier between the various Resistance groups. She was successful because she knew people in the right places—higher-ups in the Nazi regime, perhaps. Or influential Parisians. It's unclear how, but she did have access. And after what my father told me about her . . ." He paused as another round of drinks arrived at our table. "Babs, do you know those ladies—"

I cut him off. "What did he tell you?" I leaned over the table, feeling his jacket slip from my shoulders and the sodden neckline of my dress gape open. I smacked it with the palm of my hand to close the gap, but it was unclear if it had any effect.

"That she may have saved many lives according to those Resistance members interviewed after the war. But to my father, she was a traitor."

"Because of the failed drop." It was difficult meeting his eyes as his gaze was now trained firmly at the middle of my forehead.

"Yes. Some sort of treasure of rubies and diamonds. And something to do with a white wolf with a cross."

"A white wolf with a . . ." My eyelids lowered slowly before I brought them back up again. "What is that, exactly?" My words seemed to be bumping into each other.

"My father never found out. Whatever it was wasn't delivered. La Fleur never showed. And when the diamonds and rubies began showing up among the Nazis, my dad was removed from the field and branded a traitor. He was never charged, but he was never sent on another mission and never received any of the medals that were his due because the cloud of suspicion never left him. He blames La Fleur, believes she's actually the one who gave the treasure to the Nazis. And then allowed him to take the fall."

"That's terrible." I managed to hold back a belch just in time to save my dignity. Even in my mental fog, I felt great pleasure knowing that La Fleur wasn't the angel she was rumored to be. "What was her real name?"

Drew shrugged, and I found myself noticing his very broad shoulders and wondering if he played football—American or British, although at the moment I couldn't recall the difference. "Nobody knows. Even my father. She's quite the enigma." He seemed to be leaning toward me, an odd expression on his face. "Are you all right, Babs?"

"Just fine, thank you," I said, grasping the edge of the table so I didn't fall out of my chair.

He studied me for a moment, as if considering my response before continuing. "After the war, did she ever try to contact your husband? A phone call? Or letter?"

I stared at the mostly full glass in front of me, hearing the strident voice of Mrs. Schuyler over the din and through the alcohol haze in my brain. "Don't be ridiculous!" she screeched. "It's the Battle of the *SOMMAY*. I thought you said you knew French." I wanted to laugh, but couldn't. Because I was thinking of the letter inside my bag. The words written by another woman to my husband. *I will always love you. Always.*

"No," I said. "There was no contact." Then I picked up my glass and drained it.

"But he called out her name," he said gently. "That must have been difficult for you." He reached over and pressed his large hand on top of mine and I didn't mind. It was the first act of compassion I'd received in a very long while. And I learned something about Drew "not connected to the university" Bowdoin right then. He knew what it was like to love someone who wasn't really his.

He leaned back in his chair. "How is your French?"

I almost blurted out *Better than yours* but thought that would be rude. "I learned French in school, but I got much better at it after Kit came back from the war. I think I was attempting to be more cosmopolitan." I swallowed, a bitter taste settling on my tongue. "So that my husband would find me more interesting than I was. He loved all things French, and I was . . . not." I hadn't meant to say all that, but there was something so kind, so understanding about the way Drew was looking at me that I felt compelled to share things with him I'd never shared with anyone else.

I straightened in my chair, aware of how incredibly attractive he was. How incredibly attractive I found him to be. I snatched my hand away, feeling as if I'd just been unfaithful to Kit, even though I'd been a widow for over a year. Reaching into my bag, I pulled out the small folder I always carried with me of my important papers and photographs of my children. I suppose it was a leftover from the war days when one wasn't sure if one's house would still be there at the end of the day.

"Have I shown you pictures of my children? I have three of them." Without waiting for an answer, I slid several photographs onto the table. They weren't the most recent ones, all being taken before Kit's illness at Robin's fifteenth birthday celebration out on the lawn at Langford Hall. I pointed to each photo, identifying the subjects. "That's Robin, the eldest. He's seventeen. He's named after his grandfather, Robert Langford."

"The spy novelist? That Robert Langford?"

"The very one," I said, inordinately pleased that Drew knew who Robert was. "And this," I said, pointing to my second son, "is Rupert. He's fourteen and very smart and very sweet. Not as athletic as Robin, but they're good friends as well as brothers. And this," I said, tapping on my daughter's face, "is Penelope, but we call her Penny, and she's eleven. She's very clever and gets along with her brothers—although she's closest to Rupert. Most likely because he enjoys playing with her dolls and dressing up. He's very kind to do that as I know Robin would never consider it."

He smiled and pointed at another figure who appeared in each photo. "And who's that?"

"Oh, that's Walnut. He's a whippet. It's sort of a requirement—having a whippet at Langford Hall. They're passed on from generation to generation. Like the Langford signet ring." I stopped suddenly, remembering.

"A signet ring?" Drew prompted.

I nodded. "Yes, it was gold with two swans engraved on it. Sadly, Robin won't get a chance to wear it. Kit came home from the war without it. He never mentioned it, so I assumed the Germans took it when he was interred in the prison camp."

"That's a shame." Drew took a moment to examine the pictures. "They're great kids. You must be very proud."

I looked into his hazel eyes, and immediately wished that I hadn't. This man was far more attractive than he should have been. And his words were sincere, which made him even more appealing. "Yes," I said, "I am. They're fantastic—all three of them."

The world seemed to tip suddenly, ungraciously sliding me out of my chair. With wobbly limbs that refused to listen, I was unable to stop myself from falling and I was quite resigned to collapsing on the floor and perhaps sleeping there when two strong arms grasped me around my waist. "Why don't I take you to your room, Babs? We can talk more tomorrow."

I tried to tell him that I didn't have anything more to say on the subject and there was no need to talk tomorrow. But mostly I wanted to let him know that I was quite all right and that I could find my own way to my room but by the time I'd figured out what I should say, I was pressed against his side and being led toward the lifts. And then Precious was there, stuffing the photographs and the folder into my bag and handing my room key to Drew. I tried to focus on her face long enough to thank her, but only succeeded in shutting my eyes completely. Drew managed to get us both inside the lift and before the doors closed I was quite sure I saw Precious wink.

Drew struggled a bit at the door to my room. He uttered a short oath under his breath before the door finally swung open. I found myself being lifted over his shoulder then carried across the room before being ungraciously dumped on top of my bed.

"Sorry, Babs. I guess I'm more used to footballs than women."

I heard the sound of zippers and then felt my boots being tugged off my feet. As I stared up at the spinning ceiling medallion—had it been doing that before?—I had the fleeting thought that he might be planning to ravish me. The thought didn't alarm me as much as it should have. Although he didn't seem the ravishing type. A man like that usually didn't have to.

"Babs, are you all right?"

He leaned over me and he looked so sweet and concerned that I had no choice but to reach up. I'd meant to just touch his cheek, but when my arms refused my instruction, I somehow managed to lace my fingers around his neck to keep them raised. "Are you going to ravish me?"

He looked startled. "Ravish?"

"You know—have your way with me?" I closed my eyes tightly, trying to remember what my brothers used to talk about when they didn't know I was listening. My eyes flew open in triumph. "Do a little rumpy-pumpy?"

His face turned an interesting shade of red. Very delicately he pulled my fingers off his neck, holding my hands together in his large, warm ones. "It's not that I don't find you attractive, Babs—far from it. But you're a bit drunk, and I'm not in the habit of taking advantage."

He placed my hands against my sides, then pulled up the bedclothes, tucking them in gently around me. Then he pulled the phone on the side table closer to me, scribbled something on the Ritz notepad, and put a small rubbish can on the floor next to the bed. "Just in case," he said. "Call me if you need anything. I wrote down my room number."

I listened as his footsteps crossed the room to the door, pausing as he shut off the light. "Good night, Babs. See you tomorrow."

I struggled to lift my head from the pillow. "Do you really find me attractive?"

But the door had already shut, the sound of his retreating footsteps my last conscious memory.

CHAPTER EIGHT

Aurélie

The Château de Courcelles
Picardy, France
September 1914

Y OU DO REMEMBER, then," said the German officer in front of
Aurélie.

"Herr von Sternburg." She had been half hoping he would deny it.
That he would be an evil twin or a strangely similar cousin.

"Mademoiselle de Courcelles." Herr von Sternburg started to hold
out a hand to her, but at the expression on her face, he let it fall. "Those
were happier times, I think."

"I take it this isn't a social call, then." She was proud of how cool
she sounded, cool beneath her rising anger, anger that this man, this
man who had eaten her mother's cakes, had pretended to be civilized,
to be almost French, could be here now, in her home, in the uniform
of the conqueror.

"No."

"You know this man?" her father asked.

No, she wanted to say. This wasn't the man she knew, the one she
remembered, with the daisies in his buttonhole and a book in his hand.

War had made a mockery of the man she remembered. The only thing unchanged was his nose, a very imperial eagle of a nose, the most assertive thing about him.

Stiffly, Aurélie said, "Father, may I present to you Herr von Sternburg. Late of Paris."

"It's Lieutenant von Sternburg now," he said apologetically, as if his uniform didn't say it loud enough, his uniform and the soldiers at his back, bumping and jostling one another as they ogled the keep and speculated on their prospects for plunder. "I beg pardon for the manner of our meeting, Monsieur le Comte. I have long desired to have the honor of your acquaintance—although I should have wished that it might occur under other circumstances than these."

"These are circumstances of your making," said Aurélie hotly. "If you don't like them, change them. Take those soldiers back again and go infest someone else's castle."

He ducked his head. "Believe me when I say I wish I had that power. It is my regrettable duty to inform you . . . no, to request of you . . . that is, I have come on behalf of . . ."

"Lieutenant!"

Lieutenant von Sternburg froze to attention. The guards fell away as another man approached. He was no more than medium height, but he made up for it with the volume of his voice, the swagger of his step.

"Sir," said Von Sternburg. All the light had gone from his eyes. He was like a statue, a very Prussian statue, all nose and chin.

The commanding officer's eyes slid slyly over Aurélie and her father, taking in her father's Scottish tweeds, her stained old dress and priceless pearl earrings. In clumsy but serviceable French, he demanded, "What are you doing standing here jabbering with an old man and a girl?" The word he used wasn't quite *girl*. It was a term more familiar on the docks than in the drawing room. "I want my bags brought up to the largest room. If there is a presentable room in this ruin."

"The *wench*," said Aurélie's father, his voice like a lash, "is the Demoiselle of Courcelles. And the *old man* is the owner of this *ruin*. Which has stood since the fourteenth century. Unconquered."

The newcomer's lip curled. He addressed himself deliberately, insultingly, to Von Sternburg. "I could blow that wall down with a sneeze. Tell the old man to move aside. I have work to do."

"Sir." Von Sternburg leaned close to his commanding officer's ear, speaking in German. "Major Hoffmeister, this is the Graf von Courcelles. His family has held these lands since Charlemagne."

"Am I meant to be impressed?" snapped the major. He spoke directly to Aurélie's father for the first time, sticking his chin up like a weapon. "You do not seem to understand the situation, Monsieur de Courcelles. Pardon me. Monsieur le Comte. This castle has been requisitioned. Everything within and without these walls is now at the disposal of the imperial German army to do with as I please."

"We shall provide you with receipts for anything taken, of course," Lieutenant von Sternburg hastened to assure them. "You shall be made whole. When they are processed, that is."

"Processed," repeated Aurélie's father with heavy sarcasm. "At least the man who last picked my pocket in Paris was an honest thief; he never pretended he meant to repay me."

"Enough of this," said the major. "Lieutenant, see the best room prepared for me—and one for yourself, of course. Dreier and Kraus will be billeted here, the rest of the men in the village. The peasants can see them settled. I want the mayors of all the villages in the district summoned here. They are to attend me at supper. I shall receive them . . ." His gaze took in the castle yard, the Italianate facade of the new wing, the bulk of the great keep. His eyes narrowed on the giant tower. He gave a sharp nod of satisfaction. "There. I shall receive them there. I want everything in place by seven. See to it, Von Sternburg."

Turning on his heel, he walked away, taking it as a given that his demands would be obeyed, leaving the Comte de Courcelles fuming behind him.

Aurélie vented her ire on Lieutenant von Sternburg. "Are we to be your innkeepers or your captives?"

"Would it be easier to think of yourselves as our hosts?"

"The same way we're meant to make a loan of our property? As if we had any choice in the matter!"

"Mademoiselle de Courcelles . . ."

"Why? Why did you have to come here? Why couldn't you have gone to . . . to the castle at Le Catelet? Surely that would be more convenient for you? Why infest us here?"

"There were reasons." Von Sternburg looked away. "Why aren't you in Paris? I had thought you were meant to be in Paris."

"There were reasons." Aurélie tossed his own words back, mocking him, while the soldiers and the retainers looked on in horrified fascination. "Why should you be thinking of me at all? It's none of your concern where I am."

"But it is. At least now, now that we're here. This is occupied territory, and you"— looking down, into her eyes, he said with disarming diffidence—"I suppose it is too much to hope you might not be entirely displeased to see an old acquaintance?"

"Are you *mad*?"

Von Sternburg smiled wryly. "The world's gone mad. It would be strange if I didn't go at least a little mad with it."

Aurélie's father was still staring after the major. His voice was like ice. "No Courcelles has ever been a servant in his own home. Never."

"Sir. Monsieur le Comte." Lieutenant von Sternburg stepped in front of him, between him and the retreating form of the major. "Whatever you are thinking . . . don't."

Slowly, Aurélie's father turned his attention to the younger man. "Is that a threat, lieutenant?"

"No—a warning, only. Before you respond, know this. My grandfather fought at Mont-Valérien. My mother's father. Perhaps you recall him, sir? The Graf von Enghein."

"He gave me my sword and my parole. He was a true gentleman. Even if he was a Prussian." The count subjected him to a long, measuring look. "You have the look of him—particularly about the nose."

"Sadly, there are not so many of my grandfather's stamp as there were."

Aurélie's father snorted. "Your commanding officer, for one?"

Von Sternburg bowed his head. "We must all find our way in this new world."

"At the cost of your honor?" demanded Aurélie.

The lieutenant looked down at her, his expression rueful. "Honor demands I serve my country."

Aurélie lifted her chin. "Honor demands I defend mine."

"Your country, mademoiselle, or your pride?" asked Lieutenant von Sternburg quietly.

Aurélie found herself, maddeningly, without an answer.

Her father replied for her. "They are the same," he said curtly. "The Courcelles and France have always been as one."

Except when they hadn't. Except when they had warred with the monarch or his favorites, when they had backed the wrong pretender to the throne or made too blatant a bid for power. But that had been in earlier, darker times, and now the enemy was clear, the enemy was standing before her.

"Are they?" asked Lieutenant von Sternburg. "There is a poet—an English poet—who says they also serve who stand and wait. It might be best to stand, sir."

"What can one expect of an Englishman?" asked Aurélie impatiently.

"Action might be a salve to your pride, mademoiselle—but can France stand to lose the last of the family Courcelles? Or," he added, with a bow in the direction of her father, "the hero of Mont-Valérien?"

Her father held up a hand. "Tell me, lieutenant. Why should I take advice from an enemy?"

"Because Herr von Sternburg is one of Maman's admirers." Aurélie's voice sounded unnaturally high in the old stone courtyard, against the unfamiliar sounds of German voices in the background. "Is that not so, Herr von Sternburg?"

"I think any man of sense would find much to admire in Madame la Comtesse de Courcelles—and in her daughter." For a moment, his eyes met hers. Aurélie felt the color rise in her cheeks, not because there was anything insolent in his stare, but because there wasn't. Turning again to her father, he said, "I may be France's enemy, sir, but I should wish not to be yours. There is a difference. My object is only to avert unnecessary strife. I should hate to see you discommoded. Any more discommoded, that is."

"You speak like a diplomat, Lieutenant von Sternburg."

"Sadly, no diplomat. Only a lowly aide-de-camp. And I must see to my superior's supper. Until then, Monsieur le Comte, Mademoiselle de Courcelles?" Bowing his head, Lieutenant von Sternburg excused himself, grave and courteous.

Aurélie watched him go, tall and straight in his uniform, furious with herself, for giving so poor an account of herself, and with him, for giving the lie to his own words. Whatever respect he claimed to hold for her and her family, his actions spoke for themselves. He was here, with his ghastly superior, preparing to sleep in their beds and batten off their beef.

And there was nothing she could do about it. Nothing.

Mad schemes flitted through her head. Poison, arson, havoc. But she knew them all for nonsense. Von Sternburg had made it clear that they were nonsense. That there was nothing to do but—how had he put it?—stand and wait.

Had her ancestors stood and waited at the Battle of Rouvray, where Jeanne d'Arc had worked her miracles? No. And nor should Aurélie. If only she could think of something, anything, to do.

"So we have been invaded." Her father's voice brought her back to herself. "How well do you know that curious young man?"

Aurélie gave her head a brisk shake. "Hardly at all. Herr von Sternburg is Maman's acolyte, not mine. He was kind enough to make me the loan of an umbrella one afternoon when I found myself without one."

Wandering among the paintings at the Louvre. Chocolate and cakes at Angelina. Delicate white-and-gold daisies and the press of a gloved hand.

It had been a matter of chance, nothing more than courtesy. He wasn't at all her sort of person; maybe that was why the afternoon had stuck in her head, the unlikelihood of it. The Louvre was her mother's province, not hers. She had always preferred to race with Jean-Marie, to play pirates with his brothers. That, she reminded herself firmly, was why she and Jean-Marie were so very well suited. He would come back from the war and they would marry and they would go on just as they always had. Lieutenant von Sternburg had nothing to do with it, nothing at all.

Except now he did. Now he held their fates in his hand.

"His grandfather was a good man," said her father thoughtfully.

Aurélie scowled at him. "Do you know what the Germans said, when they came to Le Catelet? 'The barbarians have come.' That is what they said. And then they made good their word. Victor told me. It doesn't matter what his grandfather might have been. He's one of them."

"One doesn't reject a sword because it is made out of the wrong sort of steel. Not when one has no other." This was a side of her father she had never seen before. Calculating. "Herr von Sternburg is no barbarian. And he has a softness for you."

"For Maman, you mean." She wasn't sure why it was so important to press that point, but it was. "I shouldn't have thought you would give in so easily."

"What am I meant to do, run them through with a lance?" Never mind that she had suspected him of planning to do just that. At the look of disappointment on her face, he gave a gruff laugh and said, "A child of my own heart. At nineteen, I felt as you. But one learns with time."

"To surrender?"

Her father winced. Surrender was a sore point with him. For all his fame, for all his legend, the French had lost at Mont-Valérien. "To bide one's time. Your German made a good point, whatever his motives."

"About waiting?"

"About the price of pride. Once, war was waged by gentlemen. But now . . . If my opponent is no gentleman, need I treat him with honor? There are some with whom one would not sully one's sword."

He was speaking to himself as much as her. Aurélie wasn't sure she liked the way his thoughts were tending. "What do you mean?"

"I mean we wait," said her father. "And we see if your Lieutenant von Sternburg may yet be of some use to us. But in the meantime, we dress for dinner."

THE MAJOR DEMANDED that dinner be laid out, not in the dining room in the new wing, with its mahogany table that seated forty, its gas lighting, its intricate plasterwork and beautifully painted murals, but in the cavernous hall of the old keep, where torches guttered in holders long rusted with disuse, wax dripped from the tallow candles in the ancient iron chandeliers, and the servants huffed in indignation as they hauled platters the breadth of the courtyard.

The mayors of the various towns who had been summoned from

all about the region had been left standing, huddled in small clusters in the great room. Some of them had struggled into their Sunday best, ill-fitting suits and too-tight collars. Others had come as they were. All seemed nervous—and hungry.

"Has no one brought refreshments for those men?" Aurélie caught Victor by the sleeve as he passed with a carafe of wine.

"We were told not to. By His Royal Uppishness." Victor jerked a thumb at the major, who sat in state at the lone table placed in the hall.

The major had placed himself in the center, above the salt, like a medieval lord. All that was missing were the rushes on the floor and the dogs nosing about for bones.

"Bring him the best wine, he demanded, as if he could tell the difference between wine and horse piss."

"Victor—" Aurélie looked at her father's old retainer with alarm.

"No, I didn't," he said with regret, although Aurélie suspected he might have spat in it once or twice.

"When you've delivered that, tell Suzanne to see that bread and beer are brought for the mayors. It's absurd to bring them here when they would be at their suppers and leave them hungry."

Victor grinned at her. "Yes, mademoiselle."

As an afterthought, Aurélie asked, "Where's Clovis?" Her father's wolfhound was always at her father's feet, but he was conspicuously absent tonight.

"In the kitchen," said Victor. "With Suzanne. His Lordship the High and Mighty doesn't approve of animals. He says they're unsanitary."

"Clovis?" Clovis had always thought himself more people than people. He was the very aristocrat of animals and considered himself well above such lesser beings as the kitchen cat. "Clovis is as much a member of the family as I!"

"I'll show him unsanitary," said Victor grimly, and spat twice in the carafe for good measure.

Aurélie rather wished she were in the kitchen with Clovis instead of in the decidedly drafty hall dressed in last summer's best, a Worth gown of rhinestone-embroidered tulle over pale pink satin. The rhinestones itched and the tulle draping her arms was more a suggestion than an actual sleeve. The prior Demoiselle de Courcelles, she thought with some annoyance, had been fortified with rather more layers of velvet and wool before being expected to dine in this hall.

There were diamond clips in her hair and on her breast. Well, paste. But they looked like diamonds in the uncertain light. One didn't discard a sword, her father had said, because it was made of base metal. One could only hope the major would be too impressed by the glitter to look to the provenance. For good measure, Suzanne, the cook, had insisted on clasping a crucifix about her neck as though they were meant to dine with a vampire rather than a Hun.

Suzanne had not been impressed by this distinction.

He was only a man. A grasping little man. Just passing through. How long could they possibly stay? A night? A week? Sooner or later, one imagined, the line of battle would move again, as it had all through the fall, and the troops would go this way or that, and the major and Lieutenant von Sternburg would rush forward or fall back, depending on the fortunes of war, but, at any event, they wouldn't be Aurélie's problem anymore.

She was stalling. She was stalling because she didn't want to step into that room, so familiar, and so strange, and be forced to sit at that high table with Germans, as though she were their hostess rather than their captive.

It wasn't that she was scared. Not of Major Hoffmeister. Aurélie pressed her cold hands together, looking at the men at the high table, Hoffmeister with his ratlike features, his subordinates, one with a flaming thatch of red hair that made him look like a turkey—and Maximilian von Sternburg, who once, in better times, had made her the loan of an umbrella and had listened to her as though her opinions had merit, as though she weren't just so much debris in the wake of the brilliant comet that was her mother.

Her father was already at table, impeccably turned out in evening dress, his Order Grand Croix proudly pinned to his breast. He had been seated, in an unsubtle form of insult, at the far left of the long table, not at the major's right hand, as his position would have commanded. There were only seven places set at the table, all facing out, so the assembled local dignitaries might see their conquerors eat as they stood hungry. All were filled but for one.

Aurélie lifted her skirts and entered the room. The mayors fell quiet as she approached. Aurélie could feel the torchlight striking off the diamonds in her hair and at her breast.

"The Demoiselle de Courcelles," announced Victor, pronouncing the words with relish, as though she were their talisman, a relic made real.

The lieutenant rose. The major didn't.

"Major. Lieutenant." Aurélie inclined her head with what she hoped was elegant condescension but felt more like a tic of the neck.

The major didn't bother to respond. He was staring at the servants, who had begun circling among the local dignitaries, offering platters of bread and mugs of the local beer.

"Who told them to feed those men?"

"I did." Aurélie's voice carried through the hall. These weren't her people, not most of them; they came from other villages, held by other families, some old, some new, but, now, in this moment, local rivalries were forgotten, extinguished. She stood for them and for France. "Those men had a long and weary walk and will have another before they see their beds."

The major pressed both palms on the table, half rising from his seat. "I did not authorize this."

"No," said Aurélie, holding herself straight and tall in the light of the torches. "I did. It was my beer and bread to give."

"Not anymore." The major turned his ire on Lieutenant von Sternburg, who had moved to pull out Aurélie's chair. "What do you think you're doing? Stop. Who said she has leave to dine with us?"

The empty chair did. It had been clearly left for her. The confusion on Von Sternburg's face told her all she needed to know. This, Aurélie realized, was reprisal. Instant and petty reprisal for having the gall to bring bread to hungry men.

Von Sternburg opened his mouth to intercede, but Aurélie forestalled him. "Is this to be one of *those* dinners?" she asked, keeping her voice worldly and just a little condescending, in her very best imitation of her mother. Never mind that she was shaking with rage underneath. "In that case, I shall take a tray in my room. I shall leave you *gentlemen* to your claret and your hunting stories."

"I don't think so." Slowly, Major Hoffmeister lowered himself back into his seat and there was something in his face that made the skin on Aurélie's arms prickle beneath her long evening gloves. "If you are so concerned that everyone be fed, you may see that we are served. You! Boy!" He snapped his fingers at Victor, who was standing, horrified, clutching a carafe of wine. "Give that to Mademoiselle de Courcelles. She will wait at table tonight. We will have our supper from her own fair hands."

The men below stopped and stared, bread and beer mugs frozen suspended, mouths open. Aurélie hoped she wasn't gaping as they were. She saw Victor's hands tighten on the handle of the carafe and feared that he meant to empty it over the head of the major. She reached, instinctively, for it, to stop him. Victor yanked it back, away from her—and another pair of hands settled around the base, removing it gently but firmly from Victor's grasp and presenting it to her.

"It was the tradition," said Lieutenant von Sternburg, his voice pitched to carry, "in the medieval period, for the daughters of the house to pour wine for the family's guests. It was seen as no diminution of honor."

She couldn't seem to stop staring at his hands, those graceful musician's hands, against the cut crystal of the carafe. He wore a signet ring on one finger, a coat of arms worn to near invisibility.

"My lady," said Von Sternburg, and the use of the title felt less a formality and more a declaration. "My lady, will you do us the honor?"

A diplomat, her father had called him. He had broken the tension, saved her pride—and she resented it bitterly. To refuse now would seem less like honor and more like temper.

"Never say that a daughter of the house of Courcelles was remiss in seeing to the comfort of her *guests*." Aurélie snatched the carafe from him with more energy than grace. Red droplets fell, marring the fine fabric of her gown. She held the carafe high. "Wine, lieutenant?"

"The major will not like it. You ought to have served him first," he murmured, as she leaned over his shoulder.

"Would you lecture me on manners, as well as history?"

He coughed as the tulle of her sleeve brushed his cheek in passing. In the light of the torches, his skin seemed absurdly fair, highlighted with a sprinkling of fine gold hair along his chin. "It is true, what I said. Your ancestresses would have done the same for their guests."

"Yes, I know," retorted Aurélie as she splashed wine into his glass, one of the precious Venetian glass goblets an ancestor had hauled home from a tour of Italy, along with a mezzo-soprano and a rather lovely triptych supposedly painted by Titian. "They also bathed them. Am I meant to take a sponge to your back?"

He glanced sharply up at her, his gaze catching hers, so that she was caught, practically nose to nose, close enough that she could see the little glimmers of light reflected in his eyes and smell soap on his skin.

"I would demand no service of you that you do not care to give."

She was staring. She was staring and wine was dripping onto the tablecloth. Aurélie jerked upright, snatching the carafe away. "Fine words, lieutenant—from an uninvited guest."

"Mademoiselle de Courcelles. Our glasses are empty." Major Hoffmeister waggled his glass in the air. In an aside, to the man he called Kraus, he said, "No tavern would hire a girl so slow."

He was, she knew, deliberately baiting them—no, baiting her father. She could see him look at her father as he said it, waiting for him to react.

They said, in Le Catelet, the major had shot men out of hand, for doing no more than object.

"Wine, major?" In the dining room—the proper dining room— there was a painting, a lush Renaissance affair, all burgeoning grapes and equally burgeoning breasts, of Judith seducing Holofernes, the conquering general who had enslaved her people, pouring wine into his goblet as he ogled her cleavage.

The major didn't ogle. He didn't even acknowledge. He let Aurélie fill his glass as though she were a servant and then stood, clanking a spoon against his glass.

He did not, she noticed, drink.

"You have all been summoned here to receive instruction," he said, without preamble. "I am Etappen Kommandant Major Hoffmeister. This region is under my control. You will report here every day at precisely seven in the morning for orders."

One man was unwise enough to speak up. "Every morning? It is an hour's walk from Villeret!"

The man at Hoffmeister's left, the tall man with the crown of red hair, called out, "Then you had best start early!"

Hoffmeister didn't dignify either man with a response. Instead, he went on as though he had never been interrupted, "All weapons will be surrendered immediately. The penalty for concealing a weapon is death. That, Monsieur le Comte, includes you."

"Would you like the shepherd boy's slingshot?" the count inquired politely. "The kitchen knives, perhaps."

"All weapons," Hoffmeister snapped. "You will surrender your swords, and your rifles, and your slingshots. A full list will be provided to you to be posted in your villages. You will also receive lists of goods to be delivered to the castle. You will provide the required amount of cheese, wine, and wheat. Do not think you can fool us by holding anything back. All homes will be searched."

Aurélie didn't miss the uneasy looks being exchanged. It was rumored that the mayor of Hargival had quite a cache of wine stored in his cellar. But it wasn't the wine that concerned her. Absently, she rubbed the calluses on her palms, picturing the bales of wheat, the wheat she had worked so hard and so clumsily to harvest, so that her people might not starve come winter. The people of the village had given all they could spare to the French soldiers that had come through, first in August, then again in September.

She could see the rustles and murmurings, but none of the men would speak out, not with the major's soldiers standing along the walls and all the might of Germany behind them.

"If you take their wheat, these men will starve." Aurélie was still holding the carafe and felt like a baroque rendering of Plenty, or something equally absurd. But someone had to speak out, and it seemed it must be she. "The people of this village cannot live without bread."

"Let them eat cake, then. That is what your people say, isn't it?"

"Marie Antoinette," retorted Aurélie, "was an Austrian."

The local men liked that. The major didn't. "You aristocrats," he said slowly, "you are not known for tender sympathy for your people. Would you give your bread so they might not starve, Mademoiselle de Courcelles?"

"If it comes to that. Yes."

For a moment, she thought the major meant to strike her. But he caught himself in time. "I forgot. You *Catholics* revel in martyrdom. All of your saints shot full of arrows—or burned at the stake."

In the back of the room, Monsieur le Curé looked nervous. He had always been more interested in his collection of curios than in martyrdom.

The major grasped the crucifix Suzanne had hung about Aurélie's neck, pulling it forward so that Aurélie was forced to come with it, or allow the chain to snap. "What bauble is this? Is *this* the notorious talisman of Courcelles?"

He gave the chain a tug and the thin links snapped, leaving him holding the crucifix in his hand.

"Well?" Hoffmeister demanded. "Is this it?"

Aurélie took a rapid step back, resisting the urge to rub her neck, where a thin, red welt had begun to form.

"The talisman," said the count, "is with the lady countess. In Paris."

Or, at least, it was meant to be. Aurélie was very glad she had never told her father otherwise.

"That is what you would say, isn't it?" said the major, and thrust Suzanne's silver-gilt cross deep in his pocket. To Aurélie, he said, "Well, what are you doing standing there? Dreier's glass is empty."

Expressionless, Aurélie took up the carafe. As she passed the major, on the way to the man on his left, the shorter, rounder one, the major, without turning around, without looking at her, deliberately jerked his elbow back, joggling her arm so that the carafe overturned, the dregs of the wine spilling like blood down the front of her dress, turning the pink silk crimson, and drowning the light of the gems.

"Clumsy, clumsy," said the red-haired one, Kraus.

There was an uneasy silence in the room, the men shuffling from foot to foot, looking at one another, all feeling they ought to do something, but no one brave enough to speak out. Aurélie's father's hands tightened on the arms of his chair, but he stayed where he was, exercising the control learned long ago on the field of honor.

"Well?" The major made a brusque gesture. "What are you all doing still standing here? You are dismissed. You report here tomorrow for further orders. Go!"

The men shuffled uneasily toward the door, glancing back over their shoulders, speaking in low voices among themselves. The major plunked back down in his seat.

Stone-faced, Aurélie lifted the empty carafe. "I shall see this refilled."

Lieutenant von Sternburg jumped to his feet. "Allow me to carry that for you."

"I can carry my own burdens," said Aurélie. "Thank you all the same."

He followed her out into the passage regardless. It was a dark and narrow corridor, joining the old keep with the newer portions of the castle. It smelled of damp and rodent droppings.

Aurélie stopped, and Von Sternburg stopped, too. "It's all of a piece, isn't it?" she said bitterly. Now that she was out of the hall, away from the major, away from the villagers, she felt her mask of calm crumbling. "I cannot refuse your aid any more than I can refuse your demands. Will you requisition my good will as you requisition wheat? I warn you, I haven't any left to give."

Her voice was beginning to crack. She forced herself to stop, painfully aware that she was still clutching the carafe. She was beginning to hate that carafe. She would have flung it, just to see it crack, but for the fact that she couldn't give them that satisfaction. And, besides, Major Hoffmeister had probably already added it to his requisition list. That was what the Germans did when they came through, wasn't it? They took and took and took.

"Mademoiselle de Courcelles." Von Sternburg took a cautious step forward. "The last thing I wish is to add to your burdens."

Aurélie couldn't help it; she began to laugh, and if her laugh was a little wild, Von Sternburg was tactful enough not to comment on it. "Oh, a regular angel of mercy, that's what you are. Did you and your commanding officer plan this together? He threatens and you soothe and together you get what you want?"

Lieutenant von Sternburg stared at her, looking as though she had struck him. "Is that really what you think of me?"

Paris. Daisies and cakes and the gentle patter of rain.

Aurélie turned her shoulder. "You serve him."

"I serve my country. Please, whatever you think of me, know that. I serve my country, not Major Hoffmeister. He is—he is a bully." She could feel his presence, close behind her. His soap smelled faintly of violets. He was, she realized, staring at the nape of her neck, where Hoffmeister's summary disposal of Suzanne's chain had left a thin, red welt along her skin. "This—this is inexcusable."

His fingers barely grazed the bruise, but Aurélie jerked away, covering the spot with her hand. "Should you be saying that of your commanding officer?"

"No." He looked down at her. Aurélie looked away, away from the appeal in his eyes, but it was impossible to ignore him entirely, not when his very presence vibrated like a bell, driving away everything else. "I shouldn't. But I wouldn't want you to think that I approve of his methods."

Aurélie's lips pressed tightly together. "Maybe not his methods, but you're not going to quibble with the ends, are you?"

"Do you mean do I want my country to win this ridiculous war? Of course. I would be a traitor to think otherwise. But do I want it to go on a second longer than it need? And destroy so much of beauty and goodness and . . . never mind." Von Sternburg gave his head a shake, looking distinctly bemused. "Do you know, you're still holding that carafe?"

"Yes. I think it might be permanently attached to my palms," said Aurélie tartly. It was all very well for him to go on about truth and beauty, as if nothing had changed, as if he were still the man she had known in Paris. He wasn't the one who smelled like a vineyard. "If you'll excuse me, I'm meant to be filling it with wine so I can go back to my oh-so-honorable duties to my *guests*."

She turned on her heel, but Von Sternburg forestalled her. "Mademoiselle de Courcelles."

His fingers barely brushed her arm, but the touch made her stop short, trembling. With rage. Only with rage.

"What?" she demanded. "*What?*"

He rescued the carafe from her before she could drop it. "Please. Don't look at me like that. I only wanted to tell you—Hoffmeister may be a bully, but he's not a fool. Don't underestimate him. Don't taunt him."

"You needn't worry on my account. I'll be the perfect picture of silent womanhood."

"Because that will madden him the most?" She wished he wouldn't look at her like that, like he knew her. Like he cared. "I shouldn't want to see you made a martyr. We shouldn't be here long. A week. A month at most. All I want is to keep you safe."

Here was a snare straight from the Devil. She could almost feel herself weakening in the face of his earnestness, that kindness that was so much a part of who he was, a man who surrendered his umbrella that others might stay dry.

A conqueror. Conquerors weren't kind.

"And what of my people? Will you keep them safe, too, or does the offer extend only to me?"

"I want only to protect you," he said softly.

"What price that protection?" Gathering the shreds of her dignity about her, Aurélie said grandly, "No thank you, Lieutenant von Sternburg. I can take care of myself—and my people, too."

She was about to depart, when Von Sternburg said, "That being said, haven't you forgot something?"

"What?" Aurélie wrapped her arms around her chest. Her dress was clinging damply to her in what she feared were rather revealing places. "That you are the conqueror? That we are here only on your sufferance? That your grandfather was kind to my father once?"

"Er, no." Von Sternburg held up a rather grimy piece of cut crystal. "Haven't you forgot your carafe?"

CHAPTER NINE

Daisy

The Hôtel Ritz
Paris, France
May 1942

The decanter in Grandmère's suite at the Ritz was made of heavy cut crystal, centuries old. The Ritz staff cleaned it daily so that dust should not accumulate in its ridges. As a child, Daisy had assumed her grandmother had smuggled it out of the collections of the Château de Courcelles, but it turned out Grandmère had bought the decanter in Paris shortly after she first moved there, along with the rest of the suite's contents. She'd wanted to start fresh, she said, and, anyway, the comte raised such a fuss over every little object, as if everything inside that damned château was a holy relic of one kind or another.

Daisy pulled out the stopper and splashed a few ounces into a snifter. Behind her, Grandmère scribbled furiously.

"That's all? You've got the names right? You haven't forgotten someone?"

"Of course I haven't forgotten," said Daisy.

"And Pierre. He thought this meeting was a great success?"

"Yes. He said something afterward about moving up in the world. A grand new apartment."

Grandmère made a noise. "A grand new apartment. And we all know where those come from. Another Jewish family stripped of everything on one pretext or another and sent east to the camps."

"Well, I would never live in someone else's apartment like that. It's grotesque."

"You think not? What else are you to do, if Pierre moves up in the world by his own low cunning?"

Daisy stared at her face in the mirror above the liquor cabinet. Her skin looked pallid, her eyes unnaturally bright. She watched herself draw a long sip of cognac—almost too long to be called a sip at all, really—and noticed Grandmère's reflection in the distance, on the sofa, watching Daisy watch herself drink cognac.

"My dear," said Grandmère. "Is there something you haven't told me?"

"Why do you ask?"

"Because you haven't poured yourself a glass of spirits since that day you discovered you were expecting Olivier."

Daisy set down the snifter and turned to face Grandmère. "Last night. There was another guest at the last minute."

Grandmère made a noise of exasperation and picked up her notepad and her fountain pen from the sofa table. "Why didn't you mention him, then?"

"Because I don't think he had anything to do with what they were discussing. He invited himself. It was a surprise to Pierre, I think."

"A good surprise?"

"Yes. He's an important man, a lieutenant colonel. But he wasn't one of them, I thought. He wasn't part of their circle. He didn't stay when the rest of them retired to the study."

"He left early?"

"Yes. Just had dinner and coffee and left."

"That's strange." Grandmère frowned and tapped the end of the fountain pen against her chin. "His name?"

Daisy turned back to the decanter, poured a little more cognac, and returned to the sofa to sit across from her grandmother's sharp eyes. Today Grandmère wore a magnificent blue silk kaftan and enormous earrings that dangled like chandeliers over her narrow shoulders, giving you an impression of extravagant frivolity that ended at the three giant, somber furrows across her forehead. "Von Sternburg," Daisy said. "Lieutenant Colonel Max von Sternburg."

"Max von Sternburg." *Tap, tap* went the fountain pen against Grandmère's chin. "Yes. Arrived here recently from some field command in the east, didn't he?"

"You've heard of him?"

"Of course I've *heard* of him. He's next in line for commandant of Paris. Don't you read the newspapers?"

"Apparently not."

"I'm told Berlin thinks highly of him. His loyalty to Germany is unimpeachable." Grandmère said this with such conspicuous irony, Daisy lifted her eyebrows and sat back against the sofa. The scent of pipe smoke wafted past her nose.

"Has your poet friend been to visit?" she said. "Monsieur Lebeouf?"

"Legrand. What makes you say that?"

"I can smell his pipe."

Grandmère pointed the fountain pen at Daisy's nose. "You notice everything, don't you? Even as a child."

"Well?"

"Yes, he was here. What can I say? I enjoy poetry. About this Von Sternburg, however. You're certain he wasn't invited?"

"Quite certain. Pierre was—Pierre was nervous about it. Happy, but nervous. Von Sternburg wasn't expected."

"Then why did he come, I wonder?"

Daisy looked down at her left hand, which rested on a sofa cushion, while her right hand held the snifter of cognac. She stroked the fabric once or twice and noticed how pale her hand looked, how bony and frail, the gold ring hanging between the knuckles. She said softly, "I met him earlier in the day, in the hotel lobby."

"*This* hotel lobby? The Ritz?"

"Yes. When I came to see you yesterday afternoon. He—he approached me and asked to see my papers."

Up went Grandmère's eyebrows again. "Did he? Now that's interesting. And it was after this little meeting that he invited himself to your dinner party?"

"If you care to put it like that."

"Von Sternburg." Grandmère frowned. "Von Sternburg. It does have a familiar ring. I'm quite certain . . . Max von Sternburg . . . a long time ago . . ."

"Perhaps he was one of your lovers," Daisy said crisply.

"Perhaps," said Grandmère, just as crisp, "but I don't think so. I generally remember the names of my lovers, even if I can't quite picture their faces. Never mind. He's interested in *you*, that's the point. You must let me know immediately if he pays you another visit."

"*Mon Dieu*, Grandmère! I'm not going to—you can't possibly expect me to—"

"You will do what you must, my dear," said Grandmère. "That's all any of us can do."

"I'm a married woman. I have a husband."

"A *husband*? My dear Daisy. We speak of Pierre."

Daisy emptied her glass between her lips. "Yes?"

"Personally, I should drink poison if I were condemned to an entire lifetime of sexual relations with nobody but Pierre Villon. But perhaps you have a stronger constitution."

"Grandmère!"

"Or else a far greater faith in some eternal reward." Grandmère waved her hand upward to the trompe l'oeil ceiling, where a pair of leering cherubs lounged against a blue sky fleeced with clouds.

Daisy slammed her glass on the sofa table and jumped to her feet. "I am not *you*, Grandmère! I'm not my mother! As I have told you a thousand times! I cannot replace the child you lost. I'm sorry, but I can't. I am just *me*. I'm Daisy, for better or worse."

Her grandmother folded her arms and stared up at Daisy from a pair of narrowed eyes. Daisy knew her cheeks were hot, that her eyes blazed, and she didn't care. This fury, where had it come from? She'd been simmering with it all morning. She'd been simmering ever since—oh, let's be honest, Daisy, at least be honest inside your own head—ever since Pierre had prodded her awake in the coal-flavored dawn and pulled down her drawers, without any preamble, without even the pretense of a kiss or two, a caress, and stuck his thing inside her, morning-stiff. Because he had drunk so much wine last night, his breath was foul, and Daisy had turned her cheek and tried to breathe in the scent of the pillow instead. The sound of his grunting, the smack of his belly on hers, the creak of the bedframe repelled her so much, she squeezed her eyes shut, and because it was dawn, because she was still half-asleep and living inside some dream or another, God forgive her, God forgive her, she thought of somebody else. Without trying, without summoning him at all, she imagined thick brown hair and clever blue eyes, she imagined lanky shoulders and a smiling mouth, and as she burrowed her nose in the pillow to escape Pierre's ecstatic puffing, she didn't smell linen or sweat or laundry soap. She smelled—almost as if it existed—the sultry echo of tobacco smoke, drawn through a pipe. God forgive her.

And now she stood before Grandmère and the guilt flushed in her cheeks and her eyes, and this grandmother of hers, what did she do? She folded her arms and gazed at Daisy and *smiled*. Not the joyful kind of smile. The smile of a mother cat witnessing her kitten catch its first mouse.

"Now, that's more like it," Grandmère said.

Daisy turned and stalked to the window. Outside, a pair of women strolled wearily along rue Cambon, glancing through the windows as if their hearts weren't in it. They passed a German soldier, who turned to stare after them, and Daisy wondered what he was thinking. Whether he stared because they were pretty and French, or because he suspected them of something, some infraction of the rules.

Behind her, Grandmère's footsteps made soft noises on the rug. Daisy smelled the familiar perfume, the blend of roses and skin that was her grandmother. She heard her grandmother's low voice over her shoulder.

"Daisy, listen to me. I received some interesting news this morning."

"From Monsieur Legrand, perhaps?"

"It *seems*," Grandmère said, ignoring the question, "that Berlin wants to remove Monsieur Vallet as head of Jewish Affairs in occupied France and replace him with someone else."

"With whom?"

"It's not clear. But I assure you, Daisy, the Germans don't mean to replace him with someone more lenient."

Daisy turned her head from the window. Grandmère stood a meter or so away, watching Daisy carefully. "*Lenient?*" she said. "Monsieur Vallet is hardly lenient."

"No, he is not. But apparently that's not enough. Apparently they're planning something bigger, some great crackdown. They want every Jew out of Paris, every Jew out of France."

"But where? Where will they keep them all?"

"*Them?*" said Grandmère. "You mean *me*, Daisy. Us."

"Stop. We're not . . . I mean, you are, we are, technically, but not . . . not . . . nobody knows—"

"They will know. That's what this is all about, don't you see? To discover who's Jewish, to find out who has even a pint or two of Jewish blood and eliminate him."

"Not eliminate, surely. The camps . . . they go to camps—"

"And what do you think happens in these camps, hmm? What do you think has happened to my dear friend Madame de Rothschild at Ravensbrück? Do you think they've been serving her coffee in a silver pot?"

"Of course not."

"I used to think I could keep us safe. I used to think our rank, at least, would hold them back, so that I could help those who aren't so fortunate. But poor Elisabeth . . . and she's a Rothschild. A Rothschild! And she wasn't even born a Jew, she married into the family, she's estranged from Philippe. So you see, nobody is safe. We are all rats in a cage, waiting our turn to die."

Daisy said nothing. She turned back to the window and ran her finger along the crease where the frame met the cool glass. Grandmère's hand reached out to cover hers.

"Come with me," said Grandmère.

Daisy allowed herself to be led from the window and across the room. The cognac had found her brain by now. A pleasant numbness dulled away the guilt and the rage, the unsettled nerves. Grandmère stopped before the curio case and reached beneath the cabinet to grope for something or other. Daisy gazed through the glass, the way she used to do as a child. The velvet was now so old and dark, you couldn't tell which color it once was, sapphire or emerald or burgundy. Nestled inside its folds, the talisman had not recently been polished—by design, Daisy thought, because you didn't want to draw attention to such a thing these days—and the jewels and the gold and the glass no longer sparkled. Still, it was a beautiful thing. Gazing down on it always gave Daisy a sense of peace.

"Ah!" exclaimed Grandmère. "There you are, little devil. Here. Daisy, give me your hand."

Obediently Daisy allowed her fingers to be guided underneath the cabinet, where they encountered a small metal bump, almost a hook.

"Lift it upward with your fingernail," said Grandmère, and Daisy caught the hook with her fingernail and pulled, an awkward, tiny movement that caused a soft click, a tremor of the glass case. "You see? That's how you open it, my dear. If something should happen to me."

"*Happen* to you!"

"You must take the talisman, of course. It belongs to you. You're the daughter of the Courcelles, the next in line. The heiress. The demoiselle."

"Oh, Grandmère. You know I don't believe in any of that. What protection did it give my mother? None at all. She made it through the war and died of the flu."

Grandmère clicked the glass case closed again. "It doesn't matter if you believe in it. It doesn't matter if I do. What matters is that other people believe in the talisman's powers. What matters is the value of those stones and that setting, which amounts to a pretty penny, believe me. You are not to leave this priceless object to the Germans, do you understand me? It belongs to you. It belongs to France."

Daisy mashed her lips together and regarded Grandmère through her cognac-glazed eyes. Her grandmother stood tall and very straight, at least so straight as her spine would allow. Her eyes flashed passionately. Her white hair resembled the clouds on which the cherubs lounged above her. Oh, that old and papery skin, so thin you could see the blood spidering beneath. When had Grandmère become so old? Daisy felt a wave of compassion. She took Grandmère's hand to hold between her own, and the lightness of it surprised her, as if someone had filled her grandmother's bones with air. "Of course, Grandmère," she said. "I understand."

"I doubt it," said Grandmère, "but I suppose that will have to do. In the meantime, my girl, I have an errand for you."

AN ERRAND. How harmless it sounded, how ordinary. Go to the bookshop and ask for Monsieur Legrand. He has a book for me. A book! How simple.

It had begun to rain, suddenly and with conviction, the way it often rains in Paris during the springtime. Daisy usually brought an umbrella with her, but today she'd forgotten—fury has a way of making you forget your umbrella—and she could only turn up the collar of her coat as she trudged past the shops, around the corner of rue Cambon, a quick dart across rue des Capucines, dodging the gathering puddles, and then—just as the rain began to lessen, naturally—rue Volney, and the familiar white lines of the bookshop, the windows, the books stacked alluringly behind the glass. Behind the books, a shadow shaped like a man.

Daisy paused beneath the tattered awning and clutched the collar of her coat. The rain dripped solemnly from her hair. Inside, warm and dry, the man seemed to be leafing through a book. Some customer, no doubt, browsing a possible purchase. Daisy stepped closer. He wore a shirt and a tweed vest but no jacket, and his right hand was so large as to dwarf the back cover. Daisy thought she caught a flash of gold on one finger, the ring finger or else the pinky. As he turned a page and moved the angle of his face, Daisy saw the pipe stuck between his lips, in the corner of his mouth.

Possibly she stood there only a second or two, watching him. But it seemed like longer, it seemed like a lifetime. She couldn't seem to pull her gaze away. She had this uncanny sensation of familiarity, as if she'd known him for years instead of minutes, as if his presence in her bed that morning hadn't been a dream at all, hadn't been her imagination, but was instead reality. As if she hadn't been married to Pierre all those years, made love with Pierre, shared a home and children with Pierre, but instead with this man. With Monsieur Legrand, whose name was most assuredly not Legrand.

She stared at his nose, his hair that shone in the golden lamplight, and thought, *What is your name?*

At that instant, he looked up, as if he actually heard the words in her head, this small and dangerous question. He was so quick, she had no time to look away, and for a second their eyes met through the glass, bedraggled Daisy and warm, sturdy Monsieur Legrand. The shock of recognition passed between them. She started toward the door and so did he, so that when she reached for the handle, it was already turning, the door was already opening, and Monsieur Legrand stood right there before her in his tweed vest and his smile. He took his pipe from his mouth. The gold ring flashed on his last finger.

"My dear Madame Villon," he said. "Come right inside. I believe I've found you the perfect book."

CHAPTER TEN

Babs

The Hôtel Ritz
Paris, France
April 1964

I AWOKE THE FOLLOWING morning to someone banging a book against my head. Or that's what it felt like at any rate. At least the pain in my head softened the ache in my heart. I'd been dreaming of Kit. We were in his library at Langford Hall, searching for a particular book, both of us becoming more frantic as we kept pulling the wrong volumes from the shelves, tossing them on the floor.

My eyes popped open, realizing two things at once—I'd left Kit's copy of *The Scarlet Pimpernel* at the bar the night before, and someone was knocking on the door. I looked around at my strange and opulent surroundings, suddenly remembering where I was. And why.

I lifted my head from the pillow, immediately wishing I hadn't. The banging on my head was actually coming from *inside* my skull, and in a horrendous flash of memory I recalled how much I'd had to drink the night before. And with whom. A particular recollection filled my mind in bright, violent colors. I clenched my eyes as if I could block out the memory, but it was there, too—right behind my eyelids. Good heavens. Had I really said *rumpy-pumpy*?

The knocking on my door continued and I stared at it in horror. What if it was *him*? What if he'd returned to take me up on my offer? Surely not. Mr. Bowdoin—Drew—was a gentleman. Although he *had* admitted he found me attractive. Hadn't he? I was finding it very hard to sort through my memories because of the competing pounding from both my head and the door.

"Barbara? Are you awake? It's Precious Dubose."

An enormous sense of relief coursed through me at the sound of Precious's voice. And a little bit of disappointment if I were to be completely honest with myself. "Coming!" I shouted, the word thumping about in my head like a cricket ball run amok and ricocheting against the stumps.

I slid from the bed in the darkened room, my foot getting caught in the rumpled bedclothes, propelling me forward onto the thankfully soft carpet. I crawled for a few paces before pulling myself up on the desk chair and making my way to the door. My eyes took a moment to focus as I made several attempts to unlatch the door and pull it open.

Precious Dubose, immaculately dressed, stood on the other side of the door. She leaned in conspiratorially and whispered, "Are you alone?"

It took me a moment to comprehend her meaning. As indignantly as I could, I said, "Of course I'm alone."

She looked disappointed. "May I come in?"

I stepped aside and watched as she removed a *Do Not Disturb* sign from the door that Drew must have placed on his way out. Precious held it up for me to see. "When I saw this, I had great hopes that your rendezvous had been a successful one."

"It wasn't a rendezvous," I insisted again, even though she was busily ignoring me by opening my drapes to let in the bright morning sunlight. Although I wasn't exactly sure it was still morning. I blinked at the mantel clock and saw that it was nearly noon.

"I brought you a cold Co-Cola and some aspirin. Nothing is better when a girl has overindulged." She set a little basket on the dressing table and with her back to me pulled out two green bottles and a bottle opener.

My mouth felt as if I'd slept with a wool sock thrust inside it and I was desperate for any form of liquid, as long as it didn't contain alcohol. "Thank you," I said as I padded toward her on the carpet and she popped off the caps with the opener.

She faced me, her eyes widening as I approached, a look of what could only be described as horror crossing her fine features. She placed the bottles on the desk with a small thump as if she no longer had the strength to hold them, then pressed her hands against her heart. "What in heaven's name are you wearing? And please tell me your gentleman didn't see you in it."

I looked down at my clothing, remembering getting up at some time in the night and pulling off my stained dress then stumbling to the dresser to retrieve something to sleep in. I wore a one-piece sleeper, something usually found in children's wear, but in a larger size for adults. It was pink flannel with a print of tiny little woolly lambs all over it and a fat wool ball toggle on the zipper. My darling children had pooled their pocket money and bought it for me at John Lewis for the first Mothering Sunday after Kit had died. They said they wanted me to wear it to keep me warm at night in their father's absence.

I'd been so touched by their thoughtfulness that I wore it often and had brought it with me to Paris to remind me of them and of home. I hadn't meant for it to frighten anyone. "It's . . . warm," I said in my defense. "And it was a gift from my children."

"Do they dislike you?"

I glowered at her as I took my Coca-Cola bottle from the dresser and took a large sip, the bubbles tickling my nose. "Of course not. And there's nothing wrong with it. It does keep me warm at night."

"As would the small bonfire we could make using it. Please tell me your gentleman didn't see it."

"Of course not. And he's not my gentleman. He's a business associate, and his name is Drew Bowdoin."

"Bowdoin—like the college?"

I stared at her for a moment wondering if I was the only person in the world who didn't know about Bowdoin College. I shook my head. "Not according to Mr. Bowdoin."

Her gaze swept over me again and she sighed audibly. "Apparently, we still have a lot of work to do." She marched across the room to the closet and pulled it open. After some consideration, she took out a bright yellow dress with large white dots that I recalled trying on the previous day. It was another short dress, but not as short as the dress I'd worn the previous evening with the drink stain on the bodice. At least I wouldn't feel as if I should be wearing trousers with it. But there'd been something else . . .

"It's got the most adorable cut-out at the top—isn't it just darling? It's very clever the way it shows just a wink of your cleavage." She held it against her chest for a moment, her eyes closed, and smiled. "Beautiful clothes can change your life, believe me."

I wanted to believe it. That my life could change just by putting on a pretty dress and feeling the sun on bared skin. But I couldn't. I felt a flicker of annoyance at this woman who'd somehow managed to barge her way into my life without knowing anything about me. "I can't wear that. It's too . . . happy."

She lowered the dress. "And why don't you feel you should wear clothes that are happy?"

"I'm a widow."

Instead of replacing the dress in the wardrobe, she began taking it off the hanger. "And your late husband wouldn't want you to be happy?"

"Of course he would. It's just . . ." I shook my head, trying to find a way to tell her how utterly miserable I'd been since Kit died. How inside I felt like the barren fields in winter, waiting for a spring that never arrived. Finally, I blurted, "You wouldn't understand. I loved him." *But I think he loved another woman.* I was thankful to have held back that last, shameful secret. Because I intended to take that one to the grave.

Precious watched me in silence, the light shifting in her eyes, her beautiful face unreadable. "I do know," she said softly. "I once loved someone so much I thought I might die from wanting him. But it was during the war." She shrugged, as if in that small gesture she could explain the years of hunger and loss. Of waiting and longing. And the eventual devastation of the heart. "Circumstances brought me to France. I never saw him again."

The room was quiet for a moment as we listened to the faint sound of traffic on Place Vendôme, the confirmation that life did go on. She continued, "I chose to do more than simply survive. I chose to *live*. To find a purpose in life. To search out the joy and happiness that is every-where, even in difficult times, if we're just brave enough to look." A wide smile illuminated her face. "That's why I choose to wear beautiful clothes and surround myself with lovely things and interesting people. To go out and *live*." She took a step closer to me. "Otherwise, what is the point of surviving?" Her expression turned serious. "I'm thinking somewhere, deep down, you understand what I'm saying. Otherwise, I don't think you'd ever have agreed to have gone shopping with me yesterday."

She held out the yellow spotty dress to me. "So come on. Wear this. I'll put a yellow ribbon in your hair and let you borrow my favorite lipstick—Cherries in the Snow. My mama used to say there was nothing besides a bright-colored lipstick to make a girl believe she could conquer the world."

For the first time since meeting Precious Dubose, I found myself wondering about her past. There was a minefield there, I was sure, with the same conviction that most of her story would remain secret. But I also knew, in some odd way, that we were somehow kindred spirits, that she *did* understand. And maybe—hopefully—I could follow her lead and find joy and happiness in my life again, and a purpose besides organizing church fetes and spearheading the Keep Britain Tidy group of the Women's Institute.

"All right," I said, accepting the dress. "Under one condition. That you stop trying to play matchmaker. I have found that having a man in my life isn't necessarily a requirement. I've become quite self-sufficient."

"I couldn't agree more," Precious said, nodding emphatically. "Although having a man can certainly make life a lot more fun." She actually winked at me as she grabbed my hand and led me to the dressing table.

An hour later I was dressed and coifed according to Precious's standards, wearing a pair of low-heeled strappy sandals and, as promised, a yellow ribbon in my hair that matched the admittedly adorable dress. I thought the lipstick too bright, preferring more of a beige tone, but Precious insisted that beige wasn't a color, and if it was, it didn't belong on the lips.

On the way out, I picked up my wool jumper from the back of the desk chair.

"What is it with you and sheep?" Precious asked. "You'll look like you have a lamb draped over your shoulders if you put that on. And it'll hide your gorgeous dress."

"What if I get chilly?"

"It's April in Paris. It's warm and heavenly." She yanked the jumper out of my hands and ungraciously threw it back on the chair. "If you get cold, Drew can loan you his jacket. Or put his arm around your shoulders."

"Precious," I said in warning, but she'd already left the room and was headed toward the lift, her voice drifting back to me.

"I'm so hungry I could eat a mule."

"Excuse me?"

She didn't slow her pace as she answered. "Let's go get something to eat. Maybe your Drew can join us. Unless you two already made plans?"

"Er, no, we didn't," I said, hurrying to catch up. "I, um, when he left I wasn't really thinking about the next day."

She turned to me with a raised eyebrow. "Well, I'm quite sure he's waiting to hear from you. Unless you finished your business last night?"

I shook my head and then stopped, not really sure. "I don't actually remember. Although I do recall that I left something on our table. I need to go to the bar and check."

The lift opened and we stepped inside. "We'll do that after we eat. Come on. They always have a table waiting for me."

"Really? So you live here at the Ritz?" I asked once we were downstairs. I followed Precious through the window-lined corridor to the restaurant, aware of heads turning in our direction. Precious walked like the model she said she'd been, her head held high, her posture straight. I felt more like a new foal in her wake, awkward and gangly.

"Off and on, but mostly on. Not like my friend Coco, who has had her own suite here since 1937. When I modeled for her, she'd let me stay in her suite. I suppose I got used to the Ritz. It's hard to live any-where else after you've experienced the best."

"Coco?" I asked, the name vaguely familiar.

"Coco Chanel. The designer. I'd be happy to introduce you, if you like."

"Perhaps," I said, not at all eager to be under the scrutiny of the famous designer. Precious was challenging enough.

A maître d' approached us and after a rapid exchange in French, we were quickly escorted to a table for four by a window overlooking the famed gardens.

Just as we were being seated, Precious waved at someone at the entrance to the restaurant, and I turned to see if it might be Drew, swallowing my unreasonable disappointment when I saw it wasn't him. Instead I spotted a slender and petite woman wearing a brilliantly colored scarf over her head and who, although not much past five feet tall, had a commanding presence that made one think of a general or a queen.

When she caught sight of Precious, the woman smiled, then began to walk toward us. She walked slowly and deliberately, as if she were an old woman, but as she got closer I could see she was about Precious's age and not yet past fifty. No hair was visible beneath the scarf, and her skin, though nearly without wrinkles, appeared ashen. Her eyebrows had been drawn in with pencil, and her lips appeared almost bloodless, yet her face, with dark, penetrating eyes, drew one's attention. She wasn't beautiful in the way that Precious Dubose was, yet I found myself unable to look away. There was something about her that made one want to stare.

"Margot!" Precious stood and the two women kissed cheeks in the French way before the maître d' appeared again and held out a chair for the newcomer. Again there was a quick exchange in French and then the word *Anglais* that made the woman's penetrating eyes turn toward me.

"If your friend doesn't mind," the woman said in English, with barely the trace of an accent. "I would love to join you."

"Please, do sit," I said, noticing her frail hand gripping the back of the chair, the way the skin on her slender fingers appeared nearly transparent.

A waiter approached with a new place setting and a menu as I half stood, prepared to help the woman should she require assistance. She glanced at me again with those dark eyes and it was very clear that she would not welcome any help from me or anyone else.

When she was settled, Precious said, "Barbara, I'd like you to meet my dearest and oldest friend, Margot Lemouron. We have known each other for a very long time, haven't we?"

Margot smiled and nodded. "We have. Since the war, no?"

"That's about right. I try not to count the exact number of years," Precious said. "Because then I'm reminded how old I am."

"Ah, age. What is it but a number?" Margot's voice was unexpectedly deep. She looked at me expectantly.

Precious placed a hand over her heart. "Dear me—where are my manners? Margot, please meet my new friend, Barbara, or Babs as she likes to be called. Barbara Langford."

Margot simply looked at me, her eyes missing nothing. "Langford?"

"Yes. My husband's family name. Do you know any Langfords? They're from Devonshire."

Margot took a moment before responding, and I thought that perhaps her English might not be as fluent as I'd assumed. Her shoulders lifted in a small Gallic shrug. "Perhaps. During and after the war, Paris was so full of nationalities—Germans, Americans, English. I met so many. And I've forgotten most of them, sadly." She smiled. "So many people passing in and out of our lives."

Her haunted eyes turned toward the window and the garden beyond, at the garish reds and blush pinks of the roses in brash contrast with the pallor of her skin. Precious beckoned for a waiter, who quickly brought a glass of water to the Frenchwoman. Margot nodded gratefully and took a sip.

"Is your husband traveling with you, Mrs. Langford?" she asked.

The question was so unexpected it was as if a small fist had made direct contact with my heart. "No. I'm afraid not." I took a deep breath, my gaze focused on the condensation dripping down the stem of her water glass. Feeling both pairs of eyes on me, I said, "I'm a widow. My husband died a little over a year ago."

"I am sorry to hear that." Her smile wobbled a bit as if she understood that sort of loss. She cleared her throat. "But how wonderful that you are here now, at the Paris Ritz, to enjoy a bit of life again, yes?"

I almost told her that I wasn't here on holiday, but on a fool's errand in search of my husband's lover. But I couldn't, of course. How could I explain something that even I didn't completely understand?

"Yes, it is," I said, picking up my menu and pretending to be hungry. "Shall we order?"

We ordered our food and when it arrived Precious was the only one who gave it justice, happily spearing a bite of *quiche paysanne au jambon* onto her fork. Madame Lemouron and I simply picked at our plates like little birds hunting for hidden seeds. I felt the woman's dark gaze on me, making me wonder if I reminded her of someone. I looked up and met her eyes only once. I smiled, wanting to banish the ghosts that seemed to surround her.

"*Excusez-moi?*" The terrible American-accented French startled me, causing me to drop my fork onto the floor. My cheeks heated as I looked up at Drew, those ridiculous words somehow finding their way into my memory at just that moment. *Rumpy-pumpy.* Oh, the indignity. Perhaps if I simply pretended that I didn't recall anything from the night before I might be able to meet his gaze again.

"I'll get that," he said as he bent to retrieve my fork at the exact same time I did so that our heads collided.

"I'm so sorry," he said, rubbing his chin. "Are you all right?"

"Just fine, thanks."

He nodded a greeting to my dining companions as I made introductions. "Would you care to join us?" I asked, not sure what I wished his answer might be.

"Thank you—but just for the company." He sat down in the chair next to me, his broad-shouldered form filling the chair and radiating heat. "I've already eaten both breakfast and lunch—I'm an early riser, preferring a little exercise before the sun." He grinned, showing his perfect American teeth, then placed something on the table next to me. "I'm sorry to interrupt, but I wanted to return this to Mrs. Langford. You left it on the table at the bar last night."

I looked at Kit's copy of *The Scarlet Pimpernel* with relief, not just for its return but for the fact that I'd thought to remove Kit's letter before I'd shown Drew the book. "Thank you so much. I was worried I might not see it again."

Precious slid it around to read the title out loud. "I will admit that I've never read the book, but I do remember falling in love with Leslie Howard in the movie. I was rather young—it was decades ago—but I remember sneaking into the theater since I couldn't afford the ticket price. I managed to sneak in three times because I was quite taken with Mr. Howard." She tapped her varnished nails on the cover. "There's something very alluring about a spy, I think—someone whose loyalties aren't always clear." She looked up suddenly, then pushed the book back to me. "Perhaps I should read the book, although I will confess to not being much of a reader. Unless it's the latest issue of *Vogue*, of course."

Her smile faded as she looked across the table at Margot Lemouron, whose face had paled even more, her hands trembling slightly. Precious leaned forward, placing a hand over her friend's. "Are you all right, Margot?"

The Frenchwoman shook her head. "I'm afraid not." She attempted a smile that looked more like a grimace. Addressing Drew and me, she said, "Will you excuse me, please? I think I need to go upstairs to my room and rest. It was a pleasure meeting you both. I hope to see you again."

Drew pulled back her chair and offered his assistance to the lift, but she shook her head and left, her gait slow and uneven. "Is she all right?" he asked.

Before Precious could answer, our attention was diverted by the *thwack thwack* of a cane being thrust against the floor and a loud imperious American voice. "Coming through. I *must* eat breakfast at precisely one thirty every day and will not be detained." Waiters scattered, not wanting to drop dishes or be hit by the cane as the old woman spotted our table and headed in our direction like a battleship under fire.

I recognized her as Mrs. Schulyer, who'd sat at the table in the bar with Precious the previous evening supplying unending drinks to the table I shared with Drew. Drew watched the approaching woman with alarm, assumingly reaching the same conclusion.

I looked at Precious, hoping she'd give us the approval to bolt, but instead she smiled in greeting as a waiter pulled out the chair recently vacated by Madame Lemouron, the place already cleared by apparently invisible waitstaff, and Mrs. Schulyer sat without being invited.

Precious began the introductions, but the old woman held out a finger, encased in a fingerless lace glove like my great-grandmother Eugenia used to wear. And might have actually been buried in since she claimed her hands were always cold. "I must have my coffee first before conversation."

A waiter appeared with a tray carrying a coffeepot, sugar bowl, and cream pitcher. Without making eye contact, he poured coffee into a cup, then added three spoonfuls of sugar and a hefty measure of cream. He dutifully waited while the woman took a sip and nodded, before stepping back so that two more waiters could place in front of her a plate full of soft eggs with runny yolks and bacon, another plate with grilled onions and small tomatoes, and a bowl of stewed prunes.

She closed her eyes while sipping her coffee, slurping rather loudly, and then with a smack of her lips, placed the empty cup on the table. "That's better." She nodded regally while Precious made introductions.

"Mrs. Prunella Schuyler is another old friend of mine. She lives here as well, so we get to see each other often."

Mrs. Schuyler tightened her lips as if seeing Precious often wasn't ideal. "That poor, poor girl," she said, indicating the direction Madame Lemouron had gone. "It's the cancer you know. Too bad she doesn't have the Pratt constitution as I do—that was my family name before I married into the Schuylers. Strong as oxen we Pratts. Takes a lot to take us down. I survived the sinking of the *Lusitania*, you know."

Without leaving space to interject a word in between her ramblings, she spoke and ate at the same time, yellow egg yolks pooling in the corners of her mouth. Precious's eyes had begun to glaze over when I felt a definite prodding of my foot. I surreptitiously gave a glance under the table just in time to see Drew's rather large foot tapping the side of my sandal. Glancing up, I saw his expression was one of a man drowning and in search of a life preserver.

From my position at the WI, I apparently had more stamina dealing with lonely elderly women than Drew did. I nodded a few times while finishing my quiche, enjoying his discomfiture, and then, around the third time of her mentioning the *Lusitania*, I made a big show of looking at my wristwatch.

"Oh my. Could it really be so late? Drew promised me he'd take me bicycling in the Bois de Boulogne, didn't you?" I stared pointedly at him.

His slow nod became suddenly earnest. "Yes. Absolutely. We don't want to be late," he said enthusiastically as he excused himself and stood, then pulled back my chair. "Ladies, it's been great and a pleasure meeting you both. Enjoy your afternoon."

Prunella stopped talking for a moment, looking nonplussed. "But I'm only up to the first day of our *Lusitania* voyage."

I stood and picked up the book so I wouldn't forget it again. "You know, Mrs. Schulyer, you really should write this all down in a memoir. There must be dozens of people who'd love to hear your story."

Her thick eyebrows shot up. "Do you really think so? I am quite a good writer, so it would make perfect sense." She raised her hand and called for the waiter. "*Garçon!*" she called, butchering the word so that the waiter had no idea he was being summoned. "*Garçon!*" she yelled, louder this time and he turned, most likely to find out what the commotion was all about. "Get me a typewriter. Immediately before I lose my muse!"

Drew took my elbow and began to gently pull me away from the table. Precious waved. "You two kids have fun." She actually winked and I blushed, quite sure that her definition of fun didn't involve riding boots and a gelding. Or perhaps it did.

I began heading toward the lift, but Drew called me back. "Where are you going? I thought we had a date."

"Oh, I just said that—" I stopped. "You don't have to take me anywhere."

"Maybe I'd like to."

"Really?" I said, feeling like a giddy schoolgirl. "I'm sure you have other things to do."

"Actually no. So if you're free, let's go."

I felt a little surge of *something* in my chest as I followed him outside.

We headed out the door and he began walking while I clutched Kit's book and wondered what I was supposed to do with it while riding a bicycle. "Wait," I said, stopping. "You're headed in the wrong direction. The park is that way, on the western edge of the sixteenth arrondissement," I said, pointing in the opposite direction.

"True. But Le Mouton Noir is this way. If we want to find La Fleur, I think that's the best place to start, don't you?"

"Of course," I said, feeling oddly disappointed and not a little foolish as I ran to catch up with him. "That's why we're here. To find La Fleur."

I forced a smile as we walked together, retracing my footsteps to the bookstore from the previous day, and fervently wishing I'd never heard of La Fleur.

CHAPTER ELEVEN

Aurélie

The Château de Courcelles
Picardy, France
September 1914

THERE WERE FLOWERS at Aurélie's place at the table when she came down for breakfast the next morning, a bouquet of daisies tied with a grosgrain bow.

"You have an admirer, I see," said her father. "One with simple tastes."

"It must have been one of the mayors," said Aurélie, slipping into her seat beneath a painting of a decidedly overdressed shepherdess. "When they came out this morning for their *instructions*."

"It was the quiet German left them for you." Suzanne slapped the coffeepot down so hard that Aurélie was amazed the porcelain pot didn't shatter. It was surprisingly sturdy stuff, Limoges. "Came right in, all please and thank you and apologies, wanting to know which was your place. I wouldn't have told him, but . . ."

But when a German asked, one obeyed.

"Of course, you couldn't do otherwise." The flowers that had been sweet a moment ago now seemed sinister. A floral tribute wasn't much of a tribute when one hadn't the right to refuse it.

Would you commandeer my good will? she had asked Lieutenant von Sternburg the night before. It seemed he intended to do just that.

"They're only flowers," she said, to no one in particular.

"He has a softness for you." Aurélie didn't miss the way her father glanced over his shoulder as he said it, watching for listeners.

Aurélie shrugged and helped herself to a miniscule portion of jam. On second thought, she recklessly slathered the bread. Better to take what they could before the Germans commandeered it. "He doesn't like unpleasantness, that's all. He's trying to pretend this is a social call."

"Then maybe you ought to assist him in that fiction." Her father regarded her over the rim of his coffee cup. "Men speak unguardedly to women they admire."

The jam stuck to the roof of Aurélie's mouth. "You want me to consort with the enemy?"

"Only one of them," said her father, as though that made a difference. "Just—lend him an encouraging ear."

"Spy, you mean."

"There's no need to be crude about it."

Aurélie frowned at her father. "Only canaille sink to such levels, you said. A gentleman goes into battle properly, honorably."

"You are a woman." Her father waved a hand, appealing to the shepherdesses on the wall, hideous, simpering things. "Women wage war differently."

Aurélie was too outraged to mince words. "On their backs, you mean?"

"Aurélie." Her father had been friends with the late English king during his wild career as the Prince of Wales. He was disapproving, but hardly shocked. "I'm not suggesting you turn courtesan."

It was exactly what he was suggesting. "Men speak unguardedly to women they admire?"

"Use the wits you were born with. When one is in extremis, one does what one must. We ate rats during the Siege of Paris." Before Aurélie could point out that she'd heard about those rats before, her father changed tack. "Your mother wouldn't balk at it."

And that meant she shouldn't either? Aurélie pushed her plate away. "Just because Maman—" she began, and broke off, unable to say the words.

"Lived her life with a man not her husband?" Her father's voice was lightly ironical. "There's no need to protect my pride, my dear. If all of Paris knew, I could hardly remain ignorant."

"Yes, but . . ." Aurélie wasn't quite sure how she had found herself in the wrong. She was meant to be the picture of outraged virtue, not a shamed schoolgirl. "I don't want to be like Maman."

"Your mother has her merits," her father said neutrally, which seemed rather rich given that her parents had been estranged for the past fifteen years. They were like the mechanical figures on a clock. When one came out, the other went in. He couldn't resist adding, "Discretion, however, was not one of them."

"What, then, am I meant to be?"

"The picture of maidenly virtue." Her father shrugged. "Take Von Sternburg for a stroll in the gardens. Show him the portraits in the green salon. You can take a chaperone if you fear for your good name."

The good name she had never had, thanks to her mother's notoriety. Other girls were considered virtuous until proven otherwise. Aurélie had been labeled fast before she had even known what it meant. She had worked so hard to distinguish herself from her mother, to prove to the gratin that she, at least, was above reproach. And now . . .

"There's no point to it. They'll be gone in a week. Herr von Sternburg said so."

Her father cast her a long, sidelong look. "You see? You've begun already."

"But I didn't—" The intimacy of that encounter, the damp dress clinging to her, the warmth of Von Sternburg's regard, all came crashing back, tangling her tongue, making the color rise in her cheeks.

Her father looked owlishly at her over his coffee cup.

Aurélie ate the rest of her breakfast in dignified silence. What her father suggested was impossible.

Besides, it would be only a week, two at most. There was no need to work her dubious wiles on Von Sternburg to obtain information that could only be of limited use. The French would push forward again, she was sure of it. And then they would be free.

But it wasn't a week, or even two. September slid into October and the Germans were still there. Twenty-four kilometers to the west, the shelling continued, a faint rumble like thunder, a storm that went on and on without breaking.

In the village of Courcelles and all the other villages under Major Hoffmeister's command, the walls of the *mairies* were pasted with overlapping notices. At first, it was almost laughable, the commands that all hens were to lay two eggs a day, all of which were to be reserved for German officers. Every wild rabbit was to be counted and listed. All molehills were to be flattened.

"Do they mean to make the chickens march in goose step?" snorted Victor as he hid jars of preserves beneath the straw of the old icehouse.

But his laughter faded as the demands continued. The mattresses, the linen, the cooking pots, the meager treasures of the families in the village were methodically stripped away. A tax was imposed, eighty-six hundred francs in so-called war contributions.

"If you mind so much for your people, you could pay it yourself," said the major when Aurélie's father complained that one could hardly squeeze blood from a stone.

"Shall I wire my banker in Paris?" asked the count sarcastically.

The major regarded him unsmilingly. "Your kind always have a bit tucked away. Don't think I don't know you've been hiding things from me. We'll find them. We always do. Like those idiots who buried their clocks without stopping the chimes."

The count sketched an ironic bow. "Be my guest. Search the castle. My humble abode is, it appears, at your disposal. I shall send my accounting to Berlin."

It was empty bravado. They all knew that here, now, cut off from the rest of the world, there was no appealing to Berlin. Her father's lineage, his position, meant nothing.

That night, Lieutenant Kraus used the Venetian goblets for target practice, laughing as they shattered, spraying wine like blood.

Major Hoffmeister said merely, "I assume you'll add it to your account?" and Aurélie knew he was taunting her father on purpose, waiting for him to break, to do something rash.

Lieutenant Kraus, she was convinced, was half-mad. A sot and a bully, breaking toys for the fun of it. Lieutenant Dreier was a sycophant, as firm of purpose as a feather mattress. He greedily guzzled the good wine when he thought no one was looking, pressing his Brownie camera onto the servants and demanding that they take pictures of him next to the gilt-limned walls of the ballroom to send home to impress his family in Darmstadt.

But Major Hoffmeister was another matter entirely. He didn't imbibe. He didn't grab at treasures. Instead, he needled. One little slight after another, small inconveniences created for no cause other than to discomfit his reluctant hosts, to show them his power. He was breaking them, or trying to.

"A week?" said Aurélie's father, as October staggered into November, gaunt and cold. "Two at most?"

He had taken to haunting the parapets with a spyglass, noting

German troop movements. He was, she knew, relaying the information to a contact by means of pigeon, even though keeping pigeons had been banned on threat of death.

Aurélie didn't know whether to be alarmed at her father's recklessness, or grateful that he hadn't engaged in more direct action.

"Who would have thought it could go on this long?" Aurélie hugged herself against the wind that bit through her thin jacket. She had always spent winters in Paris, never at Courcelles. Her wardrobe was a summer wardrobe, unsuited to dawn parapets. "It can't go on much longer. It can't."

"Can't it?" said her father, and Aurélie thought that if he mentioned the Siege of Paris in '71 again she might scream. "We might know more—if you took the pains to learn."

"I doubt that," said Aurélie sharply. "What might Lieutenant von Sternburg know other than the numbers of hens who failed to lay their required quota of eggs?"

Whenever she saw him, he was hurrying past with a ledger under his arm. He looked as though he had a perpetual headache. She rather hoped he had.

The children in the village said he gave them bars of chocolate. This, Aurélie thought, would have been rather more heartwarming if he hadn't also been one of the men in charge of robbing those children's parents.

"His uncle is a member of the high command. Haven't you noticed the letters that arrive for him every week?"

"I hadn't realized you went through their mail."

"Of course I don't," said her father impatiently. "Henri does."

Henri was the old butler, eighty if he was a day, the constant butt of the Germans' jibes. Aurélie felt an idiot for not having thought of it herself.

"If Henri is reading his letters already, why do you need me?"

"Because Henri can't always get to them. He's loyal but he's not—what was that American's name? Houdini. Your mother made me see his performance," he added as an aside, his lip curling slightly, although whether at the magician or her mother, Aurélie had no idea. "It would be more effective to go to the horse's mouth, as it were."

She really shouldn't be thinking about Lieutenant von Sternburg's mouth. "If the opportunity arises."

"True daughters of Courcelles," said her father, "make their own opportunities."

She might have told him that all she had seen of Von Sternburg recently was the back of his head. She might have told him that she thought the German was avoiding her—or perhaps she was avoiding him. Or maybe they were avoiding each other.

Instead, she pushed away from the parapet. "I need to go to the village."

Her father turned to look at her. "You can't stop a dam with a loaf of bread."

"Who would waste good bread on a dam?" said Aurélie tartly, and stomped down the stairs, annoyed with the world and her father in particular. She didn't know if he had only lately developed a habit of aphorism or if she had just never noticed it before. If it was the latter, she was beginning to have slightly more sympathy for her mother.

Or maybe she was annoyed because she knew, on some level, that he was right, and that her own efforts were a poor excuse for action.

No, that wasn't entirely true. Aurélie stopped in the kitchens, taking the prepared basket from Suzanne as the cook glanced furtively behind her to make sure no loitering German soldiers were about. What she was doing did matter. Even if it was only a loaf of bread here, an egg there.

All of the grain, their hard-won grain that she could reckon in calluses on her palms, had been confiscated. The mill ground only for the

Germans; the bakery turned out loaves and cakes for the conquerors. The people of Courcelles were surviving, barely, on gruel and thin soup, flavored with what roots the Germans considered beneath them. Starving, the villagers had taken to gleaning any stray grains of wheat they could find and grinding them into coarse meal in their coffee grinders.

On hearing of this, Major Hoffmeister had ordered all the coffee grinders in the village confiscated.

Never mind that all the able-bodied men had long since gone. Never mind that he was starving old men and young children and expectant mothers.

So Aurélie had taken matters into her own hands. The Germans kept copious records, but could they say, truly, how many eggs had gone into their souffle, how many chickens into their stew? Suzanne had become an expert at making shift, spiriting food from the pot into Aurélie's basket. Every day, she would wait until Hoffmeister and his two favorite flunkies were out hunting her father's forest, pretending to be the very grand seigneurs they claimed to despise. Then she would creep down the hill, distributing her makeshift charity to the people of the village.

"Angel," they called her, and "Demoiselle," and she felt like the world's greatest hypocrite, to accept their praise when she had done so little. If she were truly a heroine, she would take a knife to Hoffmeister as Charlotte Corday had done to Marat—although preferably not in his bath. Whatever Lieutenant von Sternburg might say about the medieval tradition of bathing guests, seeing Hoffmeister naked was a humiliation she had so far been spared.

And if she did stab him? They would only shoot her. Shoot her and burn the entire village in reprisal. All would be lost and for what? Another Hoffmeister would be sent to administer the charred remains of what once had been Courcelles, and the wild grass would grow over the houses that had been and the people who had died for her foolishness.

No, she had to be cleverer than that. But how?

The stories of her youth had all been of bold action or virtuous resignation, Joan of Arc or Patient Griselda, neither of them noted for their subtlety. Aurélie wondered, fleetingly, what her mother would do. Hold a salon for the conquerors? Twist their words until they found themselves agreeing with her despite themselves?

She wasn't her mother.

She had always been so proud of that, that she was a Courcelles to the bone. For the first time, Aurélie caught herself wondering, uneasily, whether she ought to have paid more attention to her mother's tutelage, to have inherited something more from her than the color of her hair.

The sun was shining, but the village felt gray, all the bustle subdued. The usual clog-clad crowd of women around the well in the village square was missing; the Germans had made it illegal to congregate in groups of more than three. There was no washing hanging on the lines; that, too, had become a crime. The smells of food cooking, the old men at the café whose voices grew louder as they drank glass after glass of *blanche*, all were gone. The villagers hid behind the curtains of their houses, out of sight of the German imperial flag that hung boldly from the front of the former police station, now a German command post.

Those women who were out and about on errands moved quickly and furtively, looking back over their shoulders at the Germans who sat at the café or loitered by the entrance to the command post.

Aurélie took the back way, past the churchyard, avoiding the square. The familiar old church felt alien, stripped bare of the walnut trees that had, for generations, shaded the graveyard. The work of centuries had been cut down in an afternoon, the wood shipped to Germany to make rifle barrels.

No smoke came from the chimney of the schoolhouse. The schoolmistress had been deported to Germany for the crime of starting classes at the traditional ten o'clock rather than the German-mandated nine. Well, that and singing "La Marseillaise" very loudly at Lieutenant Dreier when he came to demand that the school time be changed. Local opinion was divided upon whether that had been heroic or foolish—or merely an affront to the ears and national pride.

Some houses had Germans billeted in them. Aurélie avoided those. Swiftly, not lingering, she went from garden to garden, past the empty runs where chickens used to peck, handing over a loaf here, a half chicken there, a few links of sausage, a sack of withered apples. Her meager offerings were hidden under the corners of shawls, whisked through kitchen doors, treated as though they were diamonds cut from a rajah's crown and not the dregs of the kitchen, one step away from pig slop.

It seemed impossible to remember a time when pigs ate as well as men, when the villagers heedlessly threw crusts to birds and peeled potatoes in great, careless strips.

The village felt empty, abandoned; the Germans were sending able-bodied men and women, the ones who defied them, or the ones who appeared to defy them, to work camps in Germany. There had been rumors in the village, wild rumors, that the infirm men, the ones whose health had been ruined by the phosphate mines and their brains by *genièvre,* were to be shot; that the women were to be organized into brothels. Rumors, just rumors, Aurélie hoped. There was so much, two months ago, that she would have thought wild speculation had she not seen it herself. The joke about goose-stepping chickens had long since lost all humor.

But what was she to do? Something, something, something. Aurélie could hear the words in time to her footsteps as she hurried back up the hill to the castle, her empty basket hidden beneath her thick shawl.

She was so lost in her own thoughts that it took her a moment to realize that something was wrong, that the door to her room, which she had left closed, was ajar, and Victor was hopping from one foot to the other in the corridor like an agitated mime.

"Mademoiselle Aurélie, Mademoiselle Aurélie . . ."

"Ah, Mademoiselle de Courcelles." Her room. Hoffmeister was in her room. The doors of the wardrobe gaped open, dresses piled haphazardly on the bed. The drawer of her dressing table stuck out like a distended tongue. She had precious few books and papers—she had always preferred action to reflection—but those she did have had been pulled from the escritoire and left gaping on the desktop.

From beside the wardrobe, Drier stood smirking at her, his arms full of her underthings.

"I . . . what . . . what are you—"

Dreier had the decency to look mildly abashed. Hoffmeister did not. He took a step forward, his movements deliberate. "You have been stealing from us."

"I . . . what?" Her confusion was genuine.

Aurélie tried to think what she might have done, what he might think was hidden in her room, that he needed to search it so, tearing apart the bindings of her books, ransacking her dressing table drawer, which contained nothing more exciting than several dried-out powder puffs and a saint's medal given to her by Victor on the occasion of her First Communion.

Her father . . . stealing information . . . the pigeons . . . had they thought she might have . . .

Aurélie felt as though she'd been carved from wood. "You are mistaken. I've taken nothing."

Hoffmeister favored her with a humorless twist of the lips. "Do you think I don't know? Everything is seen. Everything is counted. You have been stealing food and taking it to the village."

"Stealing *food*?" Was that what he was doing, scrabbling through her chemises looking for madeleines? Aurélie removed her thick shawl, dropping it over the dressing table chair, and, coincidentally, over her empty basket. "I have given to the villagers of my own rations—as I believe you yourself suggested, major. If I choose to part with my bread, it is none of your concern."

"Everything that occurs in this region is my concern, mademoiselle." Hoffmeister was a spare man, barely her own height, but the self-importance that radiated from him made him seem larger. "I did not authorize those disbursements."

Aurélie refused to be cowed. She lifted her chin in approved style, taking advantage of her height to look down her nose at him. "I gave only what was mine."

The major was not impressed. "You do not seem to understand, Mademoiselle de Courcelles. There is nothing that is yours. Nothing."

He smiled at her, a narrow, thin-lipped smile. That smile made Aurélie suddenly very nervous.

"This room. This room is required. You will no longer occupy it. I find my current chambers inconvenient. This will do better." He raised a hand, and Dreier obediently scuttled forward. "Lieutenant. Help Mademoiselle de Courcelles with her things."

"Yes, sir," said Dreier, and before Aurélie could say anything, before she could move, he turned and wrenched open the window, dropping an armload of her most intimate garments into the courtyard below.

"I—" Aurélie would have stepped forward, but Hoffmeister was between her and the lieutenant. Dreier gathered up an armload of her dresses.

"A moment." Hoffmeister arrested his subordinate with a gesture. "Leave us."

Us, as though he were the Sun King, throned in state.

"This is unworthy of civilized men," said Aurélie, doing her best to keep her tone level.

"This is war, Mademoiselle de Courcelles. I do not know what chivalric tales your deluded parent has fed you, but there are no knights—and very few ladies. I have an exchange to propose to you."

"My honor or my life?" Aurélie felt she would make a better account of herself if she could stop her arms from clutching around her chest. Deliberately, she unclenched them and lowered them to her sides.

Hoffmeister looked almost amused. "What would I want with either? I have no desire to make a martyr of you. As for the other—no. No. There is a relic. A . . . talisman, I believe you call it."

"A talisman," Aurélie repeated dumbly. "The talisman?"

Hoffmeister suppressed his irritation at the idiocy of the conquered. Speaking slowly and clearly, in atrocious French, he said, "Give me the talisman and you may keep your accommodations. And I will turn a blind eye to your activities in the village."

"Do you truly believe I would trade my patrimony for silk wall hangings?" She had never liked those wall hangings. They had been chosen by her father's mother, whom Aurélie suspected might have been color-blind. Either that, or she had exceedingly dreadful taste in drapes. "I wouldn't, even if the talisman were here, which it isn't."

"I could have you shot for stealing."

There was a time when it had seemed rather romantic to be martyred for France. Now that the moment was here, Aurélie discovered that she strongly preferred not to be shot.

"I can summon fifty men—including your own subordinates—

who can vouch that you advised me to share my own rations with my people." Aurélie struggled to show a brave front, the front her people would expect. "If you want to shoot me, shoot me. Make a martyr of me. Let the world know that the Demoiselle de Courcelles died for France."

Died for a few eggs and half a chicken, which wasn't nearly so impressive, but still.

"Is this talisman so important, then?" Hoffmeister seemed to think he had stumbled on something; she could see his eyes light the way they did when he thought he'd discovered an accounting anomaly.

"The talisman," said Aurélie, "is in Paris."

"Is it?"

There was no way he could know. No one had seen it beneath her shirtwaist, that day she arrived; no one had seen her hide it. Unless . . . The thought made her cold.

They liked to pretend that no one would betray them to the conqueror, but people did. All the time. Sometimes for as little as a bag of coffee beans, a block of chocolate.

"If you rediscover it, you will come to me." Hoffmeister paused for a moment, surveying the wreck of her room. "In the meantime, since you find the kitchens of such interest, I suggest you find lodging there."

He took up the dresses Dreier had abandoned and dropped them, casually, out the window. Then he stood there, looking at her.

"Yes?" said Aurélie, her nerves on the verge of fraying. She just wanted him to go, to go and leave her be.

He gestured with a parody of courtesy, indicating that she was to go. "This room, mademoiselle. It is no longer yours."

"Oh." The color flared in Aurélie's cheeks. Somehow, the reality of it hadn't quite hit her. She turned and exited, avoiding Hoffmeister's eyes.

It was just a room. Just a room with very ugly wall hangings. But it was her bolt-hole, her hideaway, and she felt strangely naked without it.

She truly would be naked if she didn't collect her clothes from the courtyard. There was no spare cloth to make anything new.

In a daze, Aurélie went down the familiar stairs. Or was she meant to be using the back stairs now, as befitted her new station? Would Hoffmeister outfit her in an apron and cap and have her serve at table? Or was she to sleep in rags at the hearth like Cinderella in the old tale?

None of it mattered, she knew that. Clothes were merely coverings for the body; a bed was a bed was a bed.

But she was shaking all the same.

Her belongings were scattered all over the courtyard. A pair of camiknickers was hanging, like a schoolboy's prank, off the arm of the cherub that adorned the Italianate fountain. Aurélie made her way around the courtyard, gathering her belongings one by one, like a peasant foraging for firewood. A chemise here, a shirtwaist there, all so sad and crumpled, such pitiful little pieces of a life, useless embroidery on her underthings, beading on her evening frocks. What good did any of that do her now? She would do better to dress in wool as the country people did.

Her favorite dress, the one with the large flower embroidered on the bodice, had landed square in a mud puddle, the delicate fabric dark with dirt.

Aurélie knelt and lifted it from the mud. No amount of washing would bleach the stain of the clay of Picardy out of that silk. She shouldn't care. She shouldn't. What use had she for evening dresses now? But she caught herself clutching the crumpled silk to her chest, hunching over it as the sobs caught in the back of her throat.

"Mademoiselle?" Someone cleared his throat. "Mademoiselle de Courcelles?"

Aurélie turned her face away, a blind instinct born of shame. She couldn't let him see her this way. She couldn't let anyone see her this way. But particularly not Lieutenant von Sternburg. Not he.

His shadow fell across the clothes; she saw the tips of his uniform boots as he crouched down beside her. Their polish seemed like an affront. "What happened here?"

"Why? Do you want to catalog it? Write the items down in a ledger? So many soiled skirts? One ruined evening gown?" It might have sounded more impressive if her voice hadn't cracked.

"I had thought," he said gently, "to render assistance."

She couldn't bear his pity. "To whom? Would you like to dance what's left into the dirt?" She wasn't being politic. Aurélie rubbed the back of her hand against her eyes. It was, she belatedly realized, streaked with mud. Which was probably all over her face. Turning away, Aurélie said woodenly, "Forgive me. I don't know what I'm saying."

She made to rise to her feet, catching one heel in her hem. Von Sternburg was immediately there with a hand on her elbow to help her. "Who did this? Did Lieutenant Kraus . . ."

Mutely, Aurélie shook her head. "I've been required to change my chamber. It appears my circumstances have been reduced. Your commanding officer was kind enough to help me move my things."

"This is insupportable."

Insupportable because the Demoiselle de Courcelles might have to live in a room without ormolu cabinets and eighteenth-century boiseries? Something inside Aurélie cracked. Wrenching her elbow away, she demanded, "Is it? Is it any more insupportable than confiscating Madame Lely's only mattress? More insupportable than taking all of Monsieur Dubois's chickens when he has a sick mother to feed? More insupportable than melting down the brasses *from the church* to make shell casings?"

His throat moved beneath his stiff military collar with its imperial insignia. "Those were for the war effort. This—"

"Were all the coffee grinders in the village required for the war effort?" Aurélie shook her ruined dress in his face. "Is that your plan, Lieutenant von Sternburg? To starve your prisoners to death? Because that's what's happening. There are children—children who haven't had a proper meal in weeks! While you dine on foie gras and the best wine from our cellars."

"I haven't been. Dining on foie gras." Von Sternburg winced, as though he realized the irrelevancy of that. "I wouldn't . . . I haven't . . . oh bother. You're right, you know. That is exactly what some people think we ought to do. Starve the occupied population into submission. Make you so weak, you can't resist."

His voice was as she'd never heard it before. Clipped. Expressionless.

"And the old men?" she asked, her voice hoarse with fear. "The ones whose wits have gone with *genièvre*?"

Von Sternburg's blue eyes met hers. She was tall, but he was taller. One seldom noticed it, because he had such an unassuming air, but now he stood straight, unsmiling.

"Shot," he said. "That's what Hoffmeister has proposed to Berlin. Unnecessary mouths to feed."

Aurélie couldn't help it. She hadn't meant to show her distress but to hear it said so baldly horrified her. The back of her hand pressed against her mouth; she bit her knuckles to keep from crying out.

"It's abominable," said Lieutenant von Sternburg. "Mademoiselle de Courcelles—please. Don't look so. This will not stand."

"But . . . if Hoffmeister . . ." Oh Lord, how had it come to this, that she was bowing to the wishes of a petty dictator? But he was supreme here. He had the power of force, the only power that mattered now.

Von Sternburg's face was set. Aurélie hadn't known he could look so stern. "Hoffmeister answers to Berlin and Berlin *will* know of this."

"That Mademoiselle de Courcelles has lost her bedchamber?"

"That Major Hoffmeister is abusing his privileges." Lieutenant von Sternburg leaned forward, his expression earnest. "I have written to my uncle. He is . . . well placed. Something will be done."

Aurélie drew back, feeling off-balance, unsure who to trust. He seemed sincere enough, but—these were his people. His commanding officer. "Why should Berlin care?"

Lieutenant von Sternburg's lips twisted in a rueful smile. "Berlin may not care about widows and children, but they will care that the population is no longer fit to work. The army needs the grain they will sow in the spring."

"Oh." That told her.

"And," said Lieutenant von Sternburg quietly, "one hopes the world still has some decency left."

He bent and began gathering Aurélie's scattered belongings out of the mud.

"You don't—you don't have to do that," Aurélie croaked. She could see Dreier watching from the window. This would all be reported back to Hoffmeister.

Von Sternburg straightened, her dresses draped over one arm. "Please. Let me do what I can to make things right. Goodness knows it's little enough." His eyes were very blue in his thin face. "You have mud on your cheek."

Aurélie's hand rose automatically to her face. "It's appropriate, don't you think? Or maybe it should be ashes."

"If I may?" His handkerchief was large, and white, and smelled of violets. He touched it gently to her cheek.

"Do you really—do you really think your uncle can do something?" It wasn't what she'd meant to say.

"I will write tonight," said Lieutenant von Sternburg gravely. "And tell you when I hear. We are not all barbarians."

See? she could hear her father say. *See how easily it's done?*

"Thank you." Aurélie felt out of place in her own skin, clumsy and awkward. She hadn't been bred for this, for scheming. "Would you . . . might you help me? With my things?"

Lieutenant von Sternburg bowed, entirely unaware that he was about to be used, betrayed. "Mademoiselle de Courcelles, it would be my honor."

CHAPTER TWELVE

Daisy

Rue Volney
Paris, France
May 1942

HONOR. IT WAS a word Monsieur Legrand spoke often, without irony. He had already said it four times since ushering Daisy into the cramped back room in which he worked, a courtyard annex, the door to which you couldn't find unless you knew where to look. Daisy noticed because *honor* wasn't a word that existed in Pierre's vocabulary, except as a joke.

"You must be an Englishman," she said.

"Nonsense. I am French, madame, as French as the tricolor itself."

"And I say you're an Englishman. Only an Englishman uses that word in that particular way, these days."

"Which word?"

"*L'honneur.*"

Legrand shrugged, and Daisy had to admit that this was indisputably the Gallic kind of shrug, accompanied by a wink even more so. He removed his pipe from the corner of his mouth and sat back in his chair. "I suppose I still have hope, that's all. A little faith in ideas.

French honor is not dead, Madame Villon. It lives and thrives. You only have to know where to find it."

Madame Villon. The sound of it, coming from this man's throat, tanned and taut, made her wince. She linked her hands together atop the table. "Call me Daisy."

"Speaking of English words."

She shrugged, the same way he had. "My grandmother's American. As you know."

Legrand stuck the pipe back in the corner of his mouth and held it there, his elbow propped on his other arm, which crossed his middle. Studied, thoughtful. He tilted his head and stared at her without shame. Daisy tried to stare back, but the sheer glamour of him was too much for her. Those cheekbones, those blue eyes. He wore the same knitted vest as he had in Grandmère's suite, over a white shirt with the sleeves rolled to the elbows to avoid staining them with ink, and all she could think was how unlike those tanned forearms were from Pierre's forearms.

They were quite alone. In the front of the bookshop, the owner and his boy Philippe took care of the customers, but they might have existed in another country. Daisy looked down at the book in the middle of the table.

"*The Scarlet Pimpernel.* An inspiration, perhaps?"

"My dear madame, I have just told you I'm not an Englishman."

She lifted the book and thumbed the pages. "A master of disguise and forgery, spiriting the persecuted out of Paris. I can't imagine any resemblance."

He reached out and pulled the book from her hands. "It's a good story, that's all."

"It was my favorite, when I was a girl. When I was thirteen or fourteen, when I had all these romantic ideas."

"Like honor?"

"Yes, honor. Among others. But we have business to discuss, I believe."

Legrand sat up, knocked the ash from his pipe, and set it to one side. "True. The first thing, we must have a name for you."

"You already know my name."

"I mean a code, a secret name, so your identity isn't compromised if some Gestapo squad should knock on my door one night and beg for a cigarette."

"Is that likely?"

"I imagine you know the odds, more or less."

He said it carelessly, but his eyes were serious, and his expression didn't move. Daisy's palms were damp. She had the feeling she was plunging off a cliff somehow, that she had closed her eyes and taken some giant, terrible leap without pausing to see what lay beneath, and now it was too late. Too late. Yes, she knew the odds. Of course she knew the odds. The odds were that she would likely die. She was going to die for this thing she was doing, let's admit it, this cause that was so futile and so fraught, this defiance of the German occupation of France. Possibly her children, too, unless Pierre could protect them. And yet the blood pulsing through her veins right now, the keen perception of every detail around her, it wasn't exactly terror, was it? It was something else. It was like coming to life. She glanced back down at the book and saw herself again, her young self, a ripening girl, all the new thoughts and emotions galloping down her limbs, all the romantic possibility, the possibility for life. And the real reason she had adored the book, which was not for the sake of the dashing Sir Percy, much as she longed for such a hero at that age, in her world made of nothing but school and home, and home being that strange, glamorous zoo of peculiar creatures known as the Ritz. She loved the book because of Marguerite St. Just. Brave, clever, irresistible French wife of the Scarlet Pimpernel. The toast of Paris. *Marguerite*, the French word for *daisy*.

"La Fleur," she said.

"What's that?"

"My code name is La Fleur."

THEY WENT TO work. Monsieur Legrand showed her the papers he had forged, the identity cards and the *laissez-passers* for a pair of Allied pilots downed over Belgium last month and now hidden in a safe house on rue de Bretagne. Daisy picked up the card belonging to one of them—new name Jean-Paul Bisset—and examined it closely. "But it's perfect," she said in amazement.

"Of course it is."

She looked up. "How did you do this? How did you find such a talent?"

"My mother's an artist. She taught me to draw and paint when I was young. And the first thing you do, when you're learning to draw and paint, you copy the works of great artists."

"Well, it's remarkable." She looked at his chin, which of course contained a small, perfect cleft, and thought, *You're remarkable*.

He waved his hand and rose from the chair to take a pair of books from a nearby shelf. Daisy strained to read the titles, but his hands moved too quickly. He opened the front cover and peeled back the paper that lined it. The gold ring caught the light from the lamp at the corner of the table.

"Now look," he said. "We tuck the papers inside the false lining of these books, here. Lay them flat, one for each cover. You see? Then just a touch of binder's glue to hold it back down again."

He took the pot of glue and unscrewed the lid and dipped in a brush. Daisy stared at his wrist as he dotted the edges of the lining paper and smoothed it back down again, on top of the papers, so delicate and flawless you couldn't see the ridges at all.

"Now you try it," he said.

"I—I can't possibly. Not as well as that."

"Just try. There may come a time when you're the only one to do it."

Daisy took a book from the stack, and one of the identity cards. Legrand had already unstuck the lining, so it peeled back easily. Daisy asked how he did it.

"Steam," he said. "Steam and a very slim knife."

Daisy laid the papers flat, brushed the glue, pressed the thick lining paper back against the front cover. It wasn't bad; she had used a little too much glue, but the edges were straight, the lump of the additional paper only remarkable if you knew where to look. If you were expecting it there. Legrand leaned over to inspect her handiwork.

"Very good," he said. "A natural."

His hair was luxurious, right next to her face. She smelled the pipe tobacco, and maybe soap. She couldn't remember the last time she had sat so close to a man who was not her husband. Certainly not alone, in this small room with its tiny window and its cozy lamplight and the stairs in the corner that spiraled up—so he said, when they first entered, with a wave of his hand—to his bedroom, such as it was. The room was lined with shelves, which were stuffed with books, muffling the sounds of the bookseller and Philippe and their customers on the other side of the wall. On the table in the middle rested the tools of his trade—the pens, the ink, the magnifying lens, the tiny chisels and knives and brushes of all shapes. They sat so close, his knee brushed hers.

She sat back a little. "So now what?"

"Now we let the glue dry, of course."

"How long will that take?"

"Generally I prefer to let them dry overnight—"

"Overnight! I can't stay overnight!"

"Hush, hush." He laid a finger over his smiling mouth. "I am deeply sorry to tell you that we don't have the luxury of time, in this case. So we shall have to make do with half an hour only."

"Will that be enough?"

"It will have to be." Legrand laid the books open, underneath the lamp. "There. That should help. Wine?"

"Wine? You have wine in this place?"

"But of course. I *am* a Frenchman, aren't I?"

Monsieur Legrand produced a bottle of Burgundy and a pair of glasses from a cabinet in the corner. The wine was superb. This in itself did not surprise Daisy—Monsieur Legrand was the kind of man who drank good wine, even in wartime—but she *was* surprised to find herself enjoying it. They talked about books, a subject that was safe but also intimate. It turned out that Legrand's father was a writer. Nothing Daisy would have read, he added quickly.

"Because these books are English, perhaps?" she said, in English.

He replied in French. "Because they are to do with men and spies, and not, I think, the kinds of subjects that would interest you. At least before now, eh?"

"What do you think interests me?"

He sucked on his pipe for a moment or two, examining her. "Not Flaubert, thank God. Perhaps Shakespeare. But in English, or translation?"

"Both."

"Dumas, of course, when you were younger. *Père et fils.* Hugo. Your grandmother started you on Balzac, but it left you dissatisfied, for reasons you could not articulate. Then you left your romantic ideas behind and started Proust."

She laughed. "You know he practically lived at the Ritz, when I was young. A strange man. He hated noise of any kind."

"Genius is usually strange. But was I right?"

"Not altogether. I quite liked Balzac."

"Ah," he said knowingly, as if that explained everything.

"And you? What did you read? Dickens, perhaps?"

"You think to trap me, do you?"

Daisy shrugged and spread out her hands.

Legrand removed his pipe from his mouth and stabbed the air with the end of it. "Dickens does not understand people. They are ideas to him, types, objects to move around his moral chessboard. I much prefer Trollope. But my favorite book of all, I think . . . now that I have had time to reflect . . ." His eyes crinkled.

"Yes?"

"I believe my favorite book of all is this one."

He touched the mouth of his pipe to the small copy of *The Scarlet Pimpernel* at the corner of the table.

HALF AN HOUR later, when the glue was not fully dry but at least no longer wet, Legrand put away the wineglasses and helped Daisy gather the books into a basket. "Congratulations," he said. "You're now employed by the Mouton Noir, delivering books to customers."

Daisy had drunk only a single glass of wine, but it landed on top of Grandmère's cognac and gave her a heady feeling. Or maybe it was the danger, the terror and the thrill of having recklessly cast her dice like this, of becoming an entirely new Daisy in the space of a day, of having spent an hour in the company of Monsieur Legrand and his pipe and his warm blue eyes. She found herself raising an eyebrow and asking, "Is that so? And where are my wages?"

His lips parted, but he didn't speak. He looked at her mouth, and she looked at his eyes looking at her mouth, and her hand slipped around the handle of the basket.

"If you need to give me a message," he said, "you should come to the bookshop and leave it inside this book." He held up the copy of *The Scarlet Pimpernel*. "It will be on the shelf of English books—Philippe can show you—in alphabetical order, and when you have put your message inside, you will replace the book next to the Dickens. I will do the same. If you see the book out of order, it means there's a message. Understand?"

She nodded.

"And if the Gestapo have come, and I am gone, then you will not see the book at all." Daisy started to interrupt, but he held up his hand. "You will leave the store immediately and return to the Ritz, where you will order a drink from the bar, rue Cambon side of course, and when you pay for this drink you will give the bartender—"

"You mean Frank? He's an agent?"

"Not an agent, just a kind of postbox. You will give him a note for the Badger."

"Who is the Badger?"

"It's not important. In this note you will simply write that the Swan has been trapped."

"Who is the Swan?"

Legrand put his hand on the lever that opened the passageway back into the bookshop.

"Me," he said.

IN THE END, it was much easier than she imagined. Mundane, even. She went to the address on rue de Bretagne, which turned out to be some apartments above a café. Inside, the foyer was modest and shabby, smelling of damp, the stonework chipped. A concierge sat at a desk, an old woman who read from a book by the light of an ancient lamp with a bowl of green frosted glass. She looked wary when Daisy approached. She folded down the corner of the page and slipped the book under the desk.

"Yes, madame? You have business here?"

"I'm here from the bookshop with a few books for Madame Bisset," said Daisy, quite cool. "Apartment 3."

The old woman tilted her head to the stairs and said to go on up.

As Legrand had told her, she knocked three times and called through the door that she was here from the bookshop with the books Madame Bisset had ordered. The handle turned and the door opened a crack.

"You are from the bookshop?" said a thin voice. "The Mouton Noir?"

"Yes. I have your books. The first is *La dame aux camélias*. Do you remember the name of the second?"

The door opened wider to reveal a woman about Daisy's age, except even thinner, in a brown dress that matched her hair. Her voice was warm with relief. "*La chartreuse de Parme*, I believe."

Daisy handed her the books, and the woman expressed her thanks.

"It's nothing, madame," said Daisy. "I hope you will enjoy them."

She turned for the stairs, feeling immeasurably lighter, relieved of much more than the weight of the volumes in the basket. As she began her descent, the woman's voice drifted down behind her.

"God bless you, madame."

DAISY RETURNED TO her apartment just in time to greet the children, home from school. It was not Justine's day to help, so Daisy made them their dinner—coarse bread, boiled turnips, a lump of cheese, a bit of meat—and helped them with their homework until it was time for bed. Pierre had not yet arrived. His dinner remained in the oven, keeping warm. She tucked the children into bed and then climbed in next to Madeleine to read a story. Her hands, she saw, were still trembling a little. Her veins still throbbed with her own audacity.

By the time she had finished, Olivier was asleep, but Madeleine remained awake, cuddled into her side. Daisy stroked the dark, straight hair, so unlike her own and that of Grandmère. The warm skin, the child smell of her.

"Maman, your heart is beating," said Madeleine. "Why does it beat so hard?"

Daisy kissed the top of her head.

"*Cherie*, don't you know? It beats for you."

CHAPTER THIRTEEN

Babs

Rue Volney
Paris, France
April 1964

M Y HEARTBEAT THRUMMED as Drew and I walked through the streets of downtown Paris, the city's rhythm absurdly uplifting, the colors, sounds, and people strange yet somehow invigorating. I'd always considered myself a country girl, and always would be, I supposed, but there was something about Paris. Something that altered one's perspective, at least for a little while.

As we crossed the street before reaching the bookshop, he quickly grabbed my arm. A motorbike sped by, narrowly missing me as I was attempting to cross the street while looking the wrong way. Again. It made no sense that the French couldn't be as civilized as the British and drive on the proper side of the road.

"*Après vous*, madame." Drew had let go of my arm and was holding open the door to the bookshop and looking at me expectantly. Which is the only reason I could guess at the words he'd just butchered.

I smiled my thanks. "You know, Drew, I don't believe the consonant *s* is meant to be applied to the end of some French words such as '*après*' and '*vous*.'"

He paused a moment to consider. "Really? My French teacher never corrected me. Of course, I was also the first person to volunteer to help her clean the chalkboards and move desks when the other guys ran out of the door first chance, so maybe that's why." His grin revealed those startlingly white teeth. "I always got As in French."

"Of course you did," I said, moving farther into the shop as he shut the door behind us and I was enveloped in that lovely scent of paper and binding glue that pervaded libraries and bookshops and made me a little homesick. As a child when my brothers and Kit had somehow managed to evade me and escape the house on one of their adventures, and Diana was too involved in one of her personal dramas to notice me, my haven had been to curl up in my father's library with a good book and become lost in a world where I could have adventures of my own.

Despite it being the middle of the day, the shop was mostly deserted. A young couple was pressed against one of the crowded shelves, their faces so close they were apparently more interested in each other's pores than in the books behind them. I glanced at Drew and he gave such a perfect impersonation of the Gallic shrug that I almost laughed out loud.

Placing a hand on the small of my back, Drew led me to a high counter at the front of the shop in the triangle of windows. A large brass cash register sat regally in the middle of the countertop, surrounded by a chaotic mixture of books teetering precariously like children's building blocks.

"Bonjour," Drew said rather loudly, as one does when speaking to foreigners. As if the volume might compensate for the lack of proper pronunciation.

Before I could suggest that the consonant *n* is also usually silent, a young man popped his head up from behind the counter. "Bonjour," he said a little warily, as if unsure of which language we were meant to be speaking.

"Do you speak English?" I asked in my best French.

His look of suspicion changed as he regarded me and my yellow spotty dress, his gaze lingering a little longer than necessary on the exposed skin of my chest before returning to my face. He was probably in his late twenties or early thirties, with dark curly hair and scruffy cheeks, wearing the ubiquitous black roll-neck sweater so common among the French youth as to be almost a uniform.

"For you, madam, of course." His English was good although heavily accented. "How can I help you?" He directed the question to me, ignoring Drew completely.

Drew pulled out the folded piece of paper of notes from his father and checked the name. "We are looking for a Jack Laypin. Does he still work here?"

Both the young man and I looked at Drew in confusion. I gently took the note from Drew and read it myself. "I believe he meant to say Jacques Lapin. We understand that Monsieur Lapin was the bookseller here twenty years ago."

"Ah, *oui*," the young man said. "Sadly, he is no longer with us. He died some time ago. I run the bookstore now."

"I'm so sorry to hear that," I said. I looked at Drew, wondering what our next move should be now that our one connection to La Fleur was dead.

"But I am Philippe, his grandson. Is there something I can help with?"

Drew let out a heavy sigh. "Probably not. We were hoping your grandfather could tell us about someone who may have once been a customer during the war."

Philippe directed a broad smile at me again, as if I were the only one who'd spoken. "I was just a little boy at the time, but I spent every day after school here in the bookshop with my *grandpère*. He even put a stool in front of the cash register so I could help him when the store got busy. I knew all the regulars. Is there anyone in particular you are looking for?"

I exchanged a hopeful glance with Drew. "Yes. My late husband, Kit Langford. Do you recognize the name?"

He shook his head. "No, madam. I'm sorry, but I do not."

I hid my disappointment. "I know he purchased at least one book here, but if he wasn't here regularly, then I don't expect you to remember him."

"Which book? My *mère* tells me I have a perfect memory—that I can remember the titles of books better than the names of the customers who purchased them." Another shrug. "It's doubtful, but possible I'd remember."

I pulled out the book tucked under my arm and placed it on top of a small stack. "It's *The Scarlet Pimpernel*." I opened up the front cover. "It has the name and address of your store stamped inside the front cover."

His dark eyes widened as he flipped the book over twice and then examined the cover. "How very strange. I remember this exact book very well, mostly because my grandfather would only ever allow one copy in the store, and if anyone tried to purchase it, he would tell the customer that it was flawed in some way and order another for them to purchase. I was also charged with shelving the books alphabetically, but if I ever saw that particular book out of order, I was to leave it alone. I never thought to question him because he was my grandfather."

"And you don't remember selling it?" Drew asked.

Philippe looked at him as if surprised to see him there. "No. It was never sold. It just . . . disappeared."

"Disappeared?" Drew's forehead wrinkled.

"Yes. There was a man who lived in the back of the bookstore. And one day *poof* he was gone, and so was the book."

My gaze met Drew's.

"This man—do you remember his name?" Drew asked.

"*Oui.* Christophe Legrand. He did special printing for my grandfather in the back room. I was never to mention it to anyone, especially to the Germans. He was a very nice man. He used to give me peppermints and play marbles with me. I was sad when he left."

I attempted to keep my voice calm. "Do you remember anything about him? Anything that might help someone recognize him?"

His face scrunched in concentration before he spoke. "He smoked a pipe and he would sometimes let me help him to light it."

My throat seemed to thicken, making it difficult to speak. "Anything else? A lot of gentlemen smoke pipes."

He shook his head, and then stopped. "There is one thing. He wore a gold ring on his little finger. It had two swans on the flat part of it. I remember that because that's the hand he'd use to hold his pipe."

I felt Drew's hand on my arm, and I realized I was shaking. He stepped away from Philippe, bringing me with him. "Kit?" he asked softly.

I nodded.

"Do you need to sit down? Or leave?"

I knew if I said yes, he wouldn't hesitate. But I couldn't stop here. We'd learned nothing, really, except that Kit had lived behind a bookseller's shop under an assumed name during the war. And had perhaps stolen a book. As much as I wanted to leave, to accept that there was nothing more to be learned about my husband's past and any association he might have had with La Fleur, I knew this couldn't be the entire story. It was as if I'd seen my husband's ghost, and I was determined to follow to see where it led.

"No, really. I'm fine. There was something else your father told you—something about a white wolf? Maybe Philippe will remember hearing a reference from his grandfather or Kit."

He continued to gaze steadily at me. "Only if you're sure. I'd be happy to walk you back to the hotel . . ."

"No," I said a little too sharply, making him flinch slightly. "I'm sorry. It's just . . ." I stopped, unsure what I was going to say. I took a deep breath. "I'd like to see this through. I've come all this way, so I might as well." I forced a smile, probably the sort that Anne Boleyn wore to the chopping block, but at least it was a smile.

Keeping his gaze on me one moment longer, Drew referred to his notepaper once more before turning back to Philippe. "Do you remember your grandfather saying anything about a white wolf with a cross?"

Phillipe scrunched his face in an expression I was beginning to recognize. "*Le loup?*"

He bared his teeth and made a low growling sound.

"*Oui,*" I said, nodding. "Wolf. A white wolf with a cross. Does that remind you of something your grandfather or Christophe might have said?"

Philippe remained pensive as he continued to shake his head slowly. "No, it doesn't. However." He came from behind the counter and led us toward the back of the shop. "A white wolf and a cross sound like objects found on family crests, no? And I know a book that might tell us more."

We stopped at the back wall lined with stuffed shelves of books. When he reached into a shelf on the far side, I expected him to retrieve a book, but instead we heard a small click as he must have pulled on some sort of lever. A section of shelves popped open and a dark, dusty room was revealed as Phillipe slid the bookcase out wide enough for a person to step through.

"One moment," he said as he disappeared inside. After we waited for a minute, the space behind the shelf flooded with light. Philippe reappeared at the opening, beckoning us inside. "Come in, come in. Please excuse the dust—we don't come in here often. It's mostly used to store older books or those that have fallen out of favor and no one is looking for anymore."

Drew followed me behind the bookcase and stopped beside me as we examined the room. The cramped, dusty space held a mottled yellow glow from the overhead bulbs and at first glance didn't appear to be anything more than a storeroom. Shelves teetered with more books, and the odd store fixtures leaned haphazardly against walls and an assortment of furniture including a large wooden desk.

I would have dismissed all of it as having nothing to do with Kit. Except. Except when I'd first entered the room, I imagined I could detect the pungent scent of Kit's pipe tobacco. "Is this where Monsieur Legrand lived?"

Philippe turned from where he was scanning one of the bookshelves and smiled. "*Oui*. There is a hidden room upstairs—the small hatch is hidden now by that bookshelf in the rear, but there are stairs you can pull down. Back during the war I wasn't allowed to mention that this all was here to anyone so no one knew about it but Grandpère and me. Oh, and the nice lady with the two children."

I shared a startled glance with Drew. "A lady?" Drew repeated.

"Um-hmm," Philippe said, running his finger along dusty spines.

"Do you remember her name?" I asked.

He shook his head without looking at us. "I do not. But I do remember that she had a little boy and a little girl around my age and when they were home from school for the summer, they would spend a lot of time here with their mother."

"And with Monsieur Legrand?" I asked, dreading his answer.

"*Oui*. I remember, too, that she was very beautiful—and very kind.

She once gave me a little stuffed rabbit, just like the one her daughter had. Because of my last name, you see. *Lapin*. It means rabbit, no?"

"How thoughtful."

Drew sent me a questioning glance, making me realize my tone sounded less than sympathetic.

"Did she return to the store after Monsieur Legrand disappeared?" Drew asked.

"*Non*. I never saw her again, or her children. I remember being very sad and missing them. My *grandpère* said I should be happy for them, since she and Monsieur Legrand were probably together. But I still missed them and cried every night."

I made a good show of looking around the room, at the old wooden floors, and the collection of spiderwebs decorating the corners like architectural embellishments. Anywhere except at Drew's face. Because even though whatever had transpired here in this room had happened before Kit and I were married, I couldn't completely forget the final words of the letter that had arrived before we'd said our vows.

My only hope is that you remember me and the short time we had together and know that I will always love you. Always. La Fleur

"Ah, here it is," Philippe said, sliding out a very thick leather-bound volume from a high shelf and stepping down the ladder. "When you mentioned a wolf and cross, I thought immediately that it sounded like something one of the grand families of France might have on their *blason*. In English I think you say 'coat of arms.'"

"Of course," Drew said. "I can't believe I didn't think of that myself. Wolves are one of the most popularly used icons in heraldic coats of arms. It's like football teams having some sort of 'eagle' in their mascot name. Of course, lots of teams put 'flying' or 'fighting' in front, but eagles still dominate in the world of football mascots."

He stopped speaking, no doubt realizing that both Phillipe and I were staring at him.

"Sorry. I was a history major and played football in college, so I kind of know a lot of useless information about both topics."

I wanted to tell him that they weren't useless, but I was mentally occupied trying to squeeze all of my thoughts and feelings about Kit and La Fleur into a little box and lock it. It was all I could do to remain in the room without running outside for a gulp of fresh air that didn't smell like pipe smoke.

Philippe approached the desk with the volume, its cover nicked and discolored in places, and plopped it on the surface in a cloud of dust. "Here. This is what I was looking for. It is damaged, but my *grandpère* never threw out anything. So we keep it back here for reference—not that anyone has ever asked for it in the last twenty years." He shrugged. "It's a history of French noble families and includes their family crests. As a little boy, I loved to look at all the pretty pictures since I couldn't read. And you are correct, monsieur. There are many with wolves— those were my favorites."

A bell rang at the front of the store and Philippe looked up. "I will leave you here with this to see if you can find what you are looking for."

We watched Philippe leave and then Drew turned to me. "I can come back alone if you want to get out of here."

I found his solicitousness comforting, and his invitation tempting, but I couldn't leave. I felt like the mouse at the edge of a trap, lured by the cheese even though it would result in the mouse's imminent demise. "No. Really, I'm all right. Besides, I'm assuming you don't read French."

"Fair point." He found a sturdy-enough chair and upended a small table with a round base, moving them both up to the desk, and we sat down. After a cursory thumbing through the pages, Drew said, "It looks like it's alphabetical by family so let's just hope the family name doesn't start with *Z*."

"Or we could start at the back of the book and go that way," I suggested.

He frowned down at the pages. "Knowing my luck, the name will be somewhere in the middle." He thought for a moment, flicking through the pages. "It looks like the pictures of the coats of arms all appear on the top right of the page. Why don't we flip through the pictures and mark the pages where we find ones with a wolf and a cross, and then go from there?"

I scavenged for pieces of discarded paper scraps for bookmarks, but after more than an hour of scouring through the pages, we'd only marked a single page. There'd been many pictures of wolves and crosses with other icons including a plethora of dragons and unicorns, but there had been only a single crest that contained a simple lone white wolf on a royal-blue background, a thick gold cross dividing the crest into quadrants.

He turned the book to face me, his finger pointing at a name. "De Courcelles," I read out loud first, if only not to hear Drew's interpretation of how to pronounce it. I ran my finger down one of the columns of small French text. "It appears their family seat is in Picardy. And there's a château." I pointed to a pencil sketch of a grand French château with rounded towers and banners flying from the parapets and a small flock of sheep gathered in a pasture behind the castle walls.

"Where is Picardy?" Drew asked. "Is it close enough to drive?"

I flipped to the back of the book where a map showed black dots indicating the seats of the prominent families listed in the book. "It appears that it's only a little more than seventy miles from Paris to Picardy. About a two-hour car ride, I should think."

"Definitely close enough, then," Drew said. "We should go. I'm sure it's a wild goose chase, but we really don't have any other leads to go on right now, so why not?"

"Oh, er . . ." I wasn't sure why my words were trying to say no when the rest of me appeared quite a bit more interested. "Today?"

"Unfortunately, no. I've got to go into the office. What about tomorrow?" He seemed so matter-of-fact and strictly business about it all. Even Precious couldn't read anything into his invitation. And then he added, "We could make a day of it, bring a picnic lunch, even."

I just wouldn't tell her about that last bit. "I, er, yes. I believe I'm free. Shall I ask the hotel to prepare the picnic basket?"

"Great idea—thank you. Ten o'clock in the lobby, then?"

"Yes. I'll be ready." I placed my hands on the desk to help myself stand, noticing the nicks and scratches in the wood, wondering if Kit had made any of them. Or La Fleur. And once again I imagined the faint scent of his tobacco, as warm and familiar to me as his touch.

"Are you okay to walk back? We could take a taxi." Drew's voice brought me back to the present.

I blinked up at him. "Yes. Quite all right. Just woolgathering."

"You look a little pale. Maybe we should grab a drink in the bar when we get back?"

I must have turned a shade of green because he immediately said, "Never mind. Maybe all you need is fresh air." He helped me stand, then brought the book to the front of the shop, where Philippe was handing a customer a package.

"Did you find what you needed?" he asked.

"We're not sure." Drew held up the book. "I'd like to buy it, just in case. How much?"

Philippe waved his hand. "Take it, please. It's one less thing to fall on my head when I'm looking for something in the back room."

"Mersy," Drew said.

Philippe blinked once. "You are welcome."

We said our goodbyes and turned to leave, but I held back. "One more question, Philippe. The woman with the children, the friend of Monsieur Legrand. You said you didn't know her name. But did you ever have reason to believe that she might have been the famous French Resistance fighter La Fleur? Perhaps something your grandfather might have said?"

"La Fleur? Oh *non*, madame. La Fleur, I would have known if I'd met her. It is said if you looked directly into her eyes their fire would blind you. The woman I knew was very womanly. Soft, yes? Not like La Fleur at all."

"I see," I said. "*Merci*." I followed Drew out onto the crowded sidewalk and we made the short walk back to the hotel. When we reached the Ritz I had no idea what we'd talked about, aware only of the scent of tobacco that seemed to follow me no matter how fast I walked.

We said goodbye in the lobby, and I was headed toward the lift in desperate need of solitude in my room to process the events of the day when the concierge flagged me down. "Madame Langford?"

"Yes?"

"Madame Lemouron has requested your presence upon your return." He indicated the lift. "If you will, I can escort you to her suite."

"I . . ." It took me a moment to recall the name, and when I did, I was at a loss for words. "She wants to see me? Now?"

"At your convenience, of course." He looked at me expectantly.

"All right," I said, stepping into the lift. "Did she say why?"

"She did not, but I suspect she would like to make a new friend. Madame Lemouron is a very special resident to us, and we try and accommodate her as best as we can. She cannot leave her room very often, so she invites friends to come see her." He lowered his voice, as if loath to share a secret about a resident but already considering me a confidant. I had that sort of face, I supposed, having been subjected to strangers' confessions and life stories on trains and in shop lines for most of my life. "I'm afraid she might be lonely."

I considered his words as I followed him down a plushly carpeted hallway, stopping at a door at the end of the hall. "We wanted her to have a quiet room," he explained. "So she can rest between treatments."

"Of course," I said, remembering what Prunella Schuyler had said about Margot being ill.

"May I put your book in your room?" He held out his hand for *The Scarlet Pimpernel* and I reluctantly handed it to him, although I was tired of carrying it. He tapped on the door, and a nurse opened it. She was a tall woman, with graying curls pushed ruthlessly under her nurse's hat, and large green eyes behind silver-framed eyeglasses. When she saw me, she smiled. "Madame Langford?"

After I'd replied in the affirmative she nodded to the concierge, who retreated back down the hallway, and then she pulled the door open wider. "Perfect timing," she said in English. "Madame has just finished her nap, and I've administered her medications, so she's ready for company." She turned toward a bench near the door and picked up a nurse's bag. "I will be back this evening at eight o'clock. I've already said au revoir, so I will let myself out."

"Yes, of course . . . ," I began, then stopped when I realized I was speaking to the door. I stood there, at a loss, uncertain as to what I should do next.

"Barbara? Is that you?" I recognized the deep voice of the woman I'd met that morning.

"Yes, Margot. May I come in?"

"Of course. And thank you so much for coming. I do apologize for my impertinence, but I'm too tired to go downstairs and was looking for company."

I walked from the entranceway, admiring the cream and gold of the suite's color palette. It was more luxurious than mine, and larger, but that would be like saying Buckingham Palace was bigger and grander than Windsor Castle. It was all relative at the Ritz.

I turned in a circle, trying to determine where her voice was coming from, and was headed toward what looked like a bedroom door when Margot spoke again. "Would you mind pouring me a glass of water? My medications make me a bit parched, and I forgot to ask my nurse before she left."

I spun toward the sound of the voice, finding myself facing an oversized upholstered chaise longue filled with satin cushions and blankets, and in the middle of it all the diminutive form of Margot Lemouron. Her head seemed even smaller against the giant lace pillow behind her, the skin on her face sallow against the white linen. Yet, despite the purple circles under her eyes, they had a light that was all their own. I wondered for a moment if that meant death was near, that each failure of the body was like candles being snuffed out one by one, until the only light left was in the eyes. It had been that way with Kit.

"Of course," I said, hurrying to her side, where a water pitcher had been filled and placed next to an empty glass. "And I don't think you're impertinent at all. I, too, could use a little company." This last wasn't completely true, but it should have been. Diana said I spent far too much time alone. Not that she'd recommend I spend time with a possibly dying woman, but at least I was trying.

I handed her the glass and watched as she took several sips, noticing again the pallor of her skin. "Are you sure you're up to talking? If you'd prefer to rest, I'm happy to just sit here and keep you company." I recalled how Kit in the last months of his illness had been too tired to talk, but had wanted me nearby, as if my presence might somehow make it all less frightening.

"You are very kind, and you don't even know me. I promise to let you know if I get tired." She looked at me closely, her dark eyes penetrating. "I would much prefer to get to know you, although I feel as if we're already old friends, no?"

"I have that sort of face. I suppose it makes it easy for me to make friends."

"Perhaps." She indicated the chair next to the bed. "Please do sit."

I glanced at the small gold clock on the side table by her chair. "It's four o'clock. Shall I order tea?"

"That would be wonderful, thank you."

I ordered tea and had sat down again when I noticed three framed photographs on the dressing table across the room. "If this is where you sit the most, wouldn't you like your photographs closer?"

"That is a very good idea, Barbara, and so thoughtful. I imagine you're an excellent mother. You have children, no?"

"Three," I said proudly as I walked toward the dresser to retrieve the frames. "Two boys and one girl." I looked down at the pictures. "Are these your children?"

"*Oui*. I also have three—but two girls and one boy."

"They are very good-looking children," I said. The oldest two, a girl and a boy, were both dark-haired and seemed to be in their middle to late twenties. The youngest girl, in her early twenties, also had dark hair, but it was lighter than her siblings'. Despite the difference in hair color, of the three she resembled their mother the most.

"Do they live here in France?" I asked as I arranged the frames on the small table.

Her face fell. "Sadly, no. They are in Canada. It is our home, and they have their lives there. I didn't want them to fret while I was in Paris for treatment. My youngest daughter is still at university. They plan to visit at the end of term."

"Something to look forward to, then," I said, leaning over and adjusting the pillow behind her head. I noticed again how thin she was, how the veins in her hand were a startling blue against the whiteness of her skin. "Can I get you another blanket? Or perhaps a sweater?"

She laughed, bringing a welcome spot of color to her cheeks. "I'm perfectly fine, but thank you. The tea is here so if you would pour me a cup I would love to sit and listen to you tell me about your family."

A waiter wheeled in the tea tray and I dismissed him so I could pour the tea. I fixed a plate of small sandwiches and pastries for Margot, although she didn't touch them no matter how many times I pushed the plate toward her.

"Tell me more about your children," I said. "Are the oldest two finished with school?"

"They are, but I'd rather not talk about them right now. It makes me miss them too much. Tell me instead about you. You said you are a widow?"

I nodded, and took a sip of my tea. "Yes. My late husband, Kit, died a year ago. He'd been ill for about a year so it wasn't a shock, but still . . ."

"But it's still as if your heart was ripped out of you without warning."

"Yes. That's it exactly."

She plucked at the satin blanket covering her knees, her tea growing cool on the table beside her. "I see you still wear your wedding ring. Because you feel you are still married to him?"

I stared at the plain gold band on my hand, remembering Kit sliding it on my finger on our wedding day. I no longer wore the sapphire engagement ring, having long ago put it away to give to Penny on her twenty-first birthday. It was too dainty, too decorative for my hands, and I'd always felt as if it should have belonged to someone else.

I met her eyes again. "I don't know. Sometimes I think I wear it because I don't know who else I am supposed to be if I'm not Kit's wife."

Her intense gaze bored into me. "You are a strong woman, Barbara. I know this already about you. Sometimes we don't know how strong we are until we are left with no other choice, yes?" She smiled. "What is it they say? Some women are lost in the fire, and some are built with it. It's too easy to quit when our lives don't turn out the way we expect. But you and I are strong enough to imagine a new life. Something different, perhaps, but even better than what we'd hoped."

A most annoying lump had formed in my throat and I forced it down with a gulp of tea so I could speak and not embarrass myself with silly tears. "I'm not sure you're right about me. I seem to have a particular gift for wallowing in my misery." I frowned. "Why are you being so kind to me? You barely know me."

She shrugged, her bony shoulders mere shadows under her bed jacket. "Perhaps because you appear to need someone to be kind to you."

I laughed nervously. "And here I was, thinking it was the other way around." Uncomfortable with her scrutiny, I pushed her plate closer to her. "You haven't eaten a thing. Should you at least try? I imagine you need to keep up your strength."

"I will try for you, although I have no appetite." She picked up a small cucumber triangle and took a tiny bite. "You are very young to be a widow. How are your children coping with the loss of their father?"

"I'm thirty-eight, so not very young. Our youngest two, Penny and Rupert, are handling it as well as can be expected. Stiff upper lip and all that." I tried to smile at my little joke, but failed miserably. "Our oldest, Robin, has had the hardest time. He and Kit—my husband—were very close. Robin was just sent down from Cambridge for drinking. He's with my sister and her husband now, which is probably the best place for him since I'm not exactly the icon of strength at the moment."

She put the little sandwich back on her plate without having taken another bite. "You do see, Barbara, that's why you are strong. A weak woman would never have admitted that her son was hurting and needed help elsewhere. And, of course, you are here on a lovely vacation. So not exactly 'wallowing in your misery,' hmm?"

"Oh, I'm not on holiday. I'm actually here to . . . well." I drew a deep breath. "I'm here to find out about my husband's time in Paris during the war."

She looked surprised. "Did your husband never talk of it?"

I shook my head. "No." *Only in nightmares.* "He was in a German prison camp and when he was released at the end of the war and sent home, he was in very bad shape. He wanted to forget about the war and everything that reminded him of it." I looked down at my teacup, the cream clumping in the now cold liquid. "So he never talked about it, and for the same reason, I never asked."

"How very difficult for you both. But then you married and had three wonderful children. It was a good life, yes?" She seemed to be genuinely interested in my answer.

"Yes," I said without having to think. "It really was. And it still can be," I added hastily. "I just need to stop grieving so I can get on with things."

"Your grief will end, I promise you. And then you will have room for joy again. I know this to be true. Just because your life will be different, that doesn't mean it can't still be beautiful."

I wanted to ask her how she knew this, but the words were stuck in my traitorous throat.

A soft smile lit her face, showing me a hint of the beauty she had once been. "I find I am getting tired, and I'm sure you are exhausted from being my nursemaid. I think I shall read for a bit. Would you mind bringing my book to me before you leave? I left it by the chair in front of the window."

I swallowed, happy for the reprieve. "Of course." I walked across the room to fetch her book, glancing at the title as I picked it up. *Les Misérables.* There was something comforting in the thickness of the volume, as if its very length showed an optimism I suspected very few battling cancer might have.

"I have found a delightful bookshop if you find yourself in need of another book when you're done with this one." I handed the book to her and she placed it on her lap. "I'm afraid we spoke mostly about me," I said. "But if you'd like company while I'm here at the Ritz, I'd enjoy coming back and you can tell me all about your beautiful children and Canada. I've never been."

She reached for my hand. "I would like that very much."

I squeezed her hand before letting go, alarmed at how brittle her bones felt, how papery her skin. "Goodbye, then. Until next time."

I started to leave but turned back, a question pecking at my head like a blackbird.

"If you don't mind me asking, Margot, what happened to your husband?"

"Gone. Like so many people during the war."

"I'm so very sorry."

"Don't be. I, too, managed to have a happy life. You see? We are both strong women because we know how to survive the worst that life can throw at us."

I smiled. "I'll let you read. I look forward to seeing you again."

I let myself out, closing the door behind me. I stood there for a long moment, feeling as exhausted as if I'd just completed a gymkhana and not completely convinced that a strong woman would feel the compelling need to run to her room and bury her face in a pillow and cry.

CHAPTER FOURTEEN

Aurélie

The Château de Courcelles
Picardy, France
December 1914

ONE SHOULDN'T FEEL so much like crying at Christmas.

It was bitter cold in the chapel, the moonlight falling jaggedly through the high old windows. Aurélie fisted her frozen fingers for warmth and tried to concentrate on the familiar ritual as the priest, in his white vestments, rustled about at the altar. But he was cold, too, cold and nervous. As the censer slipped through his fingers, clattering to the floor, everyone in the small congregation froze, looking over their shoulders.

"Go on," Aurélie's father commanded, and everyone exhaled again, their breath showing in the frosty air.

The Germans had contrived to rob them even of Christmas. Hoffmeister had plastered his posters on the wall of the *mairie* and the doors of the cafés: there would be no midnight mass on Christmas Eve. Everyone was to be in their homes by six o'clock. For safety's sake.

But it wasn't safety, it was pure meanness. They had so little left, so precious little, couldn't he at least have left them this? There would be no réveillon, the traditional midnight feast, no bûche de Noël. Not that the Germans were stinting themselves. The orders had gone out weeks ago, every available duck, goose, or chicken was to be sent to the château, to be boiled, roasted, and stuffed for the Germans' own feast. Every remaining bottle of wine, every hidden stock of brandy, had been ferreted out and claimed. But it wasn't enough for them, was it? It wasn't enough that they had the villagers' feast. They had to take their devotions from them as well.

Aurélie's father had gathered together the castle servants and bidden Monsieur le Curé to say midnight mass anyway, here, in the old chapel.

"They ordered us to keep to our homes by six?" her father had said, with a glimpse of his old arrogance. "This is my home, all of it, every hectare. Let them turn me out of my own chapel."

Yes, but it wasn't only his pride at issue. There was Monsieur le Curé, who might be punished, or Suzanne or Victor for attending. Aurélie knew her father was relishing his small rebellion, but she found herself wishing he had chosen to express his discontent in some other way. He thought he was pulling the wool over Hoffmeister's eyes, chalking up a point in their grudge match. He seemed not to realize there was no game. There was only the business of survival. That Hoffmeister knew of this and was choosing, for his own purpose, to ignore it, Aurélie had no doubt.

She also had no doubt that he would enact his revenge. When and how it suited him.

Her father was enjoying himself, playing the grand seigneur, and Aurélie felt guilty, so guilty for grudging him that—but also frustrated, frustrated that he couldn't see what she saw. When had he become so childish? She oughtn't think that about her father. It was unfilial. But there it was, and it wouldn't go away.

She didn't want to doubt her father's judgment. He had always been her touchstone, a model of stability against the giddy nonsense of her mother's fashionable urban existence. But this . . . There was no consolation in it. They ought to have waited, ought to have gone to the morning mass in the village that Hoffmeister had grudgingly deigned to permit because he could find no good reason to refuse it.

The mass was concluding, a strange, gabbled mass without music, without light. Her father, with the air of a conjurer, drew out a bottle of brandy.

"Let's see them keep us from our réveillon!" he said, and Aurélie could see the flash of teeth as Victor grinned and took the bottle.

The bottle came around and Aurélie took a swig, hoping it would warm her. Together, they tottered across the blighted grass from the old chapel, ducking beneath the lighted arrow slits of the old keep, where Hoffmeister held his own Christmas court. They could hear the voices, German voices, singing songs in their own barbaric language.

Was Maximilian von Sternburg one of that boisterous company? Undoubtedly. It was at moments like this that she was forcibly reminded that he was the enemy, alien, no matter how friendly he professed to be, no matter how their strolls in the dead garden conjured the memories of gentler times.

Aurélie ducked her head and blundered into the warmth of the kitchen.

"This will warm you right up, my love." Suzanne unearthed some cider and began warming it on the hearth, handing out steaming cups.

Perhaps there was something in it, in this illicit celebration. It seemed to be bucking up her father's retainers, at least.

"There," said Victor. He took the baby Jesus from his hidden place behind the crèche, placing the wooden baby in the cradle in the manger. "Now it's truly Christmas."

The crèche was a crude one, whittled locally, decorated with paper flowers, a brave attempt at festivity in the midst of despair.

There had been a crèche in Aurélie's mother's rooms at the Ritz. It had amused her mother to adopt that old tradition. The crèche had been baroque, featuring exquisitely carved and painted figures: delicately gilded halos on the holy family, streetsellers juggling apples, gossips chatting across houses, the wise men on their camels, bearing their precious burdens of gold, frankincense, and myrrh. Throughout the Christmas season, guests would come to ooh and aah over it. It had become a tradition of sorts. Aurélie had hated it, had hated their home being made so public, constantly on display.

Now she found herself wondering if her mother had put up the crèche as usual. She had loved it as a child. She would make the camels canter and dangle the angels from their golden halos. And her mother had never once complained, not even when Aurélie chipped a wing on an angel.

What was her mother doing now? Was she wondering about Aurélie? Worrying about her? When Aurélie had run off, all those months ago, it had seemed like a grand act of defiance, but it had never occurred to her that the war would go on so long or in such stalemate, that she would find herself so entirely cut off from Paris, unable even to let her mother know she was alive and unharmed.

Clovis, her father's wolfhound, butted his head against her hand, and Aurélie absently scratched him behind the ears, noticing how gray he had become, how stiffly he bent his knees to settle at her side.

The heat of the kitchen, the taste of the cider woolly on her lips, her father's unaccustomed shabbiness, Clovis's stiff knees—it all felt unreal, dreamlike. And not a good sort of dream.

She had always sulked over Christmas at the Ritz, scowling at the artificiality of it, the chocolate-box prettiness, but now she would have given anything to open her eyes and be back there, to turn back the clock to last year, when she had suffered through her mother's réveillon in a dress that was too tight in the collar, making half-hearted conversation with the wits of Paris. If only they could put everything back as it was, make her father himself again, take the gray hair from Clovis's coat, make the village a peaceful, happy place, a place of refuge in contrast to the bustling, smoke-stained city.

"Do you know what Nicolas told me?" Suzanne said, as she topped up Aurélie's steaming beaker of cider.

"Nicolas the baker's son or Nicolas the schoolmistress's nephew?" asked her father.

"The baker's son." Suzanne splashed cider into her father's cup. "He said he'd had a letter from Father Christmas. Father Christmas wrote that he was mistaken for an airman and shot in the foot and that was why he wouldn't be delivering any gifts this year—but not to worry, he'll be all recovered by next Christmas. Wasn't that clever, now?"

"That was Madame Lelong, the postmaster's wife," said Aurélie's father. "She wanted to make sure the little ones wouldn't be crying for their presents."

"But it's horrible," Aurélie burst out. Her cup was empty; she couldn't remember drinking it. Her tongue felt thick with the cloying taste of the cider. "Father Christmas—shot. What have we come to?"

"It was a kindness." There was a warning in her father's voice.

"Kind? To tell the children we've killed Father Christmas?"

"Not killed," said Victor patiently. "Only wounded."

It was monstrous. "Don't you think Father Christmas ought to come after all?" She looked around at the others, their faces slightly blurry in the candlelight. She hated herself for not having thought of it before, for not having contrived something. It hadn't occurred to her. Because she had been taking too many walks with Lieutenant von Sternburg? Max. He had asked her to call him Max and she had, because it advanced their cause, that was all. "The books from the library . . . I could give every child a book."

"Do you really think the village children yearn for Aristophanes?" asked her father.

More than her father ever had. He had never been a great reader, another rift between him and her mother.

Guilt made Aurélie fierce. "At least it would be *something*."

"With our arms in it? They would know where it was from in an instant."

Yes, but they would also know someone had cared.

Aurélie tried desperately to think what else they might bring. If she'd had her old room, she might have ransacked the useless trivialities, the little luxuries she had taken so for granted. But now she slept in a garret above the kitchen, sparsely furnished. A coin for each—if they'd had the coins to give. If they wouldn't have to worry about the coins being confiscated, the children punished for receiving them. So many things had been made illegal, it was hard to remember them all.

"Here," said Suzanne, coming unexpectedly to her aid. "We've some nuts put by. If we tie them up in a bit of cloth with some string, it will be enough. Just so they can see Father Christmas made the effort after all."

"Give them here," said Victor. "I'll parcel them out."

Aurélie's father looked at her sideways. "And who's to deliver these parcels?"

It felt like a challenge. "I shall."

"After curfew?"

"Didn't you just say there's no curfew for a de Courcelles?" Ordinarily, she'd never have spoken so to her father. He was the head of his house, and due respect.

But he didn't take her to task for it. "I didn't say it quite like that. All right, then. If you're determined."

She hadn't been determined, but he seemed to have determined it for her. Aurélie squinted at her father. The fire in the kitchen smoked; she couldn't tell, but she thought he was, obscurely, pleased. Because she was thumbing her nose at the Germans?

But this wasn't about the Germans, she reminded herself. It was about the children. And Father Christmas.

Why, then, did she feel as though she had been managed?

"You will be careful?" said Suzanne, handing her the basket. She was beginning to look worried. "If they've sentries out . . ."

"They'll all be at the feast." Aurélie wasn't quite as sure as she sounded. She doubted Hoffmeister would ignore so obvious a precaution. He'd probably enjoy denying some man his Christmas revels, making him sit outside in the cold. "They wouldn't shoot a woman."

Never mind that they had before and probably would again. Why did they say these things when they all knew them to be untrue? But Suzanne and Victor were nodding along as though they didn't know as well as she it was all lies, as if any of them believed what she had said. Was it because the truth was too unpalatable to bear? Like lying to the children about Father Christmas, only they were lying to themselves, trying to make themselves believe that the old rules still applied.

"It could wait until morning," suggested Suzanne, uneasy. "Until light. Even Father Christmas loses his way sometimes."

"Especially with his wounded foot," said her father, expressionless.

He was testing her. She wasn't sure why, but he was.

"Do you need a light?" asked Victor.

"No. I know the way well enough." What was a twisted ankle among friends? She didn't need her father to tell her that to carry a light would be folly. She might as well pose as a grouse and invite hunters to take turns shooting at her. "I won't be long."

Another lie. She had no idea how long she'd be.

It felt colder outside than before, the air crisp with the scent of frost.

Once out of the old walls, through the gap her father had shown her when she was a child, it was almost eerily silent.

No bells. The Germans had torn the bells from the church, had shipped them to Germany to be melted into instruments of war.

But no, that wasn't it. It took her a moment to realize that the shelling had stopped. For the first time in months, the guns from the front had fallen silent.

It ought to have been beautiful, but it wasn't. It was eerie, terrifying. She felt like a rabbit in a clearing, caught out of concealment.

Through the silence, she heard the crunch of footsteps on the hard ground and froze. Not just footsteps. Boots. German boots. A man in uniform appeared at the other end of the lane, by the graveyard, where the walnut trees no longer grew.

"Don't shoot!" It seemed really quite imperative not to die just now. "I can explain!"

The steps quickened, the moonlight glinting off the silver insignia on a peaked cap. "Aurélie?"

"Lieutenant von Sternburg. Max." Aurélie gulped in air, the cold burning her lungs. The nearness of her escape made her dizzy. She resisted the urge to sit down hard on the cold ground, holding tight to her basket instead. "What are you doing out here? Shouldn't you be feasting on stolen brandy and plundered geese?"

"I hadn't the stomach for it." The moonlight played tricks, obscuring familiar features, but his voice was the same, cultured, rueful. "What have you got there?"

Aurélie shifted the basket in her arms, twisting it away. "Some nuts for the children. That's all. They're from our own store."

She couldn't see his face, but she could sense his sudden stillness, hear the change in his voice. "Did you think I was going to report you to the major?"

"I—I don't know." She had hurt him. It seemed strange to feel guilty for it, when he was one of the conquerors, one of the barbarians. "You have your duties. If you aren't going to report me—then I have some packages to deliver."

"For the children?" Max shook his head. "You're too late."

"Too late?" A hundred horrid images scrolled through Aurélie's cider-fuzzed brain. "Wait. You don't mean——"

"Don't look like that! It's nothing like that. All I meant was, Father Christmas already came."

"He did?" Aurélie looked up at him, the meaning of his words finally sinking in. "I thought—I thought he had a wounded foot."

Max smiled unevenly. "He managed to hobble out of bed. He brought little enough. Chocolates. Tops. Balls. But something."

Aurélie gave up the pretense. "Why?" she demanded, staring up at him, trying to make out his expression in the moonlight. "Why?"

"Father Christmas wouldn't . . . ," he began, and then stopped. "Why? I don't believe in making war on children. There's so little that's truly precious. To destroy like this—to take away their peace, their innocence—how can we do that? This isn't what war ought to be."

"What ought it be?" There was a bench by the denuded graveyard. Aurélie sat on it, feeling the shock of cold straight through her dress and drawers. "Two rows of men shooting at each other?"

"Yes!" Max's face was earnest in the moonlight. "Exactly that. Men who chose what they chose, fighting by recognizable rules. Not—not this trampling of innocents for sport!"

His confusion made something twist in her chest. She had been like that, too, what felt like a very long time ago. She had thought that war was bugles and glory. Jean-Marie had known otherwise the last time he saw her, had tried to tell her. But she had ignored him.

Aurélie thought of the stories that had nourished her childhood:

their glorious ancestor who had followed Joan of Arc, her father dashing into battle against the Prussians. But those were only the bits they sewed into the tapestries, sanitized and edited.

"Was it ever otherwise, do you think?"

Max let out a long sigh, folding his tall body onto the bench beside her. "Probably not. Not if you believe Voltaire, at any rate. Candide asks if men have always massacred each other, if they have 'always been liars, cheats, traitors, ingrates, brigands, idiots, thieves, scoundrels' and so forth. His friend replies, 'Have hawks always eaten pigeons?'"

"Your commanding officer has banned pigeons," Aurélie pointed out. "So the hawks might be out of luck."

Max choked on a laugh. "This is a metaphorical pigeon."

"I don't believe that makes a difference," said Aurélie. "It's contraband, all the same. You'd best get rid of it."

Max stifled a yawn, rubbing his eyes with the back of his hand. "Shall I put it in the book? Item: one pigeon, metaphorical, executed. Of course, that raises the question of how one executes a metaphorical pigeon."

It was the sort of debate they used to carry on by the hour in her mother's salon. Aurélie had never been part of those discussions; no one had ever thought her worth having them with. And, to be fair, she had thought it all nonsense, pointless nothings. Now there was something strangely bittersweet about it. It felt like a luxury to sit here, in the dark, in the cold, and talk nonsense. "How does one execute a metaphorical pigeon?"

Max stretched his long legs out in front of him. Aurélie could see the mist of his breath in the cold air, the rise and fall of the silver buttons on his coat. "By removing all irony," he said at last. "Killing all thought. Draining dry wit. Reducing the world to the imposition of blind obedience, with no sense or justice in it. No kindness. No mercy."

Aurélie glanced up at him sideways. "How did we get from pigeons to this?"

He grimaced. "How did we get from anything to this?"

"I keep wondering that, too," Aurélie admitted. "I had thought, at the beginning, that it would be a few weeks, and then everything could go back to normal. But now . . . I don't even remember what normal was anymore."

"Rainy days at the Louvre," Max said softly. "Cakes at Angelina."

"You left. You left after that. I looked for you at my mother's salon . . . to return your umbrella," she added hastily. "But you never came back."

"No." He looked down at his hands. "I was called back to Berlin."

"And it was only an umbrella." Aurélie rather wished she hadn't said anything. She wasn't sure why she had. But it was Christmas Eve and the shelling had stopped and everything was strange and edged with ice. "Not the least bit important. One can find a new umbrella anywhere."

"Not anywhere. There are some umbrellas—there are some umbrellas that matter more than others." Max leaned forward, his eyes pale in the moonlight. "I ought to have written . . . I meant to write . . . I would have written . . . but it was too hard. It was my sister, you see. Elisabeth . . ."

"You mentioned her." At the Louvre. He had shown Aurélie the picture he kept in his watch.

"She was the heart of our family, our good angel. For the longest time, it was only me. My mother—she lost child after child. I wasn't meant to know, you understand. But . . ."

"Nursemaids talk," Aurélie provided for him. She knew it well. It was how she had learned of the peculiarities of her own position, that "Uncle Hercule," who lived in the suite with them, was, in fact, her father's cousin and her mother's lover.

"Yes," said Max gratefully. "And when Elisabeth was born . . . she was such a little thing, so delicate. They'd had the mourning bands ready, but she lived. She lived and everything was bright again. My mother had headaches; she had kept the curtains drawn and I was meant to be quiet and not disturb her, but once Elisabeth arrived, it didn't matter anymore. Suddenly, everything was light and we could run and laugh as much as we liked and there were flowers in all the rooms. I was nine already when Elisabeth was born. But it was like living in a whole new house, as though my life started again with Elisabeth. Does that sound strange?"

"No," said Aurélie. There had been a life before the Ritz, she knew. She could still vaguely remember the slamming doors, her mother's raised voice, the flat of her father's palm against a tabletop, making her jump. Her life, her life as she knew it, had begun when she was four years old, when her mother had taken up permanent residence at the Ritz. "Did she . . . is she—"

"It was a chill," said Max. "Just a chill. All of our science, all of our advances in medicine, and not one doctor could save her. I was in time to see her. But just."

"I'm sorry," said Aurélie. Without thinking, she put her hand on his, squeezing hard. "I'm so sorry."

"That was why I left, you see. Why I left and didn't come back. My mother . . . she was in a bad way." He shifted to face her, turning his hand so that they were palm to palm, his hand holding hers. "That's what I don't understand, about any of this. There is so much misery we cannot prevent. Why do we go out of our way to cause more?"

"I don't know." Aurélie ran her tongue along her dry lips. "I was never philosophical."

"No," said Max, lifting his eyes from her lips. "You only put us all in our places with a few well-chosen words."

"I didn't," Aurélie protested. She pulled back, looking at his face, his familiar, careworn face. "Did I?"

"It was beautiful to behold." His voice was so low she could hardly hear. "You were beautiful to behold."

"Were?" Aurélie asked hoarsely. This was folly, she knew. Worse than folly. But she couldn't seem to help herself. Not when he was looking at her like that. No one, not even Jean-Marie with his clumsy affection, had ever looked at her like that before.

"Are." The word was torn from his throat. Aurélie wasn't sure how it had happened, but both her hands were in his, their knees bumping together. "I wish—I wish we were anywhere but where we are. I wish I had come back to Paris."

"For your umbrella?"

"It was never about the umbrella." His eyes were very pale in the moonlight.

"That's good," Aurélie said unevenly. "Because I think one of my mother's friends filched it."

Max's hands tightened on hers. "I hate this. I hate what we've done here. I hate the cruelty, the waste of it. But, most of all, I hate being here, with you, knowing that to you I must always be the enemy."

Never mind that it was exactly what she'd been thinking not an hour ago. "You're not my enemy."

"Aren't I?"

"I don't know." It should have been simple. It should have been easy. Aurélie glowered at him. "It's your own blasted fault. If you'd just be like the rest of them, it wouldn't be so hard to remember that I'm meant to hate you."

"I'm sorry." He smiled crookedly at her, that wry, rueful smile that was so his own. "I'll try harder to be hateful if you like."

"Don't," said Aurélie fiercely, and kissed him.

CHAPTER FIFTEEN

Daisy

Avenue Marceau
Paris, France
July 1942

THE KISS SHOCKED her. Pierre had long ago fallen out of the habit of kissing Daisy when he left for work. Or when he returned. Or at any time at all, really, except at the specific moment when he required sex.

At one time—again, long ago—Daisy had missed that small gesture of affection and what it meant. Then she became used to its absence, as human beings do, and stopped even caring that he didn't offer it. Now?

Now she was busy! She was getting the children ready for school, the last day of the term, making sure they ate their breakfast and packed their little gifts for the teachers in their satchels. (Not *little* gifts at all, actually—Daisy had secured some coffee, real coffee beans, which she wrapped in cheesecloth and tied with ribbon. The teachers would be so delighted!) She was giving instructions to Justine, who now came daily, and checking the larder for the day's shopping, and checking the clock, because every minute counted. As she raced about the apartment in the sticky July heat, as she performed all the myriad small chores that made up her mornings, she was thinking about kisses, all right. Just not from her husband.

"Where's my hat?" Pierre had thundered from the hallway, the grand foyer of the gigantic new apartment on avenue Marceau, into which they had moved six weeks ago when Pierre took up his new position in the Jewish Affairs Bureau. Pierre loved hearing his voice echo from the soaring ceilings and the plasterwork. Daisy hated it. Daisy had put Olivier's satchel back on the kitchen floor and hurried out to find the hat, which had fallen off the commode and behind the umbrella stand. She brushed off a speck or two of dust and handed it to him.

"Here you are, dear."

She'd fully expected him to rage and grumble and storm out the door, smashing the hat down as he went, but he didn't. Instead he said—yes, it's true!—he said, *Thank you, Daisy,* and placed the hat on his head. He'd inspected himself in the oval mirror, nodded with satisfaction, and just as Daisy had turned to hurry back down the hallway, he reached for her shoulders and kissed her. On the lips!

"Oh!" she gasped.

"When I return from work this evening, I want you to wear your best dress, my dear. That blue one, perhaps?"

Daisy resisted the urge to wipe her lips. "Whatever for?"

"We're going out to dinner, of course. At Maxim's."

"Maxim's!"

"Yes. I have something to celebrate!"

Daisy stared at her husband for the first time that morning, and she realized Pierre was smiling, actually smiling, and his eyes were as bright as if he'd taken some kind of drug. Had he? Or was he coming down with a fever, perhaps?

"Celebrate?" she asked.

He laid a finger over his damp lips. "Shh! It's a secret." But because he was Pierre, he went on. "Let's just say that a certain project I've been working on for the past two months is coming at last to its fruition. By the end of the week—well! You'll see. You'll read about it in the newspapers, my dear wife, and you will be very proud of your Pierre, I promise!"

A chill went down Daisy's limbs, thick and slow, as if her heart were pumping slush instead of blood. "That's—that's wonderful," she whispered.

"All this"—Pierre gestured to the hall around them, the gilded furniture and the shining parquet floors, the intricate ceilings that yawned above—"it's only the beginning, my love. And it's all for you. For our children. I have done all this for your sakes."

"Pierre, I don't want this, I don't want luxury—"

"Hush! None of this. Just wait. A few more days only." He adjusted his hat and smiled again. "And remember tonight! Your best dress!"

"But what are we celebrating? What's this project?"

"I can't say. It's very secret, very important." He leaned forward and whispered, "It will take care of this Jew problem once and for all."

"I didn't know we had a Jew problem in Paris."

He laughed. "My dear little wife, who doesn't read the newspapers! Never mind. It's for your husband to take care of these matters for you. Goodbye, now. I must be off."

Then he kissed her again—again!—and swept out the door.

ON THE DAY Pierre had returned home from work, not long after the May dinner party, and announced that (as he had foretold) a beautiful new apartment had been found for them, an apartment fit for their new exalted place in the world, Daisy had protested vehemently. Daisy had said she would move with the children to the Ritz, to live with Grandmère, but Grandmère herself had blocked this plan. Grandmère had said she must put up with this grotesque arrangement, living in some-body's confiscated apartment, because Daisy would be perfectly placed in such an echoing place to hear whispers from the very inner circle of the occupation. Grandmère was right, of course, but Daisy still hated herself for giving in. Wherever she went in that house, she felt the ghosts of the former occupants staring at her, whispering *J'accuse!* Every chair, every wardrobe, every lamp, every bed and sheet and pillow seemed to recoil from her touch, to recognize that she was an interloper, a thief.

The only thing Daisy couldn't help appreciating about this new apartment was its location. Years ago, she had fought Pierre to put the children in the École Rousseau, one of the best primary schools in Paris, for which they couldn't afford the fees. For once, she'd put her back into it, and Pierre had finally relented. Grandmère had paid the fees, naturally, and Daisy had gladly walked the daily two kilometers with Madeleine and Oliver, back and forth from their apartment in the less-fashionable environs of rue Portalis. As the years passed, she had walked them not so gladly. A half kilometer was a pleasant morning stroll, time to chat with the children and enjoy the sights and smells of Paris. Two kilometers was just plain tedium.

But this new apartment, this grand and guilty new abode the Villon family now called home, lay only a few streets away from the *école*. Daisy hated that this was a relief to her, but it was. A quick jaunt past the heavenly smells of the boulangerie, the café that served mostly German officers, the tidy facades of the fashionable shops, and there they were. She could bustle the children inside and hurry down the Champs toward rue Volney, to the bookshop. To Monsieur Legrand.

In her own defense, Daisy reminded herself that this shortened dis-tance allowed her more hours to do her work, to deliver more forged papers to more hidden airmen, more intelligence agents, more Jewish families facing deportation to Germany. Still, as they reached the steps and the open door, the mothers and children streaming inside, she had to swallow back her own shame, as always, and concentrate her attention on Madeleine and Olivier. She knelt to kiss them and remind them about the presents for their teachers.

"Of course, Maman," said Madeleine.

"Good morning, Madame Villon!" It was the headmistress, Madame Duchamps, who had developed a habit in the past few weeks of addressing Daisy personally, each morning and afternoon, in a manner you might call obsequious. "And how are my sweet children this morning, eh?"

Olivier said, "Wonderful, madame! It's the last day of school!"

Madame laughed. "Well, well. Very sensible! And you, Mademoiselle Villon?"

Madeleine, it must be said, hadn't trusted this recent mood of Madame Duchamps's from the beginning. She looked up and said coldly, "Not quite so well as my brother, thank you."

Madame didn't know what to make of this. She moved her jaws like she was chewing on an especially tough cut of meat.

"Ah yes. Well," she said at last. "Clever child."

"Madame Duchamps," Daisy said, as the children hurried through the door and into the courtyard, "I've been meaning to ask you something. I need to speak to Madame Levin about the mothers' committee next year, but I haven't seen her at all this week. Perhaps you can give me her telephone number?"

The doughy, pleasing face of Madame Duchamps turned to stone. "I'm sorry, madame. I'm afraid the Levins are no longer enrolled at this school."

BY THE TIME Daisy turned the corner of rue Volney and saw the familiar signboard—*Le Mouton Noir* in dignified Roman letters, set around a faceless black sheep—the July air had already grown oppressively warm. The heat brought out all the smells of the bookshop, leather and wood and binder's glue, and especially the scent of pipe tobacco. Daisy paused in the doorway and gathered these flavors at the back of her throat. Her dress stuck to her skin. Her heart hammered in her chest, but of course that was just because of the long, brisk walk from École Rousseau. Wasn't it?

"Hello?" she called out.

A dusty silence answered her. She stepped forward and closed the door behind her. Her gaze went to the shelf of English novels, where the brown-and-red spine of *The Scarlet Pimpernel* sat in perfect alphabetical order on the shelf of English-language books, between the O. Henry and the Ovid. Daisy let out a long breath and brushed back her damp hair with her fingers. A small object hurtled across the room and struck her middle.

"Philippe!" she gasped.

"There you are, madame! I have been waiting all morning!"

Daisy laughed and unwrapped the little boy's arms from her waist. "I am not so late, am I? Where is your grandfather?"

Philippe shrugged. "Out. I am minding the shop." He said this proudly, straightening himself to his full hundred and fifty centimeters.

"Very good." She took her pocketbook from her shoulder and opened it. "Do you know what I have for you?"

"Sweets?"

"Not today, I'm afraid. Something else."

Daisy put her hand inside the pocketbook and drew out a small stuffed rabbit. Philippe shrieked.

"For me?"

"Yes, for you! What other little boy is named Lapin? You must take very good care of him, do you hear me? There are not so many such rabbits to be found these days."

Philippe drew the furry toy reverently from her hands and stroked its back with his finger. "He is just like Mademoiselle Madeleine's rabbit."

Daisy smiled and knelt down, so her head was on the same plane as Philippe's dark head, all peaks and angles, eyes like the glossy chocolates they served on tiny, exquisite plates at the Ritz. "Not quite. Hers is spotted, and yours is brown all over. Like you, my little lapin." She rose and kissed his hair. "Now, tell me what . . ."

Her words trailed away, because there on the other side of the room, where there had been nothing but shelves, Monsieur Legrand now stood in his shirtsleeves, damp with heat, a pen dangling from one hand and a book from the other. Staring at her.

Daisy went again to brush her hair from her forehead, but of course she had already done this, and there was nothing to brush. She tucked a few strands behind her ear instead. "Good morning, monsieur."

"Good morning."

"A little hot, isn't it?"

"Miserable. Especially in that stuffy little hidey-hole of mine."

"Is there somewhere else you can work, perhaps?"

"You can work in my room!" said Philippe.

Legrand gave the little boy a kind look. "No, no, my good man. We wouldn't dream of intruding. We'll just find a way to bear it, that's all." He stood back from the entrance to the hidden office. "Madame?"

Legrand was right. It was terribly hot in their workroom, almost intolerable. "I open up the window at night, to let in some air," he said, "but I'd rather not take the chance during the day."

"It wouldn't help, anyway. The air's no cooler outside."

Legrand put the pen behind his ear and held out the book. "There are two more on the desk, still drying. Addresses are right here." He squinted at her. "Is something wrong?"

"Yes. Pierre was in a very good mood this morning."

"And this is bad news?"

"He wants to take me to dinner tonight. He wants to celebrate, he said."

"Celebrate what?" Legrand said sharply.

"I don't know. He wouldn't say, exactly. I tried to draw it out of him, but he only admitted it was something to do with work, some big project that's about to come to fruition and—one presumes—further advance his standing among the Germans."

Legrand swore. "For a man working in the Jewish Affairs office, that can only mean one thing."

"The rumored roundup?"

"What else could it be?"

Daisy pulled out a chair and sat. "The Levins have disappeared."

"The family at school?"

"Yes. I asked the headmistress this morning, and she told me the children were no longer enrolled, that's all. And her expression when she said this, it was like . . . it was like marble." Daisy looked up at Legrand's grim face. "I don't suppose you've heard anything?"

"Nothing. I can only hope the move was of their own planning." He sat down in the chair next to her and lifted his pipe from the tray where he kept it. From his pocket he took a matchbook and lit a match, which he stuck carefully in the pipe's bowl until the tobacco inside had caught and the rich perfume seeped into the air. Daisy had watched him perform this ritual at least a hundred times by now. It meant that he was thinking about something, turning over some problem in his head. She tried not to stare at his fingers, or the play of tendons in his forearms, which his rolled sleeves exposed. But it didn't matter, did it? Each shape of him, each bone, each color and shadow and hair of him was like her own. She could close her eyes, she could stare at the wall, she could bury her head in the thickest pillow and still she would know what he was doing, what he looked like at any particular moment, from any particular angle. Now he settled the pipe in his palm, wrapped his fingers around the bowl, set his mouth at the end.

A hundred times, and more. A hundred hours, possibly two hundred—who counted? Day after day they had met, they had labored without speaking, they had labored *while* speaking. It was a charity project, she told Pierre. For residents of Paris in these hard times, when paper was rationed and nobody could afford a new volume, the Mouton Noir had a kind of lending library, and Daisy delivered books and brought them back again. Which was true. The soundest lies, as Legrand told her, were the ones built on a foundation of truth. So she could look at Pierre and tell him, without blinking, how she spent her days. Not that Pierre really listened, or even cared. Pierre was too occupied with his own work.

Madame Levin. A handsome woman, a little reserved, dignified and correct in all her manners but sometimes funny, when you least expected humor. Daisy knew her in the way she knew any or all of the other mothers at the École Rousseau. They were more than acquaintances, less than friends. Still, Daisy had always liked Madame Levin. Her children were clever and maybe a little boisterous, but always polite in a genuine, unaffected way. Now they were no longer enrolled at the *école*. Daisy pressed her fingertips together and inhaled the smell of Legrand's pipe and tried not to imagine the police— the *French* police, the shame of it!—pounding on the Levins' door, dragging away Madame Levin and the two little girls, Marie-Rose and Geneviève, in their pinafore dresses and brown curls. Their pale, innocent skin.

A hand landed gently on her shoulder. "Now, then. Don't despair," said Legrand.

"Not despair? There's nothing we can do. They will be deported to Germany, they'll be interned in those terrible camps."

"What do you know of these camps?"

"From my grandmother. How many do you think, in this roundup? Hundreds?"

"Thousands, possibly. Some of our agents are picking up terrible rumors. The Germans have got something up their sleeves, and they're pushing the French to demonstrate their loyalty by cooperating."

"Like Pierre."

"Like Pierre. Like a great many officials in occupied France, many of whom have no love for either the Jews or the British. You cast your lot with the victors, it's the way humans have survived and thrived through the centuries."

Daisy drove her fists into the table and rose. "But what can we do? Isn't there anything we can do? If I could just—just . . . stick a bomb in Pierre's briefcase . . ."

"That would be brave and stupid and solve exactly nothing, besides killing the father of your children."

Daisy made a noise of agony and sat. She put her head in her hands. "There must be a list of names. He must have a list somewhere."

"Of that, I have no doubt at all."

Daisy turned to look at him. Legrand sat back in his chair, perfectly relaxed, one curl snoozing over his forehead, undone by the heat. Only the whiteness of his knuckles, clenched around the pipe, betrayed his anxiety.

He continued in that reasonable voice of his, as if discussing the weather. "In fact, it's likely what he's been working on all these weeks. Compiling a list of Jews and their places of residence, so his masters can strike on the appointed day."

"And if we had that list in advance . . ."

"We could save a few. Not all, not even most, but a few."

"It's so little. To save a few? It's nothing, it's a raindrop in a thunderstorm."

Legrand had been staring at the window that—when not concealed by a curtain—opened into the courtyard. Now he turned to her and drew the pipe out of his mouth. His hand moved to cover hers on the warm wood of the table's surface. "It's not nothing. Not to those we save. To them, it's everything. Each identity card I create—each one you deliver—represents a unique and singular life, a person, an airman or an agent or a Jew who has another chance to survive. Don't ever forget that. Don't ever lose yourself thinking of the ones you couldn't save. Think instead of the ones you did."

Daisy's eyes were so full, she was afraid to blink. The tears would just overflow if she did, and once she started weeping, they were both in trouble, because she wouldn't be able to stop. Tears for the war, for those in hiding, for those already dead, for those about to die. For the family in whose home she now lived, God forgive her. For her marriage, for her children, for her own unique, singular life that was probably doomed. And she had not yet begun to live! She was only just now glimpsing what was possible! And she would die. Sooner or later, they would get her. That was inevitable. Yet she had never wanted life so much.

Underneath Legrand's hand, she curled her thumb around his thumb.

"To get this list from Pierre," she said. "You understand what I must do."

There was no answer. She couldn't look at his face.

She went on. "I think sometimes that I hate him. My own husband. I can't even remember what it was like to love him, to care for him at all."

"Daisy—"

"I look at him and feel nothing but disgust. I loathe every hair of him. He kissed me this morning, before he left for work, right on the lips, and I wanted to vomit. Do you know what that's like? To submit to the kiss of somebody who disgusts you?"

"Almost as hard, I think, as to be unable to kiss somebody you adore."

"No." Daisy stared at her thumb, entwined with Legrand's thumb. "Because there is some pleasure in denial. There is some hope. When you give your body to the use of somebody you loathe, there is nothing. Nothing. Your soul is black and empty."

Legrand moved his thumb against hers. She thought, *Say something!* Say you want to kill him for me, tell me you can't stand the thought of him touching me, say that you would rather die than let Pierre kiss me again, have me again. But maybe he *was* saying it. Maybe that small movement of his thumb contained it all, every word.

"What does this make me?" she whispered.

"What does it make *me?*" he answered. "To let you do it."

"Is it so hard?"

Legrand lifted her hand and kissed it.

Daisy stared at her fingers, which he continued to hold, not far from the lips that had kissed them. Then she looked at the lips, and finally up at his eyes, which were warm and very blue, and seemed to be communicating something important to her. It was terrifying, looking at someone like that, eyes meeting eyes, but Daisy forced herself to hold Legrand's gaze. He had to *know,* he had to understand, just in case. What if the Gestapo swooped in, the next moment? He had to know that she prayed for him, she dreamed of him, she thought of him every moment, she was in love with him, she loved him.

"I don't even know your real name," she said.

Legrand rose to his feet and pulled her up with him. They stood face-to-face, mere centimeters between them. Daisy felt his breath on her skin. She smelled his sweat, his soap, his tobacco. She thought, *We're going to kiss.* At last, I am going to kiss him. And then what? But there is so much work to do.

He took her other hand and leaned forward. Daisy closed her eyes.

But the kiss, when it arrived an instant later, met her forehead. He held his lips there for a moment or two, while the heat of the July air melted them both, and Daisy was disappointed and grateful, both at once.

"You have the strength of a lioness," he said. "My brave, beautiful Daisy. You must be strong enough for us both."

In the whole of Daisy's life, nobody had ever called her strong or brave, not even after she gave birth to Olivier, who was four and a half kilos and nearly split her in two. It gave her strength. It made her feel as if she actually were as brave as he thought her.

She stepped back and released his hands. "I'll deliver the books," she said, "and I'll find that list. Whatever it takes."

WHATEVER IT TAKES. It was an easy thing to say, an old cliché. A promise you made before you really considered what you might be called upon to do, and how hard it would be.

In the scheme of things, it wasn't that hard to put on a pretty dress and go out to Maxim's with your husband and make cheerful conversation with him, to flatter and flirt with him. Yet to Daisy it was agony. It was torture, each word dragged from her lungs, each smile pinned on by brute force, the performance of her life, sustained only by the thought of Legrand and the sensation of his hands holding hers, his lips on her forehead, telling her she had the strength of a lioness.

By the time they returned to the grand apartment on avenue Marceau, Daisy was exhausted. Still, she persevered. She poured Pierre some brandy—he had already drunk a bottle and a half of wine at dinner—and curled herself tenderly around him on the sofa. She praised once more all his hard work at the office and teased him about this big secret he was keeping from her.

"No, no, no!" he said, wagging his finger, loosening his necktie. "It's all locked up tight in the safe."

"Not the safe in your own study! As close as that?"

"To leave it in the office would be madness," he told her, in an air of great condescension. "There are spies about, you know!"

"No! Who would do such a thing?"

"But never you fear, my dear. They can't outwit me."

"You're so clever, Pierre. But can't you show me? I want to see this extraordinary thing you've done."

Pierre stuck his hand under her dress. "I have much more extraordinary things to show you right now."

"Pierre, wait—" The word choked off in a gasp, as Pierre's finger jabbed between her legs.

"Ah, ah, look at this! Someone's a little aroused by her husband's success, no?"

Not exactly by that, Daisy thought. She tried to squirm away from the jabbing finger. "Pierre! Not here! The children . . ."

"The children are in bed," he said. "Justine's gone home for the night."

Daisy's dress made a deep V at the neckline. Pierre removed his hand from between her legs, only to jerk down her sleeves, to jerk away her brassiere so her bosom came free. In reflex, her hands came up to cover her naked breasts, but she checked herself. She wasn't supposed to deny him, was she? She was supposed to submit; she had to soften him up, to make him vulnerable, to give him what he wanted so she could take what she wanted. She made herself cup her breasts instead, to present them to Pierre as a delectable gift. Naturally Pierre didn't question this bounty, no more than a child questions the sudden appearance of a bag of sweets. He grabbed a breast in each fist and squeezed, he slobbered his tongue all over her skin and pushed her right back on the cushions.

"Wait, Pierre . . . the diaphragm—"

He was not going to wait, not for the diaphragm and certainly not for her. His breath stank of brandy, his skin stank of perspiration. Luckily he didn't expose much of it, just the essentials. Daisy stared at the ceiling while he unbuttoned his trousers. The air in the room was so hot, so close, she couldn't breathe. She gathered the sofa cushions in her fists as he flopped down on top of her like a large, wet fish. Because he'd drunk so much, it took forever. He made her turn over, and then back again, humping and stopping for breath, humping and stopping until Daisy was ready to scream, was ready to take one of those heavy silver candlesticks from the mantel and bash him over the head. His sweat dripped on her face. At last he came in a howl of relief. He sank on her chest, drooling a little, snoring, and Daisy's gaze traced the intricate petals of the plaster rose some four meters above her and imagined another body pressing her into the cushions, another pair of arms, another sound, another smell entirely. The scent of pipe tobacco, the sound of a man's soft chuckle.

Whatever it takes, she had promised. If only she could have taken her scarf and strangled Pierre instead.

CHAPTER SIXTEEN

Babs

Picardy, France
April 1964

PRECIOUS TIED DIANA'S Hermès scarf in a provocative bow on the side of my neck, smiling as she stepped back to admire her handiwork. "Well, now, don't you look prettier than a mess of fried catfish."

I wasn't quite sure what that meant, but I had other concerns as I stared at my reflection. "It's a little frivolous, isn't it?" I asked. "A scarf is meant to be useful, I believe. Not decorative."

She gave me a knowing smile as she adjusted the extravagant bow. "Whatever it takes, dear. Whatever it takes."

I pulled back. "To attract a man, do you mean?"

With a quick admonishing shake of her head, she said, "Not at all. I want to make you see yourself as a woman who is not only beautiful and stylish, but who knows her own worth. When you're wearing your new clothes, you stand straighter and walk more confidently. You are an intelligent and strong woman who has survived adversity and who still had enough pluck to agree to come to Paris for an assignation with a man you'd never met before."

"It's not an . . ."

Precious cut me off. "How you present yourself to the world should alert people that you're a force to be reckoned with. Not someone who should be overlooked because she still dresses like a refugee despite the war being over for two decades." She leaned close to my ear. "You are a formidable woman, Barbara Langford, and your beauty and style should reflect it. Never forget that."

I swallowed, not exactly sure I agreed with her but wanting to try. I met her eyes in the mirror's reflection. "How did you get to be so clever?"

A secretive smile crept across her lovely face. "Life. I refused to let fate dictate my future. I reinvented myself as many times as I needed to succeed." She spun me around so that we were face-to-face. "Every day you learn, Babs. You learn, and learn, and learn. And the day that the universe has nothing left to teach you, you can stop."

She turned quickly away and began organizing the cosmetics on the dressing table while I returned to my reflection. The peacock blue in the silk scarf matched the skirt ensemble Precious had selected for me, making me feel more scandalous than confident. The skirt was too short and if I reached my arms up, my bare midriff would peek out from over the waistband. *You are a formidable woman.* I would keep repeating that to myself until I could almost believe it.

"Are you ready?" she asked, pausing by the door. "I hope you don't mind but I took the liberty of ordering a few extras for your picnic basket."

"Like what?" I asked, beginning to worry. Her idea of picnic items was most likely far different than mine.

She opened the door, looking innocently up at the ceiling. "Oh, just my favorite champagne. And a few of my favorite foods. Like oysters—on ice, of course. Strawberries. And chocolate. Chocolate is always a good choice."

"Thank you," I said slowly. "Although that really wasn't necessary. I'd already ordered baguettes and cheese. It's just the two of us."

"Exactly," she said with a smile I could only describe as wicked.

She exited the room first, allowing me to snag my trusty jumper off the back of the desk chair when she wasn't looking. I was bound to be chilly with all of the exposed skin.

As we exited the lift downstairs we heard the unmistakable sound of a typewriter as Prunella Schuyler typed away at her memoirs. She'd taken my suggestion to heart and even though we were now subjected to the constant clacking whenever we were entering or exiting the hotel, at least she wasn't accosting us and shouting out the story of how she'd survived the sinking of the *Lusitania*. If I didn't think she'd corner me for an entire day, I might have mentioned that my husband's parents had both been survivors, too, and that they hadn't felt the need to talk about it every waking moment.

I spotted Drew before he saw me, and I felt a momentary surprise at the interruption of my breathing as I watched him leaning against a wall with his hands stuffed into his pockets, his feet casually crossed at the ankles. His hair was damp, sending improper thoughts about him showering, and I couldn't help but admire his broad shoulders under a knit long-sleeved shirt in a lovely shade of green that I knew matched his eyes. Assuming I remembered the color of his eyes. Which I did.

"That man is *fine*," Precious whispered in my ear. "Now you two go on and have fun. I'll go see what Prunella is up to." With a kiss on each cheek and a wave in Drew's direction she was off.

"Good morning," Drew said as he approached, an appreciative smile on his face. "I've already put the picnic basket in the car, so I'm ready if you are."

"Yes, of course. Let's go play detective, shall we?" I sounded so much like a schoolmarm that I hoped that Precious hadn't heard me. I followed him out of the hotel and into the beautifully sunny spring day.

A dark green sporty-looking coupe—borrowed from a friend at the office—sat at the curb, a valet holding open the passenger side door. As Drew slid into his seat next to me, he said, "I'll keep the windows up if you don't want to mess up your hair."

I was prepared with my automatic response, which would have been yes, but stopped myself. Why shouldn't I be driven through the French countryside on a beautiful day with a handsome man with the sun on my face and the wind in my hair? A *formidable woman* certainly would, and she wouldn't worry about her hair, either. "Absolutely not. Please keep them down. Just allow me to put on my jumper because I'm sure the wind will feel chilly." I should have put the scarf over my head, but the bow had been so beautiful that I didn't want to undo it, knowing I couldn't recreate it later.

I wiggled forward in my seat, trying to fit my long arms into the sleeves of the jumper, only realizing that my top was baring my midriff when my hands were no longer free to pull it down.

"May I help?" Drew asked, his face looking as stricken as I felt.

"No thank you. I'm quite all right." It was only after failing to wiggle my arms free that I felt Drew gently tugging on the shoulders of the jumper and pulling them over my arms.

"There," he said, patting me gently as if I were a dog.

I pulled down my top and nodded without looking at him. "Ready."

Drew was a careful driver, expertly maneuvering the car through Paris traffic and then north toward the motorway, following signs to Amiens. The wind made conversation difficult, and I was happy to sit back and enjoy the scenery, reminding myself more than once that the driver wasn't part of it and I should stop staring.

"Have you been to Picardy before?" Drew asked, his voice loud enough to be heard over the wind.

"No, I haven't." I shook my head to emphasize my words. "I've

never been to the French countryside—only Paris with my mother
and sister. But that was a very long time ago. All I know is that it's
where the great Battle of the Somme was fought." I didn't add that I
only knew that because of my dear brother Charles, who had loved to
play with his toy soldiers as a boy and reenact battles. He loved the
strategizing and the organization of armies, the bright uniforms and
shiny cannons, and I suppose it should have consoled me to know that
he'd died doing something he loved.

"I hope we have time to drive around a bit, then. It's not one of the
big tourist spots but it should be. It's the birthplace of Gothic architecture and has six of the world's greatest examples of Gothic cathe-
drals, which span the entire history of Gothic architecture. Imagine
that! Amiens Cathedral is the largest cathedral in Europe and two
Notre-Dames could fit inside. Hard to believe, isn't it? If you climb
up in the cathedral you get amazing views of the city and the river
Somme."

I found myself smiling and not just because I was truly interested
in what he was telling me—I was—but because of the boyish exuberance he exhibited in the telling. I was thoroughly charmed and
not a little surprised.

He caught me looking at him and frowned. "What? Did I pronounce
something wrong? Should it really be '*Sommay*'?"

I let out an unexpected bark of laughter, quickly covering my mouth
with my hand, then allowed myself to laugh when he grinned back at
me. "Yes, well, I hope we have time today, and if not, then we'll have
to come back." I don't know what had possessed me to add that last
part, unless Precious's words had made more of an impact on me than
I'd thought, but I was glad I'd said them. I was just too embarrassed to
look at him to catch his reaction.

We drove in a comfortable silence for another quarter of an hour or so when the car began slowing and Drew signaled a turn off the motorway and onto a narrow road marked only with a sign indicating a village called Piscop.

"Are we here?" I asked, looking for a grand château and seeing nothing but green fields.

"Sorry, no. I'm starving. I thought we should go ahead and stop for lunch."

I looked at my watch. "But it's only half past eleven."

He grinned sheepishly. "Yeah, I know. But my stomach tells me it's lunchtime. Do you mind?"

"Of course not. Do you know this place?"

His face seemed to close and darken for a moment, so briefly that I thought I might have imagined it. "Yes, I've been here before. Just once. But I remember how pretty it was and that it might be a good place for a picnic." He continued to drive along the curving road that seemed to be carved into a hill before stopping in a small inset, the wheels of the car just barely off the roadway.

Drew opened my door and we stood in the middle of the road, surveying the rolling green hills interspersed with fat leafy trees dotting the landscape. A flock of sheep grazed happily in a neighboring field, seemingly the only living creatures besides us for miles. It wasn't too terribly different from Devon, yet despite the same blue sky and bright sun that hovered over both places, it felt foreign to me. And not just because of the large American I'd arrived with. There was just something about the scent of the fields, or the sounds of the insects, or maybe the birds sang in a foreign language. Or maybe what Dorothy had said in Diana's favorite film, that there really is no place like home, was true.

Drew took the picnic basket from the boot and then crossed the road to the field of green grass, where he carefully set the basket. "I think this is about as perfect as we can get," he said confidently as he opened the lid and pulled out a red plaid blanket.

"Let me help," I said, grabbing two corners of the blanket. We spent the next few minutes setting out the food while neither one of us commented on the vast amounts of it, or the curious items. He may have raised his eyes at the oysters packed in ice or the bottle of champagne, but I made myself busy breaking the baguette in half and preparing plates of bread, cheese, and fruit.

The sound of a cork popping brought my attention back to Drew. Holding up the frothing bottle he grinned. "I didn't want it to get warm. If you'll hold the glasses, I'll pour."

I wanted to say no, because women like me didn't drink champagne in the afternoon. I didn't drink champagne at all, really. Before that disastrous night in the bar with Drew, the last sip of alcohol I'd had was at my own wedding, and that was in the evening. But I thought of Diana and Precious, and I knew that they wouldn't have hesitated. And if I were to be a *formidable* woman, I'd drink champagne in the afternoon. With a man. On a hillside in France while eating oysters and chocolate. I picked up the two champagne glasses and held them while Drew poured generous amounts into each.

Drew held his up in a toast. "To finding the answers we seek."

I raised my glass then took a sip, the bubbles filling my nose and causing my eyes to water. I hesitated a moment before I swallowed, not sure I really wanted to know those answers anymore.

We began to eat, the warm sun and the champagne loosening my bones and allowing me to breathe deeply for the first time in a very long while. I was reminded of Diana's last words to me, at the train station seeing me off. *Recklessness might be the thing we need sometimes to see our lives anew.* As I looked across the blanket at Drew and took another sip of my champagne, I wondered if this had been what she'd meant.

Feeling warm, I rolled up the sleeves of my jumper. "You said you've been here before," I broached as I spread brie on my baguette with a tiny silver cheese knife so thoughtfully supplied by the Ritz. "When was that?"

His face darkened again, and it took him so long to respond that I was already thinking of a change in topic before he spoke. "I was on my honeymoon."

I choked on the bread and cheese and had to take a gulp of the champagne to wash it all down. "You're *married*?"

"Oh no. No, I'm sorry. I didn't mean to imply . . ." He stopped, looked embarrassed. "I'm divorced. I was married eight years ago and have been divorced for three." He grimaced. "I found out after we were married that she didn't want children. And since I do, well . . ." He reached for the bottle and refilled our glasses.

"That's awful." I closed my eyes, the memory of our conversation in the Ritz bar filling me with mortification. "And that night we met, I kept going on and on about my children. I even forced you to look at their photographs. How perfectly dreadful you must have thought me."

"Not at all. I actually liked hearing about them. Since I will most likely never be a father, I live vicariously listening to other people telling me about their kids."

"What do you mean you'll never have children? You're still quite young. What are you, thirty?"

He grinned that toothy grin of his that I was beginning to find quite irresistible. "Either you're trying to flatter me, or you're a terrible judge of people's ages. I'm actually thirty-five."

"Oh, I assumed you were so much younger than me . . ." I quickly took another sip of champagne to hide my blush. "Sorry, it's just that I have always felt I was the oldest person in the room, even when I was a child. I think I have an old soul or something. Or maybe I'm not sure how old I'm supposed to feel because I didn't have the girlhood I was meant to have had. I was never a debutante because of the war, and then I was a wife at nineteen, a mother at twenty, and running the Women's Institute at twenty-one. I went from pinafores into tweeds it seems and skipped all that middle part of being a girl."

He nodded slowly, his brow furrowed in concentration. "I'm not sure exactly what you mean, but it doesn't sound like a lot of fun. However, it's not really my age that makes me reluctant to think of future fatherhood." He slowly slid an oyster into his mouth and I couldn't avert my eyes from his lips as they moved around the bivalve. After chewing slowly and deliberately, then swallowing, he continued. "About a year after we divorced, my ex-wife remarried and now has two children. So it wasn't that she didn't want children, she just didn't want any with me."

"Oh, Drew—no! I'm sure that's not it at all. Who wouldn't want to have children with you?" His eyes widened. "Oh, er, I meant that I think you'd make a wonderful father, that's all. With anyone. Or I mean, your wife. Not your ex-wife, of course, as she's married to someone else, but your new wife. I mean, if you had one."

At the look of confusion on his face, I drained my glass and reached for my baguette.

"And I just found out that she's pregnant with baby number three." He sighed. "I think that's why I was so eager to come to France. Yes, I want to do this for my dad so he can have peace before he dies. But hearing about my ex . . ." He shook his head slowly. "It's made me feel so unsettled. Not unhappy or anything—I love my job, and I enjoy living in New York, but it just feels incomplete somehow. Like I should do something to shake up my life a bit, you know?"

"I know exactly. It's why I didn't throw your letter away." Our eyes met as a spark of mutual understanding passed between us. Flustered, I returned my focus to eating my baguette. A clump of brie clung to the end and as I lifted the bread, the cheese began to fall. Despite all of my mother's teachings, I couldn't stand the waste and instead of allowing it to fall to the blanket, I caught it with my tongue and licked the cheese off the tip of the bread.

I glanced over at Drew, who was watching me closely, his face gone suddenly red.

"Are you all right? Was it the oyster?"

He swallowed and shook his head, then crossed his legs. "No. I'm fine." He cleared his throat. "But it's getting late and we should go." He began hastily wrapping up the food and I joined him, even though I wasn't finished eating. The champagne and the warm sun had made me feel heated so I discarded my jumper as we packed up, curious as to Drew's silence and hoping it wasn't anything I'd said.

When the picnic basket was securely stored in the boot and we were once again in the car heading toward Picardy, we reverted back to silence. I attempted to start conversation, but Drew apparently wasn't in a talkative mood. He kept sending me short glances then swerving as he jerked his attention back to the road. I wondered if he might be thinking of his ex-wife and was upset with me for forcing out unpleasant memories. I spent the remainder of the drive replaying our conversation and thinking of the best way to apologize.

After driving for another half hour, he slowed the car to turn off the motorway and into a small village. The cobbled street winding gently through the town was surrounded on both sides by charming stone buildings, many with iron balconies climbing with bright flowers and vines. Several of the buildings still possessed thatched roofs and it felt as if we'd traveled through time instead of just seventy miles from Paris.

Drew parked the car on the street. "You can wait here if you like. I just need to ask for directions to the château."

"I'll come with you," I said. "I'd like to stretch my legs."

A pained look crossed his face as he approached my side of the car.

As he opened my door, he pointed at me while seeming to study the car's paint at the same time. "You might . . ." He circled his finger in the direction of my stomach.

Looking down I realized that somehow my top had disengaged itself from the waistband of my skirt again and seemed to be comfortably rolled up against the bottom of my brassiere, exposing my entire midriff. I quickly pulled it down, smoothed my skirt, then exited the car with as much dignity as I could muster. I gathered my composure and as we began walking, being careful not to get one of my new sandals stuck between cobbles, I said, "It must have happened when I got into the car. I promise you it wasn't intentional."

Drew stopped in front of a café and held the door open for me. "I didn't think it was." And then, just as I passed in front of him, he added, "But I wouldn't have minded if it were."

I was still blushing when we left the café ten minutes later after obtaining directions—in French—to the Château de Courcelles. The owner hadn't spoken a word of English, for which I was eternally grateful because Drew couldn't understand all the innuendoes and assumptions about our relationship the man was comfortable sharing with me despite my protests that we were merely acquaintances. When we returned to the car, I quickly put my jumper back on despite the heat and wondered if I'd imagined the look of disappointment on Drew's face.

With only one wrong turn, I managed to direct Drew out of the village and just a couple of miles to where the man had told me we'd find the château. Except it wasn't there. I looked down at the pencil marks the man had scribbled on a paper napkin for me.

"This is definitely the right place." We'd left the car in a clearing at the edge of a dense forest, near a rocky path leading up a slight rise through the trees. I looked down at the drawing again, turning in a circle to reorient myself. "I'm quite sure of it. Although I'm beginning to understand the man's look of confusion when I told him where we wanted to go. I'm wondering . . . ," I began. I took a step toward the rocky path. "He kept on repeating the word *brûle* and I thought he was trying to get us to stay for dessert. But now I'm left wondering if he really meant *burned*—as in burned ruins. Because that would certainly explain why we're not seeing turrets over the trees."

"True." Drew shoved his hands in his pockets and nodded at the path. "You up for a hike?"

I fought back disappointment. How were we to learn anything about a French spy inside the burned-out ruins of an ancient château? "We might as well. Maybe the view from the top will be nice." With a sigh of resignation, I headed toward the path, wishing I had my brogues instead of the strappy sandals Precious had made me wear. At least I'd won the battle over high heels versus low ones or else Drew would have to carry me. Which had probably been her idea all along.

Drew insisted on walking behind me in case I fell, and I kept my jumper on despite the sheen of perspiration clinging to my skin from the exertion. By the time we emerged from the forest, I was panting heavily. Drew showed no strain whatsoever, making me almost wish that I had asked to be carried.

Parts of the wall that had once encircled the castle and its outbuildings remained, a sporadic puzzle with enough stacked stone pieces to be able to envision the length and breadth of the old château. Here and there an abbreviated set of brick steps rose to empty spaces. But of the château itself, there was nothing but random bricks protruding from the earth like little raised hands to remind the world that it had once existed.

"It's rather sad, isn't it?" I asked, watching as Drew picked up a small stone from the grass, then carefully replaced it in the exact same spot.

He simply nodded, and I knew he understood what I'd meant.

How someone's history could be obliterated in the space of a single day, with only the vague lines in the dust to testify that anything had been there at all.

He indicated a simple white stone structure, nearly hidden by the shadow of the encroaching woods, its walls streaked with lichen, the masonry cross atop the peak of its gabled roof indicating its significance. "It appears that the chapel didn't share the same fate as the château despite being within the perimeter of the defensive wall."

"Come on," I said, walking toward it with renewed determination. "I don't want the destruction of my brand-new shoes to have been in vain." I hadn't meant it to be funny, but he smiled that devastating grin again anyway.

We climbed the front steps toward the arched door, the middle of each step sagging from the imprint of centuries of footsteps. He pushed open the door, hinges groaning, and a welcome respite of cool air from inside wrapped around us.

Our eyes met. "Do you believe in ghosts?" he asked.

I grimaced. "Not the dead kind." I stepped inside, ready to confront the other kind.

Drew allowed the door to shut behind us, making us blink in the darkness as our eyes adjusted from the bright daylight outside. It wasn't a large chapel, but the soaring ceiling lent it a grand airiness that made it appear bigger. A ribbed vault cradled an alcove at one end, where I imagined an altar had once stood. Ribbons of colored light slipped through the stained-glass windows behind it, gradually showing us two short rows of wooden pews facing the alcove. As I moved inside, I could see effigies lining the walls, narrowing the nave.

Disturbed dust rose from the ancient stone floor causing me to sneeze—rather loudly since I'd learned from my brothers.

"Bless you," Drew said at the same time another male voice said, "*À vos souhaits!*"

Startled, we both turned to look behind us in the narthex, where an old man, stooped with age and wearing a dark brown cassock and sandals, peered out at us from the gloom. He was so thin and bent I wasn't surprised that we'd overlooked him when we'd entered the chapel. A miasma of dust and disintegration clung to him like a garment, as if he were slowly moldering along with the ancient walls and floors.

I wasn't Catholic, but I wondered if we'd committed some sort of faux pas by not genuflecting or whatever they did. I'd had a Catholic friend at school and had been very perplexed by the list of rules of her faith that she'd shared with me and made me very glad I was Church of England.

The man didn't appear angry, merely curious as to our presence and began speaking in a barrage of French at Drew, who looked more confused than the old man. I shook my head and pointed at Drew. "Americain," I said in explanation, and the man nodded with understanding.

"I hope we are not intruding," I said in French, after introducing Drew and myself. "We were looking for the Château de Courcelles and have discovered this is all that is left."

"You are not intruding, madame. I am Monsieur le Curé, and have been associated with this chapel since I first took my vows as a lad. Sadly, the château is no more, and this chapel is no longer consecrated. Which is oddly fitting, seeing as how it was once used as a pigeon coop—hardly a way to honor such a place. The last Courcelles was lost in the most recent war and the property now belongs to the state. I just come to tidy up and pay my respects to le comte, Sigismund the First." He indicated the effigy of a man wearing medieval chain mail and holding a sword. A large wolfhound lay obediently at his feet. "He was a very great man, went on Crusade with Louis the Fat. He shouldn't be forgotten."

"You're right. He shouldn't be," I agreed wholeheartedly. I wanted to ask about the effigy next to him, apparently the great man's wife, and the fluffy little dog at her feet that seemed so out of place in the gloom. But my feet were hurting so I focused on my task. "Does anyone know what happened to the family?"

He shook his head, his eyes sad. "After the château was destroyed during the first war, there was no home for the family to return to. So they stayed away, although the taxes were still paid on the property. The Courcelles were a proud and old family. They would not walk away from their responsibilities. It was my understanding that the demoiselle would return one day to the château and rebuild what was once here. And then the Nazis invaded France, and the Courcelles were no more." He gave me a familiar Gallic shrug.

"The demoiselle?"

"Yes. The daughter of the family. She was the last of the line, you see. She had no brothers or sisters. So after she was gone, there was no one."

I translated for Drew, who nodded with interest, his attention focused on the stained glass in the alcove. "Ask him if he knows why Joan of Arc is featured in the window—if there's any significance there."

"*Oui*." Monsieur le Curé nodded sagely after I'd asked the question. "The comtesse was blessed by Saint Jeanne herself and when the saint was martyred, the comtesse obtained a relic of cloth dipped in the blood of the blessed saint and made it into a talisman. The talisman is very powerful, but only if held in the hands of the demoiselle. The legend dictates that it can only be passed down by females in the de Courcelles family, and that France will never fall as long as the demoiselle holds the talisman."

Drew's eyes narrowed as I translated. "Ask him where the talisman is now."

The curate waited for me to speak, then slowly shook his head. "It disappeared sometime in the last war. No one knows what happened to it."

Drew and I were silent for a moment, digesting this news, wondering how it all fit together. "One last question, if you don't mind," I said. "Have you ever heard of a connection between the famous spy of the French Resistance, La Fleur, and the Courcelles?"

His eyes widened in shock. "No, madame. And I would know, having been intimately acquainted with the family for so many years. I never met La Fleur. I would have known her if I had. It is said her eyes could kill a man with their intensity, and that she spit fire from her mouth." He made the sign of the cross. "It can't be blasphemy, as she was on God's side."

"Of course not." A loud rumble of hunger pains came from Drew, who was busily studying the ceiling. After a quick glance in his direction, I said, "Merci, Monsieur le Curé. You have been most helpful."

"Thank you for visiting. Please come back." He looked so singular and lonely that I almost promised that I would.

Instead I thanked him again then waited for Drew to say his goodbyes before we exited the chapel together, the bright sun nearly blinding us. His stomach let out another loud rumble.

"So," I said. "What do you think?"

"I think I'm hungry," he said. "And I can't think on an empty stomach. Let's go eat."

"But we just ate," I protested, following him back toward the path. "How can you possibly be hungry again?"

He stopped to grin at me, making something in my chest flutter. "Well, Babs, that's something you should know about me. I'm *always* hungry."

There was something in the way he'd said it that made the blood rush to my face. I quickly ducked my head, then led the way to the path, ignoring him until he reached for my hand, bringing me to a halt. I looked up into his eyes, wondering—or hoping—for something I could not name.

"It will be more slippery on the way down. Hold my hand so if you slide, I'll be there to keep you upright."

Too embarrassed to speak, I allowed him to wrap his large hand around mine and hold it until we'd reached the bottom of the path and entered the clearing, not daring to look at him until both of his hands were firmly on the steering wheel of the car, and we were headed to a café en route to Paris.

CHAPTER SEVENTEEN

Aurélie

The Château de Courcelles
Picardy, France
December 1914

I T WOULD HAVE been unthinkable in Paris, kissing Maximilian von Sternburg in a graveyard, at the dead of night. Kissing Maximilian von Sternburg anywhere, really. Not just because she was a well brought up young lady—well, somewhat well brought up—but because he was Herr von Sternburg, polite, attentive, reserved.

He wasn't reserved now.

Maybe it was because the rest of the world had been stripped away. Maybe it was because it was Christmas Eve, and a time for magic. Maybe it had always been there and she just hadn't seen it. He kissed her the way she drove a car, with complete assurance and more than a little recklessness. Aurélie found herself clinging to his shoulders, feeling as though they were careening down a mountain road, screeching along the corners, the wind in her hair and the world blurring around her, her pulse leaping, feeling alive, so very alive, dizzy and excited and drunk on it all.

He smelled of violets, like springtime in the midst of winter. His hair was surprisingly soft beneath her fingers, not slicked back and stiff with cream the way some men wore it. The ends tickled her palm.

Somehow, her hands found their way beneath his greatcoat, under his scratchy uniform jacket. She could feel the warmth of his skin beneath the linen of his shirt, not cold at all, but warm, so warm, his muscles shifting beneath her fingers—who knew a scholar could be so well-muscled—the whole animal apparatus of him that she had never noticed before, had never allowed herself to notice, because it was his mind one noticed first, his clever, clever mind. But under it all, all the learning, was this, this animal drive, that pulled them flesh to flesh and stripped her raw with pure, physical desire.

"Aurélie. *Aurélie.*" Max pulled back, his voice hoarse, shaking. "Wait."

"What?" She rather minded the interruption. She felt cold without him, suddenly aware of the mess of her hair and the fact that her shawl was hanging drunkenly from one shoulder. She didn't want to talk. She just wanted to go on like this, not thinking, not having to think. She held a finger to his lips. "Whatever it is, don't."

He kissed her finger, took her hand in his and pressed a kiss to her palm, before, reluctantly, folding his hand around hers. "There's something you need to know."

"What can possibly be that important?" The magic was fading. It was midnight again and cold and the graveyard was sere and grim, the stumps of the old trees raw and ugly. "Do you have a wife back in Berlin?"

"What? No! Nothing like that! Do you think I would . . . no!"

"Men do."

"I don't." Before Aurélie could feel the relief of it, Max blurted out, "I was the one who told the major about your talisman."

Aurélie leaned as far back as she could, squinting at him in the moonlight. "You . . . what?"

"I was the one who told him. About the talisman and the jewels and the legend around it . . . I never meant you to be harmed by it. I had thought we would move on in a few days, a week, at most. And you and the talisman were safely back in Paris. . . ."

Except that she had come from Paris and the talisman with her. Aurélie felt rumpled and scattered and thoroughly confused. "I don't understand. Why would you tell him about the talisman?"

There'll be fortune hunters, her mother had warned her once. *Men who want what you have.* Not her personal charms. It was clear her mother hadn't meant that. But the jewels that were part of her patrimony. The jewels embedded in the talisman.

"It seemed to make sense at the time," said Max helplessly. "The major was going to destroy the château. One less center of resistance, he said. He meant to find a pretext to torch the castle and your father in it. So I told him—I told him there was a treasure hidden in the walls. He didn't know Paris well enough to know that the talisman is the centerpiece of your mother's salon. That isn't his world. But he liked the sound of priceless jewels—and mystical powers."

"You told him it was here." So much began to make sense. All those veiled comments. Hoffmeister's determination to oust her from her quarters. She wondered if he had yanked the boiseries from the walls, torn up the boards from the floor.

Max grasped her cold hands. "I only meant to prevent him destroying the château. He had meant to place headquarters in Le Catelet, but once he heard there was a treasure at Courcelles . . . I wanted you to have a home to come back to."

"You're saying you did this for me?" She didn't know whether to be touched or appalled. "You're saying all of this—this occupation—is because of me?"

"No! Courcelles would have been occupied anyway. Just by other people. And the castle would have been destroyed and all its history lost."

Her father in it, he had said. Yes, she could see her father refusing to leave his citadel, immolating himself on a principle. "So this was meant as a kindness, then?"

She must have sounded as incredulous as she felt. "Don't you think I'd go back and change it if I could? There's so much I would change if I could. I lie there at night wishing I'd gone back to Paris before all this started so that I might have told you—"

"Told me?"

It was as though her voice recalled him to their circumstances. She felt his sudden stillness, his indecision.

Quietly, without inflection, he said, "That I love you."

Without the sound of the guns, the night was painfully quiet and still, the air sharp with frost. "Love."

"Love," repeated Max. His hands tightened on hers. "Do you think I don't realize what effrontery it is to speak the word to you here? If I had come back to Paris, if I had spoken before, I might have said something without the sentiment being loathsome to you. But now . . . How can it be anything but an imposition?"

Aurélie registered the passionate tone of his voice, the press of his hands, but the words themselves seemed to ricochet around her like billiard balls, all scattershot.

"Love," she said again.

"It seems an absurdity, I know, here, in these circumstances. I wouldn't have said anything . . . I didn't mean to say anything . . . but . . . you kissed me," he said, and it sounded like a question. It was a question. And Aurélie didn't have an answer for it.

Love.

What did she know of love?

Oh Lord. It had been one thing to walk with Lieutenant von Sternburg, to allow him her company and pretend it was duty, pretend she was doing it for what gleanings she might gain for the war effort.

Pretend she didn't enjoy his company, didn't look forward to the sound of his voice, the feel of his arm through hers as they strolled.

But love . . .

"It's late. I should be getting back." Aurélie stood so abruptly she almost tripped over her basket.

"I see," said Max, but she knew he didn't see, not at all. How could he when she didn't understand herself? But he mastered his emotions all the same, standing at once. "I'll see you to the keep."

"There's no need." The path up the hill had never seemed longer. How could she walk it with Max beside her, feeling whatever it was between them, knowing how he felt? It was impossible. "I know the way."

"I don't doubt that. It's just that the sentry is less likely to shoot you if you're with me."

"Yes, but he'll think . . ." The sentry would think they'd been doing exactly what they'd been doing. The memory of their kiss, of the power of it, made her voice unnecessarily harsh as she said, "He'll think I'm your trollop. Just another French whore."

Max stiffened, every bit the outraged Prussian nobleman. "You can't imagine I would ever let anyone think—"

What a damnable mess it all was. Aurélie began walking, faster and faster, too fast, her words crisp and sharp as frost. "You can't control their thoughts. And why should they think otherwise? It's common enough. A bit of real coffee, a pair of silk stockings . . . chocolate for the children."

Max hurried to catch up to her. "Do you think I expect payment . . . in any kind? It was for the children, of my own account. I would never—"

His goodness shamed her. She was ashamed of herself, of everything. "I know you wouldn't. But other men haven't your scruples. Or your kindness. Haven't you noticed the world is made of wolves?"

They walked in silence for a moment. Max said, in a low voice, "I never meant to put you in an impossible position."

How had he thought it anything but impossible? He was German; she was French. It was as simple as that. At least, it was supposed to be. Oh yes, he might try to steal a kiss, that was the sort of thing the conqueror did, but she wasn't meant to kiss him. Or enjoy it. And he wasn't meant to speak of love. He certainly wasn't supposed to mean it.

"When did you decide you loved me?" The words escaped her before she could think better of them.

"I'm not sure I would call it a decision." They walked in silence a moment more, before he said, "It was a Tuesday in May, a year and a half ago. I'd come to your mother's salon because I was told it was one of the sights of Paris, like the Comédie Française or the Tour Eiffel. That didn't come out quite right, did it? Rather, I should say, I was told that her salon was a cultural experience, that in her suite in the Ritz, one met all the cleverest writers and wisest men, all the most eloquent poets and visionary painters. I came for that, thinking I would visit once so that I might say I had, and then never come again."

"Are you going to say you saw me and loved me?" said Aurélie doubtfully.

"No, nothing like that. Not that one wouldn't," he added hastily. "But I've never understood men who are struck by a pair of fine eyes not bothering to know what's going on behind them. No. It was about an hour after I had arrived. Monsieur Proust was reading from his manuscript, and you were standing in the back of the room, commenting. I nearly snorted madeleine up my nose."

Aurélie had never heard anyone refer so tenderly to the occasion of getting food up one's nose. "I didn't know," she said.

"I tried not to choke too obviously," said Max gravely. "But I came back again to your mother's salon for you, to see what you would say next. Sometimes you weren't there, but mostly you were."

"Standing in the back of the room." She had never noticed, at least, not consciously, how often Maximilian von Sternburg had found his way to the back of the room beside her. If she had considered it, she would have thought only that the best seats, the sofas and settees and spindly Louis XV chairs, were already taken as of right by her mother's regulars. "You came for me?"

"If I had wanted poets, I might have found them at any café," said Max. "But you were only to be found at the Ritz, so to the Ritz I came. If not for Elisabeth . . ."

The grief in his voice was so palpable that Aurélie, without thinking, put her hand on his arm. The touch went through her like a shock. Never mind that she'd walked arm in arm with him a hundred times before. It felt different now. Dangerous.

"I'm sorry," she said, and she wasn't only talking about his sister.

She wrapped her hands in the folds of her shawl, as if she could blot out the memory of his skin. The sentry was watching them from his box. She had no doubt what he was thinking.

She blurted out, "I don't think we should see so much of each other anymore."

Max went very still. She could see him looking at her, trying to read her face. "If that's what you want."

It wasn't, not at all, but that was precisely why she needed to stay away from him. At least as much as one could within a set of medieval walls.

Max said something to the sentry in German, a command, and then turned and bowed stiffly to her. "Goodnight, Mademoiselle de Courcelles."

He turned, but not toward the keep. Away, back toward the bare hill and the sleeping village, where no church bells rang.

"Wait," said Aurélie, knowing it was weakness to prolong their parting. "Where are you going?"

He seemed very remote, and very German, in his big greatcoat and uniform cap. "To deliver your packages."

Aurélie bit her lip, remembering the basket, abandoned by the bench. Her duty, forgotten. "I thought Father Christmas had come already."

Max looked at her steadily. "These children deserve all the joy they can get, in small packages or large. And how could I not—after you risked so much?"

She thought of those pitiful little packets of nuts, scattered when the basket had fallen in the heat of their kiss. "So much for so little, you mean."

"It isn't little, to care." Max's eyes were very bright in the moonlight. He doffed his cap to her, the torchlight glinting off his silver-gilt hair. "Joyeux Noël, Mademoiselle de Courcelles."

Avoiding the eyes of the sentry, Aurélie began walking rapidly across the courtyard, back toward the new wing. No, it wasn't so little, to care. Not at all. And that was what scared her.

THERE WAS A hollow place where Max von Sternburg had been. Aurélie hadn't realized how much time she spent with him, how much she relied upon his company, until he wasn't there anymore. January shivered into February, cold, bitter cold, her ears numb to the sound of distant shelling, her hands perpetually covered with chilblains. The coal had been diverted to Germany, the trees in the forest felled to make planks to line trenches. The walls of the castle had never seemed so gray, or the world so bare.

It might have been better had she had an occupation, if there were fields to till or crops to harvest, but this was the quiet time of year, when the ground was frozen hard. If there had been wool, she might have spun—if one of the women had taught her. There was mending to do, always, but Suzanne was a far better hand with a needle than she. Hoffmeister hadn't thought to forbid her the books in the library, so she read, puzzling over difficult words, wishing she had applied herself more to her studies, trying to avoid the suspicion that she was striving, in some strange way, to impress Max von Sternburg, even though she went out of her way to avoid him and he her.

She tried to find her father, but he, too, proved remarkably elusive. That he was engaged on some grand project, she had no doubt. That he didn't trust her enough to include her, she also knew, and it stung. He was protecting her, she told herself, but she didn't really believe it, not entirely.

In the end, Aurélie took refuge in the chapel, going on her knees on the worn old stones engraved with the names of long-dead Courcelles. She tried to pray, but her thoughts remained stubbornly of the earth. In her strange, solitary childhood, she had come to the chapel frequently. She would evade her governess and sit on the floor beside the effigy of the first countess, absently stroking the carved fur of the lady's lapdog as she poured out all her thoughts and concerns to her ancestress. Aurélie had never thought herself fanciful, but sometimes she imagined she could see the lady herself, standing there insubstantial in the shade, smiling down at her in the warm silence.

But that had been summer, always summer, when the air was sweet with the scent of roses and jewel-toned light fell through the old stained-glass windows, dappling everything with color. Try though she might, Aurélie could find no sense of presence here now, either human or divine. Where was the Lord, to have visited such horrors upon them? The children of the village grew wasted, frail. Where were her ancestors, as Germans reveled in their keep, shaming their shades? Where was her father, keeping her in ignorance when she burned to do something, anything?

She felt lost, deserted by everyone on whom she had relied.

Everyone except the one person she had the least reason to trust.

Love. It was absurd to think of love at a time like this. She shouldn't be thinking it. It made her chest hurt and her head ache.

"It was a Tuesday in May," he had said, sounding sure, so sure. No wild declarations of passion, just that calm certainty.

So sure in his love for her.

For her.

Jean-Marie loved her, Aurélie knew, but he loved her because it was expected. He loved her because their families had known each other for generations. He loved her because it was less bother than finding a wife for himself.

But Max had no obligations to her, no ties of family or history. If he loved her—Aurélie made sure to stress that *if*—it was purely because of some quality in her. Because there was something about her that called to him. Or something he thought called to him.

She had to keep telling herself that, because if she were to allow herself to believe that he saw her, truly saw her, as he had seen her in the corner of her mother's salon, away from the throng, impatient with their philosophies, and still loved her anyway—that was heady and dangerous stuff, and she shouldn't be allowing herself to consider even the possibility of it, not with a German, not when she was all but promised, never mind that she'd never felt any more passion for Jean-Marie than he felt for her.

Certainly nothing like the passion she'd felt on Christmas Eve, in the churchyard, with Max von Sternburg.

Aurélie rested her forehead against the cold stone of the countess's pet dog, praying for clarity, for a sign, for anything.

The cold wind whistled through the cracks in the windows. And then Aurélie heard a noise that wasn't the wind at all.

She froze against the stone, her body chilled and alert at the same time.

There was a flutter and a cooing noise. Slowly, Aurélie lifted her head—to see a white pigeon perched on the breastplate of Sigismund the First.

For a moment, all disbelief fled. Here was fairy tale, indeed. A sign from her ancestors. A dove bearing—a metal canister?

Sense returned with a vengeance. This wasn't a metaphor or a message. Not that sort of message, in any event. This was a carrier pigeon, banned on pain of death, bearing intelligence, and if Hoffmeister found it here, they'd all pay for it.

"Hello," said Aurélie to the pigeon. "If I may?"

The pigeon submitted to having its cylinder removed. Inside was a tiny scrap of foolscap, rolled into a scroll thinner than a knitting needle. Aurélie was just about unroll it when a shadow fell across the nave.

Hastily, Aurélie placed herself between the intruder and the pigeon, as though that would make any difference.

"Father! Thank goodness," she said. "I thought—"

"The German dogs would never come in here," said her father dismissively. He wasn't, Aurélie noticed, as well groomed as usual. His valet had gone for a soldier back in August, and Victor, while enthusiastic, was hardly skilled. There were nicks on her father's chin, clumsily covered with sticking plaster. But his manner was as imperious as ever. He held out a hand. "I believe that message is intended for me."

Aurélie didn't surrender it. "You should be more careful. What if someone else had found it?"

"Who else comes here? Monsieur le Curé?" Her father gave a snort. "He prefers to practice his devotions in the comfort of the green salon. That pig of a major? He doesn't want the stench of papistry on his skin."

"He'd risk it if he knew what you were keeping in here." The pigeon was pecking at the count's breastplate as one who had pecked there before. A bell tower with no bell, close to her father, under the Germans' very nose. "You are keeping the birds here, aren't you? I ought to have guessed it before. I'm amazed no one else has."

"Why would they?" There was a warning in her father's voice. "Are you planning to inform him?"

Aurélie drew herself up very straight, one hand on the countess's stone foot. "How could you suggest such a thing?"

Her father regarded her narrowly. "Pillow talk, perhaps?"

"I'm not on those terms with any of our captors," said Aurélie, trying not to think of Christmas Eve and the kiss. That had been a long time ago. Max had been true to his word; he had stayed away as she had asked. "Besides, you were the one who wanted me to get close to Lieutenant von Sternburg!"

"Ought I to have specified how close?" Her father appeared every inch the grand seigneur, looking down his nose at her. "I saw you returning together on Christmas Eve."

"He was trying to keep me from getting shot, that's all." After her father had all but pushed her into the line of the guns. Did he want her a martyr for France? It was a decidedly disconcerting thought, that her father might think her of more use dead than alive. Aurélie swallowed over a lump in her throat. "Whatever you're suggesting, I assure you, it isn't the case. Lieutenant von Sternburg is . . . *was* a friend."

"No. He's the enemy." Her father snapped his fingers at the paper in her hand. "I'll take that."

Aurélie glanced down at the paper with its tiny writing. It was coded, of course, but she recognized the hand, the distinctive angle of the 4, the lack of a central slash on the 7. She looked up at her father in surprise. "This is my mother's writing."

Her father looked annoyed at being questioned. "And what if it is?"

All these weeks, wondering if her mother knew she was alive, feeling both guilty and irritated by her own guilt, trying to convince herself her mother didn't care, while knowing that she did . . . And, all the while, her father had been communicating with her mother and never bothered to tell her.

Aurélie clutched the bit of paper. Maybe it was her imagination, but she could smell her mother's perfume, the scent made just for her by the house of Caron. "I hadn't thought that you and my mother were on writing terms."

"They say war makes strange bedfellows." Her father made an expansive gesture with one tweed-clad arm. "Just because I can't live with your mother doesn't mean I don't have the greatest admiration for her abilities. Why do you think I let her have charge of you?"

"Because I wasn't a son."

She'd never said it, never even allowed herself to think it, but there it was. Her mother, her despised mother, had wanted her. Her father hadn't.

Her father clasped his hands behind his back, looking distinctly uncomfortable. "A girl needs her mother."

"A mother who isn't received because her husband won't live with her? They shunned me in the Faubourg. They treated me like a mongrel. If you had been there—" Years of hurt came pouring out. Her father never thought of her, not then, not now. She was crushing the precious message in her hand. Aurélie forced herself to relax her fingers, before she smudged the writing beyond repair. "If you admired my mother so much, why couldn't you bring yourself to live with her?"

"Your mother was the one who left me," her father snapped.

That wasn't quite how Aurélie remembered it. She remembered the fights about everything, about her mother's friends, her dress, her lack of refinement. And her mother fighting back with complaints about her father's mistresses, his gambling, his horses. She would, her father had told her, in the ultimate insult, have understood if she were French. And, somehow, they had been left alone in the great house in the Faubourg. Her father's brushes and shaving soap had disappeared from his dressing room, along with the valet who had let Aurélie build houses out of her father's used playing cards and sniff all the mysterious lotions in his dressing case. He had gone on an extended trip, and the next thing Aurélie knew the house had been shut up around them and she and her mother had, like refugees, taken up residence in the Ritz, where her mother's Americanness wasn't quite so foreign.

"That was all a long time ago," said her father, as if it could be dismissed so easily as that. "Your mother and I understand each other. May I have the message?"

"Will you tell me what's in it?" Aurélie asked.

"Nothing you need to know."

Just as she hadn't needed to know all those years ago. Go back to the nursery, they had told her. This is no matter for little girls. But it *was*. It was her life, her country, her concern.

"I could be a help to you," Aurélie said. "I want to be a help to you."

Her father put a hand on her shoulder. It was the sort of gesture that would once have made her wiggle like a puppy wagging its tail. "You are a help to me," he said. "Your work in the village—it keeps the little major in a stew. And as long as he's looking the wrong way . . . the real work can go on."

"That's all I've been? A distraction?" She wondered what it was he had done on Christmas Eve, that he had needed to chivy her down to the village, a decoy. She had thought it was because she was his daughter, the lady of the house, carrying on in the fine tradition of the ladies of Courcelles. Because these were her people, too. But, no. She was just a distraction. A pawn.

"Not just a distraction," said her father, plucking the note from her limp hand. "An excellent distraction. Your friend was the only one with brains enough to have noticed what we're doing, but you've kept him in such a froth, he scarcely remembers his own name."

He smiled at her approvingly, but Aurélie didn't feel the warmth of it. Her chest felt tight, as though she'd received a blow.

"We?" she echoed. "What we're doing?"

"Don't ask me more," said her father, as though she were six again and begging for sweets. "The less you know, the safer it is."

Safer for whom?

Aurélie watched her father go, wondering just what it would take to make him trust her—and if he had ever viewed her as truly his own.

CHAPTER EIGHTEEN

Daisy

Jardin des Tuileries
Paris, France
July 1942

MADELEINE BESTRODE HER horse calmly, but Olivier wouldn't sit still. He kept turning and pointing as the carousel went around, laughing and straining and almost falling off. Daisy, her nerves shredded, kept starting forward from the bench, but Legrand stopped her.

"You have to trust them," he said. "You have to let them make mistakes."

"Easy to say when they're not your own."

Legrand removed his hand from her elbow and leaned forward, resting his forearms on his thighs. "That's true."

"I'm sorry. That's not what I meant."

He twiddled his thumbs for a moment, staring at the carousel as it revolved endlessly before them. The delighted screams of children. Mere yards away, the German staff cars rolled up and down rue de Rivoli, across the Place de la Concorde, ferrying the enemy from café to office to luxury hotel, but here in the Tuileries, in front of the ancient carousel, you could almost pretend that Paris was as it had always been, that the occupation was just a terrible dream. That you were just sitting here on this bench to watch your children play, and that the man beside you was not some agent for the Resistance that you met by arrangement, but your lover, your husband, the father of these children you watched together.

"My parents left me to my own devices, more or less," said Legrand. "They were both artists."

"Yes, I remember. Your father was a writer, and your mother a painter."

"Yes. Well. They were devoted firstly to their creative passions and secondly to each other. Children came a rather distant third."

"I'm sorry."

"Don't be. We knew they loved us, and we had each other. I learned how to fend for myself, how to get myself out of scrapes. And I never had to strain against the straitjacket of parental expectations, or whatever you want to call it. They allowed us to become pretty much whatever we pleased."

As he spoke, Daisy stared at his latticed fingers, and the gold of the signet ring that glimmered dully between them. The two swans, necks entwined. She thought of her own childhood within the walls of the Ritz, which had sometimes felt like a playground—if a decidedly adult playground—and other times like a prison.

"Then you were fortunate," she said. "I grew up always in the shadow of my grandmother. And my mother, who had all my grandmother's love, so that Grandmère never really forgave me for living when my *maman* had not. The Demoiselle de Courcelles, the last in a long line of heroic women, whom I could never hope to equal."

"No, that's true. You aren't their equal."

Daisy looked away.

"You're not your mother or your grandmother, or any of these ancestors who lived before you. You're yourself." Legrand straightened and put his hand on his leg, so that his pinky finger nearly touched the side of her thigh. "You're Daisy, astonishing and irreplaceable. A formidable woman."

He said the word exactly as a Frenchman might, *formidable,* with exactly a Frenchman's meaning. Daisy blinked her eyes several times.

"What have I done that's so astonishing?" she said. "I've delivered a few papers. I've slept with my husband in order to get some information from him. Hardly the actions of a formidable woman."

"No? Whereas I sat in my room last night and forged a few papers and drank myself to sleep. Of the two of us, you are much the more heroic."

"I felt like a whore."

"You're not a whore."

"I said I felt like one. I hated him the whole time."

"He didn't hurt you, did he? Force you?"

There was a new, terrible note in Legrand's voice as he said this, and it thawed her a little, although it also showed he hadn't really understood her meaning at all. Daisy looked at the narrow seam of bench between her left leg, which was covered decorously by a floral dress, and Legrand's right leg, much thicker and covered in trousers of light wool. "Of course not," she said. "He didn't need to. I just lay back and let him do what he wanted. Just as I was supposed to do."

He leaned forward again, arms on legs, staring at the carousel. Daisy thought she heard a groan from the back of his throat, but she might have been mistaken. It might have been the wind in the trees, or some ancient gear in the carousel.

"Anyway, it wasn't all in vain," she said.

"Wasn't it?"

"Of course not. He was drunk, and I got him to talk a little. He's keeping something in his safe."

"Keeping what?"

She shrugged. "He wouldn't say, and I didn't think it prudent to press him. But it's something to do with his project at work."

"The roundup."

"So we must assume. It fits, anyway."

Legrand was wearing his favorite hat, a newsboy's cap, which Daisy always thought looked a little bit too English, not the kind of hat a Frenchman would wear. She'd warned him, but he always said he liked the cap too much to give it up. It was comfortable, he said. Now he took the brim between his thumb and forefinger and worried it up and down, as if it weren't comfortable at all. "What kind of safe?" he asked. "Does it have a key?"

"No, it's a combination lock. I don't know the numbers."

"But that's no trouble at all. I can crack it, if you can get me inside."

"Inside the apartment, you mean? My apartment?"

"Yes." Legrand paused. "It's going to be tricky, though, sneaking in during the day. Especially if the children are there. How late does Pierre work?"

Daisy linked her hands neatly in her lap. She wasn't wearing gloves, because of the heat, and her finger joints were pale and tense. The smell of pipe tobacco drifted from the clothes of the man beside her. Around and around the carousel went. Her children passed by in flashes, in a blur, out of focus. Her mouth was dry. She had been anticipating this moment. She had been anticipating this question of timing and logistics, ever since Pierre had mentioned the safe, and also something else, as he had lifted himself off her last night and straightened his trousers and shirt: another piece of interesting information that had made her heart stop for a second or two. Now she found she couldn't quite put the words together to answer Legrand's perfectly reasonable query.

After a moment, Legrand straightened and looked at her. She felt his blue gaze on her cheek. "Daisy?" he said.

She replied, in as normal a tone as she could manage, "Actually, there's no trouble to do this at night. Pierre leaves for Vichy this afternoon. He'll be there until Friday. I could have the children stay with Grandmère, so they don't talk."

There was a brief silence before he answered. "That would serve."

"Shall we say tonight, then?"

He started to answer her, but in the next second he bolted from the bench. Daisy jumped to her feet and watched in confusion as he leapt toward the carousel, arms outstretched, and scooped something from the air that turned out to be Olivier. He set the boy down on his little lean legs atop the dusty ground. Daisy made a cry of distress and rushed to take her son in her arms.

"Just in the nick," Legrand muttered in English, but he was smiling.

The carousel slowed and stopped, and Madeleine jumped off in tearful distress. "I tried to stop him!"

"It's all right, darling. Monsieur Legrand caught him in time."

"It's just the kind of trouble I used to get into, when I was a boy," said Legrand. He looked at Daisy and winked. "The bane of my mother's nerves, I was."

Daisy buried her nose in Olivier's hair and inhaled his sweet, little-boy scent. But he was already pulling away, wanting to run down the gravel toward some new mischief. Daisy got to her feet and went after him, glad for the distraction. Otherwise she would have agonized over the way her son had narrowly escaped disaster at the exact instant she had invited Legrand to visit her apartment, knowing her husband would be away.

LEGRAND RETURNED TO the bookshop and Daisy continued to the Ritz, where she and the children were to have lunch with Grandmère in her suite. By the time she got the children through the rue Cambon entrance (they still couldn't quite understand why they weren't allowed to enter through the front and chose this instance to complain about it) and then up the stairs and down the various corridors, the waiters had already delivered the meal under shining silver domes. Grandmère sat at the dining table, drinking her wine and laughing with a companion, who rose and straightened his jacket as a hot, frazzled Daisy bustled the children into the room.

"Madame Villon," he said politely, but he was looking at Madeleine and Olivier, who spilled across the carpet toward their great-grandmother.

"Lieutenant colonel!"

Max von Sternburg wasn't wearing his uniform, because German officers weren't supposed to do so on the civilian side of the Ritz. Still he managed to look impressive in his double-breasted suit and gleaming silver-gold hair, his stern features and the shiny, rippling scar that disfigured the side of his face. He waited for the children to tumble past before he stepped toward Daisy and took her hand.

"It's a great pleasure to see you again," he said gravely.

"Is it? You don't look especially pleased."

That made him smile a little, at least from one side of his mouth. "But I assure you, I have looked forward to seeing you again for some weeks. Since that enchanting dinner party in May, in fact, I have thought of little else."

He held on to her hand as he said this and led her forward to the dining table, where Grandmère embraced the children and brushed the Tuileries dust from their clothes. She looked up as Max settled Daisy into a chair, and her eyebrows shot skyward in no small bemusement.

"Enchanting? I'm afraid your memory must be showing its age," said Daisy.

Grandmère, who had just lifted her wineglass to her lips, sputtered into the Bordeaux.

"Perhaps I misspoke a little," replied Von Sternburg. "It was not the party itself that was enchanting, but its hostess."

Now Grandmère recovered herself and sat back in her chair, revolving the wine in its glass. She looked from Daisy to Von Sternburg, who circled the table, pulling out chairs for Madeleine and Olivier, whom he seated with the same grave courtesy he showed their mother. "I'm sorry I missed all the fun," Grandmère said.

"There wasn't any fun, don't worry," said Daisy. "I spilled my wine, and Pierre . . ." She was going to say that Pierre had insulted her in front of all the guests, but she remembered the children just in time and checked herself.

"And Monsieur Villon did his best to entertain his friends," Von Sternburg finished for her. "May I offer you wine, madame?"

Daisy pushed her wineglass forward a few centimeters. "Please. I'll do my best not to spill it."

Again Grandmère started and looked back and forth between them, but Von Sternburg seemed not to notice anything out of the ordinary. He returned to his seat and politely answered some question Olivier posed to him. Grandmère, recovering her composure, drank some more wine and said to Daisy, "I'm sorry to have surprised you with our guest. Herr von Sternburg found me in the lobby this morning and reminded me of a previous acquaintance."

"A previous acquaintance?"

"I used to visit your grandmother's salon here, before the war," said Von Sternburg. "The previous war, I mean. Of course, that was in her old suite. Not the war, of course, but the salon."

"And I told him that I remember him well," said Grandmère.

"Which was not true at all," Von Sternburg said, "but terribly polite of her. I didn't speak much, I must admit. I was only there to observe."

"Observe what, I wonder?"

Von Sternburg shrugged. "I was a young man in Paris at an interesting time. There was so much to fascinate me. But then my sister died, and I returned home to Germany. I doubt anyone noticed my absence."

"And now here you are," said Daisy. "Returned in triumph. The great Teutonic conqueror. It must be so satisfying for you."

"Immensely satisfying, but not—I suspect—for the reasons you think." He was looking at Madeleine as he said this, frowning a little. He twiddled the stem of his wineglass between his thumb and forefinger and said, "I have a little confession to make."

"Oh?" said Grandmère. "The interesting kind, I hope."

He turned to her and smiled, but it was not an especially happy smile. "Interesting to me, at least. Did you know I was billeted at the Château de Courcelles at the beginning of the last war?"

Daisy made a little gasp. Grandmère narrowed her eyes.

"I don't believe I did. You must have known my daughter, then."

"I knew her well. Who could not admire the fine spirit of the Demoiselle de Courcelles?"

"Who, indeed?" Grandmère said softly. She tilted her head. "I certainly hope you were not still there during the terrible fire."

"A night I have spent years trying to forget."

"How dreadful. But surely this is not how you acquired that unfortunate cicatrice?" Grandmère motioned to the side of her own face.

"It is."

"I'm sorry to hear it. You must have been very badly injured. Such wounds are dangerous, I understand, and difficult to heal."

He shrugged. "At first, the doctors thought I might not live. I wanted very much to survive, however, and proved them wrong. But I learned there are scars one bears on the inside rather than the outside, and sometimes these are the most painful of all. The slowest to heal, at any rate."

Von Sternburg was not smiling now. He hadn't touched his wine, either, at least since Daisy had entered the room. Just washed it around the sides of his glass. Madeleine and Olivier, utterly awed by his presence, sat on either side of Daisy and ate their sandwiches quietly, round eyed, watching the volleys back and forth as one might watch a tennis match.

"It is all a matter of perspective, of course," said Grandmère. "Some would say that the occupiers get what they deserve. That these scars you speak of—"

"I beg your pardon," Daisy broke in. "Do you mean to say that you *knew my mother?* That you occupied her château?"

"Yes, it's true."

"And you said nothing to me of this before?"

"I told you I had heard of her. But it took me a little by surprise, you see, when your husband announced this connection at the dinner party. And I did not wish to discompose you in public with my importunate questions."

"How kind of you."

"But I have been reflecting, you see, over these past weeks. I have been thinking about those months at the château, and the time that came earlier, when I was in Paris before the war, a time I count among the happiest days of my life—"

"Surely not," said Grandmère. "Surely you have since married and had a family."

He stared at her. "In fact, I have not."

"I am sorry to hear that. My daughter, as you know, was fortunate to escape the horror of German occupation and the terrible fire that destroyed her ancestral home, to make her way to Paris, God be praised, and to marry a good French husband and bear his child, though poor Monsieur d'Aubigny was killed soon after. But at least those two had some joy together, fleeting though it was. She deserved it, after all she had endured at the hands of the Germans."

"I have no doubt of that. And when the product of this union is a woman so charming as Madame Villon, who can begrudge them their happiness?" said Von Sternburg.

"Who, indeed." Grandmère rose from the table. "Children! *If* you have finished your sandwiches, we shall now play at cards."

BUT OLIVIER DID not want to play some stupid cards. He was hot and fretful and restless and wanted to go back to the park. Max von Sternburg bent on one knee before him.

"I suppose you want to go on the carousel, young man," he said. "Isn't that right?"

"Yes, sir."

"But a ride on the carousel costs two francs, doesn't it? Have you got two francs?"

"No, sir."

"Hmm." Von Sternburg peered at Olivier's right ear, and then his left. "That's strange," he said.

"What's strange, sir?"

Von Sternburg reached behind Olivier's ear and drew out a coin. "It seems you've been hiding something from us, eh?"

Olivier squealed and clapped his hand over his ear. Madeleine ran over and clamored, "Check my ear, Herr von Sternburg!"

"Hmm. I don't know." He looked carefully at her right ear. "No, I'm sorry, there's nothing there. It's a very pretty ear, of course, but I'm afraid it doesn't . . . now, wait a moment . . . hold very still . . ."

Olivier jumped up and down. Madeleine tried very hard not to move, but her mouth twitched and twitched. Von Sternburg took a piece of her brown hair in his fingers and tucked it gently behind the curve of her ear, the better to peer inside.

"Here we are!" he said triumphantly, and out came a coin from

Madeleine's ear. He presented it before her, and she stared at him in astonishment.

"For me?" she breathed.

"Of course it's yours. Did it not come from your own ear?" He turned back to Olivier and handed him the first coin. "As for *you*, young fellow. You will now take better care of this valuable object, won't you? Not go leaving it carelessly inside your ear again?"

Olivier was giggling so hard, he could hardly speak. "Yes, sir!"

"Very good." Von Sternburg glanced at Daisy and lifted an eyebrow. She found herself nodding. He turned back to the children and lifted the scattered deck of cards from the sofa table, which he gathered in a stack between his long, elegant fingers. The children watched, mesmerized, as he spread them out in a fan. "Now, let's see. These playing cards of yours. A very interesting pack. These are pictures of France's great heroes, aren't they? That's Henri Quatre, and there's . . . er, Robespierre. And who's this, Mademoiselle Madeleine?"

"Joan of Arc!" she exclaimed.

"Very good. Now, mademoiselle. I should very much like you to do me the favor of selecting a card from this stack. Yes, yes. Quite at random . . ."

Daisy folded her arms and turned to Grandmère. She spoke in a voice that was soft enough to go unheard, but not so soft as to draw suspicion. "Can you keep them with you tonight?"

"Of course. Why?"

"You'll find out tomorrow, I hope." She watched Madeleine—her grave, reserved Madeleine!—pluck a card eagerly from the array. Her face was round and soft with excitement. Von Sternburg's eyes were closed, as if he were concentrating very hard, or else drawing inspiration from the ether. In the same quiet voice, Daisy said, "I have a book for you in my handbag."

"That's wonderful. From that lovely bookshop?"

"Yes, the one on rue Volney."

"Splendid. I've been needing a good book lately."

Both children squealed and turned to each other, jiggling up and down. Apparently Von Sternburg had guessed Madeleine's card correctly. Daisy uncrossed her arms and padded to the commode near the door, where she had dropped her handbag upon entering the suite. She rummaged inside. Behind her, Von Sternburg was explaining to Madeleine, with faultless logic, how he had known she picked the seven of hearts. Daisy's brain was still a little numb with the knowledge that this man, this German officer, had known her mother. Had briefly occupied the Château de Courcelles with her, during the war. All those stories about her mother's heroism—had he witnessed them firsthand? The abuse she had suffered? The pigeons, the chapel, the great fire? The terrible Courcelles fire that had destroyed her ancestral home—*this* was what had caused that terrible scar on his face? She had a thousand questions, and she couldn't think of a single one to ask him.

She found the book and slid it free from the handbag, and she saw that her hands were shaking. With anger? Why hadn't he told her, why hadn't he said something? My God. He had known her mother; he had seen her daily, probably, when Daisy hadn't known her mother at all. She couldn't remember the curve of her mother's cheek, or the sound of her voice, all those precious things a daughter craves from a mother, but this damned German could. Von Sternburg could remember them. He had no *right,* she thought. No right to her mother, when Daisy herself had nothing of her, not a single memory. The book turned blurry. Daisy blinked her eyes and returned to Grandmère.

"Here." She thrust the volume into Grandmère's hands. "It's what you wanted, isn't it?"

Grandmère turned it over. The leather binding gleamed in the hot sunlight that spilled through the nearby window. "Thank you. One of my favorites."

"Ah, *The Scarlet Pimpernel*," said Von Sternburg.

Daisy started. He had moved like a ghost, this tall, sturdy German, rising from the rug and joining them without a sound, while the children remained near the sofa and exclaimed over the cards, burrowing through the deck to discover his secret. Now he ran his finger over the letters on the ancient binding in Grandmère's hands.

"English books are so rare in this city," he said.

"It's nice to read in my native language, from time to time," said Grandmère.

"Yes, of course. You were born in America, I remember. May I?" He didn't stop for permission, but rather drew the book from Grandmère's fingers and settled the spine in his palm while his other hand thumbed through the pages. "I read this when I was a boy. My tutor wanted me to improve my English, you see, and it had just been published to great sensation. I must have fallen in love with Marguerite Blakeney a thousand times over."

Daisy glanced at Grandmère, who made an almost imperceptible shake of her head.

"Ah yes," said Von Sternburg. "Here it is. 'Pride had given way at last, obstinacy was gone, the will was powerless. He was but a man madly, blindly, passionately in love; and as soon as her light footstep had died away within the house, he knelt down upon the terrace steps, and in the very madness of his love, he kissed one by one the places where her small foot had trodden, and the stone balustrade there, where her tiny hand had rested last.'" He looked at Daisy. "How must it affect a man, do you think, to love a woman so deeply?"

"I can't imagine," Daisy said.

"Uncomfortable, I should think," said Grandmère. "What if it had rained, and the terrace steps were wet?"

Von Sternburg shut the book and handed it back to Grandmère. "You are not a romantic, I see. But then, you never were. All those fellows in your salon, they were resolutely Modernist. This is why I learned not to open my mouth there."

"Very wise."

He looked back down at the book tucked between Grandmère's hands. "Marguerite," he said. "That's your given name, isn't it, Madame Villon?"

"You have an excellent memory, lieutenant colonel."

"Not so excellent as that. It's the name itself that has a particular meaning for me." He smiled at Daisy. "As I said, I must have fallen in love with her a thousand times, when I was young."

DAISY LEFT AN hour later, having kissed both children several times in the fullness of her guilt, in her anxiety and excitement for what was to come, and told them to behave themselves for their great-grandmother. When she closed the door at last and started down the corridor to the stairway, she thought her heart might punch through the wall of her chest.

At the bottom of the stairway, a man rose from the bench. Von Sternburg, of course, waiting for her in his immaculate double-breasted suit, his solemn, scarred face. Bernard, standing at his post near the door, looked at them both and raised his eyebrows to Daisy. Did she require some assistance, perhaps? Daisy shook her head.

"Lying in wait for me, I see," she said to the German.

"I beg your pardon, madame. There was something I wished to communicate with you, and I found no opportunity upstairs. Shall we walk out together?"

Daisy didn't reply, only started walking across the lobby, heels clicking against the marble. Von Sternburg kept pace beside her. He said nothing until they had stepped through the doorway and onto the pavement outside. Rue Cambon lay hot and quiet on either side of them.

"I only want to say—as a well-wisher—that I admire your spirit very much," he said. "I admire, in particular, your selfless work at this bookstore of yours. Delivering books to those in need of them."

Daisy's mind went numb. She kept walking, however. Feet now clicking against the pavement, the same precise rhythm as before. "How on earth did you know I work at the bookstore, lieutenant colonel?"

"You may call me Max, if you like."

She said nothing.

He continued, "I confess, since I learned of your connection to a person—to a place that keeps its own particular shrine in my memory, I have made it my business to—how shall I say this?—to assure myself of your continued welfare."

"You've been spying on me, you mean."

"That is a terrible word."

"Well, you have. And what have you discovered, hmm? Do you suspect some nefarious motive? Coded messages hidden in these books I deliver to the infirm and the elderly, plotting the destruction of the Reich? Do you mean to report me to the Gestapo?" She spoke recklessly. Without noticing, she increased her pace, while Von Sternburg loped along persistently beside her.

"You remind me so much of your mother," he said.

Daisy stopped and wheeled to face him. "I'm not a bit like my mother. Anyway, I have a father. Nobody ever thinks of *him*, but he's there. He was kind and good, and he loved my mother. He created me with her, and then he marched off to Verdun to be killed by some German. *He's* part of me, too, and I expect I'm a great deal more like him than *her*. The so-heroic Demoiselle de Courcelles."

Von Sternburg simply stared at her, and it occurred to Daisy that his blue eyes had grown glossy, that his expression had become one of immense longing. He wore an ordinary trilby hat with this civilian costume of his, and it cast an arc of shadow on his face. Suddenly he seemed human, diminished. Even a little old.

"Of course, I wouldn't really know, either way," she heard herself say, sounding for an instant like the old Daisy instead of this new, impudent one, who felt unaccountably free to spar with German officers. With *this* German officer. "They're both dead."

"I am so sorry," he said hoarsely.

"So am I. Have you anything else to say to me? Is it now forbidden to bring the comfort of literature to the destitute of Paris? Can I expect the police to knock on my door in the middle of the night and raid my children's rooms?"

"Of course not. I only mean to tell you *this*. If you have need of a friend at any time, for any reason, I hope you will consider me that friend." He took a small rectangular card from his pocket and pressed it into her hand. "I live at the Hôtel Meurice, on rue de Rivoli. The number is here."

Before she could reply, he walked away, in the opposite direction. The heat shimmered around him. Daisy watched him go, until his trilby hat and his broad shoulders simply disappeared around the corner, leaving her alone and unsettled, yearning for something she couldn't name.

CHAPTER NINETEEN

Babs

Paris, France
April 1964

I SAT WITH DREW at a table outside a small café on rue de Richelieu feeling rather alone and unsettled, yearning for a cup of strong tea that seemed strangely absent from the café's menu. I felt very out of place surrounded by beautiful, chic people at neighboring tables, most smoking and chattering loudly in French while they sipped coffee or wine. Even Drew, with his large Americanness, seemed to fit in. He wore sunglasses, and his long legs were stretched out under the table, his ankles crossed, making him look quite bohemian. Except for the broad shoulders and tan, of course.

When we returned from Picardy the day before, Drew had rushed off to his office, so we hadn't had the chance to go over everything we'd learned at the ruins of the château. Or the reason why I still felt his hand where it had clasped mine as we'd descended the hill. I found myself stroking my hand with the other and immediately sat on them. It had been a successful strategy to stop biting my nails when I was a child, after all.

The hand stroking had started the night before when I'd gone to

Margot Lemouron's room to read to her from *Les Misérables,* but she'd fallen asleep after just a few pages. I'd stayed with her for a long while, to see if she might awaken and need something, and as I sat I'd replayed the day in my head, still feeling Drew's hand on mine.

"Are you all right?" Drew asked, his dark glasses masking his eyes so I couldn't tell if it was real concern or if he might be laughing at me.

Realizing that I must look like a schoolgirl waiting outside the headmistress's office, I immediately returned my hands to my lap. "Quite. I'm just a bit eager to see what you've turned up. You weren't really clear in your message."

He took a sip of his coffee, the tiny cup looking Lilliputian in his hand. "I'm not sure yet, myself. Someone from the office should be here shortly to bring the papers I requested. It's a nice day so I figured we'd mix a little business with pleasure."

He grinned at me, as if the word *pleasure* held all sorts of meanings. Which it did, of course, but surely not in the way I was thinking.

I looked down at my coffee cooling in its cup, the cream beginning to stick to the sides. I took a brief sip, trying not to make a face. The war years had taught me not to waste anything, which meant if I ordered a coffee, I would drink it.

A waiter approached our table with a teapot, creamer, and a clean cup and saucer. He set it before me and nodded before turning away. I looked at it with surprise.

"I asked for them to make you tea. I'm not sure what kind it is, but at least it's not coffee, right?" Drew's boyish grin made me want to kiss him, right there in the middle of a Parisian sidewalk. "I made sure they included cream since I know you like that with your tea."

"Thank you," I said, oddly teary. I couldn't remember the last time someone had considered what I wanted.

I focused on making my tea, recalling something he'd said the day before after I'd told him that I hadn't exposed my bare skin to him on purpose. *But I wouldn't have minded*. I blushed at the memory.

With the fortifying tea bolstering my courage, I looked up at him. "Drew, yesterday when you said that . . ."

"Andrew, there you are!" An extremely long and leggy woman approached us from the sidewalk. She wore an elegant suit of cream camel hair, her long, blond hair pulled back in a high silky ponytail. I wanted to shrug out of the lumpy cardigan I'd thrown over my new yellow sleeveless dress with the low neckline so I wouldn't feel like this exquisite creature's mother.

Drew stood and they kissed cheeks before Drew turned to me for introductions. "Barbara Langford, this is Gigi Mercier. She's the law firm librarian here at our Paris office—she's an absolute genius at organization and management, and just about everything else." He winked at Gigi and she smiled back.

I took a long sip from my cup, if only to avoid looking at her.

"But Andrew is the real legend at our office," Gigi protested. "He's just too modest."

They regarded each other for a moment of mutual admiration while I stared stupidly. Finally I held out my hand. "Barbara Langford. It's a pleasure to meet you."

Her grip was surprisingly strong, her face friendly. "So nice to meet you. We've been wondering who Andrew has been meeting. He's been gone from the office so much since he's arrived, we knew a woman must be involved. Nothing wrong with a little afternoon assignation, *oui*, Andrew?"

The woman actually winked at Drew, and I wasn't sure if I was more embarrassed or jealous. Which was ridiculous, really. Drew and I were certainly *not* having assignations, in the afternoon or otherwise. "We're not . . . ," I began.

Drew spoke at the same time. "Oh, Gigi—you wound me. Isn't

it natural for a man to admire two intelligent and beautiful women? Especially one who appears to have a folder for me containing the information Mrs. Langford and I are quite interested in."

I'm sure Drew had meant the *Mrs.* part to construe respectability, but instead Gigi raised an already perfectly arched eyebrow as if to imply otherwise. "Anything for you, Andrew. I didn't mind spending a few extra hours last night scouring those dusty shelves for what you requested. It's a good thing I love the smell of the ink from the mimeograph machine because I certainly used a lot of it." She handed Drew the thick folder she'd been carrying.

"Thank you, Gigi. I knew you wouldn't disappoint. I owe you another drink—or two—for this."

"Just don't forget. Although I know I won't." She winked again before turning back to me. "It was a pleasure meeting you, Mrs. Langford. Please make sure our Andrew isn't all work and no play—as that would make him a very dull boy, *non?*" Her French accent seemed to add so much insinuation to her words that my ears actually felt scorched.

I took another sip from my tea to avoid answering and just gave a slight nod. "It was nice meeting you," I said, forcing a smile I hoped didn't appear too feral.

Drew returned to his seat and opened up the folder, his expression as enthusiastic as a little boy's on Christmas morning. The heavy smell of the bright purple ink on the pages crinkled my nose before the coffee scents masked it enough to allow me to lean closer. I squinted, trying to decipher the words.

"Here," Drew said, removing his sunglasses and placing them in his shirt pocket. He stood and grabbed the arm of my chair and pulled it and me along with it around the table as if I weighed nothing. "Much better," he said, his arm pressed against mine as he slid the folder between us. "Looks like some of these are in English, but the rest are in French so I'll need you to translate."

"Yes, of course." I felt oddly disappointed, which was ridiculous. I carefully slid my cup and saucer in front of me, wondering if it would appear rude if I moved my chair away ever so slightly, but not entirely convinced that I wanted to. "What is all this?" I leaned over his arm, recognizing the header for the newspaper *Le Petit Parisien*.

"So yesterday, on the way back to Paris, you and I were discussing what we'd learned at the chapel and from Monsieur Le Curé. You said that we needed to focus on my father's 'white wolf with a cross,' that everything else was circumstantial—but not necessarily meaningless. And I think you're right. As you pointed out, the coat of arms of the de Courcelles with the white wolf and cross might be circumstantial—or might not be. So I asked Gigi to pull up any news article or piece of information she could possibly find regarding the family, going back as far as she could."

He handed me half of the stack of papers. I pushed my teacup out of the way to make room, the pungent smell of the ink assaulting my nose again. "So that we could determine if there might be a connection between the de Courcelles and whoever had the talisman."

He grinned that grin again. "Beauty and brains, Babs. Your husband was a very lucky man." My stomach did funny flipping motions. I squirmed in my seat, hoping I wasn't getting ill.

The waiter returned with a fresh cup of coffee and another pitcher of cream, along with more croissants for Drew, whose stomach had begun to rumble again. I focused my attention on the pile in front of me, finding quite a few mimeographs from *Le Petit Parisien* as well as from *Le Figaro* and *Vogue*. The largest article, a full page from the *New York Times* society page, featured a wedding photograph from 1893.

Curious, I pulled that one out to start, taking a fortifying sip of tea first. I studied the photograph of the couple, unable to take my eyes away from the bride. She was small in stature, or perhaps it was because the man standing beside her seemed to dominate the photo. He was tall and at least two decades older than his young bride. He wore a dark military uniform with medals and ribbons decorating the front pockets like a Christmas tree, his face angular and stern. Neither was smiling.

I leaned forward to look at the woman, seeing the spark behind her beauty. And perhaps a bit of defiance in the angle of her jaw, the light in her dark eyes, the way she stood a little in front of her husband. A pale hand rested in the crook of the man's elbow, looking delicate and helpless. But something about the woman's face made me quite convinced that she was neither. I sat back studying this odd couple and wondering what had brought these two together.

"What is it?" Drew was so close I could feel his breath on my neck in a not unpleasant way. "You made a noise in the back of your throat."

"Did I?" I said absently as I skimmed the article. "It's a wedding announcement for the Comte de Courcelles and an American, Wilhelmina Gold of New York."

"The Golds of New York? Quite a famous family—I think they owned half of the city and probably still do. Lots of money there. I'm sure that has a lot to do with them getting married. He looks old enough to be her father."

"I was thinking the same thing. It wasn't uncommon for many of the aristocratic families in England and Europe to bolster their sagging coffers with new American money through marriage."

"At least she got a beautiful château in the deal." Drew pulled out a sheet from his own stack from what appeared to be an architectural design book showing the rendering of a fairy-tale castle, complete with banners fluttering from the turrets.

"Still," I said, lost in thought, "I can't imagine marrying for such a reason. I wonder if there could have been something else."

"Besides the promise of becoming a wealthy widow while still young?" Drew asked.

"Possibly. But if the Golds were as wealthy as you suggest, Wilhelmina could have bought her own château. There's just something about her that makes me think she'd need a better reason."

I began flipping through the pile again, trying to sort by date and pulling out the oldest ones to read first. Drew slid a page toward me. "Well, our Comte de Courcelles—Sigismund—wasn't a complete bore. His horse won the Grand Prix in 1902 so that's something."

"True, but I'm finding much more on Wilhelmina—called Minnie, by the way—than on Sigismund. Lots of photos in the gossip rags coupling her name with men other than her husband." I skimmed yet another article in *Le Figaro* about Minnie de Courcelles née Gold then slid it over to Drew. "They had one daughter, Aurélie. She was raised at the Ritz, where her mother apparently lived." I looked at Drew and immediately wished I hadn't because my nose narrowly missed his.

"They were divorced?"

I shook my head. "Not that I've discovered so far. It appears that they might have been living separately since their daughter's birth. I'm beginning to think that Sigismund preferred to rusticate out in the country, whereas Minnie preferred a more cosmopolitan life."

"Ah. That would explain this one," Drew said. "It's all in French, but that's her photograph with the name Comtesse de Courcelles in the caption, and I recognize the word *Ritz*. And *Suite Royale*. But that's about it."

I skimmed through the article, presumably from a gossip rag masquerading as a newspaper. "This is from 1938, before the last war, and it's about the long-term residents at the Ritz. Apparently she lived there prior to the first war. It doesn't mention her daughter, but there's something about a granddaughter. A Marguerite Villon. There's nothing about either woman's personal life, but according to this, our Minnie liked to redecorate the suite often."

Drew flipped through his pile, pausing over one of them. "Here's another name I recognize—Cartier." He pronounced the final *r*, but I was beginning to find his imperfect French rather endearing.

I glanced over at his page and nodded before returning to my own stack. "Yes, I'm finding a lot of material connecting Minnie to jewels. She must have had a fondness for them. And lucky for her, the funds to support her habit." I flipped over the page and went to the next, skimming as I was quickly losing hope of finding anything connecting the de Courcelles with the talisman and La Fleur. "Apparently after Sigismund and Minnie were married, Minnie spent a small fortune in jewels that caused quite a stir according to many articles written about it. Minnie transformed an important de Courcelles family heirloom into a gaudy trinket that was ridiculed by many. One would think that such an old French family would have enough jewels . . ." I flipped a page and stopped.

"You made that sound again. What is it?" Drew leaned over my shoulder and made his own sound. "Oh."

We both stared at the mimeographed photograph, the purple hue doing nothing to disguise a picture of the white wolf and cross of the de Courcelles coat of arms engraved in what appeared to be a medallion. Next to it was the other side of the medallion, a small circle of crystal set in the middle and large jewels, the size of small rocks, encircling the edge, their actual color hidden in purple ink. I cleared my throat and read the caption out loud. "'A holy relic, a remnant of fabric dipped in the blood of St. Jeanne, is contained within a gold pendant surrounded by rubies and diamonds. The comtesse purchased the relic, previously lost as a gambling debt, thus restoring it to the de Courcelles family through their marriage.'

"It's the talisman," I said quietly. "It must be." I looked at the petite bride. "It's why she married him, I think. As a sort of bribe." Turning back to Drew, I said, "What was it that Monsieur le Curé said?"

"Hang on." Drew frantically reached into his briefcase and pulled out a pad of legal paper. "I made notes last night in the hotel so I wouldn't forget anything." He quickly flipped through the pages. "Here it is. He said that the de Courcelles talisman is very powerful, but only if held in the hands of the demoiselle. The legend dictates that it can only be passed down by the females in the family, and that France will never fall as long as the demoiselle holds the talisman."

He looked at the article in front of me. "Does it say anything else?"

"Not this particular one, but there's this." I pulled another article from the pile and quickly scanned it. "The talisman was stolen back in 1942. Minnie accused the Germans—who were at that time using the Ritz for quarters for the Luftwaffe—of stealing it." I tapped a line of text with my finger. "It says here that the granddaughter, Marguerite Villon, was interviewed as well, but neither she nor the Germans confessed to any wrongdoing or any knowledge as to its whereabouts."

"So where is it now?" Drew asked, sounding not a little desperate.

"Monsieur le Curé said it disappeared during the last war. Which could also include being stolen."

"Or maybe it didn't disappear. My father said to look for the white wolf and the cross." He scratched the back of his head, making the hair stand straight up in an attractively disheveled way. "He must have been talking about the talisman. There are too many coincidences to say it couldn't be." He looked at me, his eyes wild, as if trying to convince himself more than me. "It *must* have been the talisman."

I slid another mimeographed page from the pile. I'd almost overlooked it as half of the page must have been torn or missing because only a picture and its caption had been copied. But I stopped now, staring at the picture. It had been taken from an article from 1915 in the *Paris-Midi* and showed a young woman, tall and slender with a cloud of light-colored hair surrounding her face, wearing a white dress with a *tricolore* pinned to her chest. It was impossible to see her expression, but it wasn't her face that drew my attention. The picture was small, but on the woman's narrow chest, dangling from a thin chain, hung a medallion surrounded by large jewels.

I must have made a noise. I heard Drew's intake of breath as he looked over my shoulder. "That's it, isn't it? That's the talisman."

I quickly translated the caption. "'The Demoiselle de Courcelles, a heroine for France and the woman who routed an entire command of German officers and liberated a French national treasure.'"

We regarded each other in stunned silence before Drew let out a shout then lifted me from my chair, swirling me around regardless of the stares of sidewalk passersby and the occupants at the nearby tables. "My father was right! The wolf and the cross are real!" Before either one of us knew what he was doing, he kissed me soundly on the lips and then did it again, which did all sorts of interesting things to my knees.

I tried my best to speak over him, but his words tumbled over each other like newborn lambs in a pasture. "This is it—I'm sure of it, Babs. The talisman is what my father was sent to retrieve from La Fleur. This means there must be a connection between the de Courcelles and La Fleur. Do you see?"

"I'm not sure . . . ," I began, but he wasn't listening. He grasped my arms and I had the stray—and not unwelcome—thought that he might kiss me again. "So what do we do now?"

His face became serious. "Well, we go back to the Ritz and find out if they ever discovered who stole the talisman."

"But surely they won't know!" I protested. "It's been over twenty years. Surely no one who worked there then will still be there now."

"It's the Ritz, Babs. Why would a person ever want to leave?" He pulled out his wallet and placed several bills on the table before quickly gathering up all the papers and shoving them into his briefcase.

I opened my mouth to explain that being a guest at the Ritz was not the same as actually working there, but found myself pulled by the hand down the sidewalk back toward the hotel.

Drew bristled with so much excitement his skin should have been glowing. I was happy for him, for getting nearer to granting his father's last wish and discovering what had really happened that night in 1942. Perhaps even finding the elusive La Fleur.

But I seemed to be dragging my feet, making him slow periodically so I could catch up. Eventually he took my hand, the warm strength of his fingers doing nothing to stanch the chill that had invaded my body. I knew the closer we came to discovering the truth, the closer I came to having to confess to Drew that La Fleur had sent Kit a letter, and I had kept it from him. My reasons at the time had been sound, heroic, and done in Kit's best interests. At least I'd thought so then. But now, imagining how it would sound to Drew in the telling, I appeared to be a vindictive, spiteful woman who kept the love of Kit's life away from him for my own selfish gain. The whole scenario made me want to pack my bags and leave now, before I had to confess my shame and endure Drew's look of disappointment and reproach. As if I didn't see it enough in my own reflection each time I looked in a mirror.

The sound of a clacking typewriter met us as we entered the hotel. Drew pulled me behind a line of potted palms to be out of Prunella Schuyler's line of vision, stopping as he surveyed the hotel's entry points undetected. "Shouldn't we be going to the administration offices?" I asked.

He shook his head. "Gigi said the best person to talk to is the hallman—this guy." He showed me a scrap of paper with the name André Deneaux written on it. "He started here in 1937 as a page and moved on to taking telephone messages in 1942 and still does. He apparently has a perfect memory and is the epitome of discretion."

"So he probably won't tell us anything," I said, trying to keep the hopeful tone from my voice.

"Not necessarily. We're not asking for state secrets, after all. We just want to know if the talisman was ever found, and where it might be now. We're looking for facts. He might be able to tell us who the likely suspects were, too. According to Gigi, he probably remembers each person who's come through the doors since 1937."

"Shouldn't we do this in a more formal way? Like in a letter?"

Drew sent me an odd look before grabbing my hand again, approaching a man I'd seen several times since the beginning of my stay. "Monshur Doonox," Drew called out as our prey emerged from the lift.

The dapper, bespectacled gentleman smiled as we approached, unperturbed by the butchering of his name. "Madame, monsieur." He nodded to us in greeting. "How may I be of service?"

Drew smiled. "I understand you have been at the Ritz for nearly thirty years. Is that correct?"

The man bowed his head. His English was perfect, of course, his French accent gently coloring his words. "It is indeed. And it has always been an honor and a pleasure."

"So you'd remember the Comtesse de Courcelles? I understand she lived here for nearly six decades."

"Of course. I remember her well. A lovely, vibrant woman. She was well-known for her salons, attracting the best and the brightest intellectuals and writers Paris had to offer throughout the years of her residency. She is greatly missed."

Drew nodded eagerly while he listened to the answer, ready to ask his next question. "When she lived here, do you remember her ever saying anything about the de Courcelles talisman?"

The man's brown eyes widened behind his glasses. "The talisman? *Mais oui*. Every true Frenchman knows of the talisman. The comtesse had it displayed in a case in her suite. I even saw it a time or two. Of course, the original talisman is just a piece of cloth, a holy relic, but the comtesse had more, shall we say, extravagant tastes and added many priceless jewels. But the true value of it was always the relic."

Drew reached into his briefcase and pulled out the mimeographed photo. "Is this it?"

Monsieur Deneaux lowered the glasses on his nose, examining the photo. "Yes. This is what I remember being in the case. It wasn't purple, of course."

"Of course," Drew said, taking back the proffered page. "It says in the article that it was stolen from the Ritz in 1942. Do you remember that?"

Monsieur Deneaux tucked his chin, making it nearly disappear into his narrow neck. "It was not stolen. Not from the Ritz. We have always had excellent security." He seemed personally affronted.

"Yes, I know," I reassured. "It's only the newspapers at the time— and you know how unreliable they can be—stated it had been stolen. Can you at least share with us what you think might have happened to it? We understand that the talisman disappeared during the war, and we are merely trying to find out what happened to it."

Apparently mollified, André nodded. "It *did* disappear, but it certainly wasn't stolen. Not from the Ritz, at any rate." He leaned closer and lowered his voice. "I believe that it was taken by the husband of the comtesse's granddaughter. Pierre Villon." He said the name with such loathing that I almost expected him to spit.

"Why do you say that?" Drew asked.

"He was a French government official, a bureaucrat without much real responsibility. But he and his family lived in a very grand apartment in the sixteenth arrondissement that his position shouldn't have afforded."

"Was there ever any proof that he took it?" I disliked this Pierre Villon but thought I should be fair.

André shook his head, his lower lip curled in distaste. "People like him always covered their tracks, like cats with their excrement." He tapped his forefinger against his graying temple. "But I know. I know his type. I know what he was capable of."

"Do you know what happened to him? After the war."

Andre shrugged. "Who knows? He disappeared at some point—I do not recall when. Like so many during the war, he just *poof*." He illustrated the word by opening his fists in a starburst of fingers.

A very large woman carrying a small dog under each arm approached, calling for Monsieur Deneaux. "Please excuse me. If you need anything else, please don't hesitate to let me know." He bowed his goodbye, then left.

"Well, hello."

We turned at the familiar Southern accent that stretched the two syllables of the last word into three.

Precious Dubose, immaculately turned out in ice-blue linen, smiled at us. "I didn't mean to eavesdrop, but I couldn't help but overhear your conversation with that lovely Monsieur Deneaux. Actually, it was the word *jewels* that caught my attention. I do so love jewelry. Is there anything I might be able to help you with?"

I recalled her telling me that she had lived at the Ritz, at times with Coco Chanel. "You were here during the war, right?"

She pressed her pink lips together and looked up at the ceiling as if thinking. "Off and on. Why do you ask?"

"We're looking for the de Courcelles talisman," explained Drew. "It was displayed in a case in the Comtesse de Courcelles's suite, then disappeared in 1942. My father, who was OSS during the war, was dropped into France to retrieve it, but something happened to it. We think La Fleur might have stolen it."

Her delicate eyebrows rose. "La Fleur? I've always been fascinated by her. Such a woman—and such a legend. My knowledge of French history is very good, you know. If you think I can be of any help, I'd love to hear the whole story."

Drew and I looked at each other and then back at Precious. "Three brains are always better than two," Drew said.

"Wonderful," Precious said, drawing out the word. "Let's go have a drink, and you can tell me all about it. I always think better with a drink in my hand." Precious winked at Drew. "Come on. The Bar Hemingway is the only place in town that knows how to make the perfect mint julep."

We followed in her perfume-scented wake toward the bar, the incessant clatter of Prunella Schuyler's typewriter like little reminders that the closer we got to finding La Fleur, the closer I got to facing the ghosts I'd told Drew I didn't believe in.

CHAPTER TWENTY

Aurélie

The Château de Courcelles
Picardy, France
April 1915

THERE WERE NO ghosts in the back corridors of the castle, only dust.
Aurélie stifled a sneeze as she crept along an abandoned passageway built into the thickness of the wall in the new wing. It wasn't a
secret passage, not as such. It had been put in when the new wing was
built in the eighteenth century, the very latest in modern conveniences,
so that servants might appear, as if by magic, without passing through
the grand chambers and anterooms, unseen and unheard. When she
was young, the passages had bustled with servants, whisking around
one another. But there were no grand house parties at Courcelles anymore. The staff had dwindled even before the advent of war.

The lack of a mistress, her mother would have said. But whatever
the reason, it meant the old servants' passageways languished unused.
Except, of course, by a rebellious girl who sometimes liked to slip from
her rooms without her governess seeing her.

It didn't matter that the passage was in darkness. Aurélie knew the
location of her own rooms in her muscles, in her bones. She reached

out and felt the handle of the hidden door just where it was meant to be, the brass worn smooth with age beneath her palm.

For a moment, Aurélie was sixteen again . . . twelve . . . nine. And this was her room, her own special place that always felt so much more her own than her lavishly decorated bedchamber at the Ritz, never mind how much money her mother had spent.

But it wasn't. Not anymore. A man's shaving set dominated her dressing table. There were spectacles beside the bed and piles upon piles of papers overwhelming the desk of the escritoire she had almost never used. Hoffmeister hadn't torn the boiseries from the wall or the hangings from the windows, but the casual debris of his belongings was almost worse, somehow, because it was still the same, all of it, but he'd marked it as his, as surely as a dog in the woods with a contested tree.

How dare he? How dare he drape his hideous uniform over her chaise longue? How dare he leave the dent of his ugly head on her pillow? Aurélie wanted to scrub it all with carbolic and lye, to fling his belongings out the window as he'd flung hers.

Her nails were making dents in her palms. Aurélie forced herself to relax, finger by finger. She couldn't scrub out the taint; she couldn't let him know she had ever been here. Hoffmeister was downstairs, presiding over another endless supper, toasting the Kaiser over a feast that would have fed the village for a week. And she . . . she was here to see what she could see. To find something, finally, that might make her father look at her again, really look at her, as though she weren't Minnie Gold's daughter, but the true heir to Courcelles. As though she were the son he had always wanted her to be.

The son she had tried to be, for him, scorning the modiste for the hunting field, racing cars and horses, practicing and practicing until she could outshoot Jean-Marie, until she could skewer any man with a fencing foil, drive the faint of heart off the road.

But it wasn't enough. It was never enough.

Of course, this wasn't about that, not really. This was about France, and the people of the village, Aurélie hastily reminded herself. It was about finding something, some snippet of information that might prove the key to ousting the conqueror. The date of the next big offensive . . . damning information about an officer . . . movements of munitions that might be intercepted . . .

Aurélie went to the overburdened escritoire, placed beneath the skeptical countenance of an ancestress who had been a lady-in-waiting to Marie Antoinette and had escaped the guillotine due to the good offices of an Englishman with an impossibly floral nom de guerre.

She started on the piles with a will, but her determination soon turned to dismay. It wasn't the language. She could read the German easily enough, thanks to the tutors her mother had hired in the forlorn hope that one day Aurélie would be seized with the urge to study Kant in the original. Nor were the papers disorganized; quite the contrary. They were meticulously, painfully detailed. All the hideous, petty regulations Hoffmeister had imposed upon the surrounding villages, all were recorded here, in ledger upon ledger. There were weekly accounts of everything from the number of eggs collected to the number of men executed.

It was chilling and boring all at the same time, which rather summed up Hoffmeister. How could one man be both so deadly and so dull?

There was correspondence, too. Letters about English soldiers found sheltering in the woods and shot; pigeons sighted and shot down.

There was, Aurélie noticed with relief, no reference to either her father or the chapel. Hoffmeister seemed to think the pigeons were coming from a deserted boathouse by the lake and was having Kraus keep it under surveillance. Which explained, she supposed, the many fishing expeditions from which Lieutenant Kraus returned thoroughly sloshed, but with no fish.

And then, at the very bottom of the pile, she saw something else entirely. The distinctive paper of a telegraph form. The writing was very dark; there were places where the nib had pierced through the paper.

Erster Generalquartiermeister W.H.F. von Witzleben. Wire soonest. Delicate matters to discuss. Yr loving nephew, M v S.

M v S. Maximilian von Sternburg?

She was frowning at the paper, trying to figure out why it was here, what it meant, when the sound of footsteps and voices made her start. Aurélie shoved the telegram back where she'd found it. Her body was faster than her mind; she was halfway to the passage by the time the footsteps stopped outside the door. A key was inserted into the lock.

Aurélie escaped into the passage, pulling the door softly shut behind her, grateful for those long-ago servants whose movements were meant to be inaudible, the door padded and the floor covered in drugget.

"—another telegram," Hoffmeister was saying. "He sent it this morning, from the village."

"Or thinks he has, eh?" Someone giggled unpleasantly. Aurélie recognized the voice as Dreier's. Putting her eye to the crack in the door, she couldn't quite see him, just a leg dangling off the edge of her chaise longue. But the voice was unmistakable. "How many does this make?"

"Four," said Hoffmeister succinctly. "All to his uncle in Berlin. Wire soonest. Delicate matters to discuss."

"Is that brandy?" said Dreier hopefully, and Aurélie heard the sound of her father's Napoleon brandy being poured into one of her great-grandmother's crystal glasses. There was silence for a moment, punctuated by slurping. "Won't he realize when he doesn't hear back?"

"Berlin has other matters to attend to," said Hoffmeister drily. "They sent him to spy on me, you know."

"Cheek," said Dreier indistinctly. "More brandy?"

Crystal clinked against crystal. "These Junkers look after one another. Never mind that their world is done. Like all this. The arrogance of them. That Von Sternburg would sell out his country for a girl."

"Or her, ahem, jewels, eh?" Dreier made a noise that was somewhere between a burp and a laugh.

In the passage, Aurélie stood as still as she could, scarcely daring to breathe, her hands like ice. The telegram she had seen beneath the ledgers. The promised intervention from Berlin . . . Intercepted. Gone. She had never quite believed in it, but it had been comforting to hope it was there, that the old laws of behavior still governed, that there would be recourse. Now, she felt marooned, as surely as Crusoe on his island. There was no law but Hoffmeister's law, and his law was no law at all.

"Get your mind out of the gutter, lieutenant," said Hoffmeister without heat. "I don't care if he's swiving her six ways from Sunday. But I want that relic."

"With those jewels," said Dreier, eager to agree, "you could buy a palace that would make this one look like a hovel!"

"With those jewels," Hoffmeister corrected him, "I could buy the men who would make me a lieutenant colonel. And then there's the relic itself . . ."

"I didn't know you believed in all that," hiccupped Dreier.

"I don't," snapped Hoffmeister. Cutting off Dreier's hasty apologies, he said, "But they do, those peasants. They think it's magic. Miracles and hocus-pocus. They say—what is it?—that France cannot fall while the demoiselle holds the talisman." He made the archaic title a slur. "So we'll show them who holds that relic. And then we'll burn it."

"Not the jewels!"

"No, you cretin. Not the jewels. The relic. That disgusting, decaying scrap of fabric they claim is saturated in the saint's own holy blood.

We'll show them it will go up in flames as quickly as your grandmother's kerchief."

It might not have been grandmother's kerchief he had said. Aurélie's German was serviceable, but it didn't quite run to vulgar colloquialisms.

"And then France will fall?" slurred Dreier.

"What, do you believe in all that rubbish? *No.* But they'll think it will. So it will."

"Perhaps we burn the demoiselle with it," proposed Dreier. Through the crack in the door, Aurélie could just see his hand holding out his glass to be filled as though he weren't suggesting her immolation as casually as one might an afternoon picnic.

"And make a martyr? No. But what will the French think when they learn that their prized demoiselle was a German officer's whore? We tell them, I think, that she gave her lover the talisman. . . . She sold her body and her country. That will take care of the demoiselle."

"Wait—you're going to give Von Sternburg the talisman?"

"Von Sternburg," Hoffmeister said calmly, "won't be alive to enjoy it. There will be an accident. In an old structure like this, there are often such little accidents."

"But . . . his uncle . . ."

"Will know only that his nephew perished serving his country. There will be no inconvenient telegrams to say otherwise. There have never been any telegrams to advise him otherwise."

Murder. He was talking about murder. Max's murder.

There was a moment of stunned silence, and then, of all things, the sound of applause. Dreier was clapping. "It's brilliant! You've thought of everything!"

"Not quite everything," said Hoffmeister modestly. "One would have to determine how such an accident might be arranged. You were a pharmacist once, were you not?"

"I, er, yes, but . . ."

"If a man were to dose himself for, oh, sleeplessness, might he not become confused and walk somewhere he ought not?"

"Ye-es," said Dreier, sounding less than clearheaded himself. "But . . ."

"It is no crime for a man to take a sleeping draught. Or another man to give it."

"No," said Dreier, relieved. "No, not at all."

"But, not, I think," said Hoffmeister, rising to his feet, "until we have the talisman. Do you understand me, Klaus? Wait for my guidance. And tell me if our friend attempts to send any more letters."

Aurélie heard the other man rise clumsily to his feet. "But what about the letters to his mother?"

"Bring them to me. If there is nothing of interest, you may replace them in the dispatch bag. We don't want his mother expressing her concern to her brother."

"Yes, sir. No, sir." Dreier made an attempt to click his heels, nearly overbalancing himself in the process. "Will there be anything else, sir?"

"Try not to break your own neck on those stairs," said Hoffmeister, as Dreier careened off a Louis XIV commode and into the side of the bed, cursing fluently. Hoffmeister took him firmly by the arm, although, through the crack in the paneling, Aurélie didn't miss the look of distaste he gave the other man. "I'll see you out."

They were standing at the door, on the far side of the room. Now was her chance, under the cover of their conversation, to retreat down the passage. Aurélie forced her sluggish limbs to move. No crime for a man to take a sleeping draught, Hoffmeister had said, as though already preparing his report. No crime.

Max, lying broken beneath the parapets.

Max, dead on his bed, with an empty vial beside him. A miscalculation, too much sleeping powder, a tragic accident, condolences wired to Berlin . . .

How? How was this happening? How could this be allowed to happen? The world had gone mad. They had opened Pandora's box and let all the demons out, given them uniforms and room to play.

Aurélie paused at the base of the passage, leaning her forehead on the roughly whitewashed wall, pressing her palms against the worn paint, feeling the scrape against her skin, raw and real. It was talk, only talk, but even such talk, that Hoffmeister could consider such a thing, was monstrous. She'd seen the Germans kill before, certainly. She and her people were the enemy, to be exterminated like vermin should they prove inconvenient. That was war.

But Max was one of their own.

This wasn't war, it was murder, murder out of self-interest and cowardice and greed, and by God, she wouldn't stand for it. She'd stop them, thought Aurélie feverishly, hurrying through the tunnels with more speed than grace. She'd stop them and Max would see them court-martialed, and it would be two birds with one stone, really. She'd save Max and free her people from Hoffmeister, and, merciful heavens, she couldn't let him kill Max.

Max's room wasn't in the new wing with Hoffmeister and Kraus; it was clear across the courtyard in the old watchtower, above the long unused guardroom. Aurélie had seen his lamp burning long into the night, the outline of Max's tall form hunched over a desk, his back bent with weariness.

Not that she'd stood in the courtyard and watched him; one wouldn't do such a thing. But it was hard not to see into a lit window in passing.

There were ways to get to the old watchtower without being seen, through the tumbledown rooms where men-at-arms used to dice and drink, back when there were such things as men-at-arms. Now those chambers were crowded with bundles and boxes, dangerous contraband like coffee grinders confiscated from the people of Courcelles;

porcelain plates requisitioned from a neighboring manor and packed into a box marked with the major's Hamburg address.

It was dark. Aurélie didn't dare to light a candle, even if she'd had one, which she didn't. The stairs to the next floor were narrow and twisting, the stones worn in the middle. Aurélie crept up carefully, hugging the wall, her long skirt tangling around her legs. There was a door at the top, made of old oak, studded with nails that had been old when the Sun King was young.

Tentatively, Aurélie pushed the door open and saw Max at his desk. He had taken off his coat and sat in his shirt and braces, sleeves rolled up to the elbow. An oil lamp sputtered beside him, flickering red and gold off his pale hair, hinting at the warmth of the skin beneath the thin linen of his shirt.

Whatever he was writing absorbed him. The coals crackled in the brazier. Max's pen scratched against the paper. Aurélie watched, reluctant to break the moment, the strange intimacy of it. He was so intent; how could she break his peace? But she must have moved, have breathed, because she saw his head go up, the muscles in his back moving. He reached for his jacket as he turned, a preemptive frown on his face.

And then he saw Aurélie.

He stood, a look of pleasure lighting his face, brighter than any oil lamp. "Auré—"

"Shh!" She didn't think she had been seen or pursued, but she didn't dare take the risk. "Draw the curtains."

He didn't question her, but rose immediately to obey, drawing the curtains over the pitted, leaded glass of the old window that looked into the courtyard, bolting the shutters of the others, the ones that looked out over the fields and village. The room seemed to shrink around them.

Only when he had made the room secure did Max come to her, his face alert with concern. "What is it? Did the major do something to you?"

"Not to me." He was still in his shirt and braces, his jacket forgotten, and Aurélie found herself addressing herself to the opening at the base of his collar, where the pulse thrummed blue against his skin.

"To your father, then?" His hands were on her shoulders. Aurélie found it very hard to concentrate.

"You have to leave, you have to go, it isn't safe for you. Your telegrams haven't gone to Berlin. The major . . . he means to kill you and make it look like an accident."

Max stayed where he was, looking at her, his expression strangely wistful. But all he said was, "I had wondered."

"You wondered? Then why are you still here?" Aurélie looked about, searching for his kit bag. She found it under his narrow camp bed and dragged it out for him with more speed than elegance. "Pack. Go. They don't mean to strike until . . . well, until something, but how do we know they'll keep to that? The sooner you're back in Berlin the safer you'll be."

"And you?"

"What about me?" The room was remarkably spare. It had never truly been intended for habitation. This was a punishment, this room. Just a narrow camp bed and a desk, with a coal brazier to warm the old stone walls. Max's belongings were minimal. Most of them, Aurélie noticed, were books. She began stacking them, haphazardly.

"If I'm back in Berlin, what becomes of you?" he asked.

Aurélie stopped, a pile of books in her arms. "I'm not the one they mean to kill. Not at the moment, at any rate."

She'd meant it as a joke, but Max wasn't smiling. "How could I leave knowing you were still here with them? Unprotected?"

"You can't protect me if you're dead," said Aurélie roughly. She wasn't sure why, but she felt as though she'd been running, her chest going in and out with the effort. She shoved the pile of books at Max. "Here. Take these. I have my father to protect me. I can protect myself. You don't believe me? Challenge me to a duel. I can outfence and outshoot you."

"I don't doubt it," said Max mildly, setting the pile of books down on the desk. "Although I would hope to at least make you work for that touch."

A touch. The moment of contact in fencing. Something about the way he said it made it sound less a blow and more a caress.

"Well, then," said Aurélie belligerently, hoping the red didn't show too much in her cheeks. "What are you waiting for?"

"A duel," Max said slowly, "is an affair of honor. These men have no honor, Aurélie. They will use whatever means they may against you. And you, you will be powerless against it, because you are not they."

"I'm half American," Aurélie protested. "My grandfather was what they call a robber baron. I can be ruthless."

"Can you? Could you send a man to his death?"

"If there were cause," Aurélie blustered, but she wasn't really quite sure. If Hoffmeister were to plummet from a parapet, she didn't think she would rush to grab his coattails. But could she be the one to push him? Something in her shrank at the thought. She glowered at Max, her voice shaking with helplessness and frustration. "And what of you? If ever there was a man crippled by honor—don't you understand? He means to poison you. To drug you, that is. To drug you so that you take a fatal fall. If you stay here, they'll kill you."

Max looked down at her, his expression wry. "One less German in the world."

"Don't be an idiot," retorted Aurélie, and she had to tilt back her head to look up at him. "You know that's not how I think of you."

"Isn't it?" He was so close, she could feel his breath against the hair bundled in a disorderly pouf on the top of her head. "I am German, you know. No matter how well I speak your language, I will always be a foreigner."

"I know but—" She pushed lightly against his chest. "You're not one of *those* Germans. You're different. You're . . . you're . . . you."

Standing with her at the back of her mother's salon, ready with an umbrella in the rain outside the Louvre, delivering toys to the children of the village because he couldn't let them think Father Christmas had abandoned them. Because he was Max, just Max, and she couldn't imagine anyone else in the world like him, with the strength to be kind in a world that drew power from cruelty, with a deep-down goodness that transcended allegiances and uniforms and all the nonsense men used to justify their baser instincts.

She was going to lose him; either he was going to leave or they were going to kill him, and she couldn't bear to think of it, of Max not being there, not loving her. She couldn't for the life of her understand why he would love her, but that he did—he seemed not to have the slightest bit of doubt. That certainty was like a raft in the middle of the ocean, the one solid thing among the waves and the sharks and the howling winds.

"Please," she said, and she wasn't sure whether she was begging him to stay or to go. "Please. Don't let them hurt you."

"I won't," he promised, and she knew it was nonsense, that he was just what he'd accused her of being, an honorable man, and what defense did he have against evil?

All she could do was reach up and cup his face in her hands, memorizing every feature, the texture of his skin, the freckle above one brow, the way the color of his eyes changed from blue to gray in the lamplight. Because this, this might be all they would have, all they would ever have, and she wanted this, this memory to hold on to once he was gone, the one man in the world who loved her really, and truly, and just for herself.

"Aurélie," he said, and that was all, but it was enough.

With one hand, Aurélie reached and extinguished the lamp, turning down the wick until only the faintest ember still lingered before it winked out against the smoke-stained glass. And then they were in darkness, safe in the darkness, in this room that was shuttered and still and entirely their own.

"Shh," she said when he started to speak, and she hooked her fingers through his braces to pull him close.

CHAPTER TWENTY-ONE

Daisy

Avenue Marceau
Paris, France
July 1942

THE APARTMENT WAS quiet and dark, husband and children far away, and Daisy felt like the only person in the world. She sat in the armchair in the drawing room that was nearest to the foyer, so she could jump up as soon as Monsieur Legrand's tap sounded on the door. Certainly it wouldn't do for him to linger outside! She must be ready for his arrival. On the mantel, an ormolu clock ticked sharply. Daisy fixed her hands on her lap and tried not to count the seconds.

When they parted in the Tuileries that afternoon, Legrand hadn't said anything about how he would gain access to the building, or evade the concierge, or make his way to her floor without awaking suspicion. These were details she left to him, as a man trained in such things. Daisy was just an amateur, a woman playing at spycraft. She was a mere housewife waiting alone in her apartment—the apartment in which she lived with her husband, her beloved children—for a real spy, a genuine agent, to slip inside and steal that husband's secrets. A betrayal of her marriage, certainly, and also a crime for which she could be condemned to death. Daisy stared down at her hands, which were clasped so tightly that the gold wedding band bit into the flesh of her ring finger. *Ticktock*, the clock said. Daisy grasped the ring and yanked it free. She was so thin, the metal slipped down her finger without effort. She opened the drawer of the lamp table and dropped the ring inside, and as she pushed the drawer shut a hand came down on her shoulder.

Daisy gasped and jumped to her feet and wheeled around, all at once, nearly falling over the edge of the armchair. Legrand stood there in neat, dark clothes and a hat. A leather satchel hung from across his chest, like a messenger bag. As she opened her mouth to speak, he laid his finger over his lips. She caught herself.

"How did you get in?" she whispered.

He shrugged and smiled a little, and Daisy realized the stupidity of her question, the stupidity of waiting here in this darkened room, in the armchair that was nearest the foyer, when he was a trained agent, of course. He could unlock doors and break into apartments at a whim. Whereas she, Daisy, was in this business far above her head. She put her hand to her chest and said, "You shouldn't sneak up on me like that."

"I'm sorry. I didn't realize I was sneaking."

There was no teasing note to his voice, no inflection, no gleam in his eyes or arch in his eyebrows to suggest how long he had stood there, and whether he'd noticed what she had just done, to put her wedding ring away in a drawer. He stood very close. He must have washed, because he didn't smell of pipe smoke or anything, except perhaps soap. Daisy inhaled carefully through her nose. Yes, soap. And toothpaste. She stepped back a pace.

"No, I don't expect you did," she said. "This is all second nature to you."

Legrand's eyes traveled rapidly around the room behind her, taking in the size and scale of it, the ornate decoration, the gilded furniture, like some kind of professional.

"I hate it," Daisy said.

"I'm not surprised." Legrand's gaze returned to her. He inclined his head to the foyer. "Shall we proceed?"

"Yes, of course. Please follow me."

Legrand stepped politely aside, as if they were together at a cocktail party, and Daisy led the way into the foyer and down the corridor toward Pierre's study. She had some idea that she should walk softly, not make any noise, but wouldn't that seem more suspicious to the neighbors than if she walked about as she always did? Legrand would know. This was second nature to him. Breaking into people's apartments, sneaking about with restless housewives. All in a day's work, confident that he was in the right, that these petty betrayals were all committed in the service of a higher cause.

Whereas Daisy, floundering in some moral swamp . . . whereas *she* . . .

They reached the study. Pierre had left the door locked, of course, but Daisy had made a copy of the key, to Legrand's own instructions, when they had first moved in. When Pierre's back was turned, she'd pressed the key in a wax mold that Legrand had given her and taken this mold to a locksmith, who hadn't asked any questions, had simply made up the key for her and taken her ten francs for it. Now she took it from her pocket and fitted it in the lock and opened the door for them both.

The air inside the study was warm and stuffy and smelled of Pierre. Daisy went to the desk and switched the lamp on. "The safe's right there in the cabinet," she said, pointing.

Legrand went to the cabinet in question and opened it without a word. The safe squatted inside. Legrand lifted the satchel over his head and let it rest on the floor, next to his feet. Daisy folded her arms and watched him. He seemed to be taking his time, but maybe that was part of the technique. The lamplight gleamed on his hair, turning it a soft, dark gold. He ran his hand over the top and sides of the safe and crouched to peer at the dial.

"Anything amiss?" said Daisy.

"No, it's a common safe. He didn't exactly go to great expense."

"No, he wouldn't."

Legrand turned to the satchel and opened it. "You can sit down, if you like. I'll just be a moment."

"I'll stand."

Legrand was as good as his word. As Daisy leaned against the desk and curled her damp, nervous fingers around the edge, he moved with swift efficiency. From the satchel he removed a small device that looked like a bell, which he placed against the door of the safe, next to the combination dial. He leaned his ear against this device and turned the dial. His eyes were closed. Daisy stared at his fingers, agile and patient, exquisitely sensitive, faint purple stains at the tips. They eased the dial one way and then the other, slowing to an almost imperceptible movement as they reached each point of friction. Daisy realized she was holding her breath and exhaled. Legrand's eyes opened. He lifted his head away from the door of the safe and opened it.

You could say this about Pierre Villon: he was a man of meticulous organization. Each stack of papers had been laid in its own cardboard portfolio and bound with string, like a Christmas gift; each portfolio was labeled in precise block letters, except the words themselves were some kind of code or shorthand known only to Pierre himself. From his messenger bag, Legrand retrieved a small camera. He positioned the papers under the desk lamp and photographed them—not all of them, but the ones he thought were significant. Most significant were the lists of names and addresses inside a portfolio marked *JULXX*. Daisy counted thirty on each page, and there were twenty-four pages.

"But this surely can't be all of them," she whispered, positioning each paper so that Legrand could photograph it. "There are only hundreds here, and your intelligence speaks of thousands."

"Possibly these are only the ones that your husband is responsible for."

"Then it won't make much difference, will it?"

Legrand snapped another photo. "To them it will. If we can act fast enough to get them out of Paris."

Daisy lifted away the sheet and arranged another one in its place, and as she did so, her gaze snagged on something written there. "Wait a moment," she whispered.

She drew the paper closer to the lamp and ran her finger down the list of names, trying to find whatever it was that had caught her unconscious attention. About two-thirds of the way down, there was a name through which a thick black line had been drawn. Daisy peered close, trying to make out the typewritten letters. Her fingers were cold and shaky. She handed the page to Legrand. "Can you read this for me? The name that's been crossed out."

Legrand took the page and held it directly under the lamp. His eyes squinted, his lips pursed. He looked back up at Daisy, bemused.

"*Wilhelmina de Courcelles, Hôtel Ritz,*" he said. "Isn't that your grandmother?"

HE FILLED THREE rolls of film while Daisy carefully arranged each stack of papers in its proper order, in its proper portfolio, bound with string in the exact same fashion, stacked back in the safe according to its original position there. Possibly no more than half an hour had passed, and now the thing was done.

Her grandmother's name, there on the list. What did it mean? Why was it crossed out? Had Pierre seen it there and drawn that black line? Had he put it there himself, and then thought better of it? And if he had, whom was he trying to protect? Grandmère? Daisy and the children? Or just himself?

And here she stood, betraying him. Not just with the papers in the safe, but with her heart. Her head, her body that craved someone else. This man, who stood with her, warm and clever and daring, taut and golden and everything her husband was not.

Legrand closed the door of the safe and spun the dial to the exact number on which Pierre had left it. He picked up the satchel and slung it back over his head and across his chest.

"Well, that's that," he said.

"Yes, it's done," she replied.

"I can make my own way out."

"No, I'll show you out. Would you—would you like a glass of water first? Wine?"

Daisy's heart thumped. She stood next to the desk, and Legrand stood in front of the safe, and several yards of open air existed between them, there in Pierre's study. They stared not quite at each other—at each other's ears, or cheekbones—and Daisy realized that Legrand was as desperate as she was. That his pulse also pounded, that his lungs were short of breath, and these physical symptoms had nothing to do with the practical acts of sabotage they had just committed together.

"I should return to the bookshop," he said at last. "So much work to do and so little time."

"Of course. You're right."

"Listen, don't worry about your grandmother. I've already made papers for her, just in case. I can get her out of Paris at a moment's notice. I promise I won't let them take her. Or you."

"I know you won't," she whispered.

Daisy switched off the lamp, leaving them in unexpected blackness. She found the crack of faint light at the bottom of the door and started toward it, only to bump into some piece of Legrand. His shoulder, from the shape of it. She said *Oof*, and he said *Pardon* and grabbed her arm to steady her, and for an instant she leaned into that arm, very nearly settling herself against his chest. But she stepped back instead, apologized, and reached for the door handle. He followed her out of the study and back down the corridor, and in another moment he would be gone, and Daisy would be left alone in her empty apartment, the long night ahead, only her spinning thoughts for company.

Wilhelmina de Courcelles, Hôtel Ritz. Surely Pierre would not have done this for Daisy's sake? Of course not. Pierre cared only for his own skin.

Whereas Legrand—*I promise I won't let them take her. Or you.*

And he would keep that promise. Legrand was not a man who broke his promises.

They reached the foyer. Without looking at Daisy, Legrand opened the door a few centimeters, looked into the vestibule, and slipped free.

Gone.

Daisy closed the door and leaned against it. Everything was dim and shadowed; night had settled fully outside the windows and in her chest as well, swallowing her ribs and her vital organs, everything. Gone. But of course he was gone; that was right. She was married. She had a husband, however monstrous, and children. She had no business taking this one good thing she had done, these few good deeds, and desecrating them with some sordid act of adultery. She closed her eyes and saw his fingers, operating the safe; she saw his eyes and smile, heard his voice, and her eyes hurt with the strain of her unshed tears.

She felt as if someone had reached inside her chest and torn her heart out, still beating.

The door moved. Daisy jumped back.

Through the opening came Legrand, his head and shoulders and then his whole body. He edged around the door and closed it behind him, while an amazed Daisy stepped back and took in the sight of him.

"The damned concierge is having some conversation with one of your neighbors in the hallway," he said. "Do you mind if I wait a few more minutes?"

Daisy turned and went down the hall to the kitchen. "I'll pour some brandy," she said.

THEY SAT NOT in the drawing room but in the little nook off the dining room, furnished with a sofa and a lamp table, where Daisy liked to read when she had a moment to herself, which wasn't often anymore. "It's my favorite part of the apartment," she explained. "The only room I like at all."

Legrand sat at the other end of the sofa, leaning forward, dangling the snifter between his hands. "I grew up in a rather grand house myself," he said. "And I had a spot just like this one, where I liked to go when I needed a bit of time by myself."

"Somewhere in England."

He looked up at her, and for an instant she thought he was going to deny it. Then he lifted his brandy in a little salute. "Somewhere in England."

She smiled. He smiled.

"Then why are you here?" she asked. "This isn't your fight."

"If you hadn't noticed, my dear, we are at war together."

"Yes, but Paris itself. Our people. It's one thing, training in an army. This, right inside occupied Paris, it's so intimate. And dangerous."

Legrand settled back against the sofa. "I spent a great deal of time in France, before the war. It's a second home to me. It was like an escape from England and all that provincial life. All those daughters of the local squires, in their cardigans and their brogues and their prim little dresses."

"Very sweet girls, I'm sure."

"Sweet, yes. But not very interesting. Not what you'd call cosmopolitan."

"Oh? Am I cosmopolitan?"

He tilted his head and looked at her, and the warmth of his gaze made it seem as if he was actually touching her. "I wouldn't say cosmopolitan, exactly. But you've seen things. You know things. You have this—this marvelous earthy quality, as if you understand much more than you let on, and it makes me . . ."

"And it makes you what?"

He looked away, at the wall, and finished his brandy. "Nothing."

"Tell me."

"You'd laugh at me. Anyway, I shouldn't say it."

"Why not?"

Legrand turned back to her. "Because you're married."

"You've said things to married women before. Don't say you haven't."

"Yes, but you're different."

"Different how?"

"You have a conscience." He set down the snifter on the lamp table and stood. "I'll just see if that talkative concierge of yours has run out of breath."

But when he cracked open the door, the noise of female chatter drifted upward from the staircase, punctuated with a cackle of laughter.

He shut the door again and looked over one shoulder at Daisy. "I could kill them, you know."

"Please don't. People will talk."

"Then I don't suppose you've got a drainpipe out back? Something I can shimmy down?"

"Can you do that?"

"I've had some practice."

"Follow me," she said.

The bedrooms were in the back. She was loath to take him into the children's room—so she told herself, anyway—or to her own bedroom with Pierre, God forbid, with its grand, canopied, ridiculous bed. Instead she led him to the guest bedroom, which was naturally unoccupied, a modest room dressed in blues and yellows. There were two windows at the back. Legrand peered at both of them and judged the distance to the drainpipe, and to the alley three stories below.

"Is it safe?" Daisy whispered.

"Safe as houses."

He started to open the window, and she put her hand on his arm.

"You're wrong," she said. "I used to have a conscience. But it was made of fear, and doubt, and this shame I had, because I had no father, no mother, this crazy grandmother, this crazy childhood inside a hotel. That's why I married Pierre. I wanted to be respectable."

Legrand turned away from the window to face her. She hadn't turned on any lamps, and the room was dark, his face in utter shadow. Probably he couldn't see her any better than she could see him.

"Do you still feel this shame?" he said.

"Sometimes. But mostly I'm afraid I will always be respectable. I'm afraid I will never know what it's like to be free."

Legrand put his hand on her hair and cupped the curve of her head. "My dear Daisy," he whispered. "My dear, brave love."

"Tell me your name," she whispered back.

"It's Kit. Short for Christopher."

"Kit." She went on her toes and kissed his lips. "Kit."

His arms went around her and pulled her gently against him. Outside the window, Paris went on and on, drinking and smoking and clattering, finding a way to survive. But here it was calm and dark, it was everything. She smelled the brandy on his breath, the soap on his skin. She thought, *This is it, I can't go back. The old Daisy is gone.*

She slid her arms around his neck and kissed him again, and this time he kissed her back. Slow and serious, because this was important.

CHAPTER TWENTY-TWO

Babs

Paris, France
April 1964

FELT MY HIGH ponytail swish slowly and gently as I walked down the gallery connecting both sides of the Ritz, eyeing the beautiful wares in the boutique windows. Precious had said I should experiment with shopping on my own here as all of the shops met with her approval, but I hadn't yet found the courage to actually enter one.

I wore another one of my new dresses, a bright green confection with a deep square neckline and short puffed sleeves, but it was so short I was afraid to sit down for fear of exposing myself to unsuspecting passersby. I'd brought my trusty jumper with me to drape over my lap if needed and that had made me feel much better. Or at least dressed. I could only hope I wouldn't run into Precious as I was quite sure she would relieve me of the jumper posthaste.

I looked down at my gold wristwatch, relieved to see that it was time to meet Drew at the Vendôme entrance, and quickly increased my pace before any of the salespeople had a chance to notice me.

My heart gave a little flip as I recognized the back of Drew's head and the broad width of his shoulders beneath a dark suit jacket. But then I spotted the leggy Gigi next to him, and my footsteps slowed involuntarily. I briefly thought of hiding behind a potted palm as Drew and I had done the previous day to avoid Prunella, but then Gigi turned her head and spotted me.

"Mrs. Langford. So lovely to see you again. I just gave Drew more of what he asked for."

There was something indecent in what Gigi said, but I was at a loss to describe exactly what. Drew turned and smiled excitedly, holding up a folder. "She found Pierre Villon. He still lives in Paris."

"How wonderful," I said, my heart sinking. I'd half hoped that we'd heard the last of the Villons and the talisman when we'd spoken to Monsieur Deneaux.

"He lives in the eighteenth arrondissement, which isn't very nice," Gigi explained. "Of course, with Andrew here you are quite safe. He's so big and strong, *oui*?"

I did my best to smile and nod nonchalantly as if I hadn't had the same thought a dozen times a day since I'd met Andrew Bowdoin.

"I must get back to the office. Give me a ring if you need anything else, Andrew. I'm always happy to help."

Gigi winked at Drew then gave a more formal goodbye to me before leaving, heads turning as she and her legs walked across the floor to the door. Drew was more interested in the papers inside the folder than looking at Gigi, making me like him even more.

"There's a lot of interesting stuff in here." He closed the folder. "Come on, let's go."

"Go where?"

"To see Pierre Villon." He started walking toward the door.

"But he'll be at work, won't he? Shouldn't we make some sort of an appointment?"

"Hardly," he said, allowing me to exit in front of him. "He doesn't have a job. Apparently the French have long memories and don't feel inclined to employ a man who spent ten years in prison for war crimes."

"War crimes?"

"I suspected as much when Mr. Doonox mentioned that the Villons lived in an apartment that was way above Pierre's pay grade. During the war, the only people who lived well were the Nazis, and those who worked with them."

"And how would you know about him being in prison?" I asked, hurrying after him in my new chunky heels.

He held up the folder Gigi had given him. "Gigi is a miracle worker when it comes to giving me what I need."

"How nice." He gave me an odd look, forcing me to unclench my jaw. We walked past the line of taxis. "How are we going to get there?"

"Metro. Have you taken it yet? It's really convenient and the nearest stop, the Tuileries, is a quick walk. It might take a while as we have to change trains a couple of times. I hope you don't mind, but it's probably best not to take a car."

I tried not to appear too excited about traveling across the city with Drew at my side. Barring my recent travel to Paris, it was probably one of the most exciting excursions I'd had since taking the trip to Cambridge to bring Robin home. "I don't mind," I said, keeping my voice neutral.

We sat side by side on the jostling train, our arms bumping against each other at regular intervals. He appeared not to notice, but I felt an odd jolt each time. I noticed a young man sitting opposite openly staring at me, and I shifted in my seat, glad I'd thought to drape my jumper over my lap for modesty's sake.

When we eventually emerged up the steps from the underground tunnels onto Paris's Right Bank, I immediately wanted to return to the Ritz. Despite the nearby white dome of the Sacré-Coeur Basilica and the proximity of the river Seine, there was certainly a seedy quality to the neighborhoods we walked through. Many of the buildings were covered with painted words and symbols, some of them quite shocking, which made my cheeks heat. Either Drew was good at pretending he hadn't noticed, or he was too focused on our errand to pay attention to anything else besides the map and the written directions on the piece of paper he held in front of him.

Young women wearing even shorter skirts than I was lurked in doorways calling out greetings to Drew in French. He asked me to translate, but I pretended I didn't understand what they were saying. He stopped in front of a drab cement building, its architectural style as obscure as its year of origin. Bins of foul-smelling garbage sat at the bottom of the steps where two tomcats wound their way around and between them, staring at us suspiciously.

"Are you sure this is the right place?" I asked, remembering what we'd read in the newspaper articles about Pierre Villon's mother-in-law living at the Ritz. Surely her son-in-law couldn't possibly live in such a place.

Drew looked at the piece of paper and then at the painted number on the side of the front door. "This is definitely it." He put his foot on the bottom step. "Stay behind me, all right? Until I know it's safe."

I nodded, feeling my heart squeeze a bit, but not wanting to tell him that as a girl who played with her older brothers and their friends I knew how to throw a punch and where to land a kick. I did as he requested and followed him through the peeling-paint door and into an entryway that smelled of boiled cabbage and Robin's room after he returned from a football match. Mail slots to the right listed the last names of tenants next to their flat numbers.

"There," I said, pointing to the top right. "Villon—number 310."

He nodded. "Come on. Doesn't look like there's an elevator so we'll take the stairs. Stay close to me, all right?"

I nodded, my heart doing that odd squeezing thing again. We

climbed to the third floor, listening to the lives of those behind the doors as we passed. A baby crying, a woman shouting. A man singing in Italian. It was all somehow sad, that the demoiselle's husband should live here in this dismal, foul-smelling place.

When we reached number 310, we stopped and stared at the door where the word *collaborateur* had been painted in thick red letters in scarlet accusation. It appeared that someone had once tried to scrub it out, but the outline of the word remained like a ghostly reminder. We looked at each other for a moment and then Drew knocked on the door, beckoning for me to stand back. It took three knocks before we heard an epithet coming from behind the door, and then slow footsteps approaching.

"Who is it?" The French words were slurred.

Before Drew could speak, I stepped forward. "My name is Mrs. Barbara Langford and I'm with Mr. Andrew Bowdoin. Are you Pierre Villon? We'd like to talk to you about your wife, Marguerite Villon, and her connection to the de Courcelles family."

"Daisy?" The door flew open, revealing an unkempt man with greasy hair that was more salt than pepper and a paunch that tested the integrity of the buttons on his dirty shirt. He was quickly trying to button the remaining buttons, the gaping holes displaying corpulent white skin and graying chest hair. The scent of cheap wine on his breath washed over us, making me almost choke. "I am Pierre. Come in, come in," he said, beckoning us into the squalor of a one-room flat that reeked of spilled spirits. Which was a blessing, really, as underneath it all the stench of unwashed skin clung to the walls and moth-eaten rug like spilled milk.

"Who is Daisy?" Drew asked.

The little man looked up at Drew, the difference in their heights almost comical. Except the expression on the man's face was anything but. The man responded in passable English. "Marguerite was her real name, but everyone always called her Daisy." His eyes welled up with tears and I couldn't help myself from touching his arm and leading him to a sofa. I sat down with him, ignoring the dark stains that could have been food or perhaps not. I preferred not to think of it.

"And what happened to Daisy?" I asked gently, holding on to his hand. I heard Drew take a deep intake of breath.

He shrugged his shoulders then returned to slumped defeat. "I don't know. She disappeared during the war, along with Madeleine and Olivier."

"Your children?"

"Yes. A boy and a girl." He shook his head sadly. "I never saw them again, either."

"I'm sorry," I said. I started to ask him to tell me more about them, but Drew interrupted me.

"Did you ever hear from Daisy or the children? To let you know that they're alive?"

Pierre perked up for the first time. "Not a letter, but a photograph. It was sent to me anonymously when I was in prison." He stood and slowly shuffled to a bedside table with a single drawer, its knob missing. With the stubby end of a finger he pried it open and then removed a single photo. He looked down at it for a long moment, letting out a sigh of despair sounding as if it had come from his every pore.

"They are older in this photograph than they were when I last saw them, which means they survived the war, yes?"

"Yes, it would," I said with as much confidence as I could muster. There was no need to crush the last hope this man had managed to cling to. I took the photograph as Drew moved to stand next to me while we examined it. They were beautiful children, the daughter with two long dark braids, a few years older and slightly taller than her brother. They appeared to be in the awkward early teen years, the evidence of childhood fading from the boy's rounded cheeks and the girl's wide eyes, their legs long and spindly like a colt's.

"They're lovely," I said, handing the photo back to Pierre.

"And you don't know who sent it?" Drew asked with an incredulous tone, his eyes narrowed slightly as if he were interviewing a witness to a crime. I wanted to tell him to stop, that Mr. Villon had already suffered enough.

"*Non*. I liked to assume it was Daisy, because that would mean she was still alive. But there was nothing to trace where it came from or from whom. That would have been so like her. She had good reason to despise me, but she would have wanted me to know that Madeleine and Olivier were safe and well."

"Why would she despise you?" I asked gently.

Milky brown eyes turned to me. "She considered me an inadequate husband. I tried to give her nice things, to provide for us in the way in which she'd been raised. She had lived at the Ritz, with her *grandmère*, her entire life, until we married. I only wanted the best for us. But she . . ." He shrugged. "She and I liked different things."

He sat down again on the filthy sofa as if remembering the past had cost him all of his energy. Unwilling to join him again on the stained sofa or to sit on the unmade bed with dirty sheets, Drew and I remained standing.

"I knew she was having an affair. I never saw them together, but she changed. She was no longer the content woman she'd been. She became someone else entirely so that I barely recognized my own wife." He stared at the blank wall, his eyes narrowing. "But I took care of that little problem."

"What do you mean?" I asked.

He looked at me as if just remembering I was there, as his thoughts moved forward from the past. He shook his head slowly. "She was still my wife, and we had the children together. A man has the right to protect what is his, doesn't he?"

"Of course." I tried to sound sympathetic. "So what did you do?"

He shook his head. "I don't talk about it. I need to find Daisy, so I can say I'm sorry. To beg her forgiveness. And then, perhaps, when it doesn't weigh so heavy on my soul, I can talk about it."

Drew cleared his throat. "Did you ever visit her grandmother, the Comtesse de Courcelles, at the Ritz to ask of Daisy's whereabouts?"

Pierre shook his head. "I was in a Nazi camp during the end of the war, and then a French prison for ten years. When I emerged, the comtesse was gone—either died, or moved, I do not know. Not that she would have ever told me anything. She didn't like me very much."

"What of the talisman?" Drew pressed. "Did Daisy ever talk about it, or show it to you?"

"Pfft. It was all nonsense, all that talk of legend. I would have only been interested in the priceless jewels that surrounded it, anyway. This is probably why Daisy never talked about it with me."

Drew sighed with his own disappointment. "I see. Well, thank you for your time. If you can think of anything else about Daisy or the talisman, we're staying at the Ritz."

"How nice for you," Pierre said bitterly.

We said our goodbyes, but as we were leaving Pierre roused himself again and stood. "If you find Daisy, will you tell her . . . tell her . . ." He stopped, reconsidering his words. "I would like to talk with her. And let her know that even though I know I don't deserve it, I would like to see the children."

Before Drew could quell all hope, I spoke up. "Of course, Mr. Villon. I will be sure of it."

"*Merci*."

When we made it outside I had to take several deep breaths to get the stench of despair and neglect out of my nose. I saw Drew watching me. "I know, I shouldn't have pity on a collaborator. But he wants to see his children. Surely that means there is *something* redeeming about him?"

"Possibly. Although I'd be curious to know what he did to Daisy's lover. I have a feeling it wasn't something nice." He took my elbow and began leading me in the opposite direction from where we'd arrived.

"Where are we going? It's a bit late to be caught on this side of town, I think. Perhaps we should head back to the Ritz?"

He shook his head. "Nope."

"No? Aren't you hungry? It's getting close to suppertime."

He gave me a grin that seemed quite lascivious. "I already told you, Babs—I'm always hungry so yes, I am. That's why I made reservations at one of the best restaurants in Paris that happens to be not too far from here."

"But it will be dark by the time we finish eating . . ."

"Stop worrying, Babs. I promise to get you back to the Ritz safely. But today happens to be my birthday, and for my present I want to take you out for a night of fun. You've had a rough few years, without a lot of fun, I think, so here's your chance."

I looked down at my jumper. "But I'm hardly dressed to go out . . ."

Before I could finish my sentence, he'd unceremoniously removed my jumper. "There. Now you look even more amazing." He shoved my jumper into a nearby dustbin, but I stumbled over my complaint as I recognized the appreciation in his eyes as he regarded me.

"But I'll be cold," I finally managed.

"Not where we're going." His lascivious smile had returned.

"We're going to hell?"

"Hardly. Just the Moulin Rouge." He took my arm again and began leading me down the sidewalk. "Have you been before?"

"No. I don't believe it's a place one goes with one's mother and sister, who are the only companions I've had on my Paris visits. Besides, my brother Charles told me that there's an aquarium where naked women swim with snakes. Not really quality entertainment, I don't think."

If I'd expected for him to turn us around at that, I would have been wrong. "Yeah, I've seen them. Don't worry. The snakes can't get out."

"It wasn't the snakes I was concerned about."

He squeezed my hand against his side. "Oh, come on, Babs. It'll be fun. You need to let your hair down every once in a while. You wouldn't begrudge a man having fun on his birthday, would you?"

"No, I suppose not . . ."

"Great. Did you know that more champagne is served at the Moulin Rouge each year than anyplace else in the world?"

"I didn't know. Although I'm not sure I should drink . . ."

"It's my birthday, Babs. Just try a glass of champagne to toast my big day, all right?"

"Just one, though." I fought back the memory of us drinking together at Bar Hemingway on the night we'd met. At least Precious and Prunella wouldn't be there to keep them coming.

As we headed down the Boulevard de Clinchy, I spotted the iconic red windmill and the bright neon lights announcing the *Frou-Frou* revue performed twice a night. I'd seen pictures, of course, of the famous cabaret dancers with their frilly skirts and high kicks, but I'd always imagined the whole experience of the Moulin Rouge as being a little naughty. Definitely not the sort of place to which Kit would deem appropriate to take me. So it was with almost a feeling of defiance that I entered on Drew's arm, determined to enjoy myself.

Tiers of white-clothed tables dressed with red table lamps surrounded the stage. A bottle of champagne was already waiting for us as we were seated near the stage, and as Drew pushed in my chair, he spoke close to my ear. "You're in for a treat tonight, Babs. I want you to enjoy yourself."

I felt a warm shiver of anticipation jump along my spine. "But it's *your* birthday," I protested as he seated himself across from me.

"Trust me. Seeing you enjoying yourself will be the best kind of present."

The waiter poured two glasses of champagne. I was about to make a small toast to his birthday when Drew raised his own glass. "To La Fleur. Without whom we never would have met."

I didn't want to toast the enigmatic La Fleur, but I didn't have a choice. I took a small sip, allowing the bubbles to tickle my nose, then another larger one, hoping to forget all about La Fleur for at least an evening.

WHEN I AWOKE the following morning, I kept my eyes closed, still feeling the rhythm of the music of the cancan inside my head. I opened one eye, and then the next, aware of two things at once. The first was that I was not in my bed. The second was that I wasn't alone. I sat up quickly, my head spinning, aware that I was fully dressed except for my shoes. I had an odd recollection of kicking them off to climb onstage with the dancers and Drew pulling me back. But surely that had been a dream?

Drew lay supine next to me, shirtless, but at least wearing his pants and socks. Certainly that meant we hadn't, well, we hadn't. The opulent surroundings told me that we were in his room at the Ritz and not still in Montmartre, although I had no memory of returning to the hotel.

He appeared to be sleeping, although he wasn't snoring. Kit didn't snore, either, so I must be a good judge at choosing sleeping partners. I allowed my gaze to pause on Drew's naked chest, at the smattering of gold-tinted hair and the pronounced muscles that moved under his tanned torso as he breathed. My fingers twitched, wanting to reach out and touch that smooth expanse of skin, to remember what a man's bare skin felt like under my hand.

Instead, I clenched my hands into fists and began to slide out of the bed, being careful not to disturb the bedclothes. I wanted to escape to my own room, to pretend this hadn't happened, but the need to use the water closet was too urgent to be ignored. I tiptoed across the carpet toward the bathroom, carefully closing the door behind me.

As I turned on the golden swan tap to wash my hands, I looked into the mirror above the vanity. For a long moment I simply stared, not recognizing the woman who looked back at me. Her fine gray eyes were wide and worldly. Knowing, somehow. Me, yet not me. The sleeve of my dress had slipped from my shoulder, revealing one of the new brassieres Precious had helped me select. It was lacy and feminine and lifted me in places where I hadn't been lifted since before my first child. I leaned forward, staring at the face of this woman who'd experienced life and love and loss. But whose eyes still shone with light. It was the face of a formidable woman. A woman who wouldn't recognize defeat.

I returned to the bedroom, quietly moving past the bed toward the door.

"Are you back for some rompy-frumpy?"

I jumped at the sound of Drew's voice. I slowly turned to see him lying on his side facing me, a sly grin on his face.

"It's rumpy-pumpy," I corrected, my mouth lifting in an involuntary smile.

He raised his eyebrows in question.

"No, I'm not. Unless . . ." I indicated the bed with my chin, hoping he'd understand what I meant.

He shook his head. "No, we didn't. Although it wasn't from lack of trying. You tore my shirt to shreds trying to take it off me. I thought it best if we slept it off before we did anything . . . rash."

I nodded, relieved and disappointed at the same time. "Yes, well. I should go."

He held his hand out to me. "Don't."

I looked at his hand and then his eyes, both telling me to stay. I remembered the woman's reflection in the mirror, *my* reflection, and smiled. I reached behind my neck and slid down the zipper of my dress, letting it fall to my ankles, revealing my new undergarments. And when I saw the look on Drew's face, I finally understood their purpose.

CHAPTER TWENTY-THREE

Aurélie

The Château de Courcelles
Picardy, France
April 1915

THERE WERE SO many bits of her body she had never quite understood the purpose of until now.

Aurélie lay curled up against Max on the narrow camp bed, in the drowsy peace of the dark room. Her head was pillowed against his collarbone, and she knew she ought to feel exactly what Hoffmeister had called her, a German officer's whore, but she couldn't muster the energy.

She didn't feel ruined; she felt as though she had always been here and always should, with Max's chest rising and falling beneath her cheek, flesh to flesh beneath his scratchy blanket.

Out of the darkness, she heard Max's voice, just above her head. She could feel the words before she heard them, feel them reverberating in his chest. "Would your mayor marry us?"

"Acting mayor," said Aurélie. "The real one's gone off to war. Wait. Did you say marry?"

Max raised his head slightly, looking down at her. "But, of course. You will marry me, won't you?"

Aurélie scrambled up slightly, or as much as she could in the narrow space between Max and the wall, the movement causing all sorts of interesting things to brush against each other. She really hadn't thought. Not of marriage, not of consequences, not of anything beyond the moment. "But you can't marry me."

Max wiggled up slightly against the pillow. "Is it because I am not a Catholic? I had thought, in France, one could marry by civil ceremony."

"Well, yes, one may. But there are other concerns—for one thing," Aurélie said, falling back on the easiest excuse she could think of, one that didn't involve complicated questions of loyalty and honor, "you haven't asked me."

Max gently curled a strand of her hair around his finger. "I had assumed, since you compromised me . . ."

"Don't be absurd," said Aurélie, blushing, and very glad he couldn't see it. She shoved her hair back behind her ears. It felt very louche, the feeling of her own, unbound hair against her bare back. "You did a fair bit of compromising on your own."

"Well, then," said Max, as though it were settled. "I would get down on my knees, but I seem to be in want of trousers."

"Don't," said Aurélie hastily. "The bed would be very cold without you."

"Also the stones of the floor," said Max. "But I would happily freeze my knees for love of you."

"I don't believe love requires such tests as that," said Aurélie absently. Max was stroking her bare arm and it was very distracting. "But, really, Max! How could we possibly marry now? It's not because you're not Catholic"—there were dispensations for that—"or because you haven't proposed properly," she added, just in case he decided to try the frozen knee approach after all. "Did you think what people would say? Hoffmeister would use it as an excuse to have you court-martialed. And my people—they would think I had betrayed them."

That was the real reason, and they both knew it. The Demoiselle de Courcelles was a symbolic figure, more so than ever after her very public defiance. Her argument with Hoffmeister at that first, horrible dinner had already become legend. Local gossip had turned her exploits into something more than they were, making her a latter-day Robin Hood.

To marry the enemy would be to betray everyone who believed in her, who clung to her legend for hope.

"I see," said Max, and the worst part was that she was fairly sure he did. Aurélie braced herself for reproaches, but all he said was, "After the war, then."

"Yes, after the war," said Aurélie, but it hurt a bit to say it, to pretend. Because surely this war would go on forever and there would be no after. Or he would go back to Berlin and realize that he had been mistaken in her, that she was just another souvenir of Paris, like a pressed flower or a theater program, a remembrance of a time that had been rich and calm, before the world went mad.

"We wouldn't have to live all the year in Berlin," said Max, and she realized he meant it seriously, quite seriously.

Aurélie drew her knees up to her chest. "Where, then? Paris?"

"If you like." There was a slight pause. "Would you like?"

"I never felt truly at home in Paris." She had always felt large and awkward next to her mother. "I've always thought I would live in the country someday, with a house full of dogs."

"Only dogs?"

"Children, too, I suppose." There had never been a husband in her imagining. Or, rather, there had, but he had been in the background, largely absent. "And motorcars, of course."

"I never had a dog," said Max. He stretched his arms above his head, finding a more comfortable spot on the pillow. "They made my mother sneeze. But I always wanted one."

"What about a half dozen?"

"Large or small?" inquired Max.

"Large." Aurélie thought for a moment. "Although I do rather like King Charles spaniels."

"And wolfhounds?"

"Of course." Her father had always had wolfhounds. Clovis was the last of his line. When she thought of Courcelles, it was of the feel of fur between her fingers, the hot moisture of a large tongue licking her cheek.

As if he could tell what she was thinking, Max said, "We could spend summers here. If your father would allow us."

Aurélie looked down at him, at the dim outlines of his face in the darkness. "If he sanctions the match, you mean."

Max sighed and pulled her down beside him, into the crook of his arm. "I'd like to think, had there been no war, there would have been nothing to which he could object."

"He did approve of your grandfather. He doesn't approve of many people." Aurélie rested her head on Max's shoulder, trailing her fingers across his bare chest. Such an interesting and alien thing, a male chest, rising and falling with his breath, lightly fuzzed with pale hair. "And if my father refuses his blessing? Will you elope with me despite his objections?"

Max's voice was very quiet in the darkness. "Oughtn't I to be asking that of you?"

Aurélie's fingers stilled on his chest; she could feel the weight of the silence pressing around her. It wasn't just marriage he was proposing now. He was asking if she would defy her father, her people, to follow him.

"My father left me." In the dark, in the quiet, with Max's arm around her, it was easy to speak honestly, to speak the truths she wouldn't even admit to herself. "Not once, but again and again and again. He would miss me, I think. When he remembered me. But I'm not sure he would. If he objected to our marriage, it would not be out of concern for me, but for what people would think—of what you are. Not who you are, but what you are."

"German," Max supplied for her.

"He would be wrong," said Aurélie, coming to a conclusion and knowing it was right. She could feel Max's breath release. "If the war were over and our countries were at peace, then, yes, yes I would run away with you. They do have lakes and meadows in Germany, haven't they?"

"And ducks and drakes and wildflowers," he said, and kissed her.

It was, Aurélie thought, rather a good thing to be ruined. It meant one could be ruined again without suffering any awkward twinges of conscience. She now began to understand why so many of her mother's great friends were fallen women, and why they seemed to so enjoy being fallen.

Some time later, some rather long time later, they nestled together in sweat-damp sheets. As if there had been no break in their conversation, Max said, "I don't only live in Berlin, you know. My mother needed to stay in town, to see specialists, but my real home is in Prosen, in a town called Rydzyna."

"Rid-what?"

Max chuckled. "Rydzyna. There was a castle there held by my ancestors long, long ago."

"Back when they went on Crusade with my ancestors," said Aurélie drowsily. She tried to stifle a yawn and failed. Being ruined was exhilarating and exhausting.

"Most likely," said Max, and she felt the press of his lips against her hair. "But we hadn't the luck you've had with your castle. Ours was destroyed during the Thirty Years' War and built up again after. It's more a manor house than a castle."

"You mean it's not drafty and riddled with mice?" said Aurélie. "I'm not sure if I can lower myself to that sort of modern convenience."

After a brief tussle, Max said, "I can't answer for the mice, but we do have close stoves in most of the major rooms, which take care of the drafts rather nicely. The house sits on a lake—a manmade one, I'm afraid. My ancestor thought it would be rather nice to live on an island, so he made one for himself."

"I understand the impulse." An island sounded quite perfect at the moment, an island where one could love and be true, without the conflicting demands of affection and honor. Where no one would trouble them, or catalogue the number of coffee grinders, or threaten them with artillery and treason. "Would we live on your island, then?"

"If you would like it. I should like it—if you would like it."

"I think I should like it," said Aurélie gravely. "Very much. We could have little boats for the children."

"And for the dogs?"

Aurélie gave him a withering look, which was rather wasted in the darkness. "*Not* for the dogs. They can swim."

"So shall our children," said Max easily. "I will teach them."

"You can swim?" said Aurélie, trying to ignore both the casual reference to their children and the image of Max stripped down to his skivvies in a sunlit stream.

"Of course. One doesn't live on an island without learning to swim. I'm not sure how old I was when I first fell into the lake. Or if I fell or was tossed." He touched a finger to Aurélie's cheek. "Shall I teach you to swim? The lake is particularly lovely in the summer twilight."

"Do you promise not to toss me?" Too late, Aurélie realized the double entendre. "I didn't mean—er. Tell me more about your home."

"Our home." Max leaned back against the pillows, bringing her with him. "There are formal gardens—my grandmother saw to those—but what I like best are the wildflowers. Fields and fields of wildflowers. The land is very flat and rather damp, and in the spring, when all is blooming . . ."

Aurélie frowned at his chin. "How could you bear to be in Paris when you had that waiting for you?"

"You were in Paris," said Max simply.

When they could speak again, Aurélie said unsteadily, "I'm not clever like you, you know. I'm not cultured or well-read. I can't debate philosophy in three languages—or even one."

"But you can outshoot me. Didn't you tell me so?" When Aurélie didn't smile, Max turned so that they were lying on their sides, on a level, looking directly at each other, his fingers twined through hers. "I don't love you for any of those things, you know. Not because you can outrace me or outshoot me, or doubtless outfence me, too. You are . . ."

"Yes?"

"You are you," he said to her, as she had said to him what felt a very long time ago. "You are remarkable just as you are. There is no one else in the world like you and there is no one else for me. And I don't care if you've read Plato or Kant or last week's *Paris-Midi*."

"I haven't got last week's *Paris-Midi*. Or last month's. And half the time I didn't bother to read it, anyway."

"You see?" said Max, and she could hear the tenderness in his voice. "You are the most honest person I know. The most honest and the most honorable."

Except when she wasn't.

She could feel the talisman between them, as if it were there. She had lied to him about the talisman; she had lied to him about everything. Except what had happened between them in this bed. That much was true.

"But I'm not." Aurélie drew back a bit, determined to disabuse him. "I was meant to beguile you, you know. To rifle your conversation for spare bits of intelligence."

"It's just as well I haven't any, then," said Max, but when she didn't smile at it, he drew her closer. "My heart, don't you think I know? You were never subtle about it."

"I wasn't?" Aurélie wasn't sure whether she ought to be offended.

Max affected a falsetto. "'Goodness, it's cold for November, isn't it, and by the way, have you heard anything about an offensive?'"

Aurélie pushed against his chest with both hands. "I never sounded like *that*."

"I paraphrased," said Max, unabashed, and Aurélie wrinkled her nose at him, even though she wasn't quite sure he could see it in the darkness. His voice changed, grew serious. "I have heard one thing, though."

"Are you really sure you should be telling me? I don't think that's a very good idea."

"You really aren't very good at being a spy, are you?" said Max tenderly.

"No," Aurélie agreed glumly. "I'd make a much better general."

"So you should. I shouldn't want to stand against you. But this isn't like that. Everyone will know soon enough."

"What?" There was something about his tone that made her very nervous.

Max stared up at the ceiling, choosing his words carefully. "The High Command has decided there are too many mouths to feed in the occupied territories. They have decided to allow a select number of people to leave. Women and children and men too old to till the fields," he specified.

"Leave for where?" Too many people had already been sent to work camps in Germany.

"To France—the other parts of France, that is. The convoy will travel first to Switzerland, and from there, back into France. They mean not to tell anyone until a few days before, so that people won't have much time to prepare. The first convoy will leave in June." There was a moment of silence, before Max said, "I should like you to be in it."

Aurélie sat up, accidentally elbowing him in the chest. "Me?"

Max looked at her gravely. "You. I would feel better knowing that you were safely in Paris."

Aurélie pleated the sheet with her fingers, trying to make sense of what he was saying. "But . . . what about my people?"

"They have your father to look after them. Isn't that what you said?"

Yes, when he wasn't risking his own skin playing with pigeons. Aurélie shoved her tousled hair away from her face. "But Hoffmeister would never let me go."

"No. But if you were to acquire forged papers, you could be gone before he realized. You would have to cover your hair. You're too recognizable as you are. But it could be done."

Aurélie stared at the outlines of his face, wishing she dared light the lamp. "You've thought of this before."

"As soon as I heard about the evacuations." They were only centimeters apart, but Max suddenly felt very far away. Quietly, he said, "If you go, I'll go."

Aurélie bristled. "That's not fair. You can't tie your survival to my desertion!"

"Aren't you asking me to do the same? To desert to save myself?"

He didn't need to sound so damnably reasonable. "I'm not telling you to desert! Only to get yourself reassigned."

"And is that not the same as what I ask of you?" Max took her limp hands in his, chafing them gently to warm them. "Aurélie, I don't know what plots and intrigues you've embroiled yourself in. I don't want to know. All I ask is that you conduct them from Paris, not here."

Paris. She had run from Paris, had come all this way, through horrors unspeakable. And what had she done? Fallen in love with a German. And served as a symbol for her people. There was that. And the food she had brought, while little, had been sorely needed. She was needed.

"And if I were to refuse?" Aurélie's voice cracked on the words.

Max didn't hesitate. "Then I stay here with you."

Aurélie frowned at him. "Is that a threat?"

"Not a threat. A promise. We protect each other, you and I."

"Even though we're on opposite sides?" Without meaning to, Aurélie found herself leaning into his warmth, resting her head against his shoulder. Max's arm curled around her, supporting her, warming her. In a small voice, she said, "I wish we were on your island."

Max's sigh ruffled her hair. "So do I. So do I." He nuzzled the top of her head. "But soon. Soon. I mean it, you know. I don't care what the rest of the war brings, I don't care who wins or loses, so long as we can be together after."

Aurélie rubbed her head against his shoulder. "That's treason, you know."

"Would I prefer that my country win? Certainly. But after this . . . ah well. There are monsters anywhere. Aren't there?" He sounded as though he were trying to convince himself. "We'll need papers for you."

Reluctantly, Aurélie said, "I know someone who might be able to acquire them."

He didn't ask who or how. It was, Aurélie realized, safer for them both that he not know. They were skirting the edges of dishonor. "Good. When you have them, tell me what name you will be going under. I will add it to the list."

"I don't recall agreeing to go." Had she? She was beginning to suspect that Max's unassuming ways hid a very strong will. He would never force her, not in anything, that she knew for sure. But, somehow, he had a way of winning an argument.

"Think about it. Please?"

"I'll think about it." Aurélie turned toward him without thinking, her bare breasts brushing against his chest. "I'll think about going."

"But please." Max made a strangled sound deep in his throat, half groan, half chuckle. In the darkness, his lips found hers. "Don't go yet."

A LOUD NOISE woke her, reverberating through her ears. Aurélie's first thought was that Suzanne had dropped a pot down below in the kitchen, and she tried to bury her head back under her pillow. But the pillow was thinner than hers, the sheets coarser, and when she rolled over, she nearly fell off the edge of the bed.

Aurélie sat up abruptly, realizing she was also not wearing any clothes, and remembering, in vivid detail, why.

Clutching the blanket to her chest with one hand, she wiped the sleep out of her eyes with the other. "Was that—"

"A pistol." Max was already in his uniform trousers, pulling the braces up over his shoulders. "Is there a way you can leave without being seen?"

"Through the storerooms." That was enough to wake her up with a vengeance. Aurélie began feeling around for her discarded garments, which appeared to have migrated to all the corners of the room.

Shrugging into his coat, Max said, "I'll go see what's happened out there. You wait a few minutes and then go the other way."

"All right," said Aurélie, feeling blowsy and bleary. She struggled to reach the buttons at the back of her dress.

With swift efficiency, Max did them up for her. And then, to her surprise, he knelt before her. Possessing himself of both her hands, he pressed a kiss to each. "Soon," he said. "Soon, we will be together properly."

"On your island on the lake," murmured Aurélie, looking down at his shining golden head. Her chest felt tight.

There was shouting outside and the sound of booted feet. Max gave her hands one last, firm squeeze. "Soon." He pressed a hard kiss to her lips. "Soon."

And he snatched up his hat and was gone.

Aurélie hastily pinned up her hair with whatever pins she could glean from the worn boards of the floor, wrinkled her nose at herself in Max's scrap of a shaving mirror—did she look as though she'd been thoroughly tumbled?—and hurried down the stairs, taking the long route back through the storerooms to the kitchen of the new wing, from which she hurried across the courtyard as though she had only just been roused from bed. From her own bed.

There was a confusion of people in the courtyard, but at the center of it, Aurélie could make out a cluster of German uniforms: Hoffmeister, flanked by Dreier on one side and Kraus's flaming red head on the other. Across from them stood her father. They were all staring at something on the ground.

Aurélie pushed and wiggled her way through, elbowing Suzanne and stepping on Victor's foot.

"Pardon me, excuse me. . . . What's this?" She arrived breathless at her father's side.

"What do you think it is, mademoiselle?" clipped Hoffmeister, and Aurélie finally looked down and saw what they had all been staring at.

A pigeon.

A dead pigeon, lying in a welter of blood-stained feathers.

"It's a bird," she said dumbly.

Behind Hoffmeister, she could see Max, looking so very official and German again in his uniform and cap.

"Not just any bird. A pigeon. Well?" Hoffmeister demanded, so suddenly and so loudly that everyone jumped. "Whose is this? Who was keeping this pigeon?"

No one spoke.

Hoffmeister's face was white with fury—but also a strange, furtive satisfaction. "I will find out. I don't care who you are, or what you think you are, I will find out, and the miscreant will be shot."

The count's hand tightened on his wolfhound's collar as Clovis snarled at Hoffmeister.

"Have you considered that it might have been passing through?" He sounded thoroughly bored, but Aurélie could see how white his knuckles were against Clovis's graying fur.

Hoffmeister raised his pistol, training it on Aurélie's father. "You do know," the major said, in a dangerously conversational tone, "that to keep a pigeon is death."

"There was a time," said the count blandly, rubbing the area between Clovis's ears, "when to keep a pigeon was dinner."

"You will not joke about this. You are lord here? Good. Then you take responsibility for your people. Any pigeons I find are your pigeons."

Max put a hand on Hoffmeister's arm. "Sir, with respect . . ."

"Enough! You want your—what do you call it?—your noblesse oblige? You take the consequences. If I find another pigeon, Monsieur le Comte, it does not matter where or how I find it. You will die for it. Do you not think I mean it?"

The only response was the shuffling of feet in the courtyard, the lowering of eyes.

Hoffmeister's lips pressed tightly together. His gun was pointing at Aurélie's father still, shaking slightly with the force of his rage.

"This," he said tightly, "this will be your fate if I find another one of these cursed birds."

He lowered the gun and pulled the trigger.

The sound of the report hammered against Aurélie's ears, broken by an agonized yelp that turned into a low howl.

"Clovis!" He was lying on the flagstones; there was blood on his fur. Aurélie flung herself down beside him, her hands moving desperately over his coat, trying to find the wound. "Clovis, Clovis."

At her voice, the old wolfhound struggled to rise, but his legs folded beneath him. His tongue lolled out of his mouth.

"Clovis!" Aurélie frantically shrugged out of her shawl, wadding the material against Clovis's side to stanch the blood.

"It's no use," said her father, his voice tight. "There's no saving him."

"Remember that." The major was standing above them, and it was all Aurélie could do not to snarl at him, not to wrench that wretched pistol from his hand and bludgeon him with it. "Remember. Next time I shoot your daughter, perhaps. Your dog, your daughter . . . and then you. Do not give me cause."

He turned without waiting for a response and marched away, his sycophants falling into place behind him. Max cast one long, concerned look over his shoulder at Aurélie. Through the fog of her tears, she vaguely saw him raise his brows at her and cock his head.

Leave, he was saying. Leave.

A hand grasped her arm, a hand considerably more twisted than she remembered, with brown splotches on it. "Come away." Her father drew her to her feet and stood for a moment, beside her, looking down at his old companion. Gruffly, he said, "He was old. He had a good life."

"You can't mean that."

Her father looked down at her and Aurélie saw that he wasn't calm at all; he was stiff with rage. He began walking rapidly toward the new wing. "Would I prefer to thrash that canaille until he is nothing more than pulp? Certainly. But now is not the time."

"He means to kill us all." Aurélie grabbed his arm, pulling him into the relative shelter of the kitchen garden. In a low voice, she said, "You can't do anything more with the pigeons. If he finds another—"

"How, pray, am I meant to send messages to Paris? Donkey and cart?"

"Send them by me." She hadn't thought it until she said it, but there it was, fully formed. "There is to be a civilian evacuation next month. Send the messages with me."

Her father looked at her assessingly. "Where did you hear this? From your lieutenant?"

"Yes," said Aurélie shortly.

Her father plucked a spear of last year's lavender, still winter gray. He rubbed it between his fingers. "He wants you to go."

"He wants me safe."

Her father tossed the mangled lavender aside. "Maybe he wants you out of the way."

Did he? For a moment, Aurélie wondered. But then she remembered Max kneeling before her, his head bowed. Soon. If he wanted her out of the way, it was for her own safety—and his, she reminded herself. If she went, he went.

But she wasn't going to tell her father that.

There was so much she couldn't tell, not to Max, not to her father.

Aurélie shrugged, looking away. "Does it matter, if it serves our purpose?"

"That depends on the *our*," said her father. He was standing very straight, as though back in the military. "You ask me to work with a German."

"I ask a German to work with you. If you provide the necessary papers, he will find me a place on the convoy."

Her father smiled without humor. "You would compromise my honor and his. You are thorough, I give you that."

Aurélie grimaced at her father. "Or perhaps no one's honor need be compromised. He removes a thorn in the flesh of the German command. And I—I get your messages through. And there's something else," Aurélie added all in a rush. "There's something I didn't tell you. I have the talisman. Here. At Courcelles."

That, at least, had the benefit of getting her father's attention. "Here?"

"Here." She didn't tell him where. The very stones of the castle had ears these days. "I thought I could do some good with it, that my very being here with the talisman would somehow make the Germans retreat."

She felt foolish even saying it, but her father didn't mock her. "I, too, once," he said, staring out over the bedded remains of last year's herbs. "I brought it with me into battle and watched my comrades fall around me."

"You were not the demoiselle," said Aurélie, and winced, because if it failed to work because he was not the demoiselle, what did it mean, then, that it had not worked for her? Was she less than the true born daughter of her father? No, her eyebrows were his, most definitely. There was no implication that her mother had played her father false until well after Aurélie had been born. No one disputed her birth, only her upbringing. "I had thought, in my hand, it would work."

Her father's hand settled on her shoulder. He gave a heavy pat, his one gesture of affection, the same he had given her when she was a girl and skinned her knees climbing the old tower stairs and didn't cry as Suzanne bandaged them up again. "These things work in ways that pass our understanding. Who knows? Maybe it is working, even now. Maybe . . ."

"Maybe?"

"Maybe you are right. Maybe we send you back to Paris with the word that you have retrieved the talisman from the hands of the enemy. We spread the message through France that the demoiselle holds the talisman and the enemy must fall."

CHAPTER TWENTY-FOUR

Daisy

Le Mouton Noir
Paris, France
November 1942

T HEY *MUST* FALL," said Daisy. "They *will* fall. This can't be for nothing."

Beneath her hand, Kit stirred, slurred, mumbled. "Fall? What's fallen?"

"The Germans. *Will* fall. They must. The news from Algiers . . ."

"*Algiers?* Why are we talking about Algiers?"

Daisy lifted her head. "Because it's the breakthrough we've been waiting for! The tide's turning, I can feel it. And Algiers is *our* doing, just four hundred of us Resistance overturning the Vichy pigs—"

"My dear. Can't you ever just *bask?* For a *moment?* Even . . . even half . . . half a *minute* . . ."

Kit's voice fell away into the pillow. His eyes were still closed, his muscles slack. This was one of the few points of incompatibility between the two of them: Kit fell into a stupor immediately after lovemaking, whereas sex tended to charge Daisy with new life. As Kit rolled away semiconscious, Daisy wanted to cuddle and talk (*chatter,*

Kit called it) and sometimes even to make love all over again, although Kit was generally willing to oblige *that* impulse, after a certain amount of encouragement. She said it was because they had so little time like this together. Almost always, when they were able to snatch an hour or two together at all, they met in the morning or the early afternoon, while the children were at school, clock ticking away, and Daisy didn't want to miss a single minute in slumber. Kit said nonsense, she was just that sort of woman. *What sort?* she asked dangerously, and Kit, without stopping to consider, or perhaps too knackered to think, walked straight into that trap. *The sort who finds sex invigorating,* he replied, and Daisy had made him pay for that careless observation, never fear.

But that was months ago. Now they'd grown used to each other's habits, to all the shades of expression and gesture and humor. Kit was so familiar that Daisy, gazing at his face, catching his glance across the bookshop or her grandmother's suite or some discreet café in the tangled alleys of the Left Bank, knew exactly what he was thinking, anticipated exactly what he would say. Lying here in Kit's narrow bed, clothes strewn around them, skin glowing furiously, she felt as if they had somehow grafted together, two seedlings grown into one, her postcoital vigor merging into his languor as two parts of the same perfect whole. She was Kit, and Kit was Daisy. As they had just established yet again. She folded her hands beneath her chin and stared at Kit's lips.

"It's been *two* minutes, at least," she said, "and I don't see how you can fall asleep at a time like this."

"I don't see how you can remain awake at a time like this."

Daisy traced the curve of his chin with her fingertip. "But don't you see? Every victory, each little advance, it's not just a victory for France. It's a victory for us."

"How's that, darling?" Kit mumbled.

"Because once the Germans are defeated, we're free, you and me. I can leave Pierre, and we can get married."

That made his eyes fly open. "Madame Villon. Are you proposing to me?"

"Of course I am. And you had better say yes."

"Oh? Do you have some notion of punishing me?"

She reached downward. "I have many ways of punishing you, *rosbif*."

"Ah! Yes! So you do. Then I expect . . . I expect . . . my God . . ." His words fell away into a groan; his eyes closed once more.

"Yes? You expect?"

"I expect . . . I expect I had better say *Oui, mon ange,* whatever you wish, I am yours to command."

"That's better."

"Ah, don't stop. Please. Go on punishing me . . . all you like . . . yes, even more . . . I deserve it . . . but tell me . . . what was I thinking? . . . tell me . . ."

"Yes?"

"What has brought this . . . God save me . . . what has brought this *charming* idea into your head, all of a sudden?"

"What idea?"

"Marriage." He turned another gasp into a sigh. "And don't say it's Algiers."

"No reason," Daisy said. "Only that I love you madly and want this stupid war to end, so we can live with the children in some sweet little cottage and make more babies together."

Kit's eyes flew open again. "What did you say?"

Daisy drew her hand away and sprang from the bed. "Nothing. We must get to work."

"You said *more babies*."

Daisy found her brassiere and fastened it swiftly. "*Mon Dieu, mon amour,* we will have time for babies later. Let's not get ahead of ourselves."

"But you said—"

"There is a war to win, after all." She yanked on her shirt, fastened the buttons, and turned to Kit, who still lay in the bed, propped on his elbow, a scrap of blanket to protect his considerable modesty, tousled and beautiful, long naked limbs everywhere, arms that had held her close a moment ago, had made love to *her*, of all women, the luckiest Daisy in the world. She bent to kiss him. He took her hand.

"Daisy," he said, "if you wish me to marry you this very instant, you know I'd do it."

"But I have a husband, *mon amour*. It's very inconvenient."

"I could kill him, if you like."

Daisy thought he was joking, but she couldn't be sure. He certainly looked grave, as if he meant it, but then the English sense of humor was often incomprehensible. Kill Pierre for her. Would he do that? Did she want him to? Her lover, to kill the father of her children? She thought of God, she thought of Madeleine and Olivier. No! A thousand times *non*. Which was why she could not tell Kit this secret of hers, even though the knowledge—while frightening her to the bone—also doused her with floods of love, as she held his hand and felt his pulse connecting to hers.

No, not yet.

But please God, let those armies triumph, now in North Africa and then all over Europe. Let the enemy fall. The sooner the better.

WHEN DAISY AND Kit had begun their affair four months ago, it was July, and the air inside Kit's cramped sleeping quarters was hot and oppressive, leaving them panting and sweating and almost outside their own skins when they made love. Now it was dank November and a very different story, but it was not just the weather that had changed.

True, they had not been able to create false papers for everybody on the list in Pierre's safe. They had not been able to find many of them, for one thing, or to forge enough identity cards, even though Kit worked day and night, even though Daisy ran her feet off carrying messages and delivering the finished papers. But because of their efforts, fifty-two Jewish families had safely left Paris before the terrible dawn of July 16, when the French police started banging on doors and dragging people from their homes, over thirteen thousand in total; nearly eight thousand of those Jews were packed into the Vélodrome d'Hiver and left to swelter in the heat for days, before they were loaded onto trains and sent into Germany, where they disappeared into night and fog.

Thank God, her grandmother was not among them.

Daisy had sobbed without control when the magnitude of the roundup became clear. She still remembered how Kit had held her, how they had clung to each other in the stifling air of the workroom. She had tried to think only of the names and faces of those they had saved, those for whom their efforts meant everything, meant life itself, but her mind kept returning to images of the horror in the stadium, the individual terror each person must have felt, multiplied thirteen thousand times. It was evening, and Pierre was in the office or out celebrating his success or something, and Justine was minding the children as they slept. Daisy had mumbled something about going to see her grandmother and just left. Now Kit and Daisy sat and cried together. Then they got drunk and made love, over and over, because what else could you do in the midst of such darkness? You couldn't just sit there facing this horror; you needed oblivion, you had to cling to something, some scrap of hope.

Anyway, the next day Daisy's eyes were dry and her body exhausted, but her soul had turned to steel. *I want to do more*, she said to Grand-mère and to Kit, and they had brought her into contact with a network of French agents, whom she knew only by their code names, which were all various kinds of animals. She had begun as a courier, but as existing agents were captured or killed, and Daisy's own reputation for daring and resourcefulness began to spread, she started gathering intelligence herself. She encouraged Pierre to give more dinner parties, she learned how to open his safe and raid his papers. She kept her ears open and her face carefully innocent; she was just some pretty, brainless Paris housewife to whom it was a pleasure for a self-important Nazi officer to brag indiscreetly. Every crumb of information that came her way, she passed along in reports that became legendary among both the British and American intelligence services. She continued to courier forged identity papers to downed airmen and to agents and saboteurs dropped in from Britain, to recruit safe houses and escort fugitives.

You are like a new woman, Kit said to her. Or rather like the real Daisy had finally stepped out of the old skin.

Daisy, drunk with risk and passionately in love for the first time in her life, could not have agreed more. Yes, the situation in Paris was bleak, the occupation more brutal by the day, agents picked off one by one, radio sets going ominously quiet, but Daisy had never felt more purpose, had never taken so much immediate, visceral pleasure in food and drink and sex and fresh air. She was alive, she told Kit, she was finally alive.

Only take care to remain so, he would reply, drawing her into bed, as the days turned cooler and the children returned to school. *Remember I would die to lose you.*

And I would die to lose you, rosbif, she whispered back, kissing his warm skin, curling her body around his, *so if we must fall, let us fall together.*

That was October. Now the trees were all bare, and the air had turned dark and cold. The Germans, enraged by the success of the Allied invasion into North Africa earlier that month, had seized back control of the Vichy free zone and cracked down ruthlessly on Resistance networks everywhere, but especially in Paris. And now Daisy was beginning to worry about Pierre.

Of course she could not have banished her husband from her bed, just because she'd taken a lover. She refused Pierre as often as she dared, but sometimes she allowed him his carnal rights, in order to keep his suspicions at bay, and also in order to chip little pieces of information from him. She treated these episodes like chores, like cooking dinner or polishing the silver, unpleasant but necessary. After all, you could think about something else while the unpleasantness was going on down below; you could simply imagine yourself elsewhere, in bed with someone else, or else occupy your brain by working out the logistics of a message drop.

Now, Daisy and Kit didn't speak of any of this, hardly spoke of Pierre at all, in the way a prostitute doesn't discuss her clients with her lover. But since October, Pierre hadn't even attempted to have intercourse with her. He'd slept on his side, his back to Daisy, and moreover he spent most of his time at the office, anyway. Was he simply committed to his work? Or had he begun to entertain some inkling of what his wife was up to in her spare time? She tried to ask, but Pierre always answered her with some noncommittal remark, some evasive change of the subject.

So Daisy was feeling wary about Pierre, and the relative safety of the free zone no longer existed, and the Gestapo was tightening its noose, and the network was fast running out of money and resources, utterly dependent on the British and the Americans. Now she was pregnant with Kit's child, due sometime around the middle of July. (She hadn't yet seen a doctor, but she was quite sure she knew when she had conceived, a rare moment of carelessness.) That wasn't all. Last week, she'd had the distinct sensation that she was being followed, and then news had reached them of a major Gestapo raid on one of their most important informants. Even her grandmother had warned her to be careful, that their luck was perhaps beginning to run out. Grandmère, in fact, had already laid down plans, in case Daisy should have to flee at a moment's notice, with or without the children. (If necessary, Grand-mère would take charge of Madeleine and Olivier, and they would all reunite in Spain or Switzerland or someplace.) Until now, Daisy had refused to listen to these plans. She didn't want to consider that she'd have to give up her work, or Kit, or both.

But now, as Daisy made her way down the stairs to the workroom, nerves still buzzing from lovemaking, and considered just how many more weeks remained until her pregnancy became obvious to both the men in her life, she thought that maybe it was time to pay a visit to Grandmère, just in case.

Kit FOLLOWED HER down the cramped hatchway a moment later, fully dressed, hair combed back damply from his forehead. He dropped a kiss on the nape of her neck, sat down in the chair, and reached for his pipe. "Darling, I've been thinking—" he began.

"Shh!"

He looked startled but obeyed. Through the walls of the hidden workroom, they heard voices from the bookshop, muffled and indistinct but masculine in timbre. And as Daisy and Kit both knew, the customers of Le Mouton Noir in these troubled times were mostly female.

They sat in silence, staring at each other, listening to the noises through the walls and bookshelves. Daisy could make out the young soprano of Philippe's voice, the firm tenor of Monsieur Lapin. But that deep, urgent, staccato baritone that answered him! This was a commanding voice, a voice that did not expect to be disobeyed. Daisy strained to hear the words, but all that wood and plaster—designed, after all, to blanket the sounds of Kit's own activities in this room—made it impossible.

Kit grabbed her hand. "Go upstairs," he whispered. "I'll destroy the papers."

"But if they search—"

"Go! I'll close the hatch behind you. They'll never see it, and even if they do, I swear they'll have to climb over my dead—"

The doorway slid open. Daisy started from the chair. Kit moved even faster, jumping forward to block Daisy from the intruders, so that she caught only a glimpse of Monsieur Lapin's haggard face and a long arm in a dark suit.

"Monsieur Legrand, I believe?" said a familiar, urbane voice.

Daisy edged out from behind Kit. "Lieutenant colonel!" she exclaimed.

He WAS NOT wearing his uniform, but the same suit of navy blue he wore on the rue Cambon side of the Hôtel Ritz to visit Grandmère in her suite and the trilby over his pale hair. He removed it now and begged Daisy's pardon for intruding. Then he turned to Monsieur Lapin and asked for a moment of privacy.

"Yes, monsieur," said Monsieur Lapin, and closed the door. They heard the soft thump of the bookshelf sliding into place, Philippe's high voice asking a question, his grandfather shushing him. Von Sternburg stepped forward and laid a book of plain brown leather on the table. *The Scarlet Pimpernel.*

"Your grandmother explained that this book is like a password," he said.

"Grandmère!"

"Who the devil are you?" said Kit.

"Compose yourself, young man. I come here as a well-wisher, nothing more. A certain piece of information has come my way, and I wished to communicate it to you without delay."

Von Sternburg's face was solemn and heavy. He put his hand to the scar on his face, as if it had begun to pain him. Daisy thought he looked like he had aged a decade or so since she'd seen him last.

"Lieutenant colonel," she said softly, "are you well? Can I get you a glass of water? Or brandy?"

Kit looked surprised. Von Sternburg merely shook his head.

"My thanks, but I'm afraid we have little time. Your grandmother has asked to summon you to her at once."

"What's the matter? Is something wrong? She's not unwell, is she?"

"She's as well as ever," said Von Sternburg. "It's your husband."

For an instant, a terrible hope took hold of Daisy's heart. "What's happened?" she demanded. "Is he dead?"

"Not dead. I'm afraid I've heard word that he's shortly going to be arrested." Von Sternburg glanced at Kit, and then back at Daisy. "For crimes against the German state."

THOUGH THE RITZ was only a few minutes' walk away, Von Sternburg did not accompany her. "I have another urgent errand," he said, glancing away, "and besides, it is perhaps best if we are not seen together, at the present time."

So Daisy continued on to rue Cambon, while Von Sternburg hurried around the corner and out of sight. The streets were cold and bare, the few pedestrians hunched over with hunger and anxiety. When she reached the warmth of the lobby, Daisy drew in a long, relieved breath. Surely nothing terrible could happen here, inside the Ritz.

Upstairs, however, her confidence drained away. Grandmère paced across the rug in her kaftan of emerald silk, pausing only to add another splash of cognac into the glass she clutched in her hand. Daisy folded her arms. "Should you be drinking at a time like this?"

"At a time like this, absolutely," said Grandmère. "Did your German friend explain the situation?"

"He's not my friend," said Daisy. "But yes, he did tell me something interesting. Pierre's to be arrested, no?"

"Within the day, according to Von Sternburg."

"And you believe him?"

"About this?" Grandmère set down the glass on the sofa table. "I do."

"I don't understand why you trust him. *Mon Dieu*, he's a German officer! It might be a trap. Probably it is a trap. And now he knows about the bookshop, about Kit, about the hidden room—"

"My dear, don't you realize? He's always known. All this time, all these months, Lieutenant Colonel von Sternburg has been your truest friend. Why do you think you haven't been discovered? Arrested, like all the others? Do you think it's because you're such a very clever spy?"

Daisy stared at her grandmother across the yards of soft, pastel carpet, the fragrant Ritz air. As always, Grandmère sparkled with jewels, on her earlobes and neck and tiny, pale fingers. She was like one of those delicate figures inside a music box, so crusted over by paste you almost couldn't see where the fakery ended and the reality began. But her face. Oh, that was genuine, all right. Her eyes glared at Daisy, fringed by overlong, overthick, bristle-black eyelashes.

"That's ridiculous," said Daisy. "Why would such a man protect me? I don't even know him."

Grandmère gave her a worldly look and turned away to stride across the room, toward the curio case. "Regardless. The game's up. They've intercepted some intelligence that could only have originated with Pierre—some report of yours—and now they're just waiting for the proper warrant to come through. Even the Gestapo, it seems, must follow certain protocols where French officials are concerned. So it gives us a little time."

"Time for what? There's nothing we can do. If we try to save Pierre, they'll only discover what's really going on."

Grandmère bent over the case and reached underneath for the latch. "It's already too late. They'll be searching your apartment—"

"The apartment's clean. They won't find anything." Daisy said it desperately, trying to hold on to some hope, some possibility of reprieve. "I know what to say. They think I'm just some empty-headed housewife—"

"Daisy." Grandmère turned to face her. "It's time to go. You and the children, you've got to flee."

"I—I can't. We can't. There's still so much work to do, and the network needs agents and money. I can't abandon them now. And Kit . . . and the children . . ."

"Daisy, the game's up. You're finished, at least for now. Legrand will be reassigned elsewhere, and you and I—"

"No!"

"—you and I will find some place to regroup, to see the children safe." Her voice turned soft. "Oh, Daisy, my darling, I understand. I can see you're in love. But it's war, and such things cannot be allowed to compromise the safety of others. Do you want Legrand to be captured?"

"Of course not!"

"And your children? To lose a child, believe me, it's worse than death."

"No!"

"Then you must say goodbye to your lover. It won't be forever. I'm sure you will find some way to—"

"I'm going to have his child."

Grandmère, who had started toward her, stopped short in the middle of the rug. "I see."

"So you see, he can't be reassigned. He must come with us. We must stay together, at all costs."

Grandmère's gaze dropped briefly to Daisy's stomach, then she continued across the room until she stood before her granddaughter. "We will see what's to be done. For now, you must listen. I've sent a message down the escape line. In a day or two, we will have arranged a safe house outside of Paris, where we can await the next move. Legrand has already made a set of papers. You and the children—"

"The children! My God, I've got to—"

"Hush. You'll stay in the bookshop until I give the signal." Grandmère held out her hand. "And you must take this with you."

"The talisman? But I can't keep that with me. If I'm searched—"

"Not to keep. I've made arrangements with an American contact of mine, in the intelligence service. Before you leave Paris, you'll take this to him."

"And what's he going to do with it?"

"He'll get us money for the jewels, which we badly need at the moment, as you know. The network's about to be starved out of existence. And with the Germans taking over the free zone, it's as impossible there as in Paris to sell the jewels. As for the talisman itself, it will be returned safely to the hands of the demoiselle."

"Oh, the old superstition," Daisy said. She took the bundle of silk cloth from her grandmother's hand and stuffed it in her pocket. "Just let me know where and when to make the drop. In the meantime, I've got to fetch the children from school."

"It's already done, my dear. They'll be waiting for you at the bookshop."

"What? By whom? When?"

"Right now. Von Sternburg's gone to get them."

Daisy thought she might explode. She whirled and turned for the door.

"Daisy, wait! Stop!" Grandmère darted in front of her and stood before the door. "It's all right. In the name of God, don't go. He'll get them out. The children know him, and Madame won't question a German officer. It's safer this way."

"I don't understand! Why do you trust him like this? With your own great-grandchildren?"

Grandmère opened her mouth and closed it. Her hand, which had found the door handle behind her, dropped away. "You'll have to ask him that yourself," she said softly. "In the meantime, keep that damned thing safe, do you understand me? Remember you're the demoiselle."

"I'm not the demoiselle. The line of the Courcelles has died out, don't you remember? It's just a fiction, Grandmère, a fairy story. There is no demoiselle."

Grandmère only stared at her, neither fierce nor pitying, a dainty old woman on the verge of frailty. The kaftan stirred a little in the draft. She made a little sigh, just like a Frenchwoman.

"Very well. Go. But remember, Daisy. It's the talisman who finds the demoiselle, not the other way around."

"I'll keep that in mind," Daisy said. "And if that Von Sternburg does not deliver Madeleine and Olivier to me within the hour, I swear before God that I will tear the both of you limb from limb. Now excuse me."

She stretched around her grandmother's iron-straight body for the doorknob.

CHAPTER TWENTY-FIVE

Babs

Paris, France
April 1964

STRETCHED LANGUOROUSLY IN the bed, evaluating my current state of affairs. Which, at that moment, consisted of a naked arm wrapped around my equally naked waist, pulling me close in a very intimate spooning position. I pressed back against the solid chest that was Drew, every inch of my skin sighing with happiness.

When I closed my eyes—something that had been done rather infrequently in the last three days—I no longer saw Kit's face. It wasn't that I had erased him from my memories. It was more like I'd moved a favored childhood doll to a high shelf in my closet; protected and cherished, but no longer a part of my life. Kit had been my first love, the object of my childhood crush that hadn't changed despite the years. It should have, I realized now. It might have saved us both a lot of heartache.

Drew sighed in his sleep, and I felt the ripple of his breath on the back of my neck like a blessing. Kit would have understood. He had loved me, in a way, and would not have begrudged my happiness.

And oh, what happiness I'd found. Quite unexpected, but there it was, lying in the bed next to me. Drew was so very different from Kit—much broader, more muscular. So American. So unhaunted. Drew slept the sleep of contentment, as if nightmares didn't exist. He never screamed a remembered torture or called out another woman's name. Perhaps it was those differences that had made my coming to terms with Kit's memory easier for me. And so very pleasurable.

"Is there a cat in the room, or is that you purring?" Drew's sleepy voice made dormant parts of my body stir.

"I beg your pardon?"

"You made that noise again. The noise you make in the back of your throat when you're thinking. It sounds like a very happy cat."

I turned in his arms and looked into his eyes. They were green today, not hazel—definitely green. "No cat. Just a very happy, happy woman."

"That makes two of us."

I raised an eyebrow.

"Well, happy man, I meant. You're an amazing woman, Babs Langford. I'm so glad you found me."

"Wasn't it the other way around?"

"I don't think so." He drew back, a questioning look on his face. "Is this our first argument?"

I pretended to think. "It might just be."

He grinned. "I guess that means we need to have makeup sex to smooth over any hurt feelings." And we proceeded to do just that.

A KNOCK ON the door announced room service bringing us another meal. After the second day, I'd ceased to put the bedclothes over my head, having been reassured by Drew that the discreet staff at the Ritz had seen far worse than two people sharing a bed.

The waiter kept a neutral smile on his face as he set out a brunch that seemed more like a holiday feast. It would take some getting used to Drew's voracious appetite, although, owing to our recent physical exertions, I'd discovered a new appetite all of my own. After the waiter left, Drew retrieved our bathrobes from the floor, where they'd been hastily discarded the night before, and we sat at the two chairs pulled out at the table by the window.

Drew filled two flutes from the pitcher of mimosas and handed one to me. "To another beautiful day," he said as a toast. I lifted my glass, then cast my gaze outside, where a heavy spring downpour was currently bashing itself against the window.

My smile faded a little. "It reminds me of England."

"Do you miss it?" he asked, tucking into a heaping plate of scrambled eggs and sausage.

"Yes, a little. I've never lived anywhere else. It's home. Even with the fickle weather, I do love it. My heart aches a bit when I think about it—which is silly, I know. Paris is rather nice. But there's something rather perfect about the sky after an English country rainstorm, when the sun has a milky glow and paints the pastures with pale yellow. One can see it best from the top floor gallery at Langford Hall. After we were married, I had a window seat built there. Kit and I would sometimes sit with our tea and wait for the rain to stop."

Drew was looking at me with such sympathy and understanding that I had to look away. I felt very close to tears and quickly swallowed them. Brightening, I asked, "What about you? Have you ever lived outside of New York City?"

"I was born and raised there, and have lived there ever since—except for six years in Boston." He watched me fix my tea, his eyes thoughtful. "Have you ever wanted to live outside of England?"

"I never really thought about it. I had a lovely childhood with wonderful parents, boisterous brothers and an older sister. And dogs. We always had dogs."

"So you love dogs."

"I do. A house hardly seems like a home without them. And you?"

He shook his head. "We always lived in the city, and my mother said it wasn't practical. But I always imagined I'd like to have one. Or three. I was an only child, and I always craved commotion."

"Well, Langford Hall was next door, so there was always quite a lot of rowdiness when all the boys were home from school. I followed them around like a lost puppy, wanting to be a part of all that. They only tolerated me for the most part. Except for Kit."

Drew's green gaze settled on me, waiting for me to continue.

"He was the only one who paid any attention to me, always made sure I didn't fall too far behind, and helped me down from more than one tree. It's why I fell in love with him. I suppose it just felt natural for us to marry when he came home from the war." I stopped there, knowing that I was close to treading into dangerous territory.

"You lived at Langford Hall after you were married?"

"Yes. I'd always loved it. All that history. It was much older than our house—it was completed in 1799. Ours only dated back to Queen Victoria. So many nooks and crannies and things to explore. And in which to hide from my brothers when they'd discovered some horrid spider to put down my back. Kit would always find me first, but he'd never tell on me. He was kind that way."

Drew took my hand. "My father only had the best things to say about Kit. I wish I could have known him."

I smiled, trying to imagine them meeting and couldn't. It was a bit like two different worlds traveling on a perpetual parallel path. "Langford Hall also has the folly where Kit's father would go write. It could only be reached by a little bridge his father had built because he refused to row across water after surviving the *Lusitania*. It was so pretty—I used to pretend a fairy prince and princess lived there." I smiled into my cup, remembering. "There was a small family of beautiful swans that lived on the lake. They were rather wretched creatures, always nipping at one's fingers when you fed them breadcrumbs. I suppose they hadn't been taught the old adage about not biting the hand that feeds you." I spread butter and marmalade on my scone as I remembered the swans and my mother-in-law's intense dislike of one of the females she named Caroline.

"There had always been swans on the lake, almost as long as there had been whippets at Langford Hall. It's why the signet ring Kit inherited from his father had the swans engraved on the top. They were the unofficial emblem of the Langfords of Langford Hall. At least until the war."

"And what happened then?" He'd stopped chewing, anticipating my response.

"We ate them." I shrugged. "We were hungry, and they were readily available and not rationed. I remember them being quite tasty."

Drew let out a hearty laugh, and I joined him, although it didn't eradicate my guilt. It was the reason we hadn't had them replaced. It was as if we'd betrayed them in some way and didn't deserve them anymore.

"Do you miss New York?" I asked, half dreading the answer although I wasn't sure why.

He sat back in his chair and drew a deep breath. "Not as much as I thought I might. But I need to get back. I was only supposed to be in Paris for two weeks. I've been dragging my feet about buying my plane tickets because we haven't solved the mystery of La Fleur. I hate to leave behind unfinished business."

I washed down my bite of scone with tea, and it all tasted like paper. "Unfinished business?"

He leaned forward, his expression earnest. "I wasn't referring to you, Babs. You are . . ." He stopped, shook his head. "I can't really describe you. Or the way you make me feel. It's like trying to describe the pull of the moon, or the light from the sun, I guess. Just seeing your face in the morning makes my day brighter. Hearing your voice, even when you're speaking in that funny accent when you're trying to speak French, makes me feel like I'm home."

I couldn't speak for a moment, afraid my raw emotions would show up as tears, or in a confession that I felt the same. But I couldn't make this—whatever *this* was—more complicated that it already was. We were separated by more than just an ocean, but also by the specter of a stolen letter that floated unseen between us. A piece of paper that would show Drew that I wasn't who he thought I was.

I swallowed. "But you need to get back to New York."

"Yes, Babs. I do. I wasn't sure how to tell you, or when the right time might be, but . . ." He drew a deep breath. "My plane leaves tonight."

A horrible stabbing pain that felt almost worse than childbirth tore at my insides as the implications of what he had just said settled on me. I took my own deep breath, bringing to mind what it was like to head a WI meeting and to bring up an unpleasant topic. "Well, then," I said, proud of how calm my voice sounded, "I say we cross that bridge when we come to it. Right now I'm going to suggest we get dressed and leave this room and see if the world outside still exists."

"If we go early enough, I might still be able to take you to Maxim's for an early dinner."

"We just ate, Drew. How can you be thinking of dinner already?"

He gave me a grin that could only be described as wicked. "What can I say? You make me hungry, Babs. But you're right. We need to bathe and get dressed."

"Ladies first." I stood, already untying my robe.

"I'd rather not wait," he said, grabbing me by the waist and pulling me to him. "I hope you don't mind sharing."

Our robes fell together in a pile of peach cashmere. I wrapped my arms around his neck and pressed my lips against his. "I don't mind a bit," I said against his mouth. "Not one bit."

AFTER MUCH DITHERING at his hotel room door about who should leave first and how much time should lapse before the second person left, we ended up leaving together. Not that it would have mattered as the hallway was deserted. A maid had brought me clothes and makeup from my room, and I'd blushed only once when she'd shown me the variety of knickers to choose from, none of which the old Babs Langford would have found in her dressing table.

As we exited the lift downstairs, I felt quite sure that everyone was staring at us, knowing what we'd been doing for the last three days in Drew's hotel suite. It bothered me a bit, but not anywhere near as much as it might have once. And even if it had, I wouldn't give up those three days for anything.

The clacking of Prunella's typewriter made us turn in unison in the opposite direction, nearly running into Precious Dubose. I almost didn't recognize her. Her hair was half loose, falling down one side of her face. Her lips were bare, her makeup nonexistent except for her mascara that had migrated below her eyes. Deep purple crescents showed through the mascara, making her appear more than a decade older. Even her usual immaculate clothing was rumpled, as if she'd slept in them.

"There you are! Where have you been?" Her voice held a note of desperation.

If she hadn't been so distraught, I would have told her that I had been at an assignation. It would have made her proud. Instead, I immediately felt guilty for asking Drew to call the front desk and tell them that we were indisposed until further notice.

"Did you find something about La Fleur?" Drew asked.

Precious leveled an odd look at him that I couldn't decipher. "What is it, Precious?" I asked. "What's happened?"

"It's Margot. She was taken to the Hôtel-Dieu hospital yesterday. We think . . . we think this might be the end. We've wired for the children to come to Paris."

"Oh no." I felt Drew's hand on my shoulder as he pulled me against his side.

"I've been with her at the hospital. She's still conscious. I believe she's waiting to say goodbye to her children. I've only come back to pick up a few things for her that I thought she might need to make her more comfortable."

"Let us do that," I said. "You must be exhausted. You can't take care of a sick friend if you make yourself sick. Stay here and try and sleep for a few hours and when you're more rested you can join us at the hospital."

It looked as if she might refuse.

"Precious," Drew said sternly. "Tell us what you were going to get and we will take care of it and then rush to the hospital. We won't leave her side until you get there, all right? She won't be alone."

She frowned as she swayed on her feet, no doubt from exhaustion. "I promise," I reassured her.

She appeared to be as grateful as she was relieved as she gave us her list of things to fetch from Margot's room, remembering as we started back toward the lift to give us Margot's key.

The room smelled of the daisies that filled every vase in the room, almost completely masking the scent of medicine. "I'll get the things Precious requested from the bedroom if you'll look in the closet for some sort of traveling case we can use to transport everything."

He nodded and while he opened up a closet door, I entered the bedroom. During my visits, I'd always kept to the living room, where Margot sat on the chaise while I read to her. The bedroom had been decorated in the same ivory palate, with a dark antique dressing table with a mirror above it. I hesitated just for a moment before pulling open one of the top drawers, hoping Margot would forgive me for invading her privacy.

Brightly colored and lacy lingerie sat in perfectly organized piles inside, surprising me. I had somehow not expected Margot Lemouron to be the type to own sexy undergarments. Or perhaps she actually wasn't and Precious had decided to take matters into her own hands.

I took out a small stack of knickers, not counting them on purpose. I didn't want to put a finite number to the days Margot might need them. I continued to open the drawers, searching for the silk scarves Margot often wore to cover her bald head. I found sweaters and nightgowns—I took a few of both—before opening the last drawer.

I recognized several of the brightly patterned silk scarves and plucked out the ones I'd seen her wear, assuming they must be her favorites. As I was lifting up the small pile, something fell out of one of the scarves, unfurling it as if it had been wrapped carefully. I stared down into the dark recess of the drawer and spotted a gold ring.

I pulled it out, planning on rewrapping it in one of the other scarves and returning it to the drawer, then stopped. Everything stopped. My breathing, the world. The earth's rotation. It all seemed to stop. My eyesight went all fuzzy and then straightened again. I sat down on the bed, unsure of the stability of my own two legs. I must have said something or called out because Drew raced into the bedroom. He wore a look of surprise, as if he already knew.

I held out the gold ring. Kit's ring. The one with the two swans engraved on the top. The ring that had been passed down by his father, Robert. The ring that wouldn't be going to Robin because Kit had lost it in France. Or perhaps in the German prison camp. I didn't know because we never discussed it. I had been afraid to bring back unpleasant memories for Kit, more fuel for his nightmares.

"Was this Kit's?" Drew asked, the ring looking small and lost in his large palm.

I nodded. "I just can't figure out why it was in Margot's drawer. It was wrapped in a silk scarf as if it were being kept safe."

As if in answer, he gave me a frame from his other hand, the photograph explaining his expression when he'd rushed into the room. "I was looking for Margot's bottle of perfume that Precious said would be in the side table drawer. I found this inside, facedown. I wondered why it was hidden in the drawer until I turned it over."

I stared at the familiar faces of the two children we'd seen in the photograph in Pierre Villon's apartment. The photograph of his two children, an older girl and a younger boy. Daisy's children. In this photograph, the girl—Madeleine, Pierre had said—held the hand of a younger girl with long hair, lighter than her sister's, held back with an enormous bow. Her face was turned from the camera, her other hand reaching for someone we couldn't see.

"I don't understand . . . ," I began. Or maybe I did and didn't want to.

Drew handed me the signet ring and began putting the piles of clothing and the framed photograph into a small valise. "Come on," he prompted gently. "Let's get to the hospital before it's too late."

I slipped the ring on my finger, feeling how loose and heavy it was. How cold. Or maybe that was just me as my teeth had begun to chatter. I smelled the overwhelming scent of the daisies as Drew and I left the room, the door shutting behind us like a little slap.

CHAPTER TWENTY-SIX

Aurélie

The Château de Courcelles
Picardy, France
June 1915

Once she went through that door, it would be for the very last time.

Aurélie was dressed. A carpetbag held her few meager belongings. They needed to be meager to be convincing, so people would believe that she wasn't Aurélie de Courcelles, of ancient lineage and American fortune, but Jeanne Deschamps, of no fortune whatsoever.

"The train will be waiting," said Max. "It's a long walk to Le Catelet."

He was dressed as well, the rumpled bed the only testament to their last night together.

So many nights together.

They had been discreet at first, but as the time for parting grew nearer, Aurélie had grown reckless, scarcely waiting for the sounds of activity from the kitchen below to fade before she crept out, along the familiar route through the storerooms, to Max's lonely tower. Once, she had had to hide beneath the bed when Kraus had come barging up early one morning with a message from Hoffmeister. She wasn't sure if her father and the others had guessed, if they were keeping silent out of kindness, or because they thought she was buying Max's compliance in age-old fashion.

She didn't really care. She should care, she knew, but she didn't.

Aurélie jammed a hat down onto her head. Under it, her hair had been dyed a deep brown with the crushed hulls of black walnuts. Suzanne had assured her the color would last a month, at least, possibly two. Long enough, certainly, to see her to Paris, no matter what detours the convoy took.

Aurélie went up to Max for what might well be the last time, wrapping her arms around his waist, feeling the strangeness of it all, the familiar made foreign again with the knowledge that she was leaving, that it was over. "You will leave as soon as I'm gone?"

"I've already put in my request for a transfer to active duty."

She knew what had happened to his requests in the past. Aurélie looked up into his face, her palms against his chest. "But the telegrams—"

Max dropped a kiss on her forehead. "I sent the messages from Le Catelet. I saw them transmitted. If anything happens to me, there will be questions. And consequences."

A cold fear clutched Aurélie. "Yes, but what use will that be to you or me or anyone if you're dead?"

Max rubbed his hands up and down her arms. "I have no intention of dying."

"I don't think intent is what matters." Even entombed in Courcelles they had heard garbled reports from the front, from the haggard troops of German soldiers that had passed through. "The front. I'm not sure if that's worse."

"At least it would be an honest death." Seeing the look on her face, Max quickly said, "But men survive the front. Or maybe they'll second me to the service of my uncle in Berlin. Be of good cheer. How could I die when I have you to come home to?"

Yes, but those other men who had died had people, too. Wives, children, mothers, sisters. It was a terrifying thought. Once, not so very long ago, she had thought it a grand thing to die for one's country. She had sent Jean-Marie off to war without a qualm, full of platitudes about honor and glory. But now, now that it was Max, it was a different matter entirely. She wanted to lock him up and keep him safe. Let those other men fight and die so long as Max was spared her.

Aurélie was quite horrified by how fierce she felt about it, how quickly her scruples dissolved when it came to Max and his safety.

She clutched his suspenders beneath his jacket. "Don't go doing anything heroic."

"Would you promise the same?" Max gave a lopsided smile, so full of tenderness that Aurélie felt as though she couldn't breathe. "I didn't think so."

There was nothing to do but to kiss him, long and hard, and then wrap her arms around him, trying to memorize the moment, the scratch of the wool of his uniform jacket against her cheek, the feel of his skin through his shirt.

Max squeezed her hard one last time before murmuring, "You should be going. The train will not wait."

Reluctantly, Aurélie disentangled herself. "I need to say goodbye to my father. And I must stop by the chapel—to say a prayer to Saint Jeanne. She has always guarded my house."

Max gave his head a little shake. "I never believed in such things before. But I would believe in anything that will see you safe to Paris. I will even pray to your saint with you, if it might help."

"That's not necessary," said Aurélie hastily. "You're not a daughter of Courcelles, so . . ."

"I understand," he said, and she was very glad that he didn't, not really. She was protecting him, she told herself. The less he knew about the talisman, the safer he was. But she still felt soiled somehow.

"Until Paris," she said softly.

He leaned forward and kissed her, one last time. "I'll come for you at the Ritz."

HER FATHER WAS waiting for her inside the chapel, as they had arranged. He thrust a pile of unattractive brown fabric at her.

"Suzanne made you a flannel petticoat," he said gruffly. "To keep you warm on the journey. It gets cold at night still."

"Please thank Suzanne for me." Her father turned his back as she stepped into the garment, pulling it up and tying the tapes beneath her skirt. In the hem and seams were sewn messages, rolled thin. A coat or a cloak might be taken, but a petticoat, next to her skin, should defy examination. Especially if she wore it from here to Paris without taking it off. She expected it would probably stand by itself at the end of the journey. "Will you tell her goodbye for me? To all of them? Let them know I'm not deserting them?"

"Once you're safely away."

"I've told Suzanne to tell everyone that I'm confined to my room with female trouble." In fact, she hadn't been troubled by female trouble, not for the last month. Fear could stop one's courses, they said, and Aurélie certainly had fears enough.

Her father, who had once made his way through the boudoirs of the courtesans of Paris, winced, his aristocratic features twisting into an expression of distaste. "You couldn't have feigned an ague?"

"They might wonder why a doctor hadn't been called. And you see?" Aurélie nodded at her father. "This is exactly why it's perfect. They won't inquire too closely. It should buy me two days, at least."

"By which time, the train will be well away."

"I don't know how long it will take." In normal times, it was a journey of three or four hours from Courcelles to Paris. Faster if one went by car. Longer if one took the slow train. But Max had warned her the convoy would be diverted first to Germany, where they would be searched and detained, possibly as little as a day, possibly as long as a month, before being sent on first to Switzerland and then, finally, into France and freedom. "Make my excuses for me as long as you can. The longer it takes for anyone to inquire the better. I've left a letter for you all on my bed saying that I'm taking my chances with the woods, making my way to Paris on foot. Be sure to bring that to the major when you find it—or make sure he's with you when you break into my room. Hopefully, they should be so busy searching the woods they'll never think of the convoy."

Her father looked at her with a strange expression on his face. "You sound just like your mother."

Aurélie grimaced. "American?"

"Assured." Her father turned away, letting his hand rest on the long-dead countess's pet dog. "It is not such a bad thing. And if I have made you feel that it was—that to be your mother's daughter was to be a lesser thing—that was my fault and none of your doing."

He did not, Aurélie noticed, deny that he had done so.

"I was angry. I was angry at the fates, at myself, at your mother. When I met your mother, I thought she was the answer to all my troubles. All that money and a quiet little mouse of a wife who would bear heirs for Courcelles without giving me any bother. But then your mother . . . She wasn't a mouse. And I was a fool. Instead of appreciating her for what she had become, I drove her into the arms of my cousin." Aurélie must have made some sound, because her father looked at her, his expression wry. "Oh yes, I knew about Hercule. Everyone did. It was too late by then. And you—you were hers. With that hair."

"I have your brows. Everyone says." She had tried so long and so hard to win her father's approval, to convince him she was his, his more than her mother's. And it had never been in her power. It was all a drama that had played out before she was even born.

Her father shrugged that away. "Oh, I never doubted you were mine. Your mother wouldn't have played me false if I hadn't goaded her into it. In her own way, she is a woman of honor." From her father, that was a great concession. "She raised you to be a woman of honor."

Aurélie's throat felt raw. "I have always wanted nothing more than to be a credit to the name of Courcelles."

It struck her only now that perhaps she might have wanted something more: her father's love instead of his approval. Or that love might not have to be earned but might be given freely, as of right.

"You are. You will be." Her father didn't seem to notice her hesitation. "The title will die with me, but the house of Courcelles will live on, through you."

Once, that sentiment would have filled her with exultation. Now, Aurélie found it hard to muster the requisite enthusiasm. Was she nothing but a womb? A sacred vessel? Like her mother, meant to bear heirs and pay the bills.

"Thank you," she said stiffly. "I shall try to live up to your faith in me."

To her surprise, her father reached out and pulled her into his arms, as he had never done, not even when she was very tiny. "My child. My little girl. Take care." And then, before she had time to lean into his embrace, her father set her upright again, saying briskly, "Now say your prayers and I shall see you on your way."

"Yes, Papa." She slipped into the childish address without thinking of it, and saw, before she knelt on the flagstones, her father press his eyes shut, as though in pain.

She knelt, not at the altar, but by the tomb of her ancestress, feeling around the base, into the hidden spot. It was there, where she'd left it, wrapped in a kerchief.

"I have not seen that in many years," said her father, in a low voice. "Not since your mother—"

"Tarted it up?" Even in the gray dawn light, the jewels were staggering, a ruby as large as Aurélie's thumbnail, diamonds the size of daisies. But it was the curved crystal in the middle that her father was staring at, the crystal that held the tiny scrap of five-hundred-year-old fabric stained with the blood of the saint.

"Is that—it is!" They both turned as an unwieldy figure came barreling into the chapel. Lieutenant Dreier fumbled for his pistol, pointing it at Aurélie. "You! Stay where you are! Schmidt! Weide! To me!"

"I don't know what you think you're—"

"Hush!" Lieutenant Dreier's voice was high with excitement. His hand was shaking so that Aurélie was half afraid the gun would go off. "Not another word out of you or I'll shoot! Men, seize that woman!"

"That *woman* is a noblewoman of France." Aurélie's father's cold authority checked Dreier slightly, but the sight of gold and diamonds sufficiently overcame any scruples.

Dreier snatched the talisman from Aurélie, shoving it into his inner pocket before the soldiers could see it. "That woman is a prisoner. Take her to the major! Him, too," he said as an afterthought, pointing at Aurélie's father. "They've both been . . . engaging in crimes against the state."

With Dreier's pistol in her back, her arms wrenched behind her, Aurélie couldn't even look at her father. To have come so close for this . . .

"Courage, my child," she thought she heard someone say, as they were marched past the effigy of the old countess, but she knew she must have imagined it, for the voice she heard was a woman's voice.

Dreier and his underlings marched them out of the chapel, past the keep, across the courtyard to the new wing. Dreier kept up a gloating monologue the whole way, although Aurélie couldn't be sure if it was for her benefit or his own or just that he was so excited he couldn't keep the words inside. ". . . knew you'd lead us to it sooner or later . . . watching for months . . . a promotion for me . . ."

"What is it? What is this?" It was Max, his voice sharp with concern. "What are you doing?"

"None of your concern." Dreier shoved Aurélie through one of the side doors that led into the new wing. Her shoulder was beginning to ache abominably; Dreier was shorter than she, and he had her arm pulled at an acute angle. "We're taking her to the major."

"Then I'm coming, too," said Max, in a voice that brooked no disagreement.

"Suit yourself," said Dreier, and kicked at the door of her father's study in lieu of knocking.

An irritated-looking Hoffmeister flung open the door. "What is it?"

"Wait until you see! You, you may go about your business," Dreier told his men. He shoved Aurélie through the door, waving Max to follow him with Aurélie's father. "Shut that door! Shut that door and bolt it! Oh. Is he here?"

"Am I here what?" demanded Lieutenant Kraus, who stood by Aurélie's father's desk.

A map of the region had been stretched out, marked with pins, her father's precious eighteenth-century bronzes of Mars and Venus serving as paperweights.

Dreier looked at him with annoyance, and then said, "Oh, never mind. If he's here, he's here. Wait until you see!"

"Sir," Max cut in, in his most Prussian tones. "I must protest. This is most irregular. If I may—"

"You may not." The lenses of Hoffmeister's spectacles glittered in the firelight. The people of Courcelles had spent the winter freezing, but Hoffmeister, who did not like the cold, had ordered a fire lit to warm the June morning. The selfishness made Aurélie sick with hatred. "Dreier? See what?"

"This!" Dreier looked down at his hand, which was occupied by the pistol. He dropped Aurélie's arm and reached into his coat pocket. "I mean, this!"

He yanked the talisman from his pocket and for a moment they all stared transfixed at the sheer glory of it, the rubies and diamonds scintillating in the firelight, the wolf and the cross standing out boldly against the gold, the pride of Courcelles.

Kraus's mouth hung open. Hoffmeister's eyes were beady with greed. Dreier, preening with pride, let the pistol dangle.

And Aurélie, without stopping to think, barreled into Dreier with all her might, snatching at the talisman with her left hand. The gun tumbled to the floor as Dreier stumbled into a small footstool, and, with an almost comical look of surprise, fell backward, hitting the fire screen and crashing through it.

There was a moment when the world seemed to go still and then the screaming began, horrible, high-pitched screaming, as Dreier fell onto the fire, the arm of his uniform catching flame. Aurélie's father dove for the pistol, and Kraus for Aurélie's father, grabbing the count's legs. And Dreier, like a human brand, rose to his feet, his back and arm flaming, stumbling this way and that, bumping into the hangings on the wall, mad with pain, screaming, screaming, screaming.

"Put him out! For the Lord's sake, put him out!" Aurélie cried, and Max sprang forward, pushing Dreier to the ground, trying to smother the flames on the Aubusson carpet.

"Water, I need water!" Max called.

Aurélie went for the bucket that she knew was kept by the fire, but she was arrested by a hand spinning her around. A palm slapped her hard across the face, making her head ring. Through her blurred vision and a growing haze of smoke, she saw Hoffmeister, his spectacles too close to her face, as his hand started rooting in her bodice, groping for the talisman.

"Off me!" Aurélie gasped, but her throat betrayed her. The words were lost in a fit of coughing. The smoke was thicker now, the flames consuming the tapestry of Venus watching over Mars's rest that had been specially woven for Aurélie's great-great-grandfather; crackling along the gilded frame of the portrait of her father; smoldering in the silk upholstery of a Louis Quinze settee. "Off—"

"Stop!" There was a horrible crack and Hoffmeister's hands abruptly loosed their grip. Aurélie's eyes stung, half blinded by smoke. Blinking, she saw Hoffmeister sprawled on the floor by the desk, a red pulp where his head had been, and Max, standing horrified, the bronze of Mars clutched in his hands like a club.

"You saved me," croaked Aurélie. He had killed his superior. He had killed his superior to save her.

"Not if you die by fire," rasped Max. His fair skin was smeared with soot, his cap lost, his hair tousled. He hustled Aurélie forward, his arm around her shoulders. "Quick!"

Using the bronze, he smashed the glass of one of the French windows, clearing the remainder with his elbow before jumping down into the shrubbery below, holding up his arms for Aurélie. Aurélie put her arms around his neck and let him swing her out, out into the relatively fresh air of the garden. They clung together, her face buried in his neck, his face in her hair, both shivering and shaking, their lungs aching, holding on to each other.

Somewhere, somewhere beyond them, there were cries of fire and the sound of booted feet running, but Aurélie was oblivious to all that. She could only see Dreier turned to living flame, Hoffmeister on the ground, dead by Max's hand.

"You saved me," she said again. "You saved me."

"I love you," he said simply. "But you must go. The train—if you're found here—"

Hoffmeister dead. Drier dead. Kraus—

Aurélie clutched at Max's arm. "My father. Max. My father. He's still in there."

Through the smoke, she could see her father and Kraus, locked in a wrestlers' embrace, rolling on the floor, each struggling for control of the pistol.

"Go," Max said. "Go now. I'll get him."

Aurélie clutched the talisman through her bodice. "But what if—"

Max kissed her hard. "I'll see you in Paris."

And then he was gone, scrambling up through the broken window, into the flames.

CHAPTER TWENTY-SEVEN

Daisy

Le Mouton Noir
Paris, France
November 1942

INSIDE THE GRATE, the flames licked over the few black coals, but the battle was lost before it had begun. Madeleine and Kit sat at the table, playing chess, while Olivier—who had grown weary of games and overturned the chessboard a moment ago—wandered around the tiny room, pulling books from shelves. Daisy replaced them, wearily, one by one. She'd given up trying to make Olivier put them back himself; he was too cross from being cooped up for the past two days.

Kit looked up in sympathy and pulled the pipe from his mouth. "We can trade places, if you like. Olivier, my little soldier, would you like to . . . er, learn a few new maneuvers, perhaps?"

Olivier cast Kit a withering look. "We've already done that."

"Then come back here and help your sister decide her next move."

"Hate chess!"

"Shh," said Daisy. "Remember, we have to be very quiet, like mice."

Olivier went rigid. His cheeks turned red, his eyes closed. Daisy lunged for him and tried to put her hand over his mouth, but it was too late. The scream was rising, she felt it gathering in his chest, unstoppable—

The door slid open.

Everybody whipped around.

"Uncle Max!" called out Olivier, and he ran all five steps across the room and flung himself into the arms of Lieutenant Colonel von Sternburg, who had already knelt to receive him.

FOR TWO DAYS they had been living inside the few paltry square meters of Kit's quarters, and their only glimpse of the world beyond came twice a day in the form of Max von Sternburg, who brought food and news and sweets and trinkets for the children. He always wore his civilian suit, so as not to attract attention and because it was well-known among his fellow officers—Max explained all this to Kit and Daisy, blushing a little—that he kept a mistress, a pretty married woman of whom he was deeply enamored, and they met for their assignations at the Ritz. And since a German officer wasn't supposed to wear his uniform on the rue Cambon side, nobody questioned why he should change into his suit of navy blue and set off from the Hôtel Meurice in the direction of the Ritz, bearing gifts. It was, in short, the perfect cover.

To the children, of course, he was like Father Christmas, and they greeted him with ecstatic enthusiasm. One by one he pulled the parcels from his pockets and his satchel—coffee, ham, bread, cheese, a bottle of wine, some toy soldiers, a hair ribbon, an enamel box. While the children examined these treasures, he turned to Daisy and Kit. His face was weary.

"Is there any news of Pierre?" Daisy asked. She couldn't help feeling a perverse sense of guilt that her husband had been arrested for a crime—if you could call it that—that she herself had committed.

Maybe it was justice, but Daisy would have preferred the right kind of justice, an accounting for the deeds Pierre alone was responsible for.

"He's being held for questioning at avenue Foch," said Max. "The Gestapo headquarters. Thus far, he has said nothing to implicate you."

Daisy shrugged. "I doubt it would even occur to him."

"Or perhaps he still harbors some little love for you," Max said gently. "Either way, it keeps us safe, for the moment."

"And my grandmother?"

"There's no word yet."

"So we keep waiting," said Kit.

"Not much longer, I expect." Max was staring at the children, who sat at the table to divide the loot. Olivier, ever ravenous, had already torn off a piece of bread, and Daisy didn't reprimand him. Let him have it. She couldn't keep anything down at the moment, anyway, and the less notice drawn to that fact, the better.

Kit checked his watch. "Look, I've got to step out for a moment, if you don't mind. Daisy? You'll be all right?"

"Yes, of course," said Daisy. Neither she nor Max inquired as to the nature of Kit's errand. For one thing, it was always better not to know, unless absolutely necessary. For another thing, there was the question of Max's loyalty, and where it came from, and how far it went. Kit accepted Grandmère's word that Von Sternburg could be trusted where Daisy was concerned, but he wasn't pleased about it, and Max himself seemed to recognize the delicacy of the situation.

Kit looked at him now, and they traded some communication between them.

"You'll keep them safe," Kit said, and it was not a question.

"Of course," Max replied.

When Kit was gone, the tension eased a fraction. He had left his pipe in the dish on the table, and Daisy knocked out the ash, mostly because that released the smell of the tobacco into the air, which made it seem as if Kit were still in the room. Max sat down in the empty chair and held up the hair ribbon. He told Madeleine that he had picked it out just for her, because it matched the color of her eyes.

"Why?" Daisy said suddenly.

Max looked up. "I beg your pardon?"

She thought, *You're risking your life for us, for a woman and two children you scarcely know. Why us?*

But she couldn't say it, not while the children sat there, all ears. Instead she walked to the other side of the room and took the poker to the few coals. A moment later, Von Sternburg came up next to her, smelling of cold November air, of damp wool and longing.

"It's because of your mother," he said softly.

"What about my mother?" Daisy's voice came out a little high.

"We knew each other only a short time, during the last war," he said. "But she was an extraordinary woman, and I have never forgotten her. Even behind German lines, we heard the legend of the Demoiselle de Courcelles, and what she had done for France. Of course, the popular story was not quite as I remembered it."

Daisy let this sink in for a moment. She felt him breathe quietly next to her, while she breathed, too, trying to gain some control over herself and her racing thoughts. Finally she turned to him.

"You were in love with her, weren't you?" she said, and her voice, almost to her own surprise, was full of pity. "That's what this is all about."

Von Sternburg gazed back with a look that shattered her.

"There was a time when I hated her because I thought she had betrayed me," he said. "And then a time, just as the war was ending, before I even had the chance to find her again, when I learned from a newspaper that she was dead of influenza, and I grieved for her and what we had lost. And then I came to understand, and to forgive."

"You haven't answered my question."

"Haven't I?" He smiled. "The answer is yes. We were very much in love. And I have never forgiven myself for losing her."

WHEN THE CHILDREN were asleep at last, tucked into their pallets downstairs, Daisy climbed the hatchway stairs to Kit's bedroom, which was now their bedroom, as if they were a family together in a very small home.

He was awake. "Everything quiet?" he said, opening the blanket for her.

"Yes, they're both asleep." She climbed in and yawned. The bed was made for only one person, and they had to lie almost on top of each other to fit inside it, which neither Kit nor Daisy minded. Especially now, when any moment might be their last. Already Kit's hands were reaching under her camisole to find her breasts. She stretched her arms up and closed her eyes. The camisole slipped over her head. Kit was kissing her neck, her breasts, her stomach, and her skin came alive, as it always did, warming them both as he raised himself above her and joined them together in the cold, silent night. As they rocked against each other, he kissed her cheek and asked her why she was crying.

"It's nothing," she sobbed.

Kit went still and studied her. "It's not nothing. Tell me."

How could she tell him? If he knew about the child growing inside her, it would only make him frantic with worry. Her darling Kit, her second self, who loved her so deeply. So Daisy swallowed back her grief and wrapped her legs around him and urged him on. She knew how to drive him out of his mind; she knew how to make him forget whatever he was thinking and lose himself in her, in Daisy. They finished in a reckless burst and lay panting together, afraid they had made too much noise, afraid they had gone too fast, afraid they hadn't gone fast enough. Kit was worried because she had left her diaphragm at the apartment. Daisy just snuggled deeper in the curve of his body and said not to worry so much.

"But if you have a child—"

"Don't think about it, all right?"

"I can't help thinking about it." He took her hand and trapped it against his chest. "I can't help thinking about what you said, the other day."

"Oh, I say a lot of things. Don't pay any attention to them."

They lay silent. Daisy closed her eyes and felt the beat of her heart, the beat of his heart. The third heart beating in the bed with them, too tiny to be felt, known only to Daisy and God and Grandmère. Kit lifted his other hand and wriggled it. Daisy felt a smooth metal shape pass over her knuckle. She lifted her head.

"What's this?"

"My ring. Now it's yours. Our engagement ring."

"Kit, don't be foolish. It's your family ring."

"Exactly. If you can't find me, you can go to my family. They'll recognize it, they'll help you with . . . well, with whatever you need. And after the war—"

"Kit, please. How can we speak of this? A thousand things could happen. It's bad luck to—"

"Listen to me. A thousand things could happen, yes, but they won't change *this*. This bond between us, how much I love you, that won't change. After the war, as long as I'm alive, I'll come for you. I'll find you, wherever you are—"

"The Ritz," she said. "We'll meet at the Ritz. If we're both still alive."

"What if there is no Ritz?"

"There will always be a Ritz," she said stoutly.

"Well, then. We shall meet at the Ritz, you and I, and never part again. We'll marry and grow old together, surrounded by a dozen children and a pair of cantankerous swans. And this ring, Daisy, is my promise to you. That I'll love you and go on loving you, whatever happens in the months to come. The years, if it comes to that. There's no other woman in the world for me. There never could be, after you."

Daisy just buried her face in his shoulder. She wished she could weep again, but her eyes just ached and ached and refused to shed any more tears. She thought, *He's here now. In this instant, we are together in this bed, and that's all that matters, that's enough for anyone.*

Kit laid his hand along the curve of her head; with his other hand, he traced the lines and dents of the ring on her finger. He smelled of pipe tobacco, of brandy, of lovemaking, of Kit. He whispered something into her hair.

"What's that?" she whispered. "I can't hear you."

So he said it louder, just enough that she could hear him before the cold air swallowed the words.

"Swans, you know, they mate for life."

SOME HOURS LATER, a hand grasped Daisy's shoulder and shook her awake.

"It's time," said Grandmère.

They dressed quickly, without sound. Max was downstairs, helping the children button their coats. Daisy's fingers were so cold, she couldn't fasten her blouse, so Grandmère did it for her while Kit splashed water on his face from the basin in the corner.

"Our contact is waiting at the safe house on rue Rossini, near the Opéra," said Grandmère. "Monsieur Legrand, you will proceed ahead as we agreed, to ensure the security of the location. Daisy, you will follow in half an hour. Von Sternburg has offered to drive me and the children to the rendezvous at—"

From the corner, Kit swore.

"Enough," said Grandmère. "I assure you, he would rather die than see any harm come to them."

"I don't doubt it. He's got some strange fascination with Daisy."

"Don't trouble yourself about it, young man. Only thank God that he does. Now put on your jacket and get out of here, do you hear me? There isn't a moment to lose. Everyone's on edge."

Kit grabbed his jacket from the floor and put it on. Before going down the stairs, he turned to Daisy, took her by the arms, and kissed her deeply, right there in front of Grandmère.

"Remember what I said," he told her, staring straight into her eyes.

"I'll remember."

Down he went, swinging through the hatchway instead of bothering with the stairs, as if the floor had swallowed him up. The last hair of him disappeared from view, and Daisy thought she couldn't breathe. She sat on the bed. A wave of nausea overtook her.

"What's the matter?" said Grandmère. "Is it the sickness?"

"A little. It passes quickly."

"Not for long. It's good we're getting you out of Paris. Your mother had a terrible time with you."

"The invincible demoiselle? Troubled by morning sickness?"

"My God, it was awful."

They listened to the gruff voices downstairs, Kit saying goodbye to the children, the door moving softly. Daisy pressed the ring into the flesh of her finger. It was too big, of course. She would have to wear it around her neck or something. The walls shuddered a little, as Kit slipped out through the front door and closed it behind him and was gone.

THERE WASN'T MUCH to pack. Grandmère had managed to bring out a few clothes from the apartment, before the police came; enough to provide them with a change or two, but not to arouse immediate suspicion. Everything fit inside a single carpetbag. Madeleine and Olivier sat sleepily on the chairs. Max checked his watch.

"How much longer?" asked Daisy. The talisman sat inside the inner pocket of her jacket, heavy and enormous in its silk cloth. It bumped against her ribs whenever she moved. She hated it; she wanted it gone. She wanted to be outside Paris, fleeing Paris with Kit, but that was impossible. She must go to Switzerland first. She would go to Switzerland with the children and Grandmère, she would have the baby there, Kit's baby, safe and sound, and then . . . and then . . . what?

She still felt unwell. She leaned against the table and stared at the floor and tried to breathe. Max frowned at her.

"Everything is well?" he asked, and before Daisy could say anything, Grandmère replied in her usual curt way.

"She's going to have a baby, that's all."

The children were so sleepy, they didn't hear. But Max did.

"She's *what*?"

"Shh! The children," said Daisy.

Max looked at Grandmère, and Grandmère made some motion with her hand to her stomach. Max said something in German, under his breath, and tore a hand through his hair.

"This is madness," he said. "She's in grave danger already, and now this."

Grandmère shrugged. "It can't be helped. We all have a burden to bear, lieutenant colonel, and we women have borne ours throughout history, without the men taking much notice of it."

"But she's not well."

"I am quite well," said Daisy. "It's passed already."

"You're pale."

"I'm not—"

All three of them heard the noise at the same time, the clap of wood, the shudder of the walls as the front door burst open. No one needed to tell them to be still. They froze like actors in a tableau, staring at one another, willing the sound to go away. The world to go back to what it was.

Now footsteps, moving quickly across the bookshop floor.

Something had come over Max, in those few seconds, some invisible air of command. He was no longer the concerned civilian, the avuncular friend; he was a career officer in the German army, accustomed to swift decision and maneuver. He slid one hand into his pocket and drew out his pistol; with his other hand, he motioned the children up the hatchway stairs, all the while staring at the doorway. Daisy hustled them up, urging silence, and when they had disappeared into the attic she grasped the handle and swung the stairs back into place.

Max glanced at her and Grandmère and motioned to them furiously, mouthed the words *Up, up,* but it was already too late. A soft knock sounded on the door.

"La Fleur!" said a voice, a woman's voice, not a Frenchwoman. English? "Open, open! It's urgent!"

Daisy looked at Grandmère. Grandmère looked at Max, who shook his head.

Again, the knock. "La Fleur! The Rat sent me! You must open! Please!"

A terrible fear took hold of Daisy's chest. She stepped forward. "Black cat?" she whispered loudly, to the crack in the door.

"Black cat? Black—oh! Black cat, white mouse. Open, please!"

"That's the password," Daisy said to Max, and she unlocked the door and pulled it open. A woman stood before her, tall, young, startlingly beautiful, and clearly anxious. Daisy had never seen her before. Her accent was most certainly not German.

"Thank God," the woman said.

"Who are you?"

"Code name Opossum. You've got to come with me. It's the drop, it's been compromised. There are Gestapo agents in all the streets nearby, waiting to pounce. It's a trap."

"Kit!" gasped Daisy.

"You can't go, it's too late."

"I have to go! I have to warn him!"

"They'll get you, too! I've got orders to take these jewels of yours and . . ." Opossum stopped and looked around the room. "Who's he?"

"He's a contact. He's . . ." Then Daisy whirled to face Max. "My God!" she cried.

It took him a second or two to understand her meaning. He looked stricken. "Don't be ridiculous! You know I would never—"

"*You!* Was it you all along? Did you get Pierre arrested? Did you—"

Max took her by the arms. "Listen to me! There's no time. You've got it all wrong. You're in danger, you and the children. Take the car, get out of Paris. Give me the damned talisman, I'll go myself."

"The devil you will!"

"Listen, I'm a German officer! I'll outrank any Gestapo agent there. I'll take Legrand into custody myself and then spirit him out. I'll deliver the talisman into safe hands. Daisy, you must trust me. You must."

She pulled his hands away. "Why? Why should I trust you? Because you had some stupid fascination for my mother, and now you've transferred it to me?"

"No! Not that. My God."

He stepped back and stared at her, and in the instant before he spoke, Daisy knew what he was going to say. Hadn't he already told her, just that afternoon? *We were very much in love. And I have never forgiven myself for losing her.* Hadn't he been showing her this, all along?

She thought, *Don't say it.*

Then Max's lips moved, and he said the words.

"Because you're my daughter."

There was an instant of silence, in which the room, the whole world, lurched around Daisy. She tried to speak, but her throat would not move. She looked at the scar on Max's face, the pink, shining, ruthless scar that disfigured his left cheek, from his temple to his jaw and right over his ear. She heard his voice that continued in agonized words.

"I never knew—I didn't realize. I thought you belonged to d'Aubigny. I thought Aurélie—your mother—I thought she had forgotten me. That she had used me and betrayed me. She died before the war ended; there was no chance to learn the truth, no hint at all that her daughter belonged to me. I never suspected you might be mine. Perhaps I should have, but I simply assumed that . . . I thought surely she would have sent word somehow . . . if she loved me as she said—"

"*Mon Dieu,*" Daisy whispered.

"And then I saw you in the Ritz that day and it was as if—as if the earth fell away beneath me. Your face, it struck me senseless." He pulled his watch from his pocket and opened the face. "It's uncanny. You look like my sister. You see? There's her portrait. Your eyebrows are your mother's, and the rest is her."

Daisy looked helplessly at him. The room kept spinning. She was going to vomit. "It's impossible," she whispered. She put out her arm, and somebody took it. Grandmère, holding her upright.

"It's true, my dear," Grandmère said. "I realized it right away. He made me promise I wouldn't tell."

"I thought you would hate me," said Max. "You should hate me."

The woman called Opossum stood dumbstruck in the doorway, looking back and forth between the two of them. "Bloody hell," she said in English. "He's telling the truth."

Daisy looked back up at Max, at his warm blue eyes that stared at her beseechingly. His terrible scar. He still held the watch with its open case. She couldn't look at that; she didn't need to, didn't want to. Some woman she would never know. A family she would never know. A father who had never known her, never raised her, never been there when she needed him; when she had wanted a father's love so terribly, she had married Pierre. Her life, her history, transformed in a flash. She pulled her arm away from Grandmère and covered her mouth. It was the hand that bore Kit's ring. The two swans dug into her lips.

"Give me the talisman," he said again, more gently. "Go, get out of Paris. Take care of the children. It's my turn. I failed your mother. I've failed *you*, my darling girl, but I swear before God, I won't fail you again."

Opossum broke in. "For God's sake. Just *go*, one of you, before it's too late! Or I'll take the damned thing myself!"

Daisy reached inside her pocket, pulled out the talisman, and handed it to Max.

"If you do fail me," she whispered, "I'll kill you with my own hands."

CHAPTER TWENTY-EIGHT

Babs

Paris, France
April 1964

I F THE CANCER didn't kill Margot, the medicinal stink mixed with antiseptic that pervaded the halls of the Hôtel-Dieu certainly would. I pressed my nose against Drew's shoulder as we walked quickly down the long corridor toward Margot's room, my emotions—anger, guilt, pity—all roly-poly and unable to separate. It was as if a red sock had been tossed in the wash along with the white ones, staining everything.

Drew remained outside the door of the private room, squeezing my shoulder for encouragement as if I were a fellow football player ready to run onto the playing field. And, I thought, perhaps I was.

The woman lying against the white pillow bore little resemblance to the woman whom I had met at the Ritz. But as I stood by the side of her bed and looked down at her, I saw that her light still existed in her eyes, and as long as that wasn't extinguished, the essence of the woman remained.

"Daisy?" The simple word felt heavy on my tongue.

Her fingers opened, and she smiled. Without hesitation she reached for my hand.

My entire prepared speech evaporated, my thoughts and feelings suddenly unimportant. All that remained of all that was past was two women who'd loved the same man with all of their hearts.

I slid Kit's ring from my finger and placed it into her open palm, a token of all the guilt I'd been carrying around like a valise for so long. "I'm sorry." All of my rehearsed words were condensed into just those inadequate two.

"Sorry?" Her voice had faded, too, like the rest of her body. But not those eyes.

"The letter you sent to Kit. I never showed it to him. I don't . . ." I stopped, knowing we didn't have enough time for me to try to explain. I wasn't even sure that I could explain it to myself. Instead, I simply said, "Forgive me."

She closed her eyes and smiled. "You loved him. You . . . gave him children. Made him happy. Nothing to . . . forgive."

"He loved you," I said, the words not hurting as much as I'd thought they would. "He never stopped. Until the day he died, he never stopped loving you."

She took my hand, the bones of her hand as brittle as a bird's. "Shh," she whispered. "He loved us both." Something warm and hard pressed against my palm as she closed her hand around mine. The indentation of the two swans pressed against my skin. Two swans, meant to mate for life. It made me oddly happy that Kit's ring had belonged to Daisy for all of these years. It was somehow fitting. "For Kit's son, yes?"

Tears fell on our linked hands and I was surprised to find that they were mine. "Thank you." There was so much more I wanted to say, but the words were thick and stale in my throat, words of apology and explanation for which this remarkable woman had already forgiven me.

The sound of approaching footsteps came from the hallway outside. I looked up, recognizing an older Madeleine and Olivier as they rushed into the room. I leaned down and kissed Daisy's forehead, her skin cold against my lips. "Goodbye, Daisy."

Then I let go of her hand, taking the ring with me, and left the room. Drew put his arm around me as he led me down the corridor, pulling me out of the way as a young woman of about twenty rushed by us. She was tall and slender, and wearing chic Parisian clothes. Her golden-brown hair, much lighter than her straight, dark brows, flew about her head in wild disarray. I knew I'd never seen her before, yet there was something so familiar. If I could only see her eyes . . .

"Maman!" she called out as she entered Daisy's room.

Drew pulled me away, leaving me no time to brood or to mourn a woman I'd barely known yet who had been a part of my life for so many years.

The ride in the taxi on the way back was subdued, which was curious considering how much needed to be said. There was Daisy, of course, but I couldn't as yet wrap my mind around all of those implications. But there was also the matter of La Fleur, and whether or not she'd been a traitor. And the talisman. But mostly, the one thing that weighed heaviest in my heart, was that Drew was leaving. It was awful, really. I was a grown woman, a widow. I'd survived privations during wartime. I'd even discovered that my husband had loved another woman. But this, this *hollowness* felt alien to me. It was like a nightmare from which I couldn't awaken, a nightmare where everything I'd ever learned, everything I'd ever loved and cherished, had been declared null and void.

We walked silently into the Ritz, the constant clacking of Prunella's typewriter making me want to screech at her to stop. That nobody cared about her stupid memoirs, that a woman was dying—if not already dead—and my heart was being broken for the second time and I wasn't sure how I was to survive it.

As if sensing my mood, Drew took my hand, stopping me as I

headed in the elderly woman's direction, intent on committing violence against a typewriter. "Babs, I'm sorry. I wish . . ."

"Is she gone?"

We both turned to see Precious Dubose, returned to her immaculate self, standing oddly composed and holding something in her hands.

"I assume so," I said. "Her children arrived, and we didn't want to intrude. Did you . . . "

She shook her head. "After I'd had my little nap, I realized that we'd already said everything we needed to say to each other, and our good-byes. I'm glad the children made it in time. They have always been her world."

"Next to Kit," I said, and I could tell that she already knew.

"Come on," she said. "These are sitting down shoes, and I've got lots to tell you." We followed her to a banquette in the long, carpeted hall and sat down. A waiter approached, and she immediately dismissed him. Without a word, she opened up her hands and what appeared to be a bundle of rags slipped onto the table.

I didn't understand until Precious began pushing aside the soiled and torn cloth, exposing a scratched gold medallion with a cracked crystal window in the center, a gold ring around it where the prongs of missing jewels still clung. I knew if I flipped it over, we'd see an engraving of a wolf with a cross.

"It's the talisman," Drew and I said in unison, our gazes moving from the table to Precious and then back again.

"Congratulations," she said. "You've found La Fleur."

We were both stunned into silence, even the sounds of the bustling hotel muted somehow. "But . . ." My brain felt waterlogged, swishing from one side of my head to the other, unable to settle on any one thought. "But what about Daisy?"

"She was La Fleur, too. She started the name, but I took over as La Fleur when her identity was compromised and she fled with her children and grandmama to Canada. I'd been working with the Resistance since I'd arrived from London, so I was already familiar with our other operatives. It made sense, and so I slipped from one persona to another." Her smile became secretive. "Reinvention is my best talent, you know."

"So you knew Kit," I said, my head beginning to hurt with all of the implications.

"I certainly did. He was a very fine man—one of the best. He reminded me very much of someone I had known in London, someone with an equally good heart and strong sense of purpose." She paused, swallowed, then allowed a small smile to tease her lips. "I knew you were his wife the moment we met and you said your last name was Langford. I had to assume you were here to find La Fleur."

"Wait a minute." Drew slapped his hands on the table, making a couple walking by startle and move away. "I can't believe I've been so oblivious." He turned to me. "Do you see? Margot is short for Marguerite—from *The Scarlet Pimpernel,* of all things—and Marguerite is the French equivalent of Daisy. How could I have missed it? Even Pierre told us that everyone called Marguerite Daisy!" He slapped his forehead with the flat of his hand. "Jesus H. Roosevelt Christ! Harvard is going to take away my summa cum laude!"

I stared at him. "Harvard? I thought you said you went to Bowdoin."

He may have actually rolled his eyes. "I already told you—I have no connection to Bowdoin, either by name or alma mater. I wasn't just a football player, you know." He sat back in his chair and leveled a gaze on Precious. "So what they said is true, then. That La Fleur took the talisman for her own gain. And let my father take the blame."

"Hardly," Precious said. "You see, the night of the drop, there was a problem where we were supposed to give your father the talisman. The Gestapo had somehow found out—we think it might have been Pierre, trying to save his own skin. Luckily for us, we had help from

Max von Sternburg, a German officer." She paused. "He was also Daisy's father—something she wasn't aware of until that very night. He took the talisman to make the transfer to the OSS man—your father, Drew—so Daisy and the children could escape. Unfortunately, the Gestapo were waiting for him. Knowing it meant certain death, he turned himself in—but only after giving me the talisman." She paused for a moment, remembering. "I hid and watched as they shot him. Even with his hands up in surrender. He died honorably. I'm glad I was able to tell Daisy that much, at least."

"But my father never got the talisman. No one showed up."

Precious placed a calming hand on Drew's arm. "By the time I received it, it was too late."

"So what happened to the jewels?" he asked.

"I spent them all on clothes, of course."

We stared at her in stunned surprise.

It was her turn to roll her eyes. "I'm just playing with you. I sold them, of course. The Resistance was in desperate need of operating funds. I was modeling for Coco Chanel at the time and had made many helpful contacts not only among the Nazis she considered friends, but also in the furriers and jewelers she used for her fashion house. One was a Jew whose last name was Reich—can you imagine? He worked right under their noses and because of his name he was above suspicion. He helped me sell the jewels on the black market to the Nazis. That Nazi money funded the Resistance for months to come, which made it doubly rewarding. Not only did we save more Jewish lives, but we had the Nazis pay for it."

She put her hand on Drew's arm. "You must understand that we couldn't expose the truth that might have cleared your father's name. It would have compromised too many people, too many operations already in place. It's why I didn't confess my true identity. Up until now, we have not been allowed to let the world know, but I have been granted permission seeing as how your father is running out of time. I hope you will be able to give him peace."

Precious frowned at me. "You're going to catch flies, Babs, if you don't close your mouth."

I immediately shut it, unaware of how long I'd been staring at her gape jawed. Probably for the same amount of time it had taken me to realize how completely wrong I'd been about Daisy. About La Fleur. She and Kit had tried to save the world together. Had risked their lives while I busied myself in the countryside running the WI and tending my victory garden, imagining I was doing my part. No wonder Kit had loved her.

"I . . . ," I began, not sure what I was going to say. Instead, I opened my purse and pulled out the letter. The one I'd been so desperate to hide. But it didn't matter anymore. Drew was leaving, and I'd learned the truth of someone I'd considered my nemesis. And for both, I found myself horribly lacking.

I placed the letter on the table next to the talisman, baring my subterfuge. The words written at the bottom taunted me. *I will always love you. Always.* I didn't cover them up. I needed them to see. I needed Drew to see so that he'd know he'd been mistaken about me, that his leaving had come at the most opportune time so that he didn't have to find an excuse to go back to New York.

"This came for Kit," I explained. "When he was recuperating after being released from the prison camp. I kept it from him. I never even told him a letter had arrived. Instead, I tucked it up in the attic and married him, telling myself it was for his own good." I swallowed the dam of tears trying to block my airway. "They could have been together all this time, but I was so selfish. When I thought she was evil, it was so much easier to justify." I looked down in my lap, unable to meet their eyes.

"Babs." Drew placed a hand gently on my arm. "Stop beating yourself up. You did it out of love, not out of selfishness. Your heart is so big, and so giving, all you wanted was for Kit to be happy. Your big, generous heart. It's what I love most about you."

A valet approached discreetly and stood near Drew. "Your luggage is ready, sir. And I took the liberty of calling for a taxi."

Drew stood, looking uncertain. "Remember at our picnic in Picardy, how we both said we needed to shake up our lives? I think this is it. I think you and I are meant to shake them up together. Come with me, Babs. Come with me to New York."

I blinked at him, my head and heart warring with each other, battling it out in my throat so that I couldn't speak.

Drew held up his hand. "Think about it. Let me settle my account, and I'll be right back."

I watched his departure until Precious pulled on my arm. "My mama used to say that to watch someone walk away means you'll never see them again. And I have a good hunch that you both will find a way to be together."

I turned around, but not because I believed her. "You probably think I'm a weak and spiteful woman. And I'm afraid that you might be right. Despite what he said, I know I don't deserve him."

"Don't ever think that. Ever." Her accent was amplified in that one word, the *r* disappearing completely. "Life is complicated, without any sort of road map. We are bound to have disappointments and setbacks, and with each one we make the choice to reinvent ourselves as a stronger version of who we are. You had a wonderful life with Kit. Your three wonderful children are a testament to that. And I know Daisy forgave you, so you don't need to carry that burden any longer. Learning how to forgive ourselves is so much harder." The last word seemed to catch in her throat, convincing me that she was on familiar terms with the struggle for self-forgiveness. She leaned closer so I could smell her perfume, recognizing it as Vol de Nuit. It was the same perfume Diana wore—made for brave and adventurous women. Of which I was neither. "Barbara, you are a formidable woman. Never forget that."

I looked into her beautiful face, wondering again about the stories that lay behind her bright blue eyes. Something dark lurked there, I recognized it now. I remembered seeing it in Kit's eyes after he'd returned from the war. I blinked away stupid tears I had no right to shed. "How did you get so wise?"

Precious smiled. "We all make decisions, Babs. The hardest part is learning to live with them."

"So how does a formidable woman decide what to do next?" I asked, feeling utterly lost.

"Well, I've decided to return to London. The hardest part will be deciding which version of me will be returning."

I didn't have a chance to ask her what she meant as Drew had come back and stood by my chair. He reached for my hand and pulled me up, looking at me with earnest eyes. "Come with me to New York, Babs. We've put our ghosts to rest, haven't we? Doesn't that mean we're supposed to get on with our lives now? To find our own happiness? Because, to be honest, I don't know how I'm supposed to live the rest of my life without you."

I will always love you. Always. Those words haunted me, accusing me. I was the worst sort of person, and Drew deserved so much better. "I can't, Drew. I have responsibilities. I can't just . . . leave. I agree my life needed to be shaken up, but I don't believe moving to New York with you is what I'd intended. It's been lovely, it has, but I think this is where we must part." Each word was like a blow to my heart, a searing, sharp pain, and I wasn't sure where the strength came from to say them without falling apart.

He continued to study me, as if looking for some weakness, some wavering on my part. But I couldn't allow that. "This won't be good-bye so I'm not going to say it." He kissed me, the kind of kiss that in the movies is accompanied by sweeping music and the couple riding off into the sunset. But this wasn't a movie.

I stepped back, my lips swollen and sore. "Goodbye, Drew."

CHAPTER TWENTY-NINE

Aurélie

The Hôtel Ritz
Paris, France
August 1915

Bonjour, Maman," said Aurélie.

Her mother was on her feet, her face gray. "Aurélie?"

"Hello," said Aurélie, since it was very hard to know what to say when one had been gone for nearly a year, when one had absconded with a priceless jewel and run away to a war zone without so much as a word.

She nodded vaguely in the direction of the other people in her mother's salon, shadow figures with neat beards and well-tailored suits. They might have been puppets or paper cutouts, so unreal did they seem, so strangely clean and tidy, well-groomed and well-fed. She had been traveling for five weeks, and everything felt a little blurry. Except the smells. She could smell her own rank sweat, her mother's perfume, the overripe flowers in a vase.

Aurélie swallowed hard against a wave of nausea. "I've come back."

"Aurélie. It's you. It's really you. I had thought . . . when I heard—" Her mother clutched the back of a chair, as though she, too, were feeling not entirely steady.

Everyone was staring. Aurélie was very conscious of her own disarray. The Red Cross had offered them baths at the Swiss border, but that had been a week ago, and the stench had long since sunk into her clothes. Aurélie began sidling in the direction of her old bedroom. "If I might . . ."

"Of course." Her mother came sharply to herself, moving rapidly to Aurélie's side. Taking Aurélie by the arm, her mother called over her shoulder, "Marie! Tell everyone to go. I'm not at home. How did you get here? What happened to you? When did you leave Courcelles?"

"In June." That seemed the easiest question to answer. June felt a very long time ago. The world had been reduced to a series of stops and searches, choking down bites of tasteless food, trying not to be ill. "I took a train. The Germans—they allowed some people to be evacuated."

"June?" Her mother stopped and stared at her. "Did they take you via Timbuktu?"

"No, to Belgium. And then to Switzerland." Aurélie drew a hand across her eyes, which felt gritty. All of her felt gritty. "It was not—it was not a pleasant journey."

They had been rounded up at the train station in Le Catelet and given numbers, strapped to their chests, then marched by armed gendarmes onto the train. No one had been permitted to say farewell, no well-wishers were allowed to approach. They were shuffled away like prisoners, like criminals. A baby had cried, and the baby's mother had quickly muffled the cry with her shawl, terrified the Germans would lose patience and hurt the child. They were all stiff and silent with fear.

The train took three days to cross into Belgium, where soldiers stripped and searched the evacuees, and anxious rumors spread that they were to be taken, not into France at all, but to work camps in Germany. Aurélie braided the talisman into her hair and slept in her clothes. Fear became numbness. They were detained one week, then two, before being sent on again. The swaying of the train, the cramped conditions and smells in the third-class compartment made Aurélie queasy; trying not to be ill took all her concentration and will.

It took over a week to reach the Swiss border, where they were met by Red Cross workers with mugs of milk, real milk, and hot coffee and tea, and bread rolls, proper bread rolls. It made Aurélie want to cry to see the wonder on the children's faces, at the food and the kindness. What had they come to that a bit of bread and a smile were a wonder?

The Red Cross workers had bundled them onto yet another train, but this was different now; there were no guards, no warders, no searches. Hours later, they were in Évian, on French soil, where hotels were put at their disposal free of charge, and people came to help them with their papers. It had seemed safer to remain Jeanne Deschamps, to make her way to the Ritz quietly, the talisman hidden close to her breast.

And all the while, Aurélie replayed those final moments, that moment when Max had scrambled back in through the window.

He was safe, he had to be. And her father, too. He had said he would save her father. He would. He had.

"But you're here now," said her mother. There were two thin lines between her brows as she examined Aurélie's face. "You're home."

Home. The Ritz didn't feel like home. The Ritz had never felt like home. But what other home did she have?

A fairy-tale castle on an island, in the middle of a man-made lake, surrounded by wildflowers, where Max would teach their children to swim. Aurélie felt dizzy, lost between worlds. *I'll come for you at the Ritz,* Max had said. *At the Ritz.* And surely he would. Not now perhaps, but in a month, in a year, when the war was over. If it would ever be over.

"Come, I'll have Marie draw a bath for you immediately." Her mother was shepherding her to her dressing table, easing her down into a chair, unpinning the soiled hat from her soiled hair. "My dear, your hair."

"The dye will wear out." Suzanne had told her that a lifetime ago, as she had steeped walnut hulls in a basin in the kitchen at Courcelles.

"It already is," said her mother, unpinning the dirty coils of hair on top of Aurélie's head, fanning them out. "You're piebald, my darling."

It was so very strange, sitting in this familiar chair, in front of her old mirror. But the face in the mirror was nearly unrecognizable. It wasn't just the hair dye, or the grime. The old Aurélie had been different. So sure of herself. So impatient. So young. "I had to travel incognito. I'm a widow. Jeanne Deschamps."

In the mirror, she saw her mother press her eyes tightly shut, letting out a breath. "That explains it."

"Explains what?"

"The clothes," her mother said, a little too quickly. "Relax, relax, don't try to get up. You look dead on your feet, my poor girl. Marie! Make up Miss Aurélie's bed. Would you like me to ring for anything? Chocolate? Coffee?"

Luxuries. They hadn't had coffee at Courcelles since the fall; chocolate had been an unknown quantity. It made Aurélie think of Max, delivering chocolate on Christmas Eve to the children of the village.

Aurélie turned in the chair to face her mother, away from her own unfamiliar face. "I scarcely know what those are anymore. We had strict rationing at Courcelles. The Germans took anything edible for themselves."

Her mother's hands rested briefly on her shoulders. "That must be why you're all skin and bone. My poor girl. I'll have Marie make up a tisane for you. Something strengthening. Let's get you out of those hideous clothes and into one of your own nightdresses. Marie!"

Aurélie's hands clamped down on her bulky skirt. "There are messages for you. In the seams of my petticoat. From my father. They shot the pigeons. I'd forgot . . ."

"There's no rush." Her mother stopped her as she started to wiggle frantically out of her petticoat, trying to get to the messages. "I'll read them in a bit. After I get you settled. You need your rest."

It had been different when she was traveling, suspended between worlds, but now that she was here, it all seemed real again, the flames, the clamor. There were no more pigeons. But somehow . . . she had to know what had happened. She had to let them know she was safe.

Her mother had Aurélie's dirty petticoat draped over her arm. "I'll just tell Marie to run your bath."

"Wait." Aurélie put a hand on her mother's arm. She'd forgotten how fine-boned she was, how small, how Aurélie felt like a giantess beside her. "Is there any way to get a message to Courcelles? To my father?"

Her mother said nothing, but Aurélie could see her knuckles go white against the coarse cloth. "Shortly. Later."

"What is it?" Fear gripped Aurélie. This wasn't like her mother. Not at all. "Do you have news from Courcelles?"

Her mother looked at her, and, beneath her carefully applied makeup, her face was that of a much older woman. "Courcelles is gone. It burned." Tentatively, she reached out a finger and touched Aurélie's cheek, as if testing that she was real. "I was told you had burned with it."

"M—someone got me out."

Go, Max had said, and she had gone, running to the chapel to grab her carpetbag, barely stopping, even with the roar of the fire behind her, running, running. He would get her father out, Max had said, and she had believed him, because he said it with such assurance, because he loved her.

Aurélie didn't remember sitting again, but she was. Her knees must have folded. She looked anxiously up at her mother. "My father?"

"I'm sorry." Her mother put her arms around Aurélie, drew Aurélie's head to her breast. Aurélie couldn't remember the last time they had embraced like this, the last time she had let her mother hold her. "I would have let you rest at least before telling you."

"He's gone?" It seemed impossible. Her father, the warrior. The autocrat.

"In the fire." She felt her mother lean against her for a moment, felt the force of her mother's own sorrow, before her mother straightened, automatically setting her hair and dress to rights. "You understand, we have no real news from the occupied territory. It's all rumor—but I have friends."

Oh yes. Her mother always had friends. And her friends were generally to be believed.

Aurélie drew in a deep breath, her chest tight. "I shouldn't have gone. I should have stayed with him."

"And died, too?" She couldn't remember ever seeing her mother look so fierce. Regaining her urbane mask, her mother said, "For what it's worth, there were German officers gone, too. Several of them. Your father would have considered that worth the sacrifice, I imagine. He always wanted to die in battle rather than in someone's bed."

German officers gone. Max.

Aurélie's gorge rose. "Oh no."

Her mother mistook her expression. "Darling, I didn't mean—I wasn't making light of it. We all have different ways of mourning, I suppose. And I do mourn your father."

"You are right. He would be proud," said Aurélie numbly. "How many German officers died with him?"

"Several. I don't believe there was anyone left to take charge. I heard all was chaos. That was why they thought—they thought you had died, too."

"I didn't," said Aurélie flatly. No. She had run away. To keep the talisman safe.

The talisman that would never have been there if she hadn't brought it. The talisman that had cost her father and her lover their lives. She had cost them their lives.

"My father sent me away. With this." Fumbling in her chemise, beneath the multiple layers of clothes bundled about her, she drew out the talisman, drawing the chain up over her head. She had removed it from her hair and returned it to her neck once she had crossed into France.

"The talisman." Her mother took it from her, holding it delicately by the chain, the relic swaying gently, still warm from Aurélie's skin, like a living thing, winking at her in the electric light. "You scared me half to death when you ran away with that, you know. I was afraid you meant to go into battle with it, as your father had. I was so relieved when your father told me you'd come to Courcelles."

"I know. He told me. I found one of your messages." All of that seemed so far away now. "I hadn't realized you were on corresponding terms."

"When it mattered." The carefully painted line of her mother's lip rouge trembled, just a bit. "He was very proud of you."

Aurélie lifted her hands to her temples, as though she could hold in the memories, the pain. "I did so little."

"That's not what your father said. He said you were a symbol of hope—and an excellent distraction."

She had been so upset by that, being a distraction. She had been so angry at her father. But now she would give anything to go back, to have him alive again. And Max . . . Max, who had betrayed everything, had killed his own superior for her. Max, who was meant to be playing on the banks of a lake with a brood of children with silver-gilt hair, not killed in a château in France. He would never even have been there but for her.

Max, who had once come to her mother's salon with daisies in his buttonhole. She wanted to close her eyes and turn back time, here, in her old room. She wanted to make them all whole again.

But she couldn't. She couldn't change any of it. And it hurt, it hurt so terribly much.

"It's my fault. It's all my fault." Aurélie pressed her hands over her mouth, but the sobs escaped anyway, not pretty, graceful tears, but horrible, ugly gulping sobs, torn from her gut, ripping her insides out. "If I'd never gone . . . if I'd never brought the talisman . . . I should have stayed with him. Why didn't I stay with him?"

Her mother chafed her wrists. "And die, as well? Your father would have wanted you safe," she said. "Safe and working for France."

Her father? Oh yes. Her father. It was on the tip of her tongue to pour out the truth about Max, but something held her back. What would people say? That she had been a German officer's whore. Never mind that he loved her, that she loved him, that he had come to her mother's salon with daisies.

She couldn't soil it. She wouldn't let them soil it.

Aurélie lifted her head, her eyes stinging, her throat aching. "My father. He wanted me to bring the talisman back, to tell the world that we had wrenched it from the Germans."

Her mother absently stroked her cheek. "The demoiselle holds the talisman and France cannot fall? It's not a dreadful notion. There might be something in it. . . . Ah, Marie. Is that the tisane? Enough of this for the moment, my darling. Bath first, and then sleep."

So Aurélie let herself be led, first to the bath, and then to the high, soft bed, where a warm drink that tasted like weeds was pressed into her hands. Because what mattered now? All her dreams were ash.

HER MOTHER MUST have put something in the tisane. Or Marie had. Aurélie, who had spent the past five weeks sleeping fitfully in a third-class train seat, or on a makeshift cot, slept and slept and slept some more. If she dreamed, her only memory of it was in the moisture of tears on her cheeks.

She had a vague recollection of waking in the night to find her mother beside her, stroking her hair, her perfume a soft presence in the air.

"Sleep, my darling," she had said, and Aurélie had slept.

When Aurélie woke again, it was broad daylight. She knew that, because her mother was vigorously opening the drapes, letting the light stream in.

Aurélie winced and held up a hand against the light.

"I'm sorry, my darling." Her mother was chic in a suit with a wide, calf-length skirt and a jacket that belted smartly at the waist. "I should have let you sleep, but you've been asleep since Tuesday. And *Paris-Midi* is coming at noon and the *New York Times* at one."

"The *New York Times* . . . what?"

"They want to photograph you with the talisman, here, at the Ritz." Her mother busied herself with an armful of garments that Aurélie did not recognize as her own, examining and discarding them one by one. Finally, she held one up and gave a little nod of approval. "White, I think. White, with a *tricolore* pinned to your chest. Innocent, but also patriotic. You'll look like Liberty on the barricades. Only without the barricades."

"I don't understand."

"You're a heroine," said her mother. "The woman who routed an entire command of German officers and liberated a French national treasure."

From under the pile of garments, her mother tugged out a folded newspaper, tossing it to Aurélie. It was *Le Matin*, and Aurélie's own face, her debutante portrait, taken two years before, smirked out at her from the front page.

THE DEMOISELLE DE COURCELLES
BRINGS HOPE TO FRANCE.
THE SAINT IS WITH US, SAYS DEMOISELLE
DE COURCELLES. FRANCE CANNOT FALL.

"According to that," said her mother, "you singlehandedly torched the German headquarters."

The words swam in front of Aurélie's eyes. She shoved the paper

aside, struggling to sit up against the pillows. She felt at a decided dis-
advantage, still half asleep. Her mouth tasted like the inside of a bird's
cage. "According to whom?"

"To me." Her mother perched on the edge of the bed, next to her.
"I called them. I told them the story. France needs a heroine right now.
It needs you."

Aurélie frowned at her, trying to gather her wits. "But that's not
what happened."

"Does it matter what happened?"

Dreier, a living flame. Max, with the bronze statue of Mars in his
hand. "It matters to me. It mattered to M—to my father."

"Your father would glory in this." Gentling her voice, her mother
said, "People need something to give them hope. There's nothing
better than a beautiful woman and an ancient relic. And diamonds."

"But I didn't do anything." Other than leave her father and the
man she loved.

"Then do something now." Her mother gave her blanket-covered
knees a brisk pat. "Inspire our armies to new victories. Give people the
courage to carry on. Be what your father wanted you to be. A heroine for France. And put some clothes on before the photographer from
Paris-Midi arrives."

Paris-Midi arrived and the *New York Times* and the *Chicago Tribune*
and papers from places whose names Aurélie didn't recognize, but who
were, it seemed, sure that their readers would be passionately interested in the story of the young aristocrat who had broken the German
hold on Picardy.

She hadn't, of course. She had only disrupted one command center,
and that had been restaffed within hours after some agitated sending
of telegrams and directions from Berlin, but the papers preferred not
to focus on that bit, so neither did Aurélie. She just tilted her chin and
looked melancholy and noble and went where she was told.

A car was put at her disposal. Not her car, her beloved long-lost car, but a stuffy black car with a driver paid by the government. Aurélie was ferried triumphantly from village to village, displayed with the talisman, the Demoiselle de Courcelles bringing hope to France. They dressed her in white with a *tricolore* pinned to her chest; she was Liberty, she was the Spirit of France, she was a living sign of defiance against the Germans.

And if she was quietly ill by the side of the road, only her mother noticed.

"Here, take this," said her mother, handing her a handkerchief to wipe her mouth. They were en route to yet another engagement, at which her mother and the local mayor would speak and Aurélie would stand there looking symbolic, holding the talisman. Then contributions would be taken for the war effort. "How far along are you?"

Aurélie looked at her blankly.

"The child," said her mother matter-of-factly. "How many months gone are you?"

"Child?"

"Yes, the child that's making you miserably ill—and will also make you lose your waist," her mother added drily. "That child."

The car was parked at the side of the road, the driver smoking a cigarette. It was September again, and the air was starting to get that autumn smell, the smell of damp earth and rotting leaves.

Aurélie stared at her mother. "I thought—I thought I was ill because I was sad."

For once, she had the satisfaction of rendering her mother entirely speechless. "I knew I shouldn't have left your education to the nuns," her mother said at last. "Have you the slightest idea how babies are made?"

"I . . . no." She supposed she should have thought it. But it wasn't something one discussed. And she'd never had female friends to share things with her.

"What about the father?" Her mother's voice was carefully neutral.

"I—I don't want to discuss it." The father. Max would have adored being a father. It was what he wanted more than anything. A family. A large family.

"Were you forced? Never mind. This isn't the place," her mother said hastily, when Aurélie looked at her in alarm. "It doesn't matter. What's a father, anyway? This is your child, not anyone else's. We'll raise it together, you and I. You're not alone in this."

"We should—we should be getting on." Aurélie couldn't help putting her hands to her stomach. It didn't feel any different. It seemed strange to think that a child might be growing there. Max's baby, their baby, who was supposed to grow up in a town with an unpronounceable name, surrounded by brothers and sisters and dogs. "Wouldn't I feel something?"

"Not necessarily. How long has it been since you've had your courses?" Her mother nodded, without waiting for an answer. "I'll have my doctor examine you when we return."

"A child," said Aurélie, testing out the notion. She didn't know whether to be alarmed or elated. Her mother might be wrong—except her mother didn't believe in being wrong. If her mother said something, it must be so. The world would conform itself to her wishes or face the consequences. Aurélie suddenly, fiercely, hoped her mother was right.

Her mother was still talking. "You've no husband, of course, but we can manage that." Her mother pursed her lips, thinking. "I saw Jean-Marie d'Aubigny's name on the casualty lists."

"Oh no." Aurélie pressed her eyes shut. Her playmate, her childhood friend. She should feel more, she should weep for him, but she felt drained of emotion. Horror had succeeded horror until there was nothing left. "Not Jean-Marie, too."

"Yes, it's very sad," said her mother absently. "Papers disappear in wartime. Marriage records, for example. Or there's that spineless priest your father keeps on at Courcelles. Surely, he could be persuaded to . . . to remember what ought to have happened. We'll tell people you were married in secret. A moonlit wedding at the chapel. A few stolen moments together before he had to leave for the front . . . Who is there to say otherwise?"

"Everyone in his regiment!"

Her mother waved that away. "He must have had leave at some point. Jean-Marie was a younger son, there's no inheritance to be disputed. And who would give the lie to the Demoiselle de Courcelles? You're an emblem of France. I'm surprised they aren't putting you on the coins yet."

"Yes, but—"

"Jean-Marie would have wanted what was best for you."

Aurélie couldn't deny that. Jean-Marie had always had a big heart. But it was Max she was thinking of, Max whose child would have another man's name.

But did she really want to raise her child with the stigma of illegitimacy? Not just illegitimacy, but a German for a father. People spat when they spoke of the Boches. So would she, but for Max.

In a low voice, Aurélie said, "Jean-Marie came through Courcelles at the end of September. I saw him then."

"Well, then. There you are." In her most persuasive tones, her mother said, "Let Jean-Marie do this one last thing for you. Your child will have a noble name. A *French* name."

Startled, Aurélie looked at her mother, wondering just what her father had put in those reports. But her mother was looking particularly guileless.

"The papers will adore it. The demoiselle's secret marriage to her beloved childhood betrothed, a child for France, blah, blah, blah."

"All right," said Aurélie slowly.

She put her hands on her stomach, trying to imagine the person inside. Wherever Max was, she liked to think that he knew, that he would be watching them. And Max, of all people, would never quibble because she gave his child another man's name. He would want only their happiness.

For the past month, she had been living in a fog, cut off from everything. Now, for the first time, Aurélie felt the fog begin to lift. She felt grief—but also joy. And a fierce, fierce love.

"All right," she said, and her voice was stronger. "For the child."

"Not the child, darling. Your child." Her mother took her hands and gave them a squeeze. "A person. An opinionated, strong-willed, fascinating person who will give you headaches and heartaches, but you'll love to distraction all the same. Who knows what sort of world your child will live in, what wonders he'll accomplish?"

"He might be a philosopher, or a poet," Aurélie said, thinking of Max, of those long, delicate hands, the way his fair hair fell across his brow as he sat reading in the candlelight.

"Or she." Her mother gave her a quick, impulsive hug. Aurélie breathed in the scent of her perfume. Instead of making her ill, it smelled of home and hope and springtime. "Let us not think of death, my darling, but life."

CHAPTER THIRTY

Daisy

Hôtel-Dieu
Paris, France
April 1964

Daisy wasn't afraid to die. That was the singular virtue of an illness like hers: you had time to prepare, you had time to accept this idea of death, you had time to suffer and wish you were dead already. And maybe she wasn't old, but she wasn't that young anymore, either. She'd raised her children to adulthood. Wasn't that all anyone could ask for?

Anyway, they had given her a very nice room, a pleasant place to die. Madeleine and Olivier sat on either side of the bed, each one holding her hand, and the April sunlight passed through the window and enshrouded the three of them. Olivier's blond hair had darkened to brown as he passed into adolescence, but when the sun shone on it, as it did now, you could see the trace of gold left behind, an inheritance from his mother's parents. What a fine boy, Daisy thought. He was in his second year of law school now, so promising. Probably the world didn't need quite so many lawyers, but Olivier would be a good one, certainly. He would marry some fine girl and raise a beautiful family.

And Madeleine, always so dark-haired and serious. Daisy couldn't see her face very well—everything had begun to dim, as if the lights of the world were going out, one by one—but that was a blessing, because Madeleine was taking this hard. Madeleine had always taken things hard. The flight from Paris had been terrible for her, losing her father and Uncle Max both at once, losing her home and everything familiar. Thank God for the baby. They had found a little house on the edge of Lake Constance, where Daisy gave birth one fine July evening, but really it was Madeleine's baby. Madeleine was just at an age when a little girl longs for a sister, and she had poured all her love and heartache into this infant, Kit's gift to them, and that was when life began to get better, n'est-ce pas? When the darkness started lifting, and they felt like a family again, Daisy and the children and Grandmère, there on the shores of Lake Constance, the warm, fresh air and the sparkling water, so peaceful and so beautiful. When Daisy could begin to imagine a world in which the war ended, and she and Kit found each other again, when she would be sitting at the dear Little Bar on the rue Cambon side and he would enter, turn his head, look for her, see her! He would walk toward her slowly, not wanting to rush this moment of reunion. He would stand before her and touch her hand, where his ring still lay snug on her finger, two swans entwined. He would be haggard and thin, so would she, but it wouldn't matter. None of it would matter anymore. They would kiss, they would embrace, they would go upstairs and remember what it was to be matched once more with the other half of yourself, to be made whole again.

And wouldn't Kit be amazed, wouldn't he be delighted at what they had made together? A small, beautiful girl-child to raise and love. Oh, how Daisy had loved to picture the way Kit's face would look, his expression of wonder when she introduced him to his daughter! That vision sustained her through all the long months of war and exile.

Her mind was wandering again, Daisy realized. She couldn't quite seem to keep herself in the present. She kept slipping back, and back. That kind couple who were here a moment ago, where had they gone? What was her name again?

This was important, Daisy knew. So terribly important. Why couldn't she remember?

Babs. That was it. Babs Langford. Of course.

Kit's wife.

Daisy closed her eyes. There was a time when she had hated this woman, who had stolen Kit's heart from her. A time, before that, when she had sat at the Little Bar on the rue Cambon side, day after day that autumn of 1945, while Frank refilled her glass. Waiting and waiting. Hope dribbling away as the nights wore on, and still her heart would leap every time a man walked in. That was the worst of it! The stupid *hope,* the surge of wild, terrible joy that fizzled into despair, a despair that burrowed deeper and hurt more each time the man was not Kit. The way she hadn't lost faith entirely, how some small part of her kept on believing against all evidence that Kit had actually meant what he said on that last night in the bookshop, their last night in Paris. That she was the only woman in the world for him. That he would love her always.

But *always* had turned out to be not such a long time, after all. Oh well. Bit by bit, from newspapers and from her few remaining Resistance friends, Daisy had discreetly put together the puzzle. Daisy's swan had found another swan to mate with. And this particular swan, this Babs of his, she had nursed him back to health! He had known her since childhood! It was right and fitting that he should have married her, after all. That Daisy's memory should be relegated to the status of a fond souvenir of wartime Paris. A brief, hot flame that belonged to a certain time and place. Probably they would not have suited, after all. Probably this relentless passion would have died into indifference amid the drudgery of ordinary life, in which toast was burned and tires went flat, in which milk was carelessly left to sour on the kitchen table and children brought home some terrible germ from school that left everyone vomiting for a week.

So Daisy had told herself as she traveled through the rubbled landscape of Europe into Poland and stood before the ruins of the castle where Max von Sternburg—her father, the grandfather of her children, who had disappeared into the Paris night to save them all, who had made his life a sacrifice for theirs—had grown up, in the years before all this war, before the Treaty of Versailles had sliced away this territory from Germany. So she had told herself in the cabin of the ocean liner as she steamed to Canada with Grandmère and the children, to start a new life away from all this ruin and heartbreak and sacrifice. And so she had told herself since, as the children grew up, as Daisy found a job as a translator and a teacher of English to the schoolchildren of Quebec, as eventually she took a discreet lover or two.

And time went on and on, the years passed, and the anguish began to fade to a dull sting, so that one day Daisy stared at the sky that sheltered them both, sheltered them all, and realized she only cared that Kit was happy, after all. Dear God in Heaven, if you're still listening to my prayers, let this woman take good care of him. Let Babs Langford give him all the love he so desperately craved, her darling Kit who had never quite been the apple of his parents' eyes, who had made Daisy his world as she had made him hers. Babs Langford. She'd seemed like a lovely girl, a shy, pretty woman, an English rose. No doubt she had taken wonderful care of Kit. They had probably been so happy together.

Except . . . that handsome fellow with her, who was not Kit . . .

Except . . . a pair of swans . . . Kit's ring . . .

Maman!

Daisy opened her eyes. Madeleine was squeezing her hand, and Daisy was just too tired to say *Ouch*. It didn't hurt, anyway, not really. Nothing hurt anymore.

The swans. The ring.

Kit loved her.

Babs had told her this, hadn't she? Babs had showed her the ring and said that Kit had loved her after all. He hadn't come to the Ritz after the war because he hadn't known Daisy was there.

Now he was dead.

Maman! Please!

Daisy looked at Madeleine and smiled. Poor Madeleine, who clung to her hand, who didn't want Daisy to go, who grieved so deeply and felt the tragedies of life like scores on her soul. Daisy wanted to tell her that it was all right, that life took these turns, that darkness came and went but that everything worked out in the end. She wanted to tell Madeleine that she was happy to go. She was ready. Just one thing. One more thing she needed. One more thing she was waiting for.

Maman!

This time, the voice was not Madeleine's. This voice came from the other side of the bed, beyond Olivier, from the doorway. A head of fluffy golden-brown hair, a pair of straight, dark eyebrows. Blue eyes like the English sky after the rain.

Daisy whispered, *Christine!*

"Oh, Maman! I'm so sorry. The flight was cancelled, and then I got lost in the hospital, went down the wrong corridor . . ."

The words flowed on. Her chatty baby, her bright Christine, words and images bursting from her seams. She was just finishing up her final year at McGill, studying art and English; she couldn't decide which she liked more. Her father's daughter. There was so much of Kit inside her. Sometimes, to Daisy, it had seemed like Kit was there in the room whenever Christine was near.

Daisy's lips moved. The words didn't seem to come out anymore, but she said them anyway.

I love you.

"I love you, too, Maman." Christine smoothed her hair on the pillow. A tear dripped from her eye onto Daisy's ear. "I love you so much."

A scent drifted past, the smell of pipe tobacco.

Daisy closed her eyes and slept.

CHAPTER THIRTY-ONE

Babs

Langford Hall
Devonshire, England
July 1964

OPENED MY EYES as the train pulled into the station. I hadn't slept at all on the two long train rides from Paris to Ashprington, hearing Precious's voice every time I closed my eyes. I began imagining that if I looked in the seat next to mine, I'd find her there, or Drew, waiting for me to do something. I just wasn't sure what that might be.

I stepped off the train with my new valise—Precious had insisted I take one of hers so that my new clothes wouldn't revolt—and looked down the platform for Diana, who'd promised to fetch me and bring me back to Langford Hall. I spotted her petite elegant form walking quickly down the platform toward me—my smile and greeting dying on my lips as she walked right past me.

"Diana?"

She spun around looking everywhere but at me.

"Diana!" I said again and this time her eyes settled on me, briefly widening in recognition.

"Babs! Good heavens—is it really you?"

After getting over the initial shock of my own sister not recognizing me, I smiled. "Yes, Diana, it really is. Still the same Babs beneath all the new clothes, though, I can assure you."

She raised an eyebrow at that, as if not quite believing me. It reminded me of something Precious had said, about how when I wore the right clothes I held my chin differently, as if I were a woman to be reckoned with. Diana had always known that. It had just taken me a little longer to figure it out.

"Well, you look absolutely amazing. I can't wait to show you off. Maybe I'll have a sort of debut party for you and invite all of our friends. The women will be green with envy."

"Thank you, Diana, but I assure you that won't be necessary. I really just want to enjoy being home again." Which was true, but I could no longer imagine myself slipping back into my old life, the Babs I'd been before Paris.

After my valise was stored in the boot of her roadster and we were speeding down the road, I asked, "How is everything in Ashprington?" although when she started answering I realized that I wasn't all that interested in knowing.

"The gymkhana is next week, but I've already done all the organizing so you won't have to worry about any of that. Just come and hand out ribbons, if you will. And there's been quite an uproar at the WI about whether or not we should allow men into our ranks. It's a good thing you're back so you can settle all the ruffled feathers."

She continued to speak as my mind wandered. I kept seeing Drew's grin and thinking about how we'd both come to France to shake up our lives. I hoped he'd succeeded. Perhaps not in the way he'd hoped, but at least partially. My heart still ached when I thought of him, which seemed to be all the time. *Your big, generous heart. It's what I love most about you.* I tried not to think about that, or Drew, at all. But that was like telling the tide to stay out, or the sun not to rise. All foolishness, really.

I became aware of Diana waiting for me to say something. "I'm sorry—what did you say?"

"I was asking you if you'd decided what to do with Langford Hall. The Dower House is lovely, and it's quite silly for you to ramble around the hall all by yourself with the children gone. Not to mention the expense of upkeep. I don't know how you manage, Babs, I really don't."

"I don't either," I said without thinking, startling us both.

"Well, that's a start, isn't it?"

"Yes, I suppose it is." I smiled to myself, feeling as if I'd just moved forward somehow, even if it had been just a few steps.

I felt her watching me and turned to meet her gaze. "What is it?"

"It's you, Babs. You're different. In a good way."

She returned to watching the road, but I kept looking at her, recalling what Daisy had said to me when I went to her suite at the Ritz to read to her. "Do you think I'm strong?"

"Oh, Babs. You're one of the strongest people I know. Have I never told you that? You have survived so much, things that would have crippled lesser men, yet here you are, stronger than ever. You're like an oak tree in a storm, never bending, and creating shelter for everyone else. I have to admit to being quite envious."

I stared at her for a long moment, waiting for her to tell me she'd been joking. When she didn't, I turned my attention to the road ahead, wondering why she'd never thought to tell me before now, and then realizing that before Paris, I would never have believed her. I watched the familiar landscape slip by, each mile bringing me closer to home. *I am a formidable woman*, I thought. And I suddenly knew exactly what I needed to do.

A CLOCK CHIMED somewhere in the house, startling me awake. I'd made the mistake of lying down, just for a moment, on the window seat where Kit and I had once watched the sunsets. Now it was two hours later, and I still had so much to do.

I stood, then straightened my skirt—one of the new ones I'd purchased in Paris—and headed for the stairs. I moved slowly as if this were the last time I'd have Langford Hall all to myself. I ran my hand down the curved bannister, pausing to admire the acanthus plasterwork that bordered the ceiling and the checkerboard pattern of the floor in the foyer. My finger absently rubbed at the nick in the wood caused by a vigorous game of jousting knights played by my brother Charles and Kit, using fireplace pokers. They were punished severely—whether for playing with actual weapons or for roughhousing indoors, I couldn't remember. What I did recall was spending many a night imagining Kit in shining armor, fighting for the honor of wearing my ribbon on his sleeve.

I continued my descent, staring at the Langford ancestors on the wall, trying to read the expressions in their frozen gazes. I had taken Precious's words to heart, the part about reinventing oneself, and had proceeded to do just that. I could now believe I had something to offer the world besides tea and gardening tips. Which I still did, of course. There were some things that would never change. The only difference being that they were things I *chose* to do.

The house seemed inordinately quiet, creaking uneasily in its new emptiness. Even Mrs. Finch and Walnut had deserted it for the Dower House to get it ready for my full-time occupancy. After my conversation with Diana, I had finally made the decision to deed the house to the National Trust, to allow tour groups inside to see the Georgian splendor of Langford Hall. They would not, however, be traipsing over the antique Exeter carpets or sitting down in the Chippendale chairs in the dining room. Everything would be roped off, the halls covered in plastic tarps, the Chinese silk wallpaper visible beneath clear plexiglass.

It was all awful, really. A house was meant to be lived in. To create new memories. But change was inevitable. For houses and people. It had taken two weeks in Paris to shake me out of my inertia. Two weeks transforming myself under the expert tutelage of a woman whose skill at reinvention was something of which I'd never know the full extent.

And two weeks spent falling in love. It seemed like such a short time to have that sort of deep connection, but there you have it. Kit had been my fairy tale, my knight in shining armor, my love a fantasy as insubstantial as the morning mist that blew across the lake. And I had been the salve for a broken heart, a place to lay his head when seeking comfort. To help him forget the love of his life. His Daisy.

But Drew was solid and real. A man whose heart was as big and giving as he'd claimed mine to be. He was the bridge over the messy lake of my life, and I'd been too blind to see it. I hadn't watched him leave, so there was that. Which, according to Precious, meant we were bound to find each other again.

Precious had written once, letting me know that Drew's father had died peacefully in his sleep after hearing that his name had been cleared. I was happy for Drew, that he'd been able to fulfill his father's last wish. Precious had given me Drew's address to write, and I did. Just a short note of condolence and my return address. I hadn't heard back from him, and I told myself that I hadn't expected to.

I moved to the kitchen, checking the cupboard to make sure the simple pottery dishes had been removed to the Dower House. Only the Limoges and Royal Doulton would remain with Langford Hall, placed on the dining table where only phantoms would dine.

I returned to the foyer and to the Langfords captured in oils on the walls, and felt no censure. It was almost as if they understood what reinvention really was. After all, hadn't the old admiral changed from seafaring profiteer to country gentleman to begin the legacy of Langfords and Langford Hall? I imagined I could hear soft, polite applause as I ran my finger along the spotless mantel.

It was perhaps the sense of peace I'd received upon my decision to move that had enabled me to finally forgive myself. Daisy—proud, beautiful, strong Daisy—had understood. And forgiven me. It was my duty to honor her by living my new life the way she would have lived her own if she'd been allowed. It was my promise to myself. And to Kit. After giving Robin the gold signet ring, I'd visited Kit in the graveyard and told him everything, needing my conscience to be clear. I imagined him and Daisy finally together, and my heart had felt as full and ripe as summer fruit. As I'd turned to leave, I thought I'd smelled Kit's pipe tobacco. I'd smiled, then whispered a soft goodbye as I let myself through the gate.

The grandfather clock chimed the hour, reminding me that I still needed to check Kit's study, to remove any personal items. I found if I kept very busy with all that needed to be done, I'd have no time to think of Drew, or even to dream about him. I was the new Babs—a formidable woman. And formidable women forged their own futures, with or without a man by their side.

I'd only made it two steps when someone banged the large brass knocker on the front door. I frowned, hoping it wasn't yet another passerby who'd heard that the house was soon to be opened for tours.

I was still frowning when I threw open the door. "I'm so sorry, but we're not yet—" I stopped speaking. And breathing. And holding my mouth closed.

"Hello, Babs." Drew stood there with that grin on his face, all broad-shouldered and tanned and white-toothed. "I was just passing through, and thought I'd stop by."

"Passing through?" I surprised myself with the calmness of my voice. "Through to where—Land's End? Because nobody passes through Ashprington. Unless they're lost."

His smile faded. "Funny you should say that. I've been feeling a little lost these last couple of months."

I held my ground, clutching the door so that it wouldn't open any further. "I told you in Paris, Drew. This is my home. I can't move to New York regardless of how I feel about you."

"Yeah?" His grin was back. "That's a relief. Because I just transferred to the London office."

I might have blinked a few times, as if to make sure he wasn't a mirage, and that I wasn't dreaming. But Drew was no fairy tale. He was flesh and blood and he was standing on my doorstep with an open invitation in his eyes.

"Oh. Well." I might have also said his name. It wasn't Shakespeare, but the words were just as sweet. I stepped back and opened the door wider. He met me on the threshold and we stared stupidly at each other before he opened his arms and swallowed me in his embrace. Our lips met and somewhere, amid the turmoil of the blood rushing in my ears, I imagined I heard the house sigh, a quiet murmur of approval.

"Would you like some tea?" I asked against his lips.

In answer he swung me up in his arms and brought me inside the house, followed swiftly by the sound of the heavy door shutting behind us.

ACKNOWLEDGMENTS

"THREE AUTHORS WALKED into a bar . . ."

So begins the answer to the most frequently asked question "Team W" receives from readers: namely, how our collaboration got its start. The second question is how we continue to create new books together and still enjoy the process. Three novels; umpteen cups of coffee (and sometimes stronger beverages—did anyone say "Prosecco"?); hundreds of hours spent plotting, writing, and rewriting; book tours; and volumes of emails and texts later, the answer is simple: the Unibrain. This is what happens when three writers share one brain as well as a passion for history and the written word. And it's magical.

Yet the Unibrain can't do it all—so a huge thanks goes to our editor, Rachel Kahan, and the rest of our amazing team at William Morrow for everything from the gorgeous cover art to the entire mechanism of getting our books into the hands of readers. We couldn't do what we do without all of your hard work and support, as well as the unflagging efforts of our brilliant literary agents, Alexandra Machinist of ICM and Amy Berkower of Writers' House, who have been our sisterhood's biggest cheerleaders from the moment we first proposed writing together. (All right, it might have taken a *little* more persuasion.)

We can't quite remember that first spark that led us to twentieth-century France for our third novel, but once we started diving into the ocean of books, memoirs, letters, and online databases on the two world wars and the Swinging Sixties, we discovered enough fascinating material for a lifetime of novels. While our main characters are fictional, the historical setting in which their stories take place is (as always) as accurate as possible, which often means hours spent chasing down all those tiny details and contemporary accounts that bring a novel to life. This space isn't large enough to list all of our research sources, but for more absorbing stories of life inside the Paris Ritz, we happily refer readers to *The Hotel on Place Vendôme* by Tilar J. Mazzeo. For insight into the operation and daily life of French Resistance organizations, Lynne Olson's detailed and riveting *Madame Fourcade's Secret War* is a must-read. If anyone wants to read more about life behind the lines in World War I, Helen McPhail's *The Long Silence* gives an excellent overview, while Ben Macintyre's *The Englishman's Daughter* provides an intimate and harrowing picture of life in one village in Picardy under German rule: readers will notice more than a passing resemblance between our Major Erich Hoffmeister and his real-life counterpart, Major Karl Evers, who really did demand that the chickens lay a particular number of eggs per day.

A vigorous nod to the Inn at Palmetto Bluff on the South Carolina coast for giving us beautiful shelter and sustenance (of the caffeinated and bubbly varieties) while we plotted out this book, and to the sunshine of the Florida panhandle for sustaining us as we finished our final revisions and typed *The End*. For the Unibrain, it is always *work, work, work*, because we believe in suffering for our craft. Thanks also to the Boden website for providing us stress-shopping during those trying times in an author's life. Our closets thank you; the delivery man doesn't.

There's nothing scarier than sending a book off into the world (see stress-shopping, above). Thank you so much to all of the wonderful readers, bloggers, reviewers, librarians, and booksellers who make what we do possible. We appreciate your support, and your emails, Facebook posts, and Instagram stories, more than we can say. Huge hugs to our fellow authors, who have been there with us through characters that won't cooperate and midnight trains to New Canaan for book events. We love you even if your name doesn't begin with W. (Kristina McWorris, you'll always be an honorary W to us!)

Finally, our grateful thanks (as always) to our husbands, children, and assorted pets for sharing your homes with our imaginary characters, and allowing us the time and space to get them on the page.

About the authors

About the book

Read on

Insights,
Interviews
& More...

Meet Beatriz Williams, Lauren Willig, and Karen White

BEATRIZ WILLIAMS, LAUREN WILLIG, AND KAREN WHITE are the coauthors of the beloved *New York Times* bestselling novel *The Forgotten Room*.

BEATRIZ WILLIAMS is the *New York Times* bestselling author of eight novels, including *A Hundred Summers*, *The Secret Life of Violet Grant*, and *The Summer Wives*. A native of Seattle, she graduated from Stanford University and earned an MBA in finance from Columbia University, then spent several years in New York and London as a corporate strategy consultant before pursuing her passion for historical fiction. She lives with her husband and four children near the Connecticut shore, where she divides her time between writing and laundry.

LAUREN WILLIG is the *New York Times* and *USA Today* bestselling author of *The Ashford Affair*, *That Summer*, *The Other Daughter*, and *The English Wife*, as well as the RITA Award–winning Pink Carnation series. An alumna of Yale University, she has a graduate degree in history from Harvard and a

JD from Harvard Law School. She lives in New York City with her husband, preschooler, and baby, and lots and lots of coffee.

KAREN WHITE is a *New York Times* and *USA Today* bestselling author and currently writes what she refers to as "grit lit"—Southern women's fiction—and has also expanded her horizons into writing a mystery series set in Charleston, South Carolina. When not writing, she spends her time reading, scrapbooking, playing piano, and avoiding cooking. She has two grown children and currently lives near Atlanta, Georgia, with her husband and two spoiled Havanese dogs. ∽

Amanda Suanne Photography

Reading Group Guide

1. Aurélie's mother tells her, "You musn't let your ancestors rule your life. There's more to you than your lineage." How does Aurélie's lineage define her? Does that work in her favor or against her?

2. When Babs revisits La Fleur's letter to Kit, she is left feeling guilty and betrayed. Why did Babs keep La Fleur's letter all this time? How would things have turned out had Kit received La Fleur's letter? Would Kit still have married Babs?

3. When Daisy's grandmother asks her to help the Resistance, Daisy responds, "I can't help you, Gradmère. . . . You're right, I'm not like Maman, I'm not brave or defiant or cunning. I can't do what she did. I'm just Daisy." How is Daisy like her mother, or not like her? Does that change over the course of the novel?

4. "We followed in her perfume-scented wake toward the bar, the incessant clatter of Prunella Schuyler's typewriter like little reminders that the closer we got to finding La Fleur, the closer I got to facing the ghosts I'd told Drew I didn't believe in." Throughout the novel Babs is constantly

reminded of the ghosts from the past. Does Babs truly break free from them? What about the other women in the novel? Who are their ghosts?

5. What did you make of Daisy's affair with Monsieur Legrand? How do you feel about the way things turned out for them?

6. In order to throw off the Germans, Aurélie's father comes up with a plan to send her back to Paris with word that she has retrieved the talisman: "We spread the message through France that the demoiselle holds the talisman and the enemy must fall." What does the talisman represent to Aurélie and her family, and France? Is it truly a magical object?

7. Characters who appeared in Team W's other novels *The Forgotten Room* and *The Glass Ocean* make an appearance in *All the Ways We Said Goodbye*. If you read those books, how many Easter eggs did you catch? Which was the most surprising?

8. What role does the Hotel Ritz play in each of the heroine's stories?

9. Were you satisfied with how each of the heroine's stories unfolded? Would you have changed anything about the way things ended for them? ᕬ

An Excerpt from *The Glass Ocean* by Beatriz Williams, Lauren Willig, and Karen White

CHAPTER 1

Sarah

New York City
May 2013

THE EVENING HAD turned blue and soft, the way New York does in May, and I decided to walk to the book club and save the bus fare. According to Mimi's Facebook message, the group was gathering at her apartment on Park Avenue, deep inside the plummy center of the Seventies—at least thirty minutes from my place on Riverside Drive—but I didn't mind. I was a New Yorker, I could walk all day. Anyway, a brisk hike (so I told myself, scrolling through the Mimi message chain for the millionth time that afternoon) would settle my nerves.

I allowed myself plenty of time to get ready so I wouldn't arrive late. Lateness was unprofessional, Mom used to tell me, dressed in her ladylike suit and smelling of Youth Dew and good manners. Select your outfit the night before, leave ten minutes early. All good advice. I'd already laid out a pair of indigo skinny jeans and a silk blouse, and I only changed my mind about the blouse twice. My favorite wedges, because they loaned me a few necessary inches without trading off my ability to walk. Collar necklace, hair in ponytail. You know, just the right kind of casual, threw-this-on-without-thinking elegance to set those Park Avenue yummy mummies back on their Louboutins.

The necklace itched my collarbone. I undid the ponytail, redid it. Changed necklace. Grabbed Kate Spade tote and tied Hermès scarf to handle. Took off scarf. Started to tie it back on and stopped, because the whole scarf-on-handbag look was kind of aspirational, wasn't it? Or was I overthinking again? Checked my phone and realized I should have left five minutes ago.

So off I went, sprinting, as usual, across the Upper West Side and Central Park, lungs burning, ankles wobbling, while the softball games wound up noisily and the lovers met after work, hand in hand, heading for wine bars and tapas, for apartments and takeout. When I wasn't in a hurry, when I was just strolling or even sitting on a bench, eating a hot dog with ketchup and mustard but no onion, I liked to study them, my fellow New Yorkers. I liked to pick someone out from the crowd, some man in a suit, loosening his tie, checking his watch. I tried to divine his life, his history, the peculiar secrets hidden in his past. Mom used to tell this story about the dinner parties they once had, before Dad left, and how I used to peek through the banister when I was supposed to be sleeping and watch the guests, and how in the morning I would bombard her with questions about them, who was married to whom, who did what for a living, who came from where and had how many siblings. And I used to think this story of hers was true. I used to think I was born for my career.

Now I wasn't so sure. Not anymore, not while I galloped past Belvedere Castle, dodging baby strollers; not while the smell of Central Park filled my mouth, warm green leaves and hot ▶

dog stands, car exhaust and pavement stained with urine. The great metropolitan outdoors. On my left, the gray-beige spike of Cleopatra's Needle loomed up, cornered by about a dozen tourists brandishing their selfie sticks, and the sight of them seized me with panic. I accelerated to a jog, then back to a speedwalk. When I burst through the gap to the horns and shouts of Fifth Avenue, I paused to check my phone and realized the panic I'd felt was genuine instinct: I'd misjudged the walking time. I was already eleven minutes late. All the other women would've arrived by now. Probably figured I'd flaked and felt pity for me. Upper East Side housewives always had their act together, checklists every morning neatly checked off by bedtime, and they couldn't understand those who daydreamed and lost track of time, whose brains and lives could not be contained inside straight, organized lines.

Mimi hadn't mentioned the cross street in her message, just the address on Park Avenue that suggested Seventies. I plunged across Fifth, weaving between two tour buses and into the path of an oncoming taxi. The driver laid on the horn. I reached the curb and dashed down Seventy-Ninth Street to Madison, waited for a gap in traffic, crossed Madison and tore east toward Park. A dogwalker blocked the sidewalk with six or seven pooches, ranging in size from a gray-and-white Havanese to an Irish wolfhound who belonged anywhere in the world except New York City. The Havanese lunged toward me like an old friend— I had this thing with dogs—and I thought, maybe I should be a dogwalker, maybe that's my calling. Not this. Running down a sidewalk to a book club meeting, hoping I wasn't too late for the hors d'oeuvres. I was counting on those hors d'oeuvres. Mimi probably catered from Yura or someplace equally exquisite. Checked phone. Fourteen minutes late.

Of course the building was all the way between Seventy-Second and Seventy-First. I counted down the numbers on the long green awnings, passed doorman after doorman, finally found the right digits. Checked them against Mimi's message, just to be sure.

When I looked up, a doorman in a sober black suit was staring at me. I straightened my back the way Mom used to make me and said, "Hi there? I'm here for the book club? Mimi Balfour? 8B? Sorry, I'm a little late!" Bright smile.

He smiled back, kind of sympathetic, hired help to hired help, and pulled open the bronze-grilled door. "Elevator's right ahead," he said.

I guess I should mention that I don't *know* Mimi Balfour, not personally. We've never met. She sent me a message on my Facebook author page, explaining that her book club was reading *Small Potatoes* in May, she noticed I was a New Yorker from my bio, would I mind meeting with them. It was the kind of self-assured message that assumed my acceptance; opposite to the messages and emails I received from book clubs in the months after *Small Potatoes* was first published, when you couldn't turn on the *Today* show or *The View* or *Live with Kelly and Michael* without watching me hold forth—brimming with wit and importance, taking Joy's fascination and Michael's flirtation for granted—about the Irish potato famine like I might break out in Gaelic any second. Remember those emails? The deference, the *how busy you must be*, the *adored your book so much*, the *forever grateful*. I passed them all on to my publicist, who picked out a few lucky winners and sent the rest my regrets and a helpful list of articles and interviews. No more than twice a month, I told her then. I just can't fit any more into my schedule.

As the elevator rose slowly toward Mimi's fl or—how I loved old Candela buildings and their small, dignified lifts—I tried to recall the last time I visited a book club. A year ago, maybe. No. Longer. That group in Greenpoint, in the tiny apartment that smelled of cat food. There was a blizzard, and they canceled the meeting without bothering to tell me, so I turned up while the woman and her roommate were binge-watching *House of Cards* ▶

on the sofa with their cats. To her credit, she apologized.
She'd just assumed no author in her right mind would venture
out in that snowstorm. Made me some hot chocolate, offered
me stale Tostitos, and asked what I was writing next. My favorite
question. By the time I left, the subways had shut down, and
I had to walk all the way back home in a pair of too-short Uggs,
across the Williamsburg Bridge to Manhattan, crosstown and
uptown while the snow bit my cheeks and piled on the sidewalks.
Good times. How could I forget a night like that?

I stared at the bronze arrow, inching its way around the arc,
and I told myself Mimi would be nothing like the cat food lady.
There would be hors d'oeuvres for my empty stomach, wine for
my empty soul. They would drench me with their enthusiasm
for *Small Potatoes*. Everybody loved the book, once they read
it. The trouble was, five years out from publication, not a lot of
people did. Long ago were the days of that Boston school district
that ordered *Small Potatoes* for the entire seventh grade and asked
me to speak at the middle school assembly.

Floor six, floor seven. I rehearsed a few key bits from my stump
speech in my head. That riff about the sheep always got a laugh.

Floor eight. The doors of the elevator parted, revealing a
small cream-and-gold foyer. To the left, 8A. To the right, 8B.
Only two apartments per floor in a building like this. Mimi's
husband was probably an investment banker or a hedge fund
manager. Maybe a partner at one of those white-shoe corporate
law firms. Wouldn't that be nice, to have someone else worry
about making all the money that kept you alive? I'd once had a
fling with a hedgie. He was in his late thirties and stinking rich,
a mathematical genius with a crass sense of humor, and also sort
of handsome in a skinny, electric, thin-lipped way. That was a
few months after *Small Potatoes* came out, when my celebrity
writer cachet briefly eclipsed my Irish freckles and too-curly
reddish-brown hair. Dinners at Daniel, sex at his sleek Tribeca
loft, private cars taking us everywhere. I'd broken it off when
I discovered he was also having flings with a couple of twenty-

year-old Victoria's Secret models, but maybe that was a rash decision, after all. I stepped forward and knocked on the door to 8B. Checked my phone a last time before sliding it into my tote. Nineteen minutes late.

The door opened. I half-expected a uniformed maid, but a tall, skinny, sharp-boned blonde stood before me, wearing white jeans, holding a glass of white wine, still giggling over some joke left behind.

I held out my hand. "Mimi? I'm so sorry—"

"Oh, *hi*! I'm Jen. Mimi's in the living room. Are you *Sarah*? Oh my *God*, you look *nothing* like your author photo!"

"Sadly, you can't take the makeup artist home with you," I said, my standard answer. "I'm so sorry I—"

"Come on back," she said, turning away. "Everyone's dying to meet you."

I realized, as I stepped after Jen into a massive paneled gallery painted in tasteful dove gray, that my silk blouse—bought during the days of plenty—was sticking to my skin. That I was still sweating from the mad dash across Manhattan, that my hair was wet at the temples, that my lungs were sucking wind. That my stomach was actually growling. I hadn't eaten since breakfast. Figured I'd be feasting tonight, so why not save a few dollars? I lifted my hand and wiped the sleeve of my cardigan against the sides of my face, along the skin above my upper lip. Jen's back wove in front of me, the bumps of her spine just visible underneath her snug navy tank. Her arms swung, improbably sleek. Probably a team of vigilant stylists kept every follicle on Jen's body under immaculate control. Blond, thick, shining hair growing rampant on top and absolutely, positively, *nowhere* else.

The foyer opened into a formal-yet-contemporary living room, shades of gray accented in crimson, containing a pair of opposing sofas and a flock of chairs in coordinating upholstery, all of them occupied by straight-haired women in skeletal white jeans identical to Jen's. Jen stepped aside and gestured to me with her wineglass. "I brought the *author*!" she trilled, and I realized she ▶

was already half-drunk, and I thought, For God's sake, how much wine could you possibly drink in twenty minutes?

I waved my hand a little. "Hi, everyone! I'm so sorry—"

A woman rose from the left-hand sofa, a brunette in a turquoise trapeze top, anticipating summer. "Sarah! I'm Mimi. Wow, you look *nothing* like your author photo!"

Jen screeched, "I know, right? That's what I said!"

"Sorry, I'm just a lip gloss and mascara girl in real life. And again, I apologize for being so late—"

Mimi checked her watch. "Oh my gosh, is it past seven *already*? Girls, we've been chatting for an hour and a *half*!"

Everybody laughed. On the coffee table lay a few trays of elegant tidbits. I spotted Lilliputian cheeseburgers crowned by single tiny sesame seeds, ceviche, some kind of bruschetta, guacamole furrowed by tracks from the blue corn tortilla chips in a bowl alongside. Glasses of white wine perched between fingers, and a Filipino woman in a uniform was refilling them methodically from a chilled bottle.

"I'll bet you're dying for a glass of wine, right?" said Mimi. "Angel, could you pour a glass for Miss Blake? And you can take all this back in the kitchen. You're not hungry, are you, Sarah?"

"Actually—"

"Just bring out the cupcakes, Angel. And the wine for Miss Blake." Mimi turned back to me and waved at a strange, high-backed wooden chair at the far end of the coffee table, painted in silver. "Sit! Omigod! This *book*! So amazing."

I tottered to the silver chair and sank on the seat. Allowed my tote to slide to the floor. Before me, Angel scurried around the table, lifting trays of beautiful, untouched food. I started to reach for a miniature cheeseburger, but she went by too quickly, and I converted the gesture into a sleeve adjustment. "Thanks," I said. "It came out of some research I did for my thesis—"

"What I loved," Mimi said, "were all the stories of the Irish women immigrating to America. That really resonated with me.

I'm totally Irish on my mother's side. My great-grandmother was a maid, can you believe it?"

"Domestic service was one of the few occupations open to women and girls who—"

"Wait, your great-grandmother was a *maid*? *Meems*! I had no *idea*!" one of the women said.

"I *know*, right? To some family on the Upper East Side. I wish I knew where. Wouldn't it be *crazy* if she worked in *this* building?" Mimi tossed her hair over her shoulder. "Anyway. Go on, Sarah."

"Um. So there I was in Dublin on this research grant, seven or eight years ago, and I actually wasn't studying the potato famine at all. I was researching the absentee landlords—Englishmen, basically, whose families had been granted land in Ireland, but they never lived there at all, just took all the rents from the tenant farmers and hired estate managers to oversee—thanks so much." I snatched the glass of wine from Angel and sipped. The eyes of the women around me had taken on a polite, glassy sheen. Jen reached for her iPhone and skidded her thumb in quick strokes across the screen. I swallowed the wine and hurried on. "Anyway, blah blah, I came across this archive—"

"So when you're doing your research," one woman said, "do you ever, like, come across stuff that nobody else has seen? Or something really valuable, like a painting or whatever from a famous artist that was, like, lost or something?"

"Um, not exactly. It's more like—"

"Oh, I totally saw something like that on a TV show once! It was like a da Vinci or like Michelangelo or something."

"*Yes*! I saw that, too! And I was like, wow, that dealer could have totally screwed that guy over, like bought the painting for five bucks or whatever—"

"Wait!" Mimi held up her hand, palm out, like she was trying to stop traffic. "Girls. Come on. The author's talking. So you were getting your master's, right? What subject?"

"Doctorate, actually. History." ▶

"Oh, obvs!" She laughed. "Where did you go to school again, Sarah? Somewhere in New York, right?"

"Columbia. It's in my bio? On the back of the book?" I looked around the room and realized, for the first time, that not one single copy of *Small Potatoes* lay on any of Mimi's expensive surfaces. "Um, I don't know if anyone brought a copy with them—"

"Oh, I've got it right here." Mimi set down her wine and picked up an iPad from the side table at her left. "Hold on a sec. Ugh. Messages. Did anyone else bring their iPad?"

"I've got it on my phone," said Jen.

"Can you open the file and find Sarah's bio? I have to answer this."

Mimi burrowed into her iPad and Jen swiped away on her phone. I swished my wine and said, "It doesn't matter, really. Long story short, I was at grad school, doctorate program in history, went to Dublin for a semester and found—"

"Oh, here it is!" said Jen. She stood up and handed me her phone. "Here, read it out for us."

I took the phone and looked down at the screen. "It's kind of blurred, isn't it?"

"Yeah, sorry about that. Mimi found this awesome website so we could all download it for free."

I looked up and stared at Jen's bright, smooth face. The upholstery behind her was some kind of gray-toned leopard print with a furry texture, like a real hide, stretched over a delicate Louis XVI frame painted in the same silver as my own chair. I found myself wondering if it was a reproduction or an antique, if Mimi and her interior designer had actually gone and refinished a genuine Louis XVI chair in silver paint.

The words looped in my head. *Download it for free.* Cheerful, triumphant. *Download it for free!* What a freaking bargain.

"I'm sorry," I said. "She found *what*?"

"That website. Meems, what was the name again? Bongo or something?"

Mimi looked up from her iPad. "What are we talking about?"

"That website where you found Sarah's book."

"Oh," she said. "Bingo. Haven't you heard of it? It's like an online library. You can download almost anything for free. It's *amazing*."

My hands were shaking. I set down Jen's phone, and then I set down the wineglass next to it. Without a coaster.

"You mean a pirate site," I said.

"Oh God, no! I would never. It's an online library."

"That's what they call it. But they're just stealing. They're fencing stolen goods. Easy to do with electronic copies."

"No. That's not true." Mimi's voice rose a little. Sharpened a little. "Libraries lend out e-books."

"Real libraries do. They buy them from the publisher. Sites like Bingo just upload unauthorized copies to sell advertising or put cookies on your phone or whatever else. They're pirates."

There was a small, shrill silence. I lifted my wineglass and took a long drink, even though my fingers were trembling so badly, I knew everyone could see the vibration.

"Well," said Mimi. "It's not like it matters. I mean, the book's been out for years and everything, it's like public domain."

I put down the wineglass and picked up my tote bag. "So I don't have time to lecture you about copyright law or anything. Basically, if publishers don't get paid, authors don't get paid. That's kind of how it works."

"Oh, come on," said Mimi. "You got paid for this book."

"Not as much as you think. Definitely not as much as your husband gets paid to short derivatives or whatever he does that buys all this stuff." I waved my hand at the walls. "And you know, fine, maybe it's not the big sellers who suffer. It's the midlist authors, the great names you never hear of, where every sale counts. . . . What am I saying? You don't care. None of you actually cares. Sitting here in your palaces in the sky. You never had to earn a penny of your own. Why the hell should you care about royalties?" I climbed out of my silver chair and hoisted ▶

my tote bag over my shoulder. "It's about a dollar a book, by the way. Paid out every six months. So I walked all the way over here, gave up an evening of my life, and even if every single one of you had actually bought a legitimate copy, I would have earned about a dozen bucks for my trouble. Twelve dollars and a glass of cheap wine. I'll see myself out."

I turned and marched back across the living room, tripping on the last chair leg. Angel stood frozen in awe, holding a tray of two-bite cupcakes and a chilled bottle of Pinot Gris. My armpits dripped; my heart thudded so hard I felt dizzy. As I opened the door, I heard somebody's voice carry down the gallery.

"What a *bitch*!"

I considered holding up my middle finger. But I didn't. My mom would have been proud, if she were still lucid enough to understand.

I took the crosstown bus back home and made some mac and cheese from the box. Told myself that was okay because it was organic boxed mac and cheese. Told myself that at least they hadn't gotten around to asking me what I was working on for my next book. Plopped on the sofa and toed off my wedges and picked up the remote. I had a few shows queued up on the DVR. Some history, some true crime. I told myself I'd be working, actually, because you never knew where your next book idea might come from. You never knew when inspiration might strike.

Oh, the things you tell yourself.

I switched on the TV and picked up my bowl of mac and cheese. From across the room, inside my tote bag, my phone started ringing. An outraged Mimi, probably. If I were lucky, she'd call Page Six or something. No such thing as bad publicity, right? Some intern would contact me to ask for details. Small Potatoes *author Sarah Blake melts down at Park Avenue book club* . . . *Sarah, whatever happened to all that movie talk around* Small Potatoes . . . *? Sarah, what are you working on now . . . ?*

A year after *Small Potatoes* came out, my editor took me to lunch and asked about my ideas. I said I was thinking about Queen Victoria's children. She frowned and said what about a racehorse, like Seabiscuit or Secretariat, only another one, obviously. She was sure there were more famous racehorses out there. I said I'd look into it. Then she called up six months later and said she wanted me to write the next *Boys on the Boat,* maybe like an America's Cup team made up of hardscrabble youths from Minnesota. Then it was World War Two. World War Two was red-hot. Some scrappy bilingual girl working for the French Resistance. Or what about Coco Chanel? The Lindbergh baby? I said I thought those were all pretty well covered already. I wanted something new. I said the story would find me when it was ready.

She hadn't called since. My agent stopped replying to my emails personally. The foreign translation deals dried up. The movie people didn't pick up the option after all. The royalty checks shrank and shrank.

Don't get me wrong. There was a lot of money that first year, or at least a lot of money by the standard of what I was used to: daughter of a divorced mother and an absentee father, grad student living on financial aid and ramen noodles. But I spent it all. I had to. Not on myself. Well, not most of it.

The phone rang again. I thought, Maybe it's not Mimi or Page Six. Maybe it's Mom.

The images on the screen shifted and flashed. I couldn't even remember what I was watching. I set aside the mac and cheese and rose to fetch my tote from the hall stand. My feet ached. Even my favorite wedges had their limits. My legs ached, my head ached. I rummaged in the tote and drew out my phone, just as the call went to voice mail.

Not Mom. The care home. They'd already left two messages.

I didn't bother listening. I just swiped the notification and pressed *redial.* ▶

For the past four years, Mom had been living a few blocks away—hence my tiny studio here on Riverside Drive, which was not my natural habitat—in a small, private care home for Alzheimer's patients. She started showing symptoms when she was only fifty-six, and it progressed pretty quickly from there. I won't bore you with the details. Long story short, I moved her into Riverside Haven about the time *Small Potatoes* went from hardcover into trade paperback, and sold the adorable Carnegie Hill one-bedroom I'd bought a year earlier in order to fund her care. The place had dedicated therapists for each patient, private rooms, views of the river. Nothing was too good for my mother, who raised me by herself after Dad split when I was four. Sure, it was expensive, but I figured I'd just write another book, right? Another blockbuster work of narrative nonfiction. No problem.

"Riverside Haven, can you hold, please?"

"No, wait—"

The hold music started. I sank back on the sofa and stared at the mac and cheese, which had begun to congeal. Turned my head toward the hall closet instead. The door. The doorknob. What lay behind it, singing like a siren. A siren I'd done my best to ignore for four long years.

"Riverside Haven, can I help you?"

"Hi! It's Sarah Blake. You were trying to reach me? Is Mom okay?"

"Oh, hello, Miss Blake. Diana Carr here. No, your mother's just fine. She's had a quiet day. I didn't mean to scare you. I just wanted to speak to you about last month's invoice."

When I finished speaking to Diana Carr—yes, I understood how many months in arrears I was, I understood that Riverside Haven would do its best not to have to resort to eviction—I set my phone down next to the bowl of congealed macaroni and went to the hall closet. Opened the door and rose on my toes. Found the small wooden trunk and dragged it from the shelf. The smell of dust filled my head, dustiness and mustiness and old wood, and above it all a slight hint of Youth Dew, even though I had removed this chest from my mother's apartment four years ago. I placed it carefully on the coffee table, squaring the edges, and sat on my knees and stared at the lid.

ANNIE HOULIHAN
593 Lorimer Street
Brooklyn, New York

I had opened this chest once before, when I was about ten or eleven. My mother found me in her closet, lifting out the contents, and that was the only time in my life she ever screamed at me. Slammed down the lid and sent me to my room. When she was calm again, she took me to the sofa and tucked me under her warm, soft arm. *That was your great-grandmother's chest*, she said. *With all your great-grandfather's things in it. All they found on him when they pulled his body out of the water. The Cunard company sent it back to her in a parcel, and she wouldn't even look at it. She had your grandmother pack everything into a chest and promise never to open it. She said it was his tomb. So you are never to open that chest again, do you hear me? Never again.*

I'd obeyed my mother, because what else could I do? I knew the story of my great-grandmother and great-grandfather, how they left Ireland together in search of a new life, how my great-grandfather Patrick had worked as a steward for the Cunard Line while my great-grandmother Annie raised five children in a small upstairs apartment in Brooklyn, saving up to buy a house of their own.

But I also knew what lay in that chest. I'd seen it with my own eyes, before Mom slammed down the lid. And my curious brain never could let it go. Never could erase that knowledge from my head, or banish the questions those objects raised. Because, my God, what a story they told. ▸

An Excerpt from *The Glass Ocean* (continued)

And I was just born that way. Mom said so herself.

So maybe Mom would forgive me for what I was about to do. Maybe she would shake her head and understand, because I was Sarah, her daughter, and I was born to wonder and to dig for answers. Maybe she and my grandmother and my great-grandmother would absolve me for breaking my word, because I was at the end of the road, nowhere else to go, and I wasn't doing it for myself, not entirely. I was doing it for Mom. I was doing it for that invoice lying in the drawer of my bedside table. For the voice in my head that said, *This is the story, the story that wants to find you. No other story.*

I lifted the lid.

The hinges creaked. The smell of brine filled the air. Brine and wool and wood. I closed my eyes and breathed it in, and then I reached inside with two hands and pulled out the little bundle.

Just a few things. All that remained on his body when they pulled him from the sea, ninety-nine years ago. His white steward's uniform, stained dark at the collar and the right arm, so stiff it crackled under my fingertips. An oilskin pouch, containing an envelope with *Mr. Robert Langford, Stateroom B-38* typed on the back, and a series of numbers and letters written in black ink along the other side.

A few coins, minted by the United States Treasury in the early years of the century.

A silver pocket watch, slightly tarnished at the seams.

And a first-class luncheon menu from RMS *Lusitania*, dated Thursday, the sixth of May, 1915, on the back of which was scribbled the following message, the ink smeared with moisture and barely legible.

No more betrayals. Meet me B-deck prom starboard side.